Old Enemies

Old Enemies

MICHAEL DOBBS

SIMON &
SCHUSTER

London · New York · Sydney · Toronto

A CBS COMPANY

First published in Great Britain by Simon & Schuster UK Ltd, 2010
A CBS COMPANY

1 3 5 7 9 10 8 6 4 2

Simon & Schuster UK Ltd
1st Floor
222 Gray's Inn Road
London
WC1X 8HB

www.simonandschuster.co.uk

Simon & Schuster Australia
Sydney

A CIP catalogue record for this book is available
from the British Library

ISBN HB 978-1-84737-288-8
ISBN TPB 978-1-84737-289-5

Typeset by M Rules
Printed in the UK by CPI Mackays, Chatham ME5 8TD

To James and Liz

Who taught my sons
some of the very best lessons in life.

PROLOGUE

Villars sur Ollon, Switzerland

She was a girl with hazel eyes and a face that with every smile reflected her happiness at being part of the world. She wasn't long past her sixteenth birthday; she lacked a cynical side, which was perhaps something of a surprise for a teenager from New York. That's why she trusted the two men sitting in front of her.

Casey didn't know them, but that seemed not to matter. Had her mother known what she was doing she would have shouted at her, and perhaps even her father would have joined in, too, if he'd been around, but she was far from home and at this age and distance the old rules didn't count. So much of what she'd found since she'd arrived at the international college in Villars was carved from a different world and she was determined to embrace every bit of it. Anyway, Switzerland was safe, everybody said so, particularly up here in the mountains, and she'd been here less than three months, barely enough time to get homesick. Soon she would be packing her pink suitcases and returning to Manhattan for the Christmas break, so before

1

her mom took over her life once more and smothered it in single-parent angst she wanted to stretch her wings and seek out a little excitement.

The two men nodded, encouraging, as she buried her nose in the sweet mist that rose from her mug of hot chocolate. A snowflake settled on her eyelashes, another high on her cheek. There had been a heap of snow this past month, so on the coming Friday, the first day of December, she planned to go heli-skiing, unseasonably early, Ruari's treat. After that, she had decided, she would sleep with him. Their first time. For the heli-skiing, too. There was so much that was new to her here and she couldn't resist sharing it, even with these two strangers as they sat on the balcony of the coffee shop, while the snowflakes melted and slid down her face like fading innocence.

The chocolate chilled in the thin air and she finished it quickly, leaving a thin line of froth on her upper lip. She was a little nervous, burbling, hadn't even got close to mentioning what she wanted, and her cheeks rose in a guilty blush.

'Not to worry, we understand,' one of the men said, his English sharpened by an accent she couldn't place, but everyone in this country seemed to have some sort of accent. 'We know what you want.'

He slid a small sachet across the table. He wore a wedding ring, which reassured her. Casey glanced nervously around her, but the three of them were alone on the balcony, looking out over snow-topped roofs that stretched like jigsaw pieces into the valley below. Inside the transparent plastic sleeve were six small tablets. Es. For her and Ruari. Another first.

'How ... much?' she mumbled, staring at them, her habitual smile replaced by a frown.

The man shook his head. 'We're not dealers.'

'Then ... ?' She was confused. They were too old to be part of the club circuit.

'Buy us another coffee. That will be enough.'

Her fingers stretched out for the sachet, covering it with her palm; it felt cold, almost clinical, and she hesitated one last time before tucking it into a pocket of the colourful Russian felt coat her mother had bought her as a going-away present. The man waved at the elderly waitress, and soon fresh drinks were steaming in front of them all. As she sipped more chocolate, freed from her embarrassment, Casey relaxed under their gentle questions before glancing at her watch and gasping in surprise. 'Wow, this girl's got to be out of here. I'll be late for class!' Suddenly she was on her feet, leaving in a fluster of thanks and apology, her hand still firmly thrust inside her pocket.

As she hurried away, her boots crunching through the crust of fresh snow, the smiles of the two men faded into rock.

'She didn't pay for the fucking coffee,' one said drily.

'She will,' the other whispered.

—∿—

Casey kept her most intimate possessions tucked inside a small silk purse. It was kingfisher-blue, and beneath its gold clasp she had squirreled away a photograph of her parents when they had still been together, and a more recent one of herself astride Trixie, her horse, along with the ring her grandmother had given her before she'd left for Switzerland. The ring was old-fashioned, too large for any of Casey's fingers, but her grandmother was one of those special people in her life who understood her better than almost anyone. Those secrets she wasn't told she still somehow guessed, in return offering Casey a gentle word of encouragement or occasional caution. But she never judged. 'I was there in the sixties, sweetheart,' she would say. 'Sure hope you have as much fun as I did.' And now the ring was nestling next to the note from Ruari. He was eight months older than Casey, almost seventeen, and when they had first grown close at the start of term he'd given her a piece of paper with her name written on it. He'd proved to be something of an artist, had turned the capital C into a face that bore a remarkable resemblance to Casey, capturing her snub nose and hair swept back behind her head, while the tail of the Y seemed looped in the form of a heart, although when she'd pressed him on that he'd grown embarrassed and pretended it was only her back-side. Boys could be such idiots.

Their ski instructor, Mattias, picked them up from the school; you got door-to-door service when your parents were laying out more than seventy thousand dollars a year in school fees. Their equipment was piled high in the back – helmets and sticks and the fat skis used on powder – and Mattias had driven them to a football pitch on the outskirts of Villars that was now covered in a blanket of thick, fresh snow. In the centre of the pitch stood a small canary-yellow helicopter. Their adventure was almost underway. As they clambered from the school van their boots sank in deep; it would be wonderful up on top, so long as the weather held. Casey glanced across the valley towards France, praying that the clouds piling up in the direction of Mont Blanc would steer clear of them, at least for the next few hours. It was glorious on this side, no wind, nothing but sun, a day that would lead to an even more perfect night.

She turned to Ruari, who already cleared six feet, way above her own height, so she had to stand on tiptoe to kiss him. He had an athlete's lean frame, streaks of red bleached into his brown hair by the Alpine sun and a razor nick below his left ear, with a dimple in the centre of a stubborn chin and strong, steady eyes that flooded with humour and seemed to undress her every time they touched her. She grabbed his arm, urging him on. She'd not told him what she was planning for later, when their friends and the teaching staff would be wrapped up in an end-of-term party, but she thought he'd guessed. She couldn't contain her excitement, squeezed his lean frame tighter, then slipped in her heavy boots, falling onto her back on a duvet of pure white, dragging him on top of her. Any excuse.

The instructor turned away, smiling to himself, pretending not to see as they scrambled to their feet, laughing.

Mattias greeted the pilot warmly; they were old friends who had made this trip dozens of times, and the pilot began helping stow the skis in a wire basket that ran along one of the skids. Mattias had already spent half an hour briefing his students, and now he instructed them yet again on what to expect, how to behave in the helicopter and on the snow, what to do in the event of an avalanche. One final equipment check to make sure they hadn't mislaid their hand-sized avalanche transceivers or the folded aluminium probes, then all was ready. 'Today is a special day,' he declared, laying his hands on their shoulders. 'I promise you, it will be one of the sweetest adventures of your lives.' Casey giggled; he didn't know, of course.

As Casey climbed into the open-sided cabin, she was too wrapped up in her own world to take any notice of the other passengers already on board, two men, one of whom sat inside the passenger compartment while the other had begged a favour and taken a seat alongside the pilot up front. They were entirely anonymous and unremarkable. Both wore reflective sunglasses with scarves around their chins and sun cream plastered across their noses. Their heads were covered by thick woollen hats so that very little of their faces could be seen, and what was visible was covered in stubble. They offered no sign of acknowledgement. So Casey couldn't be blamed for what was about to happen. She was young, had eyes for Ruari, no one else.

There was no way she could recognize these men as the pair she had met at the coffee bar a couple of days before.

And there were other distractions. The turboshaft engine began to whine, the giant rotor blades above their heads turned, Casey's world began to tremble and scream. Even when Ruari shouted into her ear she had trouble making out what he was saying, so she used it as an excuse to lean on his shoulder and look into his laughing eyes, unaware. No, you couldn't blame Casey for that. She was in love and on the verge of one of the sweetest adventures of her life. Or so Mattias had promised.

—⟪∿⟫—

Casey sat next to Ruari, facing the rear of the helicopter, with Mattias and the stranger opposite. Their knees almost touched, there was so little room. Outside, through the open door hatch, the scenery grew more rugged and spectacular as they climbed past the treeline and up towards the peaks. She pulled out a camera and began taking photographs, wanting to share the experience with her grandmother. The view of Villars was extraordinary, with wood smoke rising from the chimneys of its huddled chalets, while beyond she could see the valley of the river Rhone as it thrust its way towards Lake Geneva, with its power-station chimney standing tall and steaming. In the great distance were the French Alps, where ribbons of ice crystals were being blown from the mountain tops like the fluttering of Tibetan prayer scarves, while behind her,

Casey knew, in the direction they were flying, lay the peaks of Les Diablerets and the town of Gstaad, where her mother had taken her shopping only a few weeks earlier, before the snows came and blocked the pass. It was where she had bought the silk purse. Her fingers searched for it once more, beneath the folds of her ski suit, and she nestled closer to Ruari.

Casey had lost herself in the beauty, the noise, her rising sense of expectation, when she felt Ruari stiffen. His body tensed. He reached for her hand and squeezed it, too hard, so that she almost yelped in discomfort. It was only when she followed the direction of his gaze that she saw why. The faceless stranger who sat opposite him had turned in his seat. He had taken off his glove and in his bare hand he was now holding a pistol. It was aimed at Mattias's chest, barely two feet away. Casey didn't understand; there had been no argument, no raised voices. Even Mattias was looking on with an expression that suggested more confusion than concern.

'Stand up,' the stranger mouthed at Mattias. The words were flung away in the downdraught yet their meaning was unmistakable.

The guide shrugged his shoulders, indicated his seat harness, still assuming this was some sort of pathetic joke. Then he saw the finger tighten on the trigger, only fractionally, but it was enough to persuade him that it would be unwise to test the stranger's sense of humour too far. Cautiously, not taking his eyes from the snub nose of the gun, he unclipped his safety belt and edged along the bench, trying to put a few more inches between him and danger.

The helicopter flew on, ever higher.

The gunman jerked the barrel, once, twice; with desperate slowness Mattias rose to his feet. His head was bowed, he couldn't stand full height in the cramped cabin. His eyes turned towards the pilot's compartment, hoping his friend had witnessed everything and would intervene. What he saw there made him suddenly sick. That's when he knew he was a dead man.

He was beginning to rage inside with the injustice of it all when, even above the racket of the engine and rushing air, he heard Casey scream. At the same moment he felt a horse kick him in the chest, smashing through his sternum. His breastbone was no match for a 9mm slug fired from a semi-automatic. It didn't hurt, there was no pain, only numbness, which was flushing all the way down through his bowels. His knees were buckling. That made him angry; he was a mountain man, his legs were his life. He was still filling up with anger when, at more than six thousand feet, his knees gave way and he tumbled backwards into oblivion.

—∿—

The pilot hadn't been in any position to help his friend Mattias. He was already dead. He'd been flying on a path that had his craft rising straight and steady through the mountain air when the passenger in the left-hand seat reached over and twisted the lever that engaged the auto-pilot controls. The pilot had barely enough time to blurt out a protest before he died. Two bullets. No one in the rear passenger compartment heard the sharp retorts, no one saw what was happening on the other side of the bulk-head until Mattias stood up and noticed the pilot slumped over his controls, but by then it was already too late. Afterwards there was nothing more than a slight kick of the aircraft, like hitting a small air pocket, to betray the fact that the autopilot had been disengaged. The passenger up front now had control.

In the compartment behind him, the three remaining passengers were lost in their own individual worlds. Casey was old enough for love but far too young for death, even to comprehend its meaning, yet suddenly her world was overflowing with it. She couldn't stop screaming. The hel-icopter had become a coffin.

Beside her, Ruari was bent forward, straining against his harness, his senses focused on the gunman so close at hand. They both knew that if Ruari found the chance he would hurl himself at the attacker, even though the man was fifty pounds heavier and nearly half a foot taller, but Ruari wouldn't get that chance, not stuck in his harness. The attacker stared from behind his sunglasses, his face a mask drained of emotion.

All the while the noise from the engine and the rotors were beating down upon Casey, numbing her mind, driving her fear still deeper inside her until it caught her senses and sent them tumbling. One instinct consumed her; she had to survive, to get away from this danger. She fumbled with the lock of her safety belt, releasing the catch, sinking to her knees as she struggled to breathe. Suddenly Ruari reached for her, trying to help, to hold her, but it was too late, she was slumped on the floor, crawling away, her ski boots slipping as she struggled.

But there was nowhere to go. She sprawled nearer the access hatch but didn't dare move any closer. She whimpered, raised her head, looked at the gunman.

'Please,' she whispered.

He made no move. The gun remained pointed at Ruari. It seemed as if Casey was of no importance to him.

Beyond the hatch she could see the mountaintops that had so excited her and the vast blue void that filled the spaces between. The helicopter twitched, she sank still lower to the floor, reached out to grab one of the metal supports beneath the seats, clinging to it in fear, afraid to move in any direction.

'Please!' she begged once more. She began to scream, piercing cries that not even the pounding of the rotors could suppress. Ruari's hand stretched out once more, shaking as he strained for her, but still he couldn't reach. The pitiful screaming continued. She was a young girl, in terror, pleading for her innocent life.

Then the helicopter banked sharply, like a fairground ride, until it was almost on its side. For a moment the screaming stopped as Casey needed all her strength to cling to the seat support, fighting the gravity that wanted to break her grasp and rip her free. She was losing the struggle. She slipped, a few inches, then a little more. Her boots were no longer scrabbling on the floor, they were dangling over the edge of the compartment, outside, in the void. No matter how Ruari strained, time and again, he couldn't get to her, couldn't touch her, couldn't save her. Her lips twisted into shapes they were never meant to make, while her hazel eyes drowned in terror.

And at last, although it was only seconds, her fingers gave way. There was nothing to hold her any longer. She was tossed from the helicopter like a sweet wrapper in the wind. That was when she started screaming again, more pitifully than ever, but this time there was no one to hear.

CHAPTER ONE

The Eastern Highlands, Zimbabwe

The events that led up to what took place in the Swiss mountains began in another time zone and on a different continent less than five weeks earlier. The chronology would eventually turn out to be important. The matters that were put in motion typically required months to plan, but time was to prove a particularly inflexible factor. Corners were bound to be cut, knuckles scraped.

Moses Willard Chombo stood at the window of his retreat perched in the hills of his country's Eastern Highlands and snorted in frustration. It was eighty degrees, the humidity that was so unexpected in these elevated parts made him short of breath and the rain that had been threatening all morning was now tearing itself from the sky and trying to batter its way through the roof. He couldn't even see as far as the military gatehouse at the entrance to his compound; the only immediate sign of life was a column of ants clinging to the outside of the window frame. Even the weather made him feel impotent.

Chombo was a significant man but he was one who, in

13

his own mind, was not yet significant enough. He was the Mr Meanwhile, His Acting Excellency, the President *pro tem* of his battered country, and the temporary nature of his title made him feel about as uncomfortable as a second-hand shoe. He had been one of Robert Mugabe's deputies and had emerged from the dung heap left behind by that profoundly psychotic despot to squeeze into the dead man's chair, but only until elections in three months' time could confirm a proper and fully empowered successor. Chombo hoped very much that proper and fully empowered successor would be him. He needed only to win an election and was in an excellent position to do so, but Zimbabwe was still a deeply troubled country, exhausted by the years of Mugabe's madness, and the acting President's mood was as overcast as the skies. He was watching a waterspout erupt from the gutter and cascade onto the lawn, where it was tearing at the roots of a hibiscus bush, when he heard a door open behind him. The wooden frame was swollen and warped, the hinges complained, like everything in this country, and through it came Takere, the head of the President's personal guard. Behind him were two white men, in their late thirties, neatly dressed and well-muscled.

'You are late,' Chombo remarked in Shona, the language he shared with Takere. It was more observation than rebuke. The President was a big man with an ox's chest who didn't rush to judgement, the sort of man who preferred to seek salvation and revenge in his own time. It was a caution that had held him back all these years while others had rushed into the hands of the death squads.

'My apologies. There are more potholes than tarmac on the roads out of Harare,' Takere responded, cautious, with a tightness in his lips that made him lisp. He was nervous, sweating, despite the fan that churned the air above his head. 'Mr President, this is—'

But a wave of Chombo's hand cut short Takere's introductions. 'We need no names, not for a meeting that has never happened. Have you searched them?'

'Of course.'

'Search them again.'

'But—'

Yet even as Takere made his protest, the shorter of the two men had raised his hands to the back of his head and patiently spread his feet. His face bore the marks of exposure to the African sun, his ears looked chewed and hugged his skull, making it appear streamlined, an impression enhanced by his close-cropped hair that was thinning, and fading red. The eyes were of the palest grey, like openings in a frozen lake, and gave no warmth. His willingness in submitting to the fresh search showed that he understood Chombo's language and felt no need to keep the fact secret. Takere patted him down, then turned to the other man, who was broader in both shoulder and belly and whose sleek, greying hair and expensive shoes suggested a softer and more blunted lifestyle. Again Takere found nothing.

'You will understand the need for caution,' Chombo said, this time in English.

'That's why I fly El Al,' the red-haired man said. 'It never gets blown out of the sky. And why? Because it gives a damn, like you.' His accent was clipped, rolling from the tip of his tongue, South African.

'You address him as Your Excellency or Mr President,' Takere said sharply, taking exception to the man's relaxed tone. 'You show him respect.'

The ice eyes stared at Chombo, examining the black leader's face, whose every feature – lips, nostrils, cheeks, eyes – seemed too large for comfort. The prominent brow gave Chombo the appearance of having a permanent scowl.

'Respect?' the white man said slowly – he always talked slowly, as though he was never in a rush. 'That is a rare commodity in this part of the world. But I assure you, my respect for the President is every bit as great as any he has for me.'

Takere twitched in agitation but Chombo burst out laughing. Flies would seek a second opinion before settling on this man, the President decided. His mind ran back to Micklethwaite, the visiting British Minister, a man of phenomenally damp palms and absolutely no trace of respect.

'Yes, the West will give you aid, enough of it to transform your blighted country,' Micklethwaite had explained over tea in the ostentatious glass-fronted embassy that looked out along Harare's Norfolk Road. 'Zimbabwe can become the flower of Africa once more.'

'Then we shall be grateful.'

'There are conditions.'

'Of course.' There were always conditions.

'These upcoming elections of yours, they must be fair and free, and seen to be so. You understand that. Not like in Mugabe's time. None of us wants to go back to the old days.'

'Mr Micklethwaite, you sanctimonious and limp-wristed white bastard,' Chombo had thought, but did not say. Instead he had offered a generous smile. 'Mr Micklethwaite, I can lay my hand on my heart' – he had done so with an exaggerated gesture – 'and assure you that there is nothing I want more than for my country to make a fresh start with you and our other Western friends. But . . .' There were always buts, too. 'I must ask for a little patience. We have our customs.'

'You know our position on corruption,' the Minister had insisted casually, reaching for a biscuit.

'Ah, yes, you mean the corruption that permits rich businessmen to buy votes in the British Parliament and in every corner of the US Congress?' Chombo had replied softly. For a big man he could speak very softly, which somehow made the words shout all the more loudly.

'I'm not interested in an empty debate, Mr Chombo. You know what I mean. Your country has a dark past in such matters.' Then the Englishman had hesitated. Even

Micklethwaite had to admit it was a clumsy turn of phrase. Biscuit crumbs fell carelessly down his shirtfront.

'And a dark future, I assure you,' Chombo had replied, smiling yet again, deflecting the tension as he rubbed the skin on the back of his hand. 'But you must understand the way we do things in this country. Zimbabwe is desperately poor. Many live on the edge of starvation. Sometimes the only thing of value they possess is their vote. And if they give it, they expect something in return.'

'And we expect something in return, too,' Micklethwaite had replied.

The white man hadn't changed, still played the imperialist, using what he called humanitarian aid as a hammer to beat former colonies into submission all over again. Mugabe had been right about that, at least, even if he had made a total fuck-up of the potholes.

Since that conversation Micklethwaite had been sacked and replaced by yet another damp palm, but it would make no difference, the British still danced to the tune of the American organ-grinder, who knew nothing of Africa. And yet Americans believed in self-help, so what better way of confronting his current problem, Chombo thought, than to use other white men. Like these two standing on the rush mat in front of him. Security consultants. The expensive name for mercenaries.

The ceiling fan turned idly above their heads, and from nearby a pair of hornbills, spooked by a guard, screeched in alarm. The two consultants stood patiently. Chombo didn't offer them refreshment or invite them to sit.

'You have discussed matters with Takere?' he asked.

'Yes. And what has been suggested is pointless,' the shorter man replied.

Takere's eyes, tired and bloodshot, flared in agitation, but he said nothing. He sensed he was out of his depth, that it might be wise to tread water for a while.

'Look, you want to . . . *change the mind* of an important newspaper owner in London, and in something of a hurry,' the mercenary continued. 'Well, there's no point in offering him money, he has plenty. If his office burns down, it will still make no difference, he will move into a new one. And if, as Mr Takere has suggested, he were to meet with a tragic accident . . .' The mercenary spread his hands wide and shrugged. 'He would simply be replaced by others. You do not change a man's mind by smashing in his skull.'

Chombo considered the point, breathing deeply to massage his thoughts. 'Then what is it that you suggest?'

'We *distract* him. Give him something else to think about. It's difficult for a man to know where his mind is when you are *ripping* out his heart.' The man had a way of emphasizing the letter 'r', rolling it around his tongue in a manner that gave his words added menace.

Takere began cracking his knuckles in confusion, but Chombo thought he was keeping pace. 'His wife, you mean?'

The mercenary shook his head. 'No, not that. They live in London, it's sewn up as tight as an antelope's arse with all

19

their anti-terrorist precautions. And if he has any sense he'll have a security company taking care of his home, fitted it with panic alarms, CCTV, that sort of thing. There could be regular patrols, maybe bodyguards. They might even have constructed a secure room inside. No, to break an operation like that would be very difficult, take time. And time, so your Mr Takere tells me, is one thing you don't have.'

Chombo didn't bother to dispute the point.

'Anyhow,' the white man continued, 'he may not even like his wife.'

A smile spread slowly across the President's face. It took considerably longer to reach his eyes, which remained fixed on the other man, who wasn't like the last pair of 'consultants' Takere had brought him – Englishmen, who'd been halfway up his backside trying to establish parking rights before the draught from the door had time to settle, which was why they had been thrown out just as quickly. But Chombo's instincts told him that the one with frozen eyes was different. Very practical.

'Yes, as you say, there are many problems, so many problems,' the President said. 'But I have a suspicion that you have brought with you a solution. An expensive one.'

'It will be double the fee that was originally indicated. Half up front, the remainder as soon as the operation is underway, and an additional ten per cent for operating costs every month it continues. No payment, or late payment, or part payment – and we walk.'

Suddenly Takere came back to life, beginning to understand that these two men had played him like a fish. 'We said only a third up front, with the final instalment only afterwards, when the job is completed.'

'We are all of us in this for high stakes, putting our necks on the line. "Afterwards"? What is "afterwards"? I may not be around to collect, while you, Mr Takere, might not be around to pay.'

Takere looked in uncertainty towards his President, waiting for his cue to throw these cheating bastards out into the mud.

'So how is it that you propose to distract him?' Chombo asked.

'Not through his wife.'

'Then . . . ?'

'His child. At school in Switzerland.'

'Ah! The snow. It hides many things,' Chombo replied softly.

'There's a lot of it in Switzerland.'

'We should have more snow in Africa.'

And so it was that Casey's fate had been sealed. She wasn't the child of the newspaper owner Chombo was so desperate to get at – that was a kid named Ruari. It was simply Casey's misfortune to be his friend, and to be in the way.

—✺—

It had been an easy affair to fall into. He was the busy entrepreneur, rich in ideas and public principles but deficient in funds, and very much up for the statutory midlife meander, while she was the money woman, self-sufficient, predatory, with exceptional legs that most men imagined in any number of contortions yet which had the capacity to escape from a situation more rapidly than even the most carefully crafted excuse. City Woman. And the two lovers had superb cover. He was the proprietor of *Newsday*, a newspaper in the middle rank of the British market, while she was a vice-president of the paper's main bank and creditor. Being seen together was as inevitable as the process of attraction was predictable, leading from extravagant lunches to more understated dinners, then on to her house on Blackheath Common – 'an excellent investment,' he had mused, following her that first time up the staircase to the bedroom.

Nothing too heavy, except the sex, which was brilliant. No emotional baggage, no demands for exclusivity, no deep entanglement, just a gentle distraction in a life that for him was throwing up more questions than he could cover with answers. Sometimes a man in his overweight forties needed to know he could still do it.

Like most of these very private entertainments, the matter fell into a pattern, one that she was mostly responsible for providing. Candles, atmosphere, crystal glasses to catch the soft light, things that could be thrown together in the time it took him to retrieve something cold and indulgent from her fridge. But this evening there had been no adornments, just sex, and in a manner suggesting her mind was elsewhere. It didn't bother him overly, not until he was finished and left wondering whether she had even started.

'Penny for them?' he asked, reaching for his glass.

'A penny?' She turned to stare at him, pillowing her head on her hands.

'OK,' he smiled, his eyes sliding slowly over her body and widening with appreciation, 'name your price.'

The smile wasn't returned. 'There isn't one.'

'Meaning?'

'You'll get a letter tomorrow declining your request to extend your credit facilities.'

'What?' The sudden tremor in his body caused a trickle of wine to spill over his chest, but he didn't seem to notice.

'The bank won't do it any more.'

'But you can't . . .' It would be like dropping him on the surface of the moon without oxygen. 'That would destroy me. You know that.'

'The bank has decided that the newspaper sector isn't one we want to play in any more.'

'But you *are* the bank!'

'Not really. You know how these things work.'

He tried to turn to face her but his feet were tangled in the duvet. As he tried to wriggle himself free, he noticed there were goose bumps on her skin and her nipples had become rock hard. This is what she got off on. He'd always known, it was her reputation, and yet . . .

23

'So this – tonight. One final fling. Just business?' he gasped.

She looked at him curiously, as though for the first time. 'Hasn't it always been?'

CHAPTER TWO

There were times when Harry Jones was fed up with being a politician. He seemed always to be in a hurry, no time to sit back and take stock – reconnoitring, he would have called it in his old army days, finding out where you were and what lay ahead before you rushed in and got important bits of you blown away. Not that it had saved him, of course. You weren't always given the time to consider what should happen next, sometimes you just had to get on with it. That's where experience came in, and he had a lifetime of that, enough to let him know he wasn't immortal, just lucky, at least so far. He took none of it for granted, which was why he hated wasting time, standing still, doing nothing. Like now. He was nudging elbows, queuing for Passport Control at Heathrow's Terminal Three and growing increasingly restless. It wasn't as if he had anyone waiting for him on the other side, yet still he fretted.

The disgorged passengers shuffled forward more slowly than ever but even here, in the midst of a crowd, Harry found it impossible to hide. He had only just turned on his iPhone and already it was vibrating, demanding his attention. His punishment for taking almost a week off.

It hadn't even been a holiday. Harry had been to the States to get himself a new right ear – he'd left a substantial chunk of the old one back in central Asia during a heated disagreement with a man wielding a scalpel. It wasn't that he minded scars too much, which was fortunate because he'd amassed a considerable collection from the various wars, riots and revolutions he'd been involved with; he'd even managed to pick up the odd one or two during several hard-fought election campaigns. But if you were carrying scars, he argued, it meant you were still walking, which was more than could be said for some of the men and women he had left behind along the way. Yet as a politician he preferred voters to look him in the eye rather than stare at his ear, so he'd decided to get himself a new one, and only in America could you do that.

Some remarkable people at a medical research facility in New Jersey had grown him a new ear on the back of a genetically modified mouse, and he'd even got to show it off to the new President, Alexander Munroe. That hadn't been part of the plan, but Harry had a close friend in the President's National Security Adviser, Charley Ebinger, and the three of them, along with an admiral turned intelligence chief and a portly man with cherry-red cheeks who turned out to be the President's personal cardiologist, had wound up around the dinner table in the private quarters of the White House. A boys' night in, accompanied by overdone filet mignon and wine from the President's old congressional district in California. President Munroe was the antithesis of his predecessor – white, West Coast, a man who had risen through the glue pot of Washington by doing 'damn' little, damn' well', which most voters had found a relief after the intensity of the Obama years. He was also a man of boundless curiosity. They'd been a couple of bottles in with Munroe about to make some profound remark when he had noticed Harry's ear, still healing from the surgery.

'Mr Jones, you had some kind of disagreement with Mike Tyson?' the President enquired in his characteristically forthright manner.

'Just a nick I picked up on my travels. That's why I'm here in the States, Mr President. A little shopping. New ear. You approve?' Harry pulled back his hair to allow a more formal inspection.

'They sell those things in Walmart?'

'It's straight out of the laboratory. The product of one of your own government programmes for the treatment of military casualties who need new accessories. Arms and legs, mostly, and facial reconstruction, but also the occasional ear.'

'So how did you get to lose the earlier model?'

Munroe was the most powerful man in the world, capable of reshaping it or breaking it apart, but he knew he was a desk warrior and envied men like Harry who got to see things from the sharp end, and for a while he and the rest of the table became transfixed by the story of Harry's ear, lost while he had been waging a private war in order to spring a friend from the condemned cell of a distant central Asian republic. 'The friend was one of yours, sir. From Michigan. A British ear in exchange for an almost whole American. It seemed like a fair deal at the time,' Harry concluded.

'Harry's always been a careless sucker,' Ebinger said as the Filipino steward started pouring a fresh bottle. 'Been collecting scratches ever since I've known him. Even managed to get himself shot in his rear end during the First Gulf War – isn't that so, Harry?'

'I guess I was a little unlucky. My backside was about the only thing the Iraqis managed to hit during the entire conflict. I shouldn't have been playing ostrich in the desert.'

The others laughed, but the silver-haired Ebinger wasn't going to let him get away with that. He knew Harry too well, from days when he'd been a visiting lecturer at Cambridge and Harry was a mid-career student still in the British army. 'I seem to recall it wasn't exactly like that,' he said in his professorial manner. 'The version I remember was that you were part of an SAS raiding party, sent into Iraq before the shooting war had begun to snatch one of their generals from his bed. There was some sort of screw-up – over-baked intelligence – and instead of one sleepy general there was a whole welcoming committee of the Republican Guard waiting for you.' The National Security Adviser puffed on his pipe and blew

smoke at the chandelier, knowing how to play an audience. 'The reason Harry's ass was sticking in the air, Mr
President, was because he'd thrown himself across a
wounded colleague, trying to protect him. Harry then carried that soldier for three days and three nights through
the desert to get him back home.'

No one was laughing any more.

'He made it OK, the other soldier?' Munroe asked.

'I'm afraid not, Mr President,' Harry replied, his voice
subdued. 'He died on the second night.'

'But Charley said you got him back home . . .'

'He was a friend. He had family. They needed to say
goodbye. You have to bring them home, if you can.'

Harry had carried the body of his friend, despite his
own wounds, until the Iraqis had lost all interest in chasing
them.

'Hell of a story, Harry,' the President said, using his first
name, stretching to lay a hand on his guest's arm. 'Privilege
to have you at my table.'

It had been a rare honour. Just two nights ago. Now
Harry couldn't get back into his own bloody country.
'Welcome home, Jones,' he muttered to himself as the
phone continued to vibrate. A blocked number. His finger
slid across the screen.

'Mr Jones?'

'Yes.'

'This is Mary Mishcon, the Prime Minister's Private
Secretary.' Her voice rose, as though in question, as if she

was uncertain her name would be recognized even though she was known to everyone in Westminster, an iron fist clad in cashmere.

'Hello, Mary, you well? That father of yours still chasing seagulls down in – Hastings, isn't it?'

'Yes, thank you, still waving his stick around. As is the Prime Minister. Wonders if you could pop in to see him.' Again the rising tone, the gentle touch.

'I hope he's not in a hurry. I'm standing in a line for Passport Control at Heathrow. Could take days.'

'Perhaps we could send a car.'

'No, not necessary, Mary. Just my little joke. When does he have in mind?' Harry asked, mentally flipping through his diary for the next couple of weeks.

'In precisely an hour.' No upward inflexion this time. She was delivering an instruction, no trace of question about it.

—⁂—

Ruari shivered. It was now bitterly cold inside the passenger compartment of the helicopter. They'd been in the air for almost an hour. They had kept to the mountains and were flying to the north of the Matterhorn, roughly following the route of the Rhone. Soon they had crossed into Italy, but no one out there knew. Air traffic control in Milan had no brief to follow a small helicopter that was no more than a fly against the massive Alpine sky, and as it was hugging the valleys at under four hundred feet they wouldn't have been able to track it even if they'd tried. As for the inhabitants of the scattered communities it disturbed along its route, it was of no more interest than the flapping crows. They were getting on with their day, embracing the brilliant winter sun, unaware that inside the helicopter growling in the distance, a young man was sitting staring at the barrel of a pistol.

'What do you want with me?' he asked, shouting across the compartment.

'We take you on a little trip,' the gunman replied. His accent was fractured, his English poor, his face utterly without expression.

Ruari struggled to gather his thoughts. The noise of the helicopter kept battering at his senses, the cold was growing acute, and he was terrified. The only thing he was certain about, which he focused on, grasped with all his strength, was that they hadn't killed him. Casey, Mattias, both gone, the pilot, too, but he remained alive. There had to be some purpose to it, although he couldn't guess what, and in that purpose lay hope. They wanted him alive.

In the lee of a nearby mountain, the helicopter flew into turbulence. It kicked as the autopilot corrected the course and Ruari was shaken back to life. His gloves were still around his neck, not on his hands, his fingers had grown to sticks of ice, so he buried them deep within the pockets of his ski suit, and that was when his hand settled around his phone. He, too, was armed. Slowly, his fingers stiff with cold and fear, he began to make out its shape, to follow the familiar contours of its buttons, and an idea began to form. The phone was switched off but if he could switch it back on, if he could identify the right buttons, and if there was a signal up here – if, if, *if*, too many of the wretched things! – then perhaps he could call home, let someone know what was happening. Even to try would have its risks, what with that unshaven shit-for-brains sitting directly opposite him only an arm's length away, but anything was better than staring numbly at the stupid gun. His mind was made up. He twisted in his harness and stared sharply out of the open hatch, as though something had caught his eye, trying to drag the gunman's attentions that way while he fumbled within the pocket of his ski suit, trying to remember which button activated the speed dial, and which one was programmed for home. But his fingers were like lead, his actions too clumsy.

'What you do? What you do, you little bastard?' the gunman demanded, suddenly suspicious.

The pistol waved menacingly and the boy hesitated. The gunman screamed again, sending flecks of spittle flying across the compartment, hitting Ruari in the face. There seemed little point in pretence. Slowly, Ruari's hand emerged from his pocket, clutching the phone.

When he saw it, the gunman nodded. 'Good, very good,' he muttered. 'That will be useful.' He held out his hand.

Ruari felt sick. Of course the bloody thing would be useful. His entire life was on this phone, names, numbers, class times, bank details, even the text he'd got from Casey

32

first thing that morning. It had been so simple. '2nite,' it had said. And now the bastard was going to get it all.

The gunman flapped his hand in impatience, once, then again, demanding the phone. Ruari saw that the screen was lit, he'd succeeded in calling someone, though he couldn't tell who.

'Give it to me, little shit!' The gunman was stretching, insisting, holding out his fingers like a bird's claw, but in the restraints of his harness he couldn't reach far enough to grab it, and Ruari didn't want to give it. He hated this man so much he'd do anything to frustrate him, and there was also another thought buzzing around inside his head. If they hadn't killed him so far, they wouldn't kill him now, not for a miserable phone. It was a gamble, but in the end his hatred proved stronger than his fear. He hurled the phone out of the open door.

The gunman stared impassively through his reflective glasses. He gave no immediate reaction, there was no obvious anger, save for a slight setting of the lips, and he said nothing. Then he hit Ruari, in the face, with the gun. It sliced through the cheekbone and across the nose. There was no pain, not at first, that would come later, but for a few seconds Ruari's senses were scrambled and a ball of light exploded inside his head, blinding him. When eventually he regained his sight, he saw blood pouring down his chest, like a stuck pig, gathering in a darkening pool on his lap. That was when the pain began. Someone was holding a blowtorch to his face. He knew his nose was broken.

33

Directly across the cabin, the gunman's lips parted, briefly spreading into the thinnest of smiles. It was the first emotion he'd shown of any sort.

Tears now began to mingle with the blood, but Ruari didn't cry out, wouldn't give the bastard the satisfaction. He sat, eyes closed, and desperately frightened, waiting for whatever was to come.

Always in that damned hurry yet, despite it, Harry was late. Not even an Old Testament prophet could have parted the traffic and made it from Passport Control to Downing Street in an hour, not when some idiot had somehow managed to turn his car over on the approach road to Heathrow, bringing the entire circus to a halt. How was it possible to *do* that in a forty-mile-an-hour zone? But Mary, having rearranged the diary to fit him in, had rearranged things yet again. That in itself made Harry's new ear tingle in anticipation – yes, he could feel it, not as well as the old one, but it seemed to respond to his mood and was telling him that something was about to erupt. It wasn't every day that the Prime Minister's diary was so blithely reshuffled. That usually meant at least a minor war or a major bankruptcy, or that something lurid and deeply personal was about to appear in the press.

'What's up, Danny?' Harry enquired as he handed his suitcase into the care of the Downing Street doorman.

'I hav'nae the foggiest,' Danny replied in a broad

Scots accent that came from somewhere north of Glasgow.

'And that is one thing I'll never believe.'

Danny saw it all, the comings and goings, the strangled tears, the less frequent triumphs. He was a master at interpreting the gyrations of the prime ministerial eyebrow that might imply delight but usually foretold of disasters to come. No matter who crossed the threshold Danny was always there to offer a smile of congratulation or conspiracy or, when needed, of condolence. The trick for visitors like Harry was to know which one it was.

'I think you'll be knowing the way, sir,' Danny said, testing the weight of Harry's suitcase as the black steel door closed behind him. 'Good luck.'

Harry's heels clipped out across the black-and-white marbled floor of the hallway. He passed the hooded leather chair in the corner that in days long past had shielded Danny's predecessors from wind and rain, and came complete with a drawer beneath it for hot coals, which during long nights of old had been used to heat tea and scones. A few strides took Harry into the long carpeted corridor with its deep primrose walls and Henry Moore sculpture that led towards the Cabinet Room, but before he reached as far as the inner sanctum he was intercepted by Mary.

'Sorry to keep you waiting,' he said.

'No, it's the Prime Minister who apologizes,' she replied.

'That'll be a first.'

She pretended not to hear. She led him not to the Cabinet Room but into the claustrophobic lift that served the five ramshackle and much reconfigured floors of Number Ten. He was surprised to see her punch the top button – the private quarters, way up in the attic. She didn't bother knocking, but took him straight in through a ludicrously small hallway and into the sitting room.

Iain Campbell was sitting on a windowsill on the far side of the room, his bottom warming above a radiator, his body twisted so that he was looking out through nearly two inches of blast-proof glass across the military parade ground of Horseguards. He seemed slow to react to the intrusion, lost in thought as he stared into the gathering darkness of the winter evening, turning stiffly and almost in surprise to face Harry, by which time Mary had already gone.

'I come up here to think,' he said, as though he felt the need to offer an explanation. 'Cabinet Room's no bloody good. Even on a clear day you have trouble seeing further than the end of the garden. Sometimes you need a little more than that.' He rose to shake Harry's hand. It was when he got to his feet that it became clear how small he was – in fact, the smallest man in the Cabinet. 'More Tom Cruise than Napoleon,' he had claimed to an election interviewer, though only idiots believed him.

'Sorry to keep you waiting, Prime Minister,' Harry said.

'No, nothing formal, Harry. That's why I chose here, rather than the Cabinet Room. No record. One of those meetings that never really took place, eh? Drink?' He waved a hand in the direction of a small collection of decanters and glass tumblers on a side table.

'No thanks, Iain. Just got off a plane. I never drink until I'm over the jet lag.'

The Prime Minister resumed his seat above the radiator while Harry perched on the arm of a sofa. 'You've been in the States.'

'Guilty.'

'Doing your impression of Marc Antony.'

Harry's brow wrinkled in confusion.

'Friends, Romans, countrymen – lend me your ears?' Campbell smiled wearily. 'No, not a very good joke. Best I could do at short notice without a speechwriter. You'll have to forgive me.'

'Perhaps you're right. A new ear. It's an inexcusable vanity, of course. I'll probably get laughed out of my seat by my electors,' Harry said.

Campbell nodded thoughtfully. 'But not by the President. I understand you made quite a hit with our Mr Munroe.'

The Prime Minister was clearly well informed. Harry said nothing; he wasn't sure where this one was going.

'Harry, something I must ask you to treat in the strictest confidence.' He didn't wait for a reply. 'We've managed to screw things up pretty sensationally with the Americans – you know, after the god-awful mess we left behind between us in Iraq and Afghanistan, and the Gulf, come to that, and all the blame we threw at them during the election. Somehow seemed like the right thing to do at the time.' He stared at Harry. 'No, not you, I know, but me, and too many others.'

Harry sniffed the guilt and the rare acknowledgement of error. No wonder the Prime Minister didn't want an official record of this.

'We went too far, Harry. We pissed in their pockets and now it's payback time. We need to renew our nuclear deterrent, which we lease from the Americans, and . . .' He curled over, head down, his hands clasped beneath his chin as though in prayer. 'They want to rape us, Harry. Make us pay full whack. Every dollar and dime it costs them, and a whole lot more on top for the tip.' He shook his head. 'And we haven't got it. Can't afford it. We'll have to throw in our hand. And Britain without a nuclear deterrent, without a seat at the big boys' table, will be no more than another hard-up off-shore under-achieving end-of-terrace island. Not even a junior partner any longer, just junk heap.' He lowered his hands and straightened up once more. 'You talk to Mr Munroe about any of this?'

Harry shook his head.

'But you did talk.'

'Over dinner. About all sorts of things.'

'And your chum Charley Ebinger. Damn it, you have a lot of private clout in Washington, Harry.'

'Am I being accused of something?'

Campbell's tired blue eyes held him for a moment. 'No. But if you think you can smell just the tiniest hint of jealousy, you're absolutely right.' The Prime Minister went back to looking out into the night, searching for something. 'You're one of those aggravating sods, Harry, who never flies in line with the other geese. Always off doing your own thing.'

'Got a thing about geese that fly in a straight line. They're usually the first to get their tail feathers shot away.'

'As the rest of us are discovering,' Campbell responded ruefully. He turned once again to face Harry. 'Help us. Help your country. I want you to use that influence you have to get us a second chance in Washington, Harry. Stick back all the pieces on Humpty.'

'But how?'

'Archie Logan is ill. You may have noticed him a little off form recently.'

Logan, the Foreign Secretary, had produced a remarkably stumbling display at the despatch box recently, but most had put it down to exhaustion after two sleepless nights of haggling in Brussels.

'He wants to retire at Christmas, give me plenty of time to find a replacement. That replacement is you, Harry, if you'll take it. I very much want you to. After my own job it's about the most important post in the country right now.'

'I've already got a job, Iain – a Member of Parliament.'

'Yes, and along the way you've also managed to pick up more honours and medals than any man in the country. Christ, you even get a personalized Christmas card from the Queen and for all I know a blow-job from every female senator in Washington. Don't give me this "I'm only a humble backbencher" crap.' His tone was a little mean; he was hurting. 'Hell, I'm sorry, Harry, I—' He broke off and pinched the bridge of his nose as he struggled to recover his composure. 'If this doesn't work out, it's not just me who's finished. It's all of us. Britain. Cut adrift and sinking. The Falklands will go, then Gibraltar, and soon everything else. Before you know it we'll end up pawning the Crown Jewels.' He stared into Harry's eyes, trying to fathom the other man's thoughts, where the current was headed.

The moment was broken by a disturbance near at hand; the Prime Minister was running late for his next engagement.

'I want you at the heart of this. On your terms. Absolutely anything you want, Harry,' Campbell repeated. 'Think about it, will you? Please.'

'I will.'

'That's great. But don't take too long, eh? I need this particular stable cleansed by Christmas. Before Santa arrives with his sodding reindeer and covers the place in even more muck.'

CHAPTER THREE

They had been forced to put together their plan with haste, yet so far it was working. Flying conditions were excellent as they emerged from the heights of the Alps and into the foothills, passing north of the ancient stone-cutting town of Domodossola and briefly re-entering Swiss airspace, all the while remaining invisible to air traffic control. They'd had to gamble on how much fuel there would be in the helicopter but it was working out. They needed another twenty minutes in the air and the pilot reckoned he could squeeze that out – just. He sat with a map on his knees, checking their route, watching the readouts from the fuel gauge as they headed for their destination at 125 knots.

The small Italian resort of Gravedona with its red-tiled roofs and intimate squares lies on the shore of Lake Como, less than ten miles from the Swiss border. Between the town and the border, where the land rises towards the Alps, is a reservoir, hemmed in by dense fir trees and sloping sides, difficult territory for a helicopter, but the site had three attributes that were essential for their purpose. It was isolated. It was unmanned. And it had a service road.

An SUV flashed its lights in instruction as the helicopter
came into view. The pilot offered up a prayer of gratitude
that the visibility was excellent and he wasn't having to
make this approach in total darkness. The landing area next
to the reservoir was tight, on a noticeable slope, covered in
snow and hemmed in by trees. Branches went flying, shred-
ded to twigs by the blades as the pilot edged forward,
keeping just ahead of the blizzard of snow thrown up by his
downwash and threatening to blind him. The incline made
it all the more difficult, forcing him to land across it with his
left skid down the slope, keeping the blades turning until he
was sure the craft wasn't going to start slipping, or settling
so deep in the snow that the bloody thing might tip up.

Ruari sat watching as the snow and pieces of thrashed fir
tree were swept around, wishing he had a plan, but his
head ached furiously from his injuries. Both eyes had
swelled up, although the prodigious flow of blood had
stopped and was now congealing in his lap. He felt relief as
the thunder of the engines began to wane, and another
man, the driver of the vehicle, signalled that he should get
out. The driver had a gun, too, but Ruari was hurting too
much to give a damn. He stumbled, they dragged him
roughly to his feet, then dumped him beneath a tree a little
way from the helicopter. As he stared at the new man,
trying to focus on this most recent face with its thinning red
hair and ears that seemed sewn flat against his skull, he felt
a scratch on his upper arm and before he knew any more
was drifting away. He didn't see them bring the SUV

behind the helicopter and push the aircraft down the slope towards the reservoir. It didn't take much. The machine had its gearbox beneath the rotor blades, which gave it a high centre of gravity, and with a little nudging from the bull bars of the SUV it was soon toppling over onto its side. The blades bent as they hit the snow, then snapped, the helicopter groaned, resisted, and began lurching down towards the side of the reservoir. There was ice on the surface but it was nowhere near thick enough to withstand a ton and a half of helicopter. The craft slipped a little more, the last few feet, then, with a stiff, almost courtly bow, toppled over and struck the ice, sinking in seconds and leaving nothing but a dark, jagged hole that would soon be frozen over.

The dead pilot was still inside, strapped in his seat.

They bundled the unconscious Ruari into the back of the vehicle and hid him beneath blankets, and only a few minutes after landing they were underway. No one yet knew that the boy, or the helicopter, was missing. The alarm wasn't raised until night had fallen, but by then they had reached their destination, a further three hundred miles away and almost in another country.

—⁓—

Campbell turned from Harry to discover Mary Mischon, the keeper of the Downing Street diary, standing in the doorway. He glanced at his watch and let out a sound of extreme weariness. 'Remind me,' he sighed.

'Reception downstairs. Pillared Room.'

'Do I have to?'

'Not if you don't mind upsetting around three hundred of the most important businessmen in the country, about two hundred and fifty of whom have been identified as potential party donors.'

He pulled a face. 'Sometimes, Mary, I don't like you.'

'I'll resign in the morning. In the meantime . . .' She held the door open wider.

Slowly, as though considerably older than his fifty years, Iain Campbell levered himself up from his warm, comfortable seat, and as he did so he seemed to go through a profound change. He shook himself, like a butterfly emerging from its cocoon, forcing strength back to his limbs, ironing out the creases and putting on his public face. When he had finished, he held out a hand. 'Come on, Harry. Join me. It'll be a good crowd, let's say hello to the heavy hitters.'

'I'm scarcely dressed for such an occasion,' Harry replied, still in the loose clothes he'd flown in. He didn't even have a proper collar, let alone a tie.

'It's a reception, not a bloody funeral. Anyway, you're Harry Jones. You get away with murder.'

There was no mistaking the edge in Campbell's humour. He had been flying in a straight line, and up front, for so long that he had no more tail feathers left, seemed to have forgotten how to relax. And from somewhere deep inside, beyond where the Prime Minister's flattery had penetrated,

Harry heard an alarm bell ringing – join the flock once again and he might end up just like this. He'd spent time as a minister before, had once been a man rising rapidly through the ranks until his own ideas got in the way. More scars. But he couldn't deny he was intrigued by the Prime Minister's proposal, and in the circumstances it would be churlish to turn down his invitation. Anyway, the delays at Heathrow had wiped out his other plans for the evening. He nodded his acceptance.

Campbell led the way with a remarkably jaunty step down the stairs to the Pillared Room, the largest reception room in Downing Street, which sported a huge crystal chandelier at its centre and Regency gilt sofas at its edge. It was on this spot that the bald-headed fascist Benito Mussolini had been entertained before the war, where during the war the windows and ceilings had been blasted into fragments, and where afterwards Winston Churchill had suffered a major stroke that was to snatch away all the glories of victory and to be the beginning of the end for him. This was also where other moist-eyed departing Prime Ministers had taken hurried farewells from their staffs at those inevitable moments of defeat and departure, yet for now at least the room filled with chatter and good humour as Campbell made his entrance, smiling, shaking hands, grabbing elbows, picking pockets, whispering in ears and dispensing humour, even drinks. 'An orange juice for Mr Jones,' he instructed one of the staff. 'No vodka in it. My wife's already marked the bottle.' He began working the room, never lingering yet making everyone feel special, and somewhere in the crowd his wife was doing much the same. Everyone had to get a piece of him, even vicariously. An eminent banker had been hovering and now she pounced, but Campbell didn't listen to her for long – the woman was notoriously even-handed, gave politicians of every colour a hard time and no money, and soon the Prime Minister had grabbed Harry's arm once more, using him as an excuse to strike out in another direction until he spied what he thought was a safe harbour.

'Harry, I'm sure you know J.J. Breslin. Impress him, will you? We need him!' And with that, he was already gone.

It was at that instant Harry knew he had made a terrible mistake in being here. He didn't care for crowds, found them claustrophobic, and he was tired, jet-lagged, distracted. That was how he came to be caught unawares. He found himself extending a hand and, as he did so, as he felt his palm and met his eye, the clamour that had taken hold of the rest of the room somehow disappeared.

'Mr Jones, I don't believe we've met,' Breslin said.

That was for sure. Harry had spent many years assiduously avoiding him.

'But I believe you know my wife.'

And there she was, standing by the ornate marble fireplace, smiling ruefully from behind her glass of wine.

Harry's head was spinning. It wasn't often he lost control of his feelings, but now he was very close. The steward was at his side with the tray of drinks; he grabbed a whisky, leaving the orange juice undisturbed. It gave him the chance to look at her. The hair was a little shorter, a more distinct shade of chestnut than he remembered, her high cheeks perhaps a little fuller, the clothes certainly better cut but she was now – what? Thirty-eight? Or was it nine? It had been so long ago, he'd tried so hard to forget.

'Hello, Harry.' Still the same breathless, husky voice, the same pouting, expressive lips. 'It's been a long time.'

'That's for sure.'

'Paris, wasn't it?'

'The Left Bank.'

'You remember.'

'Every detail.'

Lapérouse, a corner table. A Friday evening, shortly after eight, with light, mist-like rain that had required no more than a turned-up collar and springing step to make sure he wasn't late – at least, that's the way he remembered it. Waiting for her, alone at the table, too long, beginning to feel awkward, exposed, before she'd arrived, flustered, fumbling with her coat and her words, telling him it was over, that there would be no more secret trips, no more stolen moments. That she was sending him back to his wife.

'How have you been . . . Terri?' he heard himself saying. Her name emerged almost as an afterthought, on an unwilling tongue.

'Fine. Really fine.'

Her husband was a tall man who might once have been

good-looking but who now sported a receding hairline and a developing stomach hemmed in by a double-breasted suit – always a mistake on a stomach, Harry thought. He was looking at them with a glint of curiosity through thick-framed designer glasses. 'I'll leave you two to catch up,' he said, turning abruptly and leaving them alone on their island in a sea of noise.

'You'll have to forgive J.J.,' she said. 'He has a jealous streak. He'll be checking up on us.'

'He knows?'

'Perhaps. I've never told him. He senses more than knows. Heard whispers, maybe.'

'You weren't the guilty party. I was the one who was married.'

She smiled, an expression which on her lips always contained an element of provocation. 'J.J.'s Irish. He never forgets the past.'

'And I'm . . .'

She nodded. 'The past.' Then she laughed, that soft, lilting sound like a trickling brook that he remembered and which had for a few terrifying months of his life so bewitched him. Yes, it had been witchcraft, for otherwise none of what had happened made sense. He'd been married to Julia, the most extraordinary of women, the great love of his life, and yet . . . Terri had come along and his life had been trashed. His fault, not hers, she hadn't particularly encouraged him, had always held back, but he had pursued her in that relentless Jones style until all he could think about was her. Yet somehow Julia had managed to forgive him. They had rebuilt the marriage, crawled their way back through the pain, little by little, until the day Julia had been killed in a skiing accident, following Harry down the side of yet another mountain, and after that he had never found a way of living with the guilt. It had burned like acid through so many other relationships. He'd hated Terri for all that, because she'd finished it, and he'd never understood why, and because it was so much easier hating her than hating himself. And now she was here, standing in front of him, beneath a portrait of the virgin Queen Bess.

'You know I've spent all these years avoiding you,' he said. 'Checking guest lists, walking out of receptions just like this, turning down invitations to dinner parties because I knew you and your husband would be there.'

'I know. Me, too.' No more laughter, only memories. 'But you're a very difficult man to avoid, Harry Jones.'

'Someone mentioned . . .' He found himself reaching for another drink. 'You have a family.'

She nodded, sipped, lowered her eyes. She was still elegant, the years had been kind, and if she had put on a few pounds since her early twenties they were spread in superb places. As he looked, and remembered, he found there was too much to say, and so he said nothing. A silence of guilt.

'I never remember you being tongue-tied,' she teased, softly, trying to break the impasse.

'I'm just not in the mood to stand here and swap small talk.'

'This is Downing Street, what else are we supposed to do?' A gentle laugh, which died. 'Or is it me?'

Harry wasn't one of those braggarts who claimed never to have crawled away from a place of danger. He could smell the stuff, knew how it lurked like a ruffian on the stairs, waiting to trip you, cast you down, kick the crap out of you and take advantage of any vulnerability. Crawl away? Hell, he knew there were times when the only wise thing to do was to run, to put as much distance between yourself and it as possible. That's why he'd survived. He swallowed the last of his drink and, without offering a word of apology, turned on his heel and left.

CHAPTER FOUR

In the taxi on the way back from Downing Street, Harry's mood proved to be as sour as the milk that would be waiting for him back home. Terri could do that for him, curdle the finest day. He told the cabbie to stop and clambered out, intending to walk the last stretch and restock his fridge at his local Asian minimarket, maybe get himself a fresh attitude, too. He felt mean.

He still had his suitcase but it had wheels and was clattering unsteadily along the pavement when up ahead in the lamplight he saw a group of youths loitering near the shop, blocking the path, deliberately making others walk round them and into the gutter. Five of them, wearing hoodies, smoking, spitting, cursing, scratching spots. A woman with a child's buggy, the wife of the minimarket owner, was asking them to move to one side. Harry wasn't close enough to make out her precise words but from the woman's body language he could see that she was nervous and hesitant, trying to be studiously polite. They looked at her, at the colour of her skin, and too long for comfort at the child, before turning their backs and ignoring her. She lowered her head in submission and began to make the trek into the gutter.

That was when Harry got involved. He had no trouble in finding justification for barging in, of course, and on another day he would have said he was being chivalrous, but the truth was he was pissed off, stirred up by his encounter with Terri, and wanted to take his dark humour out on somebody. The mop-heads made a convenient target. These kids were feral, the type of wild, unassimilated creatures that nowadays were found in every town and on too many corners. Broken families, of course, that was always the excuse, but so what? His family hadn't been exactly a festival of fun, either, yet Harry had got over it, hadn't he?

Or maybe not. Family was something he'd never done well and sometimes, when night pushed aside the clutter of the day, Harry wondered why he'd never been able to find the right place for a woman in his life. Was that because he had no role model, because his own father had so often been absent, erratic and untrustworthy, an emotional waterhole that had dried up and left those around him gasping? It would all have been so different for Harry, of course, if Julia had lived. She'd been pregnant when she died, carrying their son – Harry always thought it was a boy, didn't know why, perhaps that was nothing more than male attitude, and Harry possessed more than his fair share of that. Dammit, maybe he was more like his father than he cared to admit. And suddenly Harry realized his own son would have been about the same age as these punks on the pavement.

The frustration boiled over. Not just with these teenagers but with his father, with Julia for going and getting herself killed, with Terri, but most of all with himself. He was normally a man renowned for his self-control but today wasn't normal, and suddenly a gear inside him slipped and he was shouting, threatening, making a stupid scene. In response the kids began laughing, mocking, gave him the finger before melting away, moving past him like a current around a stone, kicking over his suitcase as they disappeared.

He'd spent years listening to any number of psychologists and sociologists, let alone fellow politicians, offering explanations for kids like these who turned into a rat pack, but right now he wasn't big on mitigation. He was burning, he hated them. For making a fool of him, and for enabling him to make a fool of himself.

The owner of the minimarket was out on the pavement now, rescuing his wife, comforting his bewildered child, looking at Harry with suspicion as though he was to blame. And at that moment Harry came to the conclusion that he was, after all, a lucky man not to have a family, not to be a father, not to be forced to put up with this sort of shit.

To hell with the sodding milk, he'd pour beer over his cornflakes. Harry kicked the pavement in fury as he picked up his suitcase, shouldered his anger and continued trudging home.

—⁓—

It was called the Karst, or Kras or Carso, depending on which of the locals you spoke to, a vast, thinly populated plateau that stretched back from the Italian port of Trieste and marked the boundary between Old Europe and the Balkans, the place where Latin met Slav, a spot where many passed through but few stopped. It was a place easy to overlook. That's why the kidnappers had chosen it. The dense oak trees that had given this area its character had long ago been ripped out by medieval foresters to provide wood for the trading fleets of Venice, just seventy miles along the coast, leaving scrub pine in their place. This was high limestone country, a landscape that seemed to be at war with itself, riddled with caverns and sinkholes gouged out by the underground streams that made the ground disappear beneath the feet, a place of neglected paintwork and crumbling stone walls where scattered rural communities struggled to eke out a living on thin soils. Such hard conditions bred independence and self-reliance, and a distrust of the many monarchs who had tried to bend it to their ways. It was a region of meagre rewards and hardy souls, and of the Bora, a savage northerly wind that generated extraordinary ferocity as it descended upon the Adriatic, like a hooligan who molested you before running off, only to return just when you thought it safe to come out again. The Carso was a place with its own laws, its own way of doing things. Policemen and officials sent up here had sometimes simply disappeared, as though they had been dropped down a hole in the ground, which in all probability they had. And that was another reason why the kidnappers had come.

It was dark when they arrived at the isolated two-storey farmhouse, darker than any place Ruari could remember. A dim glow from behind drawn curtains was the only light he could see in any direction. They heaved him from the car, dragged him inside, his legs still numb from the drug, his mind like treacle, and someone was trying to drive a chisel into his skull. A room, flagstones on the floor, with old wooden beams and rough plasterwork, and sparsely furnished – a table, a dresser, a mixture of ageing wooden chairs, little more. A wood fire was spitting in the corner. On the table Ruari could see dirty plates and empty beer bottles, along with a laptop computer. There were also several weapons, including an assault rifle. A smell of wood smoke and stale cooking fat hung in the air.

He counted seven men in total, the three who had brought him here and four others. As he struggled to regain his senses he quickly became aware of the order of things; five of them were dark-eyed with olive skins and a rough, wild look. They mostly spoke poor English and a language that Ruari didn't understand. He thought it sounded a little like the Latin spoken by some Catholic priests; he later discovered it was Romanian. The two others were different, lighter in hair with fairer skin beneath the tans and accents that carried the unmistakable clip of South Africa. This pair – the red-haired de Vries, and Grobelaar, the pilot – were the men in control, the remainder the hired hands. Oil and vinegar.

Almost as soon as Ruari was dumped upon his chair one of the Romanians lifted up his chin and took a couple of photographs.

'I am not happy,' de Vries declared as the photographer finished his work and Ruari's chin sank back onto his chest. 'Damaged goods. You bought back damaged goods.'

'It's only a busted nose,' said the gunman from the helicopter. His name was Cosmin. 'You should see what I did to the others.'

He laughed, crudely, baring his teeth; the rest of the Romanians joined in, a great joke, but not de Vries.

'So why did you break his nose?'

'The little shit was trouble,' the gunman replied, scratching at his dark stubble. 'He threw away his phone.'

'He had a phone? That would have been useful.' The South African began prowling, walking behind Ruari's chair. The boy became apprehensive; there was a sense of menace in this man, of anger seething just below the surface, and Ruari wondered if he was about to be on the end of it.

'And he threw it away?' de Vries continued.

'Sure.'

The South African had finished circling and was back

56

standing in front of Cosmin, rubbing his hand over the cropped hair of his skull, as though trying to slick back hair he no longer had. The gunman smiled, exposing large crooked teeth. That's when de Vries hit him, very hard, on his nose, sending him crashing to the floor. The man began protesting, but the flow of blood and the hand that was trying to staunch it made his words incomprehensible. The other Romanians had stiffened in alarm, fingers flexing in agitation; at the margins of the affair a hand began moving towards one of the many weapons, but Grobelaar had beaten them to it. His gun was already covering them all.

'You pillow-biters have to understand,' de Vries said, in a relaxed tone that suggested this violence meant nothing to him. 'You let him mess about with a phone. That makes me very unhappy. We all stand to make a considerable amount of money from this young man, so I don't want you bringing back damaged goods. I don't want him messing around with telephones. I don't want him even breaking wind without my permission.'

Cosmin began mumbling through the pain and his leaking fingers, looking up from the floor like a dog. 'But I thought—'

'I don't want you thinking,' de Vries spat, standing over his victim, cutting off the protest but not raising his voice. 'That's the last thing I want from you. It's not what I am paying you for. You want to think, you fuck off to university. Otherwise, you stay here and do what I pay you for. Is that clear?'

Ruari had watched the Romanian kill two people in cold blood. Now he saw him nodding in submission. This was a power play, not so much a battle of weapons as a struggle of wills, and there was not the slightest doubt who had won it. It was a lesson that everyone in the room understood. De Vries was a very dangerous man.

'A pity about the phone,' he continued, 'but what the hell. We have the boy. He will give us everything we need.'

Ruari shivered. He wanted to throw up. Meanwhile, the photographer began downloading the photographs onto the laptop.

—⟶ww⟵—

Chombo gazed from the window of Harare's State House, out across the cricket ground with its jacaranda trees to the golf course that lay beyond. It was raining again, stifling hot, weather for hippos, and the air conditioning was working only fitfully. The electricity had failed yesterday, twice. Praise be to Comrade Mugabe.

On the windowsill lay a red leather-covered file, emblazoned with the title of ZIM-1. Its pages detailed the financial dealings of the late departed President, courtesy of the weevils who ran Zimbabwe's Central Intelligence Organization, and the file was thicker than even Chombo could have imagined. The acting President was no saint, power in this godforsaken continent didn't fall into the hands of the innocent, but even he had thought there were limits. The file said otherwise. Maybe, just maybe, Chombo thought, he could do a better job, if he managed to survive.

The President's barrel chest heaved, pumping up and down as he tried to clear his mind of his troubles. In a country almost starved to extinction Mugabe had built himself a palace in the northern suburbs of Harare that had cost more than the entire education budget. It had pillars of marble and taps of gold in its twenty-five bathrooms, with crystal chandeliers to decorate the ceilings in the bedrooms, even while half the population lived in shacks of corrugated tin and sheets of plastic without a single window. They had also discovered rooms in the basement whose stains told of unspeakable horrors. The man seemed to have taken a personal delight in inflicting suffering.

Such things troubled Chombo. His political ambitions were straightforward, but power was not, even if Comrade Mugabe had made it seem so. Chombo sincerely wished to do good for his many countrymen, but for that to happen he must first do good for himself. He had to win the forthcoming election, whatever it took, for without that he could do nothing, change nothing. So to serve his country, he had to serve himself – yes, whatever that might take. He turned from the window to where Takere was waiting.

'You are sure?' Chombo grunted.

'They have sent a picture.' He handed across a photograph, not very good, of a white boy with a busted face.

'It is a very great deal of money they ask for,' Chombo insisted.

'They will not move another finger without it.'

The President sighed. Perhaps one day this photo with his fingerprints upon it would end up in another file, one like Mugabe's, but he vowed his file would never be as thick.

'Do the bugs you have inserted up the great British backside still work?'

The former colonial power's new embassy on Norfolk Road was glass-fronted, never the most sensible option in a super-heated place like Harare. Its construction had incurred extraordinary cost overruns yet that hadn't saved them from finishing it off in an unseemly and poorly supervised hurry, and this had provided Mugabe and his men with all sorts of opportunities for burying Bulgarian-supplied listening devices within its many cavities and miles of ducting.

'It seems they have discovered most of them,' Takere replied. 'Either that or they have been eaten by termites. But we still have our more traditional sources of information.'

'I need to know, do they truly mean it? Will they and their Western friends deny us what we need, just because we do not run our elections in the way that will allow them to sleep at night?' the President demanded urgently.

'Their bullying is like the summer rains. It passes, yet it always returns.'

'They still wish to play the imperialist. These Englishmen, they all threaten and posture, when in reality they are weak and mostly homosexuals.'

'I think they mean what they say. Anyway, that is what our sources tell us.'

'Our *traditional* sources?'

'The woman who serves the Ambassador's tea.'

Chombo snorted in contempt. The British took their servants for granted, as if they were invisible or stupid. 'In your view, Takere, this matter with the boy. It is necessary?'

He was deliberately putting the man on the spot, intimidating him, making him responsible. It meant that if anything went wrong he would have someone to blame.

'There is no other way.'

The President's words, when they came, emerged softly. 'Then let it be so.'

Takere nodded, unable to resist a smile of satisfaction, and Chombo noticed. He didn't very much like Takere. He was a necessary man and his job was necessarily unpleasant, but he took too much pleasure in it. Why, look at the man, he was wearing a new uniform, one he'd designed himself, which bore enough braid to decorate a Christmas stall. And he was standing in a studied way that was too informal, not sufficiently subservient, as if he regarded himself as being almost a partner with the President. He would learn.

'We have arrested a journalist,' Takere continued, leading the conversation in a new direction. 'We caught him near the border, trying to sneak back to South Africa. He has been running round asking questions about you, and your past.' Ah, Chombo's past, which Takere knew was a murky and sometimes moveable feast, which was why he raised the matter. Two could play this game of intimidation, it seemed.

'What did he discover? What did he say?'

'He is working for your enemies in the West. He claims he was only trying to add a little colour to the stories they will print about you at the election. Colour?' Takere snorted. 'I will give him colour, as much as he wants, until it trickles down his ankles and into the gutter.'

'But what does he know?' Chombo demanded, impatient.

'The bastard says he knows nothing, of course, but I will encourage him to refresh his memory.'

'And after you have finished with your . . .' Chombo searched for an appropriately ambiguous word – ' . . . discussions?'

Takere paused. This man might be President but he was slow, almost a dullard. He had to be led along gently, but give him enough time and he would get there eventually. They always did. 'Those who paid him should be discouraged from sending another in his place.'

'How?'

'He is from South Africa.'

The President frowned, not picking up the other man's meaning.

'He entered our country illegally,' Takere continued, 'so he would be making his way back home in the same manner. Across the Limpopo. It is a great river. Very difficult to cross in the rainy season. A place of many tragedies.'

Ah, now Chombo understood. 'A river of tears.'

'If that is what you want, Mr President.'

Now it was Chombo who was on the spot, the place that all leaders in these parts came to eventually. He had never before been directly involved in ordering the killing of another man, a rare concession in Africa, but the concession was about to run out. A rite of passage, a page in his file. His chest heaved yet again, in uncertainty, then in reluctant decision. He nodded. A man condemned, a brother lost, one African life in exchange for so many futures. It was how it had to be. Yet it bothered him, and considerably more than the fate of a European boy in a far-away place, and that, to Chombo's mind, was also how it should be. Outsiders who meddled with his country had to bear the consequences, no matter how painful. Such things were inevitable, in rough waters where so many crocodiles swam.

He crumpled the photograph of Ruari in his fist and threw it in the waste bin.

CHAPTER FIVE

Switzerland is a country of order. Matters move at a pre-scribed and regular pace, like their cuckoo clocks, and it was some time before anyone began to wake up to the fact that there was a tragedy in the making. Initially neither the helicopter nor its pilot was missed. It was Friday, the weekend was fast approaching, and the heli-skiing had been the last trip on the programme. The pilot was divorced, a solitary bugger, and he spent many weekends up in his mountain hut, which he reached using the heli-copter. The aircraft's owners weren't expecting to see either him or it until the following week. No one fretted, not even Mattias's wife, who was visiting her sick mother down the valley in Aigle, while at the college it was the end of term, the Christmas party, an evening full of dis-tractions. In any event Casey's closest confidantes thought they knew the reason for her absence only too well. The college declared its brief to be 'experiences beyond the classroom', and Casey had whispered her intention to follow it to the full.

Even when it became clear the following morning that

neither Casey nor Ruari had slept in their beds their friends covered for them, and when the college house-parents eventually discovered their absence it was at first met with little more than mutterings about teenagers and distracted musings about appropriate punishments. It was only as the day wore on and Ruari failed to turn out for the last ice-hockey match of the term that the first shoots of real concern began to emerge. A conversation took place between the college bursar and his friend the police inspector in his office further down the Avenue Centrale, a quiet word, strictly informal, nothing made official, no black mark recorded against the college. But enquiries began to be made and by mid-afternoon a picture began to appear that placed matters on a far more serious footing. None of those involved in the heli-skiing could be traced, and the helicopter was missing, no radio traffic, no radar contact. It should have been noticed earlier, but even inside Swiss clocks sometimes the cuckoos go off song. Inevitably fears of a tragedy began to take hold but by that time it was too late, and too dark, for anything but a perfunctory search. The serious stuff would start at first light the following day, Sunday – except a warm front came over and the weather closed in, leaving fog clinging stubbornly to the sides of the valleys and making flying impossible.

It was Monday before the search got underway. That was also when the college principal, after a desperate and utterly sleepless night, picked up a telephone that was growing heavier with every hour and made calls to the two families. He said only 'something has happened'. He didn't want to give vent to his inner fears, to leave the families without hope. It was entirely possible, he reassured them, that Ruari and Casey were cold and hungry, sitting in a disabled helicopter and complaining how long it was taking to rescue them.

Monday was also the day that Pieter de Vries had it confirmed that the second tranche of his fee had been deposited.

—⁂—

Ruari woke in the bedroom at the back of the farmhouse that had become his cell. He had nothing but an old mattress on a metal-framed bed, which had neither sheets nor cover, not even a pillow. They had taken his blood-stained ski suit from him, but at least the place was well heated. The pain from his nose was still ferocious, but it was as nothing compared to the agonies he felt inside. Fear, anger, self-loathing, nausea, frustration, grief, resentment; they were like demons leaping out from every shadow to pierce him and snatch away any last shred of resistance. Every time he closed his eyes, every time he tried to escape within himself, the images of what had happened came floating back on a floodtide of guilt. There was Mattias, his face staring quizzically at Ruari, his lips twisted in indictment, demanding an explanation for what he had done. Why had he done this? Got him killed? His fault! The face was drained and ghostly, the cheeks sunken, the eyes large and burning with the injustice of it all, then slowly they fell to the hole in his chest, which seemed to be growing like a spider's web until it had all but eaten the rest of Mattias away. Ruari tried to drag his own gaze away to another corner, but there was no escape. Mattias was everywhere, lurking in every corner, waiting to accuse him.

So Ruari closed his eyes, screwed them firmly shut, looking for comfort, and there was Casey. Beautiful, wonderful Casey, the girl he loved so much and lusted after still more, who had led him to the brink of manhood and whom he had so disastrously let down – no, not let down. Betrayed. That was the word, the only word. He shook his head, trying to free himself from his overwhelming sense of guilt, but still she was there, her face twisted in horror, pleading for him to save her, her soft lips frozen in a silent, endless scream.

He tried to hide still deeper within himself but they pursued him without respite – Casey, Mattias, Cosmin, de Vries, the other guards, all screaming, pounding away at him. They wouldn't let him go. He curled himself into a foetal ball and in the recesses of his mind he caught distant glimpses of his mother, flitting between the shadows. He shouted at her, calling for her to come closer, but she didn't seem to hear him so he raised his voice, louder and still louder, until he found himself whimpering upon his rank, stinking mattress, crying out for her. 'Mummy, Mummy . . .'

Whatever chance Ruari might have, he knew there was none to be had in crawling back to his childhood. He blamed himself for what had happened, but he blamed his captors more. As the furies in his mind drew closer, chasing him down in every hiding place, suddenly he turned on them and gave a roar of inner defiance that caused him to bite deeply into his lacerated lip. The pain jolted him back to the real world as once more blood began smothering his tongue and trickling from the corner of his mouth. And when he looked out once more he saw not Casey or Mattias or his mother, but a guard with stone-dead eyes watching him from the other side of the room, sneering, and for the first time in his life Ruari knew what it was to hate.

—ᴍ—

The searchers from the mountain rescue service spotted Casey first. She was lying spread-eagled on a rocky out-crop, her pink and sky-blue jacket vivid against the sunlit snow. Access by land was impossible; the rescue helicopter was forced to hover while a crewman was lowered. He found Casey's head resting on a pillow of snow, her face turned to the heavens, her eyes open, utterly lifeless.

There was no sign of catastrophe in the immediate area, no broken machine, no further bodies, and this caused much confusion at rescue control. How – and why – a six-teen-year-old girl could have fallen from a helicopter didn't bear thinking about. What sort of calamity was this?

They intensified their search in the surrounding area and a couple of hours later found their answer. Mattias's body was poking at an unnatural angle from a pile of freshly disturbed snow at the bottom of a ravine. The injuries were pitiful, he had bounced and tumbled down a rock face for many hundreds of feet, but this had clearly been no accident. The small, circular and ferociously angry hole in the centre of his chest told its own story.

In the circumstances, and in the snow, it was a stroke of fair fortune for the Swiss authorities to have found and recovered both bodies. It was the only luck they were going to have as they searched ever wider, and found nothing.

—⚓—

Harry sat in a chair, towel around his neck, facing the mirror. A frown of indecision was beginning to worm its way across his forehead.

'So what's it to be, Harry?' the tall, middle-aged woman enquired, running exploratory fingers through his hair.

'I dunno, Tessara. What do you think?'

Harry's hairdresser stepped back and stared at his reflection in the mirror. 'Let's find a cuppa something warm first, then we'll decide.'

Tessara ran a modest but remarkably popular unisex salon on a backstreet of his constituency, from which she dispensed good cheer and endless cups of tea. Like all good listeners she was remarkably well informed about what was going on in the neighbourhood, and Harry would have been happy enough simply to drop by for the local updates, but she also cut his hair more skilfully than any place he'd found in the West End at five times the price. His hairstyle during his army days had inevitably been unadventurous and over-short, and that had become a matter of habit, but the loss of his ear had required a fundamental rethink, and under the guidance of Tessara's dexterous fingers he had grown it considerably longer in order to cover the scar. But now he had a new ear. A decision needed to be made, and Harry sat staring at himself in the mirror. The first gentle brushstrokes of middle age were beginning to show through. It happened, dammit, one of those turning points. Perhaps it was a sign of what was meant to be, a new hairstyle along with a new life, with Harry once again flying alongside the other geese, being part of the team. The Prime Minister's offer had been weighing heavily on him, he knew he would very soon have to decide.

He had drifted off. When he opened his eyes once more he was shocked to see what he thought at first was the face of his father staring back at him. He'd been not much older than Harry when he died, leaving behind a wagonload of money and a lifetime of colourful and often exquisitely painful memories. And Harry, of course. Thinking about it all left Harry feeling suddenly vulnerable, not at the thought of death but at what he would leave behind, and who the hell he would leave it to. People assumed he had everything – status, wealth, a reputation more formidable than almost any man of his time, and yet . . .

'So what's it to be, my love?' Tessara demanded, returning from the kitchen with his tea.

'Your choice. In your hands.'

'Leave a bit of length in it, if you ask me,' she replied, holding up a strand. 'Ride the waves, as my son always says.'

He closed his eyes once more, accepting. He had so many other decisions to make. At least for the next twenty minutes he had the chance to switch off, allow someone else to take the strain.

'Come on, then, let's get you washed,' she declared, wheeling him to the sink.

She had finished with the shampoo and was halfway through administering a head massage when his phone rang. He groaned, swore under his breath. Idiot, should've switched the bloody thing off, would do now, whoever it was, even Downing Street. Stuff 'em. He pulled out the phone and was about to send it to sleep when he noticed the number. He didn't recognize it. He hesitated, and curiosity did the rest. With a muttered apology to Tessara and considerable caution he put the phone to his new ear.

'Harry Jones,' he announced.

'Hello, Harry.' The voice was soft, throaty, a little breathless, female. Just as it had always been.

He froze, his contentment stripped like flesh from his bones. It was Terri.

—⁑—

Harry derided himself for his weakness as he dodged the winter puddles that gathered on the paving stones of Notting Hill in the western reaches of central London. What the hell was he doing? Despite the weather he'd decided to walk from his home in Mayfair across the rain-kissed acres of Hyde Park to Terri's. He needed to clear his thoughts, but he hadn't got very far with the process by the time he found himself walking up the Portobello Road with its jumble of pastel-fronted urban cottages and antiques emporia. He passed a small dwelling that when it was built had been a dairy farm-house in the middle of open fields; now its powder-blue wall was covered almost to the point of obliteration with fly posters for wannabe rock bands. He hurried on. Soon he was turning into a more elegant crescent of tall, stucco-fronted Victorian houses backing onto a private garden square that had once formed part of the short-lived Hippodrome racecourse, a notorious track of clinging mud where fortunes were lost before the developers took over and, in unfavourable times, lost fortunes new. It had been an area of slump and slum until the idle classes took over; now it required a fortune simply to park your car on the street.

He didn't love her, of course, not after all these years, but she still aroused feelings in him – of hurt, anger, shame and, he had to admit, curiosity, like discovering a forgotten scar. She had reappeared to shine a light on part of him that he didn't understand, one that he didn't very much like. And now he was almost at her doorstep.

She had once talked to him about her dream of a cottage with honeysuckle and roses climbing over the door, but this place wasn't anything like that. It was talking millions. Much of the front garden had been given over to a driveway that led to an underground garage, while the rest was hidden behind a thick high hedge for privacy. A Mercedes roadster was parked on the paved standing, a clutter of umbrellas and road atlases spread across the back seat and a pair of woman's sunglasses – Terri's sunglasses – dangling from the mirror. Harry found it a short but weary climb up to the front door.

He'd expected a cleaner or nanny, but she answered it herself, her eyes raw from crying. Neither said a word as she led the way up the stairs to a reception room on the first floor overlooking the garden at the rear. Harry hadn't even taken off his raincoat. She crossed to the window, stared for some while; he saw her body shuddering while she struggled for control. As she remained silent, her arms clasped tightly around her, his eyes danced around the room and soaked up the objects that were the markers of her life – the books, the family photographs, a stack of jigsaws and games on a bottom shelf, the scattering of personal ornaments and heirlooms. A Christmas tree was leaning in one corner, waiting to be set and decorated.

She sighed and moved away from the window. 'It's my son, Ruari. I think he's been kidnapped.'

It was his turn to stand silent for a moment. 'What makes you think that?'

'Ruari went for a heli-skiing trip from his school in Switzerland four days ago. He hasn't been seen since. Now they've discovered the bodies of two of the friends he was with.'

'I'm so sorry . . .'

'One of them had been shot.'

He had come here dragging his own feelings of anger behind him, but now her fear swept those aside. He sat down on the sofa but still she stood, rigid, as though afraid that if she tried to move her legs would give way.

'On the day it happened I got a strange call from Ruari – or at least from his phone. Just noise, really, and muffled voices. I thought he'd pressed the speed dial by mistake and I erased it but . . . Now I think it was made from the helicopter. And today I got another message.' She walked stiffly towards a side table on which stood a laptop. 'On this. A voice message. Over the Internet. On Skype.'

'You didn't record it, I suppose.'

She shook her head. 'But I remember almost every word. "We have your son, bitch!" it began. Then it said if we called in the police or anyone like that, we'd never see him again.' The memory was beginning to twist inside her. 'It said we should do nothing except wait for their next message.' The tears were flowing now.

'Did it give you any clues? Who they were, or where they were?'

She tried to bite back her anguish. 'The voice was white South African, that would be my guess, but apart from that – nothing. Except at the end of the call . . .' She was struggling. 'At the end there was just one long scream of pain!' Now Terri was sobbing her heart out, her manicured fingers ripping at the buttons on her sleeve, her shoulders heaving, her head hanging in despair. Harry wanted to put his arms around her, to comfort her, but he couldn't. She seemed as though she would break in two, fall in pieces to the ground, but she was battling with her fear and eventually she let forth one final lung-bursting sob before scrabbling for a handkerchief and wiping her eyes, which once more fell on him.

'Forgive me, but . . .' He was hesitant, reaching for the appropriate words. 'Why are you telling me this? What about your husband?'

'J.J.'s away, out of contact, I don't know precisely where. There's some important deal he's trying to tie up, it's all ridiculously hush-hush. He's even taken his head of corporate security with him. I didn't know who else to call and . . . Meeting up with you again the other day seemed like a sign. Call Harry Jones! Why not? Everyone else does.' She tried to make light of it, came to sit on the far end of the sofa, her lips struggling to shape themselves into a brave smile. 'I didn't know who else to call, Harry.'

He wanted to leave, but couldn't. She wasn't the only

one at war with their emotions. 'That cry,' he said, 'are you sure it was him?'.

'Yes. A mother knows.' Her voice snagged on something sharp inside. She began trembling.

'*Don't, Harry,*' he told himself. '*Don't you dare touch her . . .*'

She wrapped her arms around herself as though she might burst apart.

'And what do you want me to do?' he heard himself saying.

CHAPTER SIX

The message that had capsized Terri's world and left her drowning had its origins earlier that morning. Ruari had woken from a sleep disturbed by many ghosts to find a guard watching him, impassively and without a word, and it wasn't long before he found the silence even more oppressive than the pain from his broken nose. He tried to engage the Romanian in conversation but wasn't even sure the dumb-ass understood him properly. He tried his French in case the guard found that easier than English, but that had fallen on equally barren soil. So when de Vries made an appearance Ruari tried a different tactic, asking if he might have something to read – 'you know, a comic, book, newspaper, anything. It'll keep me quiet,' he promised. But de Vries ignored him, too.

Then the South African returned to the bleak bedroom cell accompanied by another guard, named Nelu, the youngest of the guards, a skinny, gangling youth who wore a crumpled Disney T-shirt and torn jeans and carried a laptop under his arm. For a moment Ruari's spirits rose.

Perhaps they had relented, he thought. It was the last time he would make that mistake.

'Pity about you throwing that phone of yours away,' de Vries began, rubbing his stubble-red chin with a knuckle. 'Could have saved us a lot of trouble. You, too. No need for that busted nose of yours. How is it, by the way?'

'Still hurts,' Ruari muttered cautiously, although in truth the pain had subsided to a dull throbbing ache.

'I'm sure it does. Nasty things, noses. Anyway, we need your parents' contact details – you know, their private phone numbers and email addresses. And since you've thrown your phone away, you'll have to give them to me.'

'I've forgotten,' Ruari replied. 'I just sort of punch buttons, you know?'

'No, no, I don't think so,' de Vries said in his clipped voice, 'not good enough, Little Shit.' They all seemed to have taken up the habit of calling him that, never Ruari. He had a name, an identity, but they refused to acknowledge it. His captors knew it would slowly wear him down. 'Kids like you are sponges, you soak up everything. So don't pretend you can't remember. Give.'

'You can ask.'

'And I shall receive.'

Ruari glared back and ran his tongue across his injured lip. His defiance seemed not to affect the man, whose tone remained casual.

'Come on, Little Shit, don't make it any more difficult

than it needs to be. Don't you want your folks to know you're OK?'

Ruari, who was on his mattress, stretched himself out full length as though he was going to sleep.

'That's a pity, one hell of a pity,' de Vries announced in the manner of a disappointed schoolmaster. He was standing over the bed. 'Change your mind?'

Ruari closed his eyes, trying to blot out the sense of fear this man always instilled in him, and turned away, stretching the arm by which he was manacled to the bed. Suddenly de Vries had grabbed his shoulder and was kneeling on his other arm, pinning it down. For a moment they stared into each other's eyes, the South African smiled. Then his fingers found Ruari's broken nose and gave it a violent twist.

It felt to Ruari as though he had been hit by a hammer. He screamed. De Vries twisted his nose a second time and all Ruari's defences were swept away. He began spilling numbers and addresses like a ripped sack of corn. He gave them what they wanted, everything, then he lay back on his mattress sobbing. He could taste the sweetness of blood in his mouth, his body was on fire, he was having trouble focusing through the bombardment of lights that were exploding inside his skull. He was only vaguely aware that Nelu was standing nearby, fiddling with the laptop, and de Vries was talking again, calling someone a bitch, talking about the police, a husband, and messages that would follow. He made sense of

81

nothing until the moment that de Vries crushed his nose once more, and he started screaming all over again.

—∿—

'What do you want me to do?' Harry repeated.

'Wave a magic wand. Make this go away. Give me back my child,' Terri whispered, her voice straining with every word.

'You have time, kidnappers don't tend to go away. You should wait until your husband comes home.'

'I can't wait,' she bit back. 'I can't just sit here and do nothing but snivel. I'm his mother, for pity's sake.'

'I don't think this is something I should get involved in.'

'You must.'

'Must?'

'You have no choice, Harry,' she insisted firmly. 'You owe me.'

'I? Owe *you*?' he spluttered.

'Oh, I know it was a long time ago, but you weren't the only one to get hurt.'

'You covered it up remarkably well.'

'You weren't around to see.'

He listened to her in a state of astonishment. For years he'd harboured an image of her as a cynical and hard-hearted woman, for no better reason than it was easier for him to pile the blame on her that way, but now she was telling him how much she had cared, felt things. She picked up a silver-framed photo of herself holding the hand of a young boy in school uniform, green blazer, cap, long socks pulled up high, with grass stains on his knee.

'Ruari?' he asked.

'His first day at school. I told him he had to be brave. I think that goes for me, too. I need you to be honest, Harry, tell me everything you can. Don't try and protect me, I need to know.' There was an urgency in her voice.

'What can I tell you?'

'A great deal, I suspect.'

He took it as a criticism. He thrust his hands deep into the pockets of his coat. 'OK. That voice,' he began.

'The South African?'

'The first thing I ask myself is why a white South African is involved with an English kid in Switzerland.' He rose, went to the window where she had been standing, where he imagined her standing looking out at a young boy on a scooter racing across the grass, making sure he was safe. 'You ever upset any South Africans?'

'Me? No. I've never even been there. Nor J.J., so far as I know.'

The lawn was empty now, nothing but a couple of lazy crows searching for worms. He turned. 'It's always possible they might be acting for someone else.'

'You mean, like a hired hand. A mercenary.' They were statements, not questions. She was impressively up to pace. Despite her pain she was thinking, already working things through.

'Possibly. We'll need to wait and see what their demands are.'

'How long?'

'Not long, I suspect.'

'But sometimes these things can drag on for weeks – months.' Her voice rose in alarm.

'You sure you want this?'

'You must tell me.'

He saw the fear in her eyes; lines of suffering were etching a path around her mouth. She was ageing a year with every hour. 'I may be entirely off target here, you understand, but why did they make him scream? It wasn't necessary, not in their first contact with you. It makes me think they're in a hurry.'

'Is that good or bad?'

He thought it was as dangerous as hell, yet he shrugged. 'It means they'll be in touch soon. That must be good, I suppose. It's the waiting that's the worst.'

'Where is he, Harry?' she sobbed, beginning to weaken once more.

'You say you got a phone call from him?'

She nodded as she wiped her nose with a handkerchief.

'Give me his number, and the time he called, as best you can. Your number, too, and the phone company you use.' She cast aside the handkerchief and began scribbling on a piece of paper. 'Then make me some coffee,' he added. Keep her busy, give her something to do.

She hesitated. 'Black, one sugar?'

Christ, she remembered. He shuddered, wondering what else she could recall. Soon he could hear the clatter of crockery and the gushing of a tap from the nearby kitchen. His eyes wandered around the room, snagging on the life she had made for herself, items so insignificant yet which seemed to be shouting at him. He didn't care to ask himself why.

The contacts file on his phone was a wizard's grotto filled with colleagues and friends who had passed through his life, and he scrolled through to the details of one of the signals officers who had served with him during the black years in Northern Ireland and who was now making a different kind of killing as the security director of one of the leading international telephone companies. He dialled.

'Glen? It's Harry Jones.'

'Harry, how the devil—'

'No time, old chum. I need a favour.'

'Somehow I know I'm going to regret this.'

'One of your phones made a call last Friday morning from somewhere in Switzerland. I need to know as precisely as possible where that call came from.'

'Ouch. If it's not your phone and you don't have a court order, I can't help you. That sort of thing's smothered in all sorts of pissy protocols and data-protection nonsense, not to mention the Regulation of Investigatory Powers Act 2000 and various provisions of the European Convention of Human Rights. Get my balls nailed to our ever-plunging share price if I was found handing out that sort of stuff.'

There was a short silence, followed by a long sigh.

'And I think, Harry, you were just about to say that the only reason I've still got balls is because you helped me when I needed it.'

'I was thinking no such thing,' Harry lied. 'Although now you come to mention it, I do remember your wife had even more lurid suspicions than the CO about what you were up to that weekend you went missing in Belfast.'

'You fight dirty, you know.'

'Yes, we did, didn't we?'

'Screw you, Harry.' But there was no venom in it.

'You know I wouldn't ask if it weren't—'

'I know, a matter of life and death.'

'A young kid's life. I'm with his mother now.'

'Damn, you *do* fight dirty,' the voice muttered in resignation.

'Thanks, Glen. I'll text you the details.'

As he ended the call, Terri appeared with two mugs of coffee. She bent down to place one in front of him and he could smell her, a different perfume than he remembered, more subtle, but back then she'd been only – what? Twenty-three? And he a few years older. Could they ever have been so impossibly young? As she leaned forward her breast tightened against the silk of her blouse. He closed his eyes, trying to forget.

'Not quite like old times, is it, Harry?' she said, sensing his discomfort.

Their eyes met, wavered in uncertainty, like rivers on

the point of bursting their banks, but before it could take hold the moment was snatched away as from below came the sounds of new arrivals. Wet feet stomping, the front door slamming, footsteps taking the stairs two at a time, then a voice bursting with excitement. 'Terri? Darling? You up there?' More steps. 'It's wonderful news, totally bloody mind-blowing! They've signed. We're saved!'

J.J. Breslin came bounding up the stairs with the energy of a condemned man who has heard the telephone ring on his way to the execution chair. And why not? His spirit was soaring, his manhood restored. He'd shown them, shown the bloody lot of them, the doubters, the destroyers of faith, the spreaders of gloom, not to mention that bitch and the other bankers. Yet the breathless enthusiasm that had carried J.J. Breslin up the stairs disappeared the moment he stepped into the room to discover his wife, in tears, sitting on his sofa with her former lover. Feet that had sprung wings now remained nailed to the polished wooden floor, excited eyes now clouded in suspicion. 'What the f . . . ?' He was a cultured man, not used to throwing out expletives, but his surprise and disappointment escaped him before he managed to strangle the rest. Jealousy defies logic, it ignores double standards, forgets its own failings, it is a voracious consumer of both light and joy, and of memory, and in Breslin's case had absolutely no recollection of hours lost in Blackheath.

'This is a pleasant surprise,' he managed, recovering,

lying, but already Terri was flying across the room and into his arms.

'It's Ruari,' she sobbed against his cheek. 'Somebody's taken Ruari.'

—∞—

Since his last beating at the hands of de Vries, Ruari had been careful not to give his captors any cause for anger. The pain that filled his face seemed remorseless, as though a thousand rats were trying to gnaw their way out through his skull, and the flesh around his eyes and cheeks had swollen to such an extent that he could only see out of one eye, and that only with difficulty. All plans of retaliation, escape, revenge, were put to one side while he tried to recover. But that didn't save him.

From below came the smells of the kitchen. Once again meat was roasting, pork he thought, if he could trust his battered nose, but they never gave him any of it, nothing but porridge and pasta to scoop around a bowl. One of the Romanians came up with his meal of mush in one hand and a cigarette in the other. As he stood over Ruari he blew out a cloud of acrid smoke, and as it hit his bruised airways the boy started choking, violently, gasping for breath as his head began screaming in insult. The guard laughed and exhaled more smoke over him.

The other guard sitting in the chair by the window with his Makarov by his side joined in. 'Hey, Sandu, your cooking make him sick!'

'What, Little Shit, you no like my food?' the cook shouted in mock despair, holding out the bowl as though for inspection.

Ruari shook his head in denial. He was hungry, the struggle for recovery from his beating had soaked up his energy and even this mush was better than loading still more pain upon his misery. He held out his hand, turning his head, blinking through his sore eye as he tried to locate the bowl, but the guard drew it back.

'You insult me,' he accused.

'No, no . . . please.'

'He hate your food,' the other guard mocked. 'Sandu, we all hate your fucking food.'

'I'm hungry,' Ruari pleaded.

'Little Shit, you do nothing but sit around all day and complain. Do no work, do nothing but complain.' He kicked the metal bedstead. 'You no deserve my food.'

He blew more smoke over the boy, leaving him twisted in another fit of coughing, yet it was as nothing compared to the pain he felt from his sense of loneliness and overwhelming despair.

'You learn,' the guard said. 'Like a dog, you learn.'

He said something in their native language that made the other guard guffaw, then he walked out, taking the bowl with him.

—⚉—

Two other men had arrived at his home with J.J. Breslin. One was in his mid-fifties, tall, with a long chin and a boxer's gnarled brow and eyes just a fraction too close. His tie was knotted so carefully that its point hovered absolutely level with his belt buckle, and his trousers were pressed so tight they threatened to squeak. Harry noticed the shoes, they were brilliantly polished but had thick composite soles, the sort of footwear that was ideal for long periods of standing, or creeping. Gumshoes. Harry was right in suspecting he was a former policeman. Three years earlier Brian Archer had been a chief super in the Met, now after thirty years and a retirement package that he always described as 'considerably less than copper-bottomed' he had 'come over to the dark side' – the commercial sector, or Breslin's bit of it, where he was employed as the newspaper's head of corporate security.

The third man wore a suit that was expensively cut yet casually worn, not as a uniform but merely as something to get him through the day. No tie. He was much nearer seventy, small, lean in both frame and face, with hollow cheeks in constant motion, agitated, like a mountain stream finding its way around rocks, but the eyes, which were remarkably bright for a man of his age, moved cautiously, staring, analysing, digesting, seeming to doubt everything they saw and disliking much of it. They stayed fixed on Harry for some time, even as Terri began explaining to her husband what had happened. As she did so, J.J. seemed to turn to stone. When she had finished, his arms closed stiffly around her, he was in shock, needing support, trying to be strong, wanting to scream, knowing he couldn't. They continued to stand in silence, in each other's arms, struggling for composure, his face buried in her hair, until he took a deep breath for courage and turned to Harry.

'And why are you here, Mr Jones?'

'I called him,' Terri answered, too quickly, before Harry had a chance to. 'I couldn't get hold of you and I thought Harry might help. He's already—'

He cut her off, but not unkindly. 'I'm sure that's particularly generous of you, Mr Jones, but Archer here is my head of security.' The gumshoe bounced up and down on the balls of his feet. 'He'll handle matters from now on. And as this is a family matter, I'm sure you'll understand if I simply offer you my thanks for coming. And ask you to leave.'

The words were well honed but the edge to his voice didn't convey much sense of gratitude. Terri's eyes widened in embarrassment. 'Please, J.J . . .'

He cut across her again, more firmly. 'Thank you, Mr Jones.'

Harry rose, shrugging off the stare that Breslin had fixed on him, like searchlights on a rabbit hunt, and shoved his hands still deeper into his coat pockets. He hadn't asked for this, didn't want any part of it. 'I'll let myself out,' he said.

'This is my son's life at stake here. I'd be obliged if you

didn't mention this to anyone. Forgot about it altogether, in fact.'

'I'll do my very best.' Harry headed for the stairs. Every step felt as though he was walking against an Arctic wind. 'Goodbye, Mr Breslin, Mrs Breslin.' She couldn't hold his eye, he couldn't use her name. 'Good luck.'

He found himself back on the street, gulping down the early winter air. Christ, tangling with Terri was like undergoing root-canal surgery with a rusty nail. The pavement seemed to agree; he stepped on an uneven paving stone that tipped and threw a jet of freezing liquid mud over his trouser leg, staining it up to the knee. It was already trickling into his sock. He swore, something very rude in Arabic. He had promised not to breathe a word and wouldn't, of course, but as for forgetting – well, that was an entirely different matter.

And something was nagging at him, something he'd heard as Breslin first came up the stairs. *They've signed. We're saved.* Odd words, with a meaning he didn't yet understand. It wasn't just a kidnap that was going on here. There were troubles aplenty for the Breslins, so it seemed, but that had nothing to do with him, he hadn't asked to be involved, had been warned off. And yet trouble always held an irresistible attraction for Harry. He strode down the street, squelching, and reached for his phone.

CHAPTER SEVEN

Breslin, Archer and the other man sat and talked with low voices and spirits that were lower still. Not until an hour later, when they were joined by two others, was any sense of organization brought to bear on their discussions. The newcomers, one mid-thirties, the other a few years older, both bore the neat, fit, understated appearance of former military officers. They were security men, from a company specializing in risk assessment and the protection of what their website rather drily referred to as 'high net worth individuals and their families' – otherwise known as rich kids and their parents. 'We underpin corporate assets and protect your competitive advantage,' it went on to proclaim. Clumsy words, yet when the corporate copywriters took their lunch breaks, those involved could be more down to earth about what it was they did. *The world out there is a pond overflowing with the most enormous quantities of shit. We help you avoid it whenever possible, or drag you out when you can't.* Kidnap, extortion, hostage-taking, ransom, murder. The sewage in their pond flowed deep. Theirs was a world in which the players were a kaleidoscopic assortment of terrorists and criminal opportunists on one side, with rich men and insurance brokers on the other, but whatever side they found themselves on, these were the sort of people who insisted on results and didn't usually care too much how they were achieved. And in between them stood guys (and a few girls) like Will Hiley and his slightly older boss, Andy Brozic.

It took a certain type of operative to work in this field, the sort who were used to situations of crisis and danger and who, when required, were willing to put their own necks on the line but who were much more comfortable putting the other bastard's neck on the line instead. It was a rough and often unpalatable business, one that operated in the shadows and too often became confused with the dark world of the mercenary, but it was always possible to tell the difference. Mercenaries didn't work out of addresses in Mayfair and Bloomsbury.

Hiley and Brozic had been summoned by Archer, the gumshoe. He knew their firm and was familiar with its ability to handle its affairs with discretion, a familiarity that had grown to enthusiasm during several serious dinners and a couple of evenings of cup football at Stamford Bridge as its guest. The men arrived laden with a collection of sophisticated electronic equipment and, charmingly, a supply of paper notepads.

'You're a sort of private police force,' Terri suggested as they introduced themselves.

'K&R, really – kidnap and ransom. That's what we specialize in.'

The risk assessors quickly took charge. They commandeered the dining room and installed their equipment, which included their own computer – 'in case your own computers have already been infected with malware. That could let the kidnappers listen to every word we say'. The computer was connected to recording and monitoring equipment, all the family's phones were inspected, the house checked for bugs. Then they began asking questions, hundreds of them. Did the Breslins have kidnap insurance? No. Might the newspaper cover the costs? Again, no. 'That's a benefit in some ways,' Brozic announced, 'it means all the decisions are down to you. No outside interference.' He didn't mention that such interference was often highly desirable in the moments when a family lost all sense of perspective, as at some point they usually did.

Had they any idea who might be behind this? Did they have any personal enemies? Was the newspaper caught up in any contentious campaigns? Why Switzerland? What did they know about the school and its staff? And a thousand other things that were scribbled down on their notepads, even though they were recording every word.

Terri didn't sit with them. Once she had handed over all the memories of the message, something they required her to do several times, she was asked to provide tea and coffee, make arrangements for their lunch, direct them to the bathroom and fetch family photographs, but she wasn't invited to join this tight-knit group or offer an opinion. The K&R men took their lead from her husband, who took her cooperation and consent for granted. It wasn't that J.J. was trying to be unkind, rather the contrary; he wanted only to protect her, to spare her the anguish, as if a mother's mind couldn't fail to see every terrifying alternative. Anyway, J.J. was suffering himself. Every question hit him like a punch from a heavyweight's fist that left him struggling for breath. His mouth and lips grew so dry that soon he could do little more than mutter his replies. The assessors took the reins.

'We need to establish a psychological profile,' Hiley said apologetically. He moved slowly and spoke softly, but his muscular outline and sense of pent-up energy suggested he was the sort who spent his weekends in continuous bouts of cage wrestling. Now he chewed thoughtfully on the end of his pen. 'How . . . *resilient* might the victim be?'

'His name is Ruari,' Terri chided, standing in the doorway with a fresh pot of coffee in her hand.

Hiley glanced up in embarrassment.

'And since the kidnapper's South African,' she told them, relying on Harry's advice and placing the coffee in front of them, 'that means he could be a mercenary. In a hurry.'

'I doubt that, Mrs Breslin,' the other assessor, Brozic, said. 'Not many mercenaries get involved in this sort of thing. Kidnap's dirty work in their world.'

'Oh, I see. They prefer the cleaner stuff, you mean. Assassinations and civil wars.'

'We can't even be sure he's South African – the voice

might well be disguised. But we'll record him when he calls back. We can find out all sorts of things through voice pattern analysis, whizz things through the computer, that sort of thing. We'll be on his trail very shortly, I promise you.'

Whizz things through the computer? She wanted to scream. The pillock was trying to patronize her and she'd have been happier pouring the bloody coffee into his lap, but they had already lowered their heads and were back to their discussions, leaving her outside the circle. Unsuitable work for a woman. She left them, returned to the kitchen, rummaged through several drawers and a cupboard, and finally found what she was looking for. She lit one of J.J.'s cigarettes. She hadn't smoked in years.

—◊◊◊—

Workmen were in the early stages of erecting a lofty Christmas tree as Harry entered the covered streets of Leadenhall Market in the City of London. He was glad to get here, beneath the glorious wrought-iron and glass canopies that kept the place dry. It was raining hard outside, threatening sleet from a steel-grey sky, and his sock hadn't yet dried. Leadenhall was a place of bustle, of butchers and cheesemakers and purveyors of provender that was little different from when the Romans had gathered on this spot at the heart of ancient Londinium. In the passage of years since then the market place had been burned, abandoned, looted, bombed, but always rebuilt,

MICHAEL DOBBS

most magnificently by the Victorians who had filled it with cobbles, soaring columns, imperial pomp and a large number of watering holes. It was to one of these that Harry was now headed. 'Brokers' was a first-floor wine bar overlooking the centre of the market. Harry found a seat at a window and watched the struggle of the workmen. They had just finished erecting the tree and were decking it out with lights when a man in a broad chalk-stripe suit, extravagant shirt cuffs and a pronounced limp placed a large glass of something white in front of him.

'Happy Christmas,' Jimmy Sopwith-Dane – 'Sloppy' to those he recognized as friends – declared as he sat opposite.

Harry ignored the comment. He wasn't in the mood, and never much was at this time of year. Christmas as a child had always proved to be a perilous festival, when his father would return, often after an absence of weeks, with an abundance of presents to fill the many gaps and missed dates that had marked the previous twelve months. At the age of thirteen Harry had discovered that most of his father's gifts had been chosen by a secretary of Scandinavian origin who had managed to misspell his name on the labels. 'It's with a *y*, Dad, not *i*,' he'd rebuked his father, but not in front of his mother. Even at the age of thirteen, Harry had learned to tread with extreme care around the suggestion that his father had another life.

'To survival,' Sopwith-Dane said, raising his glass.

'Hope springs eternal,' Harry responded, pursing his lips in appreciation of a fine Burgundy.

It was easy to misjudge Sopwith-Dane. He had a manner that some would regard as foppish, almost Edwardian, and the limp slowed him down, but only physically, yet those who underestimated Sloppy normally ended up trailing far behind. He had served with Harry in the Life Guards and forged their friendship in the bandit country of Armagh. One night on patrol he had taken a bullet intended for Harry; it had made a monumental mess of Sloppy's knee, and with it his military career. 'No more arse-kicking for me, I suppose,' was all he had ever said by way of complaint. So he'd taken his gammy leg and Etonian humour off to the City where, with an extravagant smile and a deft hand, he'd managed to carve out a big enough niche to salvage both his marriage and the ancestral home. He also kept a close watching brief on Harry's very considerable investments.

'So, dear boy,' he declared as a waitress placed a bowl of whitebait in front of them, 'how the blazes are you?'

'On the scrounge, Sloppy.'

'Good. Glad to see that nothing's changed. What is it this time? The car, the villa, the wife – no, Harry, I draw the line at any of the daughters, even for you, old chap.' His eyes sparkled along with his cufflinks.

'J.J. Breslin. Know him?'

'The newspaper chappie, you mean? Met him a couple of times. Rather dour, not the ideal companion for a long voyage, if you ask me. Surprisingly worthy for a media tycoon. Remember his wife rather better, though.

Oh, yes, desperately distracting, that one. In a word – hot!'

'What about the newspaper?' Harry asked, hoping he hadn't visibly flinched.

Sloppy's brow wrinkled. 'Ah, not so hot. The man is Napoleonic in ambition but desperately overextended. Currently engaged in the long retreat from Moscow and got himself firmly stuck in the snows, by all accounts. Assets on the point of being frozen. Wolves snapping at his heels.'

'Bad as that, eh?'

'You know what the newspaper industry's like, robbed blind by the Internet, blood everywhere. He's not as big as the other players, doesn't have as much fat to live off in these harsh times. Mr Breslin needs the luck of his Irish ancestors, otherwise my fellow looters and pillagers will be upon him and he'll be belly up by next spring. Off to a prolonged exile in St Helena with his Josephine.'

'Terri,' Harry muttered distractedly as he rolled his glass between his palms.

'What?'

'She's called Terri.'

'Is she, by golly? I can think of worse ways to spend my old age.' He was chuckling once more, but his keen eye had spotted the firm set of Harry's face. 'You all right, old chap?'

'Of course,' Harry lied, but not well, looking out of the window and examining the ancient meat hooks for the rabbits, ducks and pheasants that still hung above a butcher's window.

'In need of some distraction, eh?'

'Something truly sinful.'

'Oh, dear, the wife's going to be no use to you there, I'm afraid.' He sighed in disappointment. 'But I know a young lady at a nearby art gallery who—'

'Just keep an eye on it, will you, Sloppy?'

'My very great pleasure.'

'No, you bloody idiot, Breslin's company. Let me know if you hear any rumblings, pick up any rumours.'

'A little light reconnaissance? My pleasure. But hope you're not in too much of a hurry.' He raised his glass and emptied it. 'Got the rest of the bottle to finish.'

So they took care of the bottle, and another. Sloppy owned a chunk of the wine bar and was anxious to deal with 'a couple of rather exotic bin ends', as he put it, 'to make space for the Christmas rush'.

And Harry was grateful for the diversion. The workmen had finished decorating the tree and the lights from around the market were beginning to burn more brightly as the afternoon faded into an early winter's evening. Harry's mood soaked up some of the rising festive spirit as he relaxed with his old friend. Then his phone rang. It was Mary Mishcon. Applying her own brand of gentle pressure. The Prime Minister anxious to hear about his decision . . .

'Mary, can't hear you well, the signal's terrible here,'

Harry exaggerated, distracted, knowing he'd had too much to drink to tackle that particular obstacle course. 'I'll call you back,' he promised.

'You used to be much better at lying,' Sloppy chided as Harry put the phone down on the table.

'Hell, I used to be better at lying to myself.'

Sloppy looked at him quizzically. 'That's all rather cryptic. I'm almost afraid to ask,' he said, reaching for the bottle and pouring with a heavy hand, 'but I will. Tell me about her.'

Harry sighed. Sloppy was a persistent bugger, and Harry didn't want to lie to him, too. He reached for his phone, intending to switch it off and avoid further disturbance, yet he hadn't even touched it when it began vibrating again. In frustration Harry glanced at the screen, then muttered another colourful Arabic oath.

It was Terri.

—⁓—

Gingerly Ruari ran his fingers around his face. The swelling was slowly beginning to subside, but not the fear, least of all the choking sense of humiliation. His sight was improving as the puffiness around his eyes faded, and at last they had relented and given him one or two things to help him pass the time, a couple of old *National Geographic* magazines and a chess set with three black pawns missing. He didn't mistake this as an act of kindness, he knew it was nothing more than a means of keeping him distracted and quiet. They had no desire to find themselves with a hysterical teenager on their hands.

What he was finding more difficult to deal with was the increasing pain from his wrist caused by his shackles – handcuffs that tethered him to a heavy chain, which in turn was fixed to the metal frame of the bedstead. Right from the first he'd tried to test it for any sign of weakness, but whenever he moved it rattled and chafed, leaving abrasions on his wrist that had already cut deeply through the skin. The chain allowed him to move no more than three feet, just enough to roll over in bed, or sit up, or use the red plastic bucket that was all he had as a toilet.

As the hours turned to days, his routine became set. They brought him three meals a day – porridge and pasta mostly, no meat, nothing that would need a knife or fork; he had to make do with a spoon. They also left him a bottle of tap water. And whether he ate, drank, peed, crapped, cried or slept, there was always a Romanian on guard, well armed, sitting in a chair on the far side of the room by the window.

Occasionally de Vries would descend upon them on a tour of inspection. He kept the guards on a tight leash, insisting they concentrate only on Ruari, snatching away the portable media players and reading material they used to while away the monotony. Harsh words were thrown in both directions. The guard was changed every two hours, but still they resented the South African's interference. Whenever these arguments erupted, Ruari kept his head down, feigning sleep, afraid the guards would be tempted to take their frustration out on him, but none did. They were too afraid of the South African to risk that.

No one spoke to Ruari, not a word, unless it was to complain about the bucket that the guards were forced to empty. Having already failed with both English and French, Ruari tried swearing at them to force some sort of reaction, but he got nothing more than a painful kick in the leg for his troubles. That was from Cosmin, whose face was swollen and blotchy and had turned vivid shades of yellow and blue. That gave Ruari a little satisfaction, even though he guessed his own face looked far worse.

His mind ran back to a film he'd once watched on his laptop, after lights out when he was supposed to be asleep, about a young girl named Patty Hearst. She was a Californian newspaper heiress who'd been kidnapped and had her mind filled with so much gunk by the pigs who snatched her that she'd flipped and gone over to their cause, even helped them rob a bank. That sort of behaviour had a name – the Stockholm syndrome. To Ruari it seemed like a form of madness. Identifying with your abductors was supposed to be a common affliction but that wouldn't happen to him, he vowed, no, never to him. Looking across the room at Cosmin, with his scraped knuckles, Ruari concluded there were many, many things he'd like to do for the bastard, but helping him wasn't anywhere on the list.

During the endless hours he spent lying tethered on a soiled mattress beside that stinking bucket, Ruari tried to

OLD ENEMIES

fathom the meaning of what they were doing to him. He had an analytical mind that wandered across the landscape inspecting many possibilities, but at the end of these journeys he arrived back at the same point. They wanted to keep him alive, at least for the moment. The one thought that jarred against this was the fact that none of his captors used a facemask or disguised their features in any way; he could identify every one of them down to that bastard Cosmin's last pockmark and crooked tooth. If a day of reckoning ever came, they wouldn't want him picking them out and providing testimony, and perhaps from the start they never intended he should see that day, planned to do away with him before this was all over. He hoped there was another explanation. Perhaps they were simply arrogant, calculating that the world was more than big enough to swallow them without trace.

His life depended on all this, on the inner thoughts of these men. Ruari had lost his innocence, no longer assumed he was indestructible. Any lingering sense of his own immortality had been wrenched from him along with Casey and Mattias. He knew his plight was desperate. Then came the moment when Sandu arrived to relieve Cosmin and started swearing – Ruari had just used the latrine bucket and the atmosphere in the room was vile. Sandu moved his chair closer to the window and flung it wide open, lit one of his throat-searing cigarettes, staring into – what? Ruari realized he had no idea what lay beyond that window, had no idea where in the world he was.

105

Slowly the cool air of early winter began to reach into the room, even as far as Ruari's prison bed, bringing with it new aromas. He could smell something sweet-sour, and remembered the aroma from the pastures above Villars. It was rotting cow shit. And on top of that there was a tang of something sharper. Fermenting cheese, perhaps? During the day the window was usually tightly closed and muffled the sounds from outside, but during the stillness of the previous night he had heard strange animal cries and the screech of hunting birds. The picture came together. He was deep in the countryside. There was still a world outside his cell.

That knowledge made Ruari determined to escape. Whether they were planning to kill him eventually, or to keep him alive, it seemed to him he had nothing to lose by trying to break out. He couldn't be much worse off than he was now. So that's what he would do. Escape.

Trouble was, he hadn't an idea in hell how to do it. Not yet, at least.

CHAPTER EIGHT

'Meet me,' she had said.

'For God's sake, why?' Harry had muttered.

'Ruari's gone. Isn't that enough?'

'Meet . . . but where?' he had replied, more cautiously.

'Our usual place.'

'Stop talking in riddles.'

'Don't you remember?'

'Why all this bloody mystery?'

'I can't talk on the phone. I think it may be bugged.'

'You're kidding. Who the hell would—'

But the phone had gone dead, leaving Harry fuming in frustration. He had no intention of moving, not an inch, least of all of seeing her again. Her husband had been right, it was none of his bloody business. He was going to stay here on his comfortable seat and continue enjoying the company of both his friend Sloppy and the bottle that stood between them. And yet he couldn't help casting his mind back to the last time they had been together . . .

Paris. Lapérouse, a restaurant that had stood on the Left Bank of the Seine since even before the Revolution, a place full of dark wood and discreet corners, of gilded mirrors and painted ceilings, of carved cherubs and dreams. How many lovers had met here, how many whispers had its walls soaked up and its waiters forgotten? That's why Harry had chosen it for another of their stolen weekends, with excuses and lies left scattered in his wake. Yet it hadn't turned out like the others. They had arrived separately, from different destinations. Harry had booked into the hotel on his own while she had come straight from the Gare du Nord. She'd arrived late, with a lame excuse about a delayed train, and no light in her face. It had been almost three weeks since they'd last seen each other and Harry thought she looked strained, was worried she was sickening for something. She had ordered distractedly and even before the first course had arrived she told him she wouldn't, couldn't, see him again. She wouldn't explain why, wouldn't look him in the eye, and he had started to protest but they had been interrupted by the waiter, and she had made an excuse to visit the ladies' room. She had never returned.

A man in the midst of an intense affair rarely has full control of either his thoughts or his emotions, and it had taken Harry many distracted months to recover, even with Julia's forgiveness, yet despite that forgiveness, and perhaps even because of it, he had never been able to forgive Terri, and least of all himself. Now she was back, along with echoes of so much pain.

Where the hell was he supposed to meet her anyway?

Once more his mind dug into the old days, the memories came roaring back on a flood tide, and he knew.

—⁓—

It was still there, beneath the railway arches on the South Bank, the cramped bar with the vaulted brick ceiling and the incessant rumble of trains passing overhead. It meant the patrons had to lean close to catch each other's words. That had been an advantage, back then. Both the lease and decor seemed to have passed through several different sets of hands since Harry had last been here; he'd remembered dark wooden tables but now there was nothing but glass and brushed aluminium, while the prices were unrecognizable, yet the atmosphere was still much the same, close, intense, private. Harry sat at the bar, distractedly making patterns with the rings of condensation from his glass of over-chilled wine. A second glass waited beside him, empty, with the bottle dribbling dampness close at hand.

'Hello, Harry.'

He poured without asking.

'Pinot Grigio. You remembered,' she said with a catch in her voice.

'I remember too much.'

She could sense his hostility. She sipped silently for a while, trying to decide where to start. 'They've taken over, Harry, those men who came out of the blue, the risk assessors. They don't know me, they've never even met Ruari, yet somehow they're now in charge. Of everything. My dining table has become the centre of what they call their Operations Room, my kitchen is like an army mess, there's a goon with a shaved head and no neck standing at my front door.' She caught her breath. 'Everything's such a mess. I don't seem to have a home or a family any longer.'

As she spoke, staring into her glass, he studied her profile, the lips that left their mark on the rim of her glass, the point of her nose that bobbed as she talked. He noticed a small mole just beneath her jaw. Had she had that when . . . ? He couldn't remember, and told himself he couldn't care less.

'I'm supposed to tell them my every move, every time I leave home, where I'm going. I didn't, not this time, of course. I don't want J.J. finding out.'

'Why not?' he asked, trying to sound disinterested, yet chiding himself for being churlish.

'Everything's so rough at home, Harry. Stifling. I can't breathe. I had to get out. J.J.'s under such pressure.' She sighed, a mournful sound that came from deep inside. 'If he knew I was here he wouldn't understand.'

'That's the thing. I don't understand, either. What the hell am I supposed to be doing in all this? It has nothing to do with me.'

'They've set up what they call a family negotiating group to decide how to respond. To decide the fate of my child, Harry. And I'm not even on it. I've been pushed aside as if I don't have a role in any of this.'

'J.J.?'

'I know he's only trying to be kind, to protect me, but . . .
He's struggling to cope. He's hurting, just as much as I am.
I think he blames me. It was my decision to send Ruari to
Switzerland, you see.' Her voice had grown subdued, less
controlled. She leaned closer to him and he smelt that per-
fume again.

'I'm sorry, Terri.' He meant it. His anger with her was
waning, her son's life was at stake, for pity's sake.

'They asked J.J. how much we were willing to pay for
Ruari's release, and he said as much as it takes, of course he
would. And they said no, they needed a figure to work
with. Five hundred, eight hundred thousand? A million?
More? That's when he shouted at them, almost lost it. "My
son," he said, "is not some sort of second-hand car with a
price tag on it." But, they said, that's precisely what Ruari
is in the eyes of the kidnappers. A commodity for sale. It's
business, and that's how it has to be dealt with. Oh,
Harry . . .'

She was on the verge of tears. It took all his resolve not to
reach for her hand.

She gasped for air, sank more of the wine. 'It seems like
there's a going rate for these things.'

'If you need any help with cash . . .' he began, remembering what Sloppy had told him.

But she shook her head sharply. 'No! That's not why I'm
here.'

'Then?'

'The risk assessor, Hiley, tells us we ought to contact the

111

police, to let them know Ruari's been kidnapped. Archer thinks so, too, but J.J. won't have it. It's the one thing the kidnappers have said so far, don't contact any authorities, otherwise . . .' She couldn't finish the thought. 'Archer says the police business would all be done very quietly, no one would ever know, but J.J. says someone always knows, that it would leak, these things always do, that there's not a town in the world where you can't find a dodgy police-man willing to sell a story.'

'To the newspapers.'

She nodded, accepting the irony. 'So J.J. says no.'

'And you?'

She turned to look at him, her eyes welling. He remembered those same, pain-stretched eyes from Paris, too. In his mind he recalled the tears as nothing more than drops of discomfort, but perhaps the moment had been harder for her than he'd realized. Her words, then as now, came slowly, as though she was having trouble forming them.

'How am I supposed to decide, Harry? How? It's my son's life at stake.' She was very close to breaking down. 'That's why I came. To ask you. For advice.'

It was his turn to gaze into his glass, to avoid the fear in her eyes that was ripping her apart and trying to drag him in, too. 'These security companies always face a dilemma. In many countries it's against the law to deal with kidnap-pers without informing the police. They can get themselves thrown in jail as accessories if they don't cooperate with the authorities, and it happens. They walk a fine line – what are they really doing, helping the family, or the kidnappers? In any event they always risk being accused of above all helping themselves, of profiteering from misery. So they prefer to do things by the book.'

'And you, Harry? I don't ever recall you being a man who did things by the book.'

'Flying in a straight line,' he muttered, thinking of geese.

'I'm sorry?'

'Nothing. Just something someone said.'

'What should I do?' she demanded urgently.

'Listen to the advice. Those men are the experts in the field. But in the end it's you who have to decide, isn't it? You and J.J., together. Ruari's your son, not theirs.'

Her nostrils flared, as they did when she was summoning up the courage to make a confession. 'That's not so easy. J.J.'s a complicated man, keeps a lot to himself, locked away inside that Irish soul of his.'

He thought she sounded bitter. The fault lines of a marriage, now being torn wide open.

'You are Ruari's parents. The buck stops with you, no one else.'

The words seemed to affect her. Her bottom lip wobbled and hesitated, as though she wanted to say more but then changed her mind. 'I must go, before they miss me and I run out of excuses.' Her eyes clung to him, trying to hold him, to close the distance between the two of them. She laid her fingers on the back of his hand but he could see nothing but the sparkle of her wedding ring. 'I'll remember what you said, Harry. I promise you I will!'

She disappeared into the night, accompanied by the wailing of some distant siren, leaving Harry staring after her shadow and wondering what on earth he had said that was so bloody significant.

—⚬—

Harry had taken a substantial amount of alcohol on board that afternoon, and although Terri's arrival had had the effect of a cold shower that rapidly sobered him up, once she had vanished into the darkness he poured another glass and allowed himself to sink well below the Plimsoll Line. He was doodling with the damp base of his glass, constructing an Olympic logo on the bar top, when a man slipped onto the stool that until a few minutes earlier had been Terri's. Harry ignored him, head down, concentrating on the rings, letting the alcohol massage his wounds, until the stranger interrupted.

'Good evening, Mr Jones.'

Harry looked up, puzzled. To his surprise he recognized the older man, who had arrived back home with J.J. and the gumshoe. Despite the well-cut clothes and the classic Omega he wore on his wrist, there was an unmistakable rawness about him. His frame was wiry, his face weathered, and if he had been an animal Harry reckoned he'd have been an old fox, the sort that is cautious, accustomed to sniffing the morning wind, never sure whether that day he would be hunter or hunted. Harry remembered the eyes from their first brief encounter, cautious, sharp, but the wrinkles around them told of a lifetime of hard living, and they were looking at Harry with contempt. And the accent was unmistakably Irish.

'We were never introduced,' Harry said, feeling at a disadvantage.

'No, but I know you, Mr Jones – or should I say, I know *of* you.'

Immediately Harry was on his guard and began trying to sober up in a hurry. His new ear began to throb along the length of its scar, not so much in pain as in warning, as if it had a sense of its own. There was little surprise in a stranger greeting him, he was a politician, a public figure, no matter how much on occasion he wished he could get a break and look at life through the bottom of a slow-draining glass, but Irishmen of a certain age who knew about Harry Jones formed a special category all of their own, the sort who were unlikely to seek him out merely to ask for his autograph.

Ireland. Harry knew the place well, too well, at least its northern chunk. Two tours during those dark days of the 1980s, one with the SAS, doing the jobs that others couldn't, or wouldn't, do. It was a dirty war, crawling through shit-filled alleyways and ditches, dragging scalps behind him. And, in all honesty, it hadn't always mattered how those scalps were claimed. There were Queen's Regulations, of course, but it was difficult to read the fine print when you were in a swamp way up beyond your bollocks and some bastard was trying his very best to kill you. It had been a dirty war in every sense, the sort that left marks which wouldn't wash away.

'You've been poking your nose in where it's not wanted. An old habit, it seems,' the Irishman said.

'I don't understand,' Harry muttered, still awash, his mind slow, a long way from being up to full steam.

'Terri.'

Ah, so she'd been followed after all.

'You're wrong. I've no desire to stick my nose in anything. None of my business, nothing to do with me,' Harry muttered. Well, it was almost the truth.

'Then for once in our lives we're in agreement,' the man replied.

So, there was history between them. The man's tone was soft, like wind through the heather, but there was no mistaking the threatened bite.

'I'll say only this to you, Mr Jones. Stay out of Terri's life. Stay out of all of our lives. Or you'll be having me to deal with.'

'Are you threatening me?' Harry looked askance but not entirely incredulously at a man who was old enough to be his father and at least six inches shorter.

'Threats? Me? Mother of God, I've always left that sort of thing to the British. No, what I'm saying is that I agree with you. This is no concern of yours. So don't go getting yourself involved.'

'And if I decide not to take your advice?'

'Then you and I, Mr Jones, will be falling out, so we will. Very seriously.'

The barman interrupted, asking if he wanted a drink, but the man shook his head. 'No, I'll not be staying. I'm finished here.' He got up from his seat. 'Good night to you, Mr Jones,' he said, turning away.

'Who the hell are you?' Harry demanded.

The stranger stopped, half turned. 'The name's Sean Breslin, Mr Jones. I'm Terri's father-in-law. Ruari happens to be my grandson.' Then he was gone.

CHAPTER NINE

Ruari suspected that the two South Africans, de Vries and Grobelaar, had left the farmhouse. He heard a car start up and drive away, and quickly the atmosphere grew more relaxed. Laughter drifted up the stairs, something Ruari hadn't heard since he'd arrived, with much scraping of chairs across the stone floor and the clatter of conviviality. The duty guard, Toma, a squat, balding man with shoulders of immense breadth and skin like a freshly plucked chicken, scowled in envy as he heard the others enjoying themselves, but soon Cosmin appeared from behind the bedroom door bearing a glass of dark red wine for him. They chatted in their native language as they drank and Cosmin began waving his arms around, theatrically, perhaps bragging – Ruari thought he heard a phrase that sounded a lot like 'South African', followed by a word that was spat out like venom and he was sure translated as 'bastards'. The captors began to relax, the creases of anxiety that had marked their brows slowly lifting as they swapped jokes. When Cosmin returned downstairs he left the door open, and soon the sounds of merriment and the smell of roasting pork began to take hold of the room. Toma sipped, cast his eyes to the door, sipped some more. After twenty minutes of fidgeting, and casting a warning scowl at Ruari, he stamped his foot and followed Cosmin out of the door. He didn't go downstairs, for Ruari could hear him, perched at the top of the staircase, exchanging banter with those below. Soon they were singing.

The local wine in these parts was called Terrano, mostly very rough, raw, which coated the tongue and got quickly to work. It was much to the Romanians' liking. And it gave Ruari his chance.

He had been spending his hours on his mattress trying to figure out how he might escape. He knew almost nothing of what lay beyond the thick stone walls of the farmhouse and had even less idea where it was located, but he'd never find out unless he could manage to slip his chains. For the hundredth time he searched for any flaw or sign of weakness in the chain, examining the handcuffs that held him to the chain and the locks that kept the chain secured to the bed, but he found nothing that might help. His attempts to fold his hand and squeeze it out of the handcuffs, even with the help of a thick smear of cold grease from his bowl, had done nothing but cause him intense pain. He had finally come to the conclusion that he wasn't going to escape the chain, so his attentions focused on the bed. It was simple, with a headboard in the design of a seashell made out of metal tubes that were welded into place. He had tested the welds as best he could whenever the guards had been distracted, but the construction was too strong. Cracking them apart wasn't going to happen. And he had no tools. For a few brief moments he tried to use his spoon to see if he could separate any of the links in the chain, but it was a desperate act that left him with nothing but a pinched finger and a pathetically bent spoon. He had no keys, no pen, nothing but the clothes that he lay in, and not even his boots. His pockets had been emptied, his watch taken from him. He had nothing but his bonds.

The bed had a cast-iron frame and metal springs, and the frame was fixed to the bed head by two bolts. The bolts were hidden beneath the mattress, he couldn't see them, but he had been able to investigate them with the tips of his fingers and estimate the size of the bolt head and the nut beneath. And it was this, he concluded, that gave him his chance. So while the singing and laughter downstairs rose in volume and covered his efforts, he took his gamble.

Kneeling beside the bed, he lifted up the mattress and found the nut. It was old, there was no chance of turning it with his fingers. He tried, of course, got a badly torn nail for his efforts. Yet he had the chain, and as he had prayed they might, the links proved to be just the right size. It was a heavy chain and he had spent most of his time in captivity cursing it, but a lighter chain would have been too small. Now he forced one of the links over the head of the bolt, and twisted.

It took several false attempts and bruised knuckles before he got anywhere. The chain kept slipping, striking against the bed frame and making a terrible clatter, and at one point the guard's suspicions were roused. He shouted from the top of the stairs; Ruari told him it was nothing, that he was only taking a leak. Toma went back to his Terrano.

Ruari had to smother the noise. He slipped his head and free arm from out of his sweater and wrapped it around the chain, then he twisted at the bolt again. It hadn't moved in forty years and was as stubborn as an Irish wind, but Ruari was persistent, too, and reluctantly, groaning, the bolt set itself free.

It was done. Ruari was sweating now, from fear, not just from the effort. His hand was shaking as he put the bolt to one side and tugged at the frame, trying to separate it from the bed head, but there were still unyielding bolts at the other three corners. As he tried to force the pieces apart, the old metal growled mightily in complaint, but the guards were singing one of their native drinking songs and the noise went unnoticed. Yet still the bloody thing wouldn't shift. So he sank to his knees, squeezing his back beneath the frame, placed his hands around the bed head and with every morsel of youthful rage he tried to separate them. And slowly, so slowly, they gave way. As they came apart, he was able to slide the links around the metalwork of the bed head and down the leg. Inch by inch, desperate not to create any noise, he coaxed them forward. A bead of sweat slid down his forehead to the tip of his busted nose, dangled, and dropped. Then the chain came away.

He was still attached to the bloody thing, of course, there was nothing he could do about that. He wriggled back into his sweater, wound the metal snake around his body, and for the first time in days was able to stand up properly. He was surprised how heavy the chain felt, how weak his legs had already become. He crept towards the window, and the old wooden floorboards creaked beneath every foot-step, threatening to betray him.

To his horror he discovered that the window was in direct line of sight of Toma at the top of the stairs, and although the man's back was turned and his concentration focused nowhere but on his glass and what was happening below, it must surely be only seconds before he would turn and spy Ruari. The boy's hands were trembling so wildly that he scraped the chair across the floor as he placed it in front of the window, while the latch and hinges took it in turn to squeal in protest. The chain made what seemed the noise of thunder as it scratched across the wooden frame. Yet, with one final heave, he was through, into the dark-ness, and found himself sliding down the tiled roof of a porch. He fell through the air and landed full on his back in slimy, foul-smelling farmyard mud.

He was free.

—⚏—

It took many moments for Ruari to recover his wits. After several days of being in a constantly lit room he was, at first, almost blind in the darkness, and suddenly very cold.

123

He had no boots, only socks, and already the dampness of the farmyard was seeping through. He struggled to his feet, sniffed the air and waited for his heart to stop pounding.

He had to get away from this place, and quickly, to put as much distance as possible between him and his captors. It didn't matter very much to him which direction he chose. There was an old moon peering from behind passing clouds and slowly Ruari's eyes grew accustomed to the demi-light. Carefully he wrapped the chain around himself once more, and set off, into the night and total unknown.

Two things became immediately apparent. While he searched in every direction, he could see lights in only one, and at a considerable distance. These lights were modest and insignificant, suggesting nothing more than a hamlet. The other thing he quickly discovered was that he would have to keep to the track. The Carso was made for hard farming, its fields scratched out on small parcels of land, while most of the surrounding countryside consisted of untamed shrub that was thick and impenetrable. Ruari didn't know it, but to wander through the Carso in the darkness could be lethal, as sinkholes would suddenly appear, threatening to suck the unsuspecting into a chaotic maze of underground caves and crannies carved out by millions of years of erosion. Even along the uneven track he was following, every footstep threatened him with violence. At one point, with the lights of the farmhouse still to be seen behind him, he tried to clamber over a low wall into a field that seemed to promise a more direct route to the distant hamlet, but the loose stonework gave way beneath him, falling apart with an outrageous clatter that raised the alarm of sleeping birds. Ruari lay still, like death, his face in the soft ground, listening for the sound of pursuit. There was still none. He turned back to the track, crept forward, and slowly the farmhouse receded into the night until he could see it no more.

Yet he wasn't alone. As his ears adjusted to the silence he heard the movements of the countryside, eddies of wind rippling through the trees, stirring them as it went, the calling of owls, the whispering of hedgerows, at one point the barking of a dog or fox. There were other sounds he didn't recognize, but nothing human, nothing that suggested rescue might be close at hand. He stumbled on, trying to find the safest path, grateful for every break in the clouds that allowed the moonlight through, and shivering with cold.

Suddenly a scream carried through the thickness of the night. It was high-pitched, repeated in several short staccato bursts, a noise of terror and of pain, and instinctively every part of Ruari's body froze. He had never heard a rabbit die before.

He hurried forward, followed at every step by the rattling of his chains. He thought he must be nearing the hamlet but it was difficult to judge distances in the dark, and the lights kept disappearing behind the thickets of trees and the hillocks. A mist had sprung up and was beginning to close in on him. He had no idea how far he had gone or how long it had been since his escape, yet he knew it had been too long since he'd last seen any sign of the hamlet. The track was winding, full of potholes that threatened to turn his ankle, and littered with sharp stones. When he came to an intersection of his track with another, he knew he had to make a decision but had no idea how to make it. He stood for many minutes, plagued by doubt, until he had forgotten even which direction he had come from. He went a hundred yards in one direction, then another, with every step adding to his confusion. And, in his tiredness, his foot slipped on a damp stone and threw him down, gashing his knee through his trouser leg and deep into the flesh. It was all going wrong. He knew he couldn't go on. His captors must already be in hot pursuit, closing in on him, and he had nowhere to run. The mist had begun to turn to a light, soft rain, and as he sat feeling the dampness creep through his clothing, sucking the resilience from his body, the warmth of his prison cell began to seem painfully appealing. He began sobbing, knowing he was beaten.

It was then that he saw the lights, advancing slowly through the mist, without urgency, bumping along the track – a set of headlights – and Ruari felt joy flooding back through his body. Fate was giving him a way out, handing him back his freedom. He hoisted himself up, hobbled to the middle of the track, and as the headlights drew near he waved his arms, shouting, demanding that the vehicle stop. It slowed and drew to a halt in front of him, dipping its front end as it hit a pothole, blinding him with its lights. He fell across the bonnet, felt its glorious warmth, wiped the tears from his eyes and hauled himself around to the driver's door. The driver's window wound down.

Ruari found himself staring into the face of his worst enemy. It was Pieter de Vries.

CHAPTER TEN

In the bar beneath the railway arches on the other side of Europe, far from where catastrophe was yet again pouring over Ruari's life, Harry had decided to make it one of those evenings. He felt he deserved it. He'd been intimidated by his old lover and threatened by a leprechaun half his size and twice his age – well, that's how it seemed halfway down the bottle, and it wasn't any better by the time he'd finished it. 'Time to say goodbye, Harry,' he muttered as he drained the final glass. He was a man who not only flew on his own but had also lived on his own, and too long for comfort.

He decided to walk back home; it would sober him up. His feet weren't working so well, but perhaps that wasn't surprising after the best part of two and a half bottles. He was sick of carrying so much responsibility, being a man stuck out on a pedestal, it was draughty and bloody lonely up there. He didn't take the shortest route back from the South Bank to Mayfair. Instinctively his tired legs carried him towards Waterloo Bridge. It wasn't the most gracious crossing on the Thames but at this time of night, when the traffic had slackened off and the lights had begun to glow on all sides, it was one of the most magical spots in London. In every direction there were symbols of what had made his country great: Wren's majestic cupola and spire atop St Paul's, beyond that the bejewelled minarets of Mammon that formed the financial heart of the City, and if he turned he could look down the river towards the art-deco triumph that was the Savoy Hotel, where he'd once spent a glorious night in the honeymoon suite with all its buttons and bell-pulls, and Julia had pulled them all, bringing staff galore knocking on the door while he was standing naked and eager. Oh, how she had laughed.

On the other side of the Thames stood the soaring, multi-coloured London Eye and beyond it, on the hidden curve of the river so that it looked as if it had jumped banks, was the gingerbread cake of a building that was Parliament – his building, where his life was supposed to be focused. *Supposed* to be. But there were times when he knew his heart wasn't in it any longer, when he wondered whether he still belonged there. Often – too often – the game of politics seemed to be about little more than filling potholes and sweeping up broken twigs. As he stood leaning over the parapet of the bridge, staring into the silt-laden waters, smelling the salt and listening to the chuckle of the ebb tide as it flowed around the piers, his mind wandered back to his conversation with the Prime Minister. It was a tempting offer that Campbell had made, one that would enable

Harry to step over the potholes and leave the broken twigs for others, and yet . . . He was hesitating. He liked getting mud on his boots, perhaps he wasn't ready for a life of chauffeur-driven lunches and over-elaborate dinners. On the other hand, maybe that was better than simply getting pissed all by himself. His life needed sorting, and fast, it all had to be settled before Christmas. Three weeks. Bugger. He walked on.

His route took him through Aldwych, where the theatres were beginning to disgorge their crowds, and onto the cobbles of Covent Garden. The piazza was already filled with Christmas revelry and one drunk, recognizing a fellow traveller, invited him to stop for a drink, but Harry pressed on, keen to get home and shut the rest of the world out.

It was only as he closed his front door that he realized he'd left his phone switched off. He'd done that when Terri arrived so that they wouldn't be distracted, and he'd forgotten all about it. Now the screen glowered at him, almost as if it was scolding him, telling him he had missed several calls. Two were from his parliamentary secretary – he suspected he'd forgotten some appointment, but right this moment he didn't care and skipped quickly on. A message from a woman with whom he'd enjoyed what might be described as a few physically ambitious evenings but who clearly wanted more. He'd overheard her describing herself as his latest squeeze, but Harry didn't particularly want a squeeze, he found the word ugly, which somehow made the girl less attractive, too. He moved on again. A restaurant confirming his booking for the following day. An invitation to squash. And three messages from Glen Crossing, his friend from the telephone company, the one he'd asked to investigate Ruari's call.

'Damn you, Harry. I've been busting my balls 'cos you said it was urgent. So call me back. Soonest. You're not going to believe what we've found . . .'

—⟋⟍—

As soon as they got Ruari back to the farmhouse they threw him into the cellar. It was small, damp, full of cobwebs and dust and stank of old vegetables. This time they chained both his arms, securing them around a thick pillar hacked from a single oak trunk that was strong enough to support the farmhouse, which meant it was more than a match for Ruari. The boy wasn't going anywhere. They also took his clothes, every stitch, until he was naked, leaving him with nothing more than an old blanket for modesty and warmth. They didn't beat him up, which he thought a good sign, it seemed he was still of value to them, but they treated him roughly and threw him down the rickety cellar stairs, and as he fell he struck his face and nose once more. More blood, much more of it, and so much pain that he threw up. No one cleaned up either him or it.

For the Romanians, the humiliation of losing the boy in the first place was compounded beyond measure by the fact that it was de Vries who had brought him back.

Nothing was said at first, they remained silent as they sorted out Ruari's new arrangements. De Vries's instructions were obeyed without either question or comment, and with eyes that avoided his. Only when they had slammed the cellar door, leaving the boy in total darkness, did the moment of reckoning arrive.

The guards gathered disconsolately in front of the fire. The smoke was drifting, blown by a downdraught from an unhelpful gust of wind that made the burning wood flare and spit. They watched as de Vries wandered across to the table that was still laden with bottles, picked up one, sniffed it, took a swig, and spat it out on the floor. 'You bastards!' he screamed. He was the smallest man amongst them yet the venom he generated suddenly made the room feel claustrophobic. The Romanians stiffened, shuffled uneasily. Then de Vries and Grobelaar gathered all the bottles and smashed every one of them in the rough stone sink, as if they were cracking heads.

When the last of the Terrano had disappeared, de Vries stood silently, leaning over the sink, his shoulders shaking. He was drawing in great, rasping breaths, struggling to control his anger. When he turned, his face was stretched white with fury. 'Who was guarding him? Who? *Who?*'

Toma swallowed several times before choking up the words. 'I was.'

The world of the mercenary is one that has no forgiveness. Guns for hire, lives for sale, there is never a comfortable ending. Someone always suffers. De Vries was standing confronting the Romanians with a pistol on his belt and his hand hanging close, too close, to it. Toma grew afraid as he watched de Vries's every move. The South African's finger twitched, a movement so slight that it was almost imperceptible, but Toma saw. Theirs was a world in which many lives were valued at no more than a handful of dollars, and he had just placed in danger an operation that he knew must stretch into millions. He expected no pity. He was like a sled dog who was of no further use, except as food for the rest of the pack.

They all knew this was the moment. There was silence but for the crackling of the fire, the silence that sometimes comes before a death. Then Cosmin stirred. He took a pace forward with a heavy, deliberate foot, until he was standing beside Toma, shoulder to shoulder. 'We all in this. It was mistake,' he muttered defiantly in his fractured English and through his broken nose.

De Vries was on the point of hurling abuse at him when he looked into his eyes, and in them he saw a reflection of his own, filled with rage, and a desire to kill. This man was dangerous and he was defiant, and he needed to be taught a lesson, the rest of them, too. Toma knew it, knew what was coming to him, and decided not to wait. He leapt to the table and grabbed a knife, waving it in front of him for protection.

'So, you want it, do you?' de Vries whispered.

Instantly Grobelaar had cocked a weapon, covering the

rest of them. This was to be a fight between the two, not the many.

De Vries couldn't get to the table with its knives, instead he picked up a chair and smashed it into the floor until he was left with a chair leg as a club. The two began circling each other, then de Vries took a step forward and the fight began.

Toma was stronger in his broad shoulders and was the better armed, he needed only one chance. One chink in the South African's defences and de Vries might never smile again. But these battles are not simply about what can be seen on the outside but how a man is prepared inside, and one look at de Vries told Toma that he was in a fight he could not win. This man had the violence of an animal, one that fought not because he had to but because he enjoyed it, lived by it. The code of the wild. That was not Toma's way, and for all his strength he was slow and lumbering. As they grappled and thrust at each other and rolled around the room, smashing chairs and glasses as they went, the Romanian knew it would take a miracle for him to win. The South African was more agile, more committed, and was a far more practised killer. Even when a lucky stab with the knife managed to slice through de Vries's sleeve and into his arm, it seemed only to increase his ferocity, as though Toma could stab him a thousand times and still he would not stop.

It ended abruptly, and unexpectedly. Toma lunged, de Vries danced nimbly on his toes and parried, catching the

Romanian on the side of the head. The blow stunned him, and de Vries was on him, pinning Toma down even though he was twenty pounds lighter. He grabbed the Romanian's arm, smashed it onto the flagstone until the hand released the knife, and suddenly it was his. He raised it, ready to strike, not to kill but to slice through the hand so that it could never be lifted in anger against him again.

But although he fought like one, de Vries was not an animal. He was a man with a job to do, one that was diffi-cult enough as it was, one for which he needed the men around him, and that included Toma. This operation had been prepared in a hurry, with corners cut, and the Romanians had been one of the economies. De Vries had chosen them because they came from the right part of the world, had the right backgrounds, the right degree of bru-tality, but they were not his men, and would be even less his men if he started butchering them. And what use would a one-armed Romanian be? He saw the fear in Toma's unshaven face, knew it was flooding throughout his body, and de Vries decided that would have to be enough. He let the bastard writhe for a few seconds more, then threw the knife away and sprang to his feet.

De Vries wasn't expecting gratitude. Instead he got Cosmin.

'It was mistake!' the Romanian said yet again, the defi-ance undiminished.

De Vries countered with a smile, condescending, as if it made no difference, but it did. He could smell the resentment on these Romanians, resentment that was binding them together, placing them as one against him, yet he had the upper hand, and hadn't he just shown it? The lesson had to be driven home, to all of them.

'A *mistake*,' the South African snarled, spitting out the word. 'You're right. It was a stupid, cretinous, Romanian half-wit's mistake. And mistakes need paying for.' He stared at them still, but now they returned his gaze, feeding off Cosmin's insolence. 'So that mistake just cost each of you ten thousand dollars. Straight off your fee. You listen to me! There will be no more fuck-ups.'

Cosmin shuddered and slowly his shoulders relaxed as the fire left his eyes. But de Vries knew it wasn't over. Despite his victory, he knew he wasn't invincible, and his slashed arm was beginning to hurt like hell. He hadn't bought these men, he'd only rented them, and he had just dropped their price. They were going to be disappointed, ten thousand times over, and disappointment had a terrible habit of breeding disloyalty. He was going to have to watch his back very carefully.

—w—

Back in his prison cellar, Ruari was at his lowest ebb. He had gambled and lost everything – his renewed freedom, his strength, and the last of his hope. His injuries and his bindings now left him in constant pain, he was desperately cold in this place where the warmth of the fire did not reach, he was in total darkness, yet he could hear the

137

scurrying of rats from somewhere close at hand, and there were times when things he could neither see nor identify crawled over him. There was to be no escape, not even in his sleep. He turned one way, only to find Mattias with a hole in his chest that was staring at Ruari like an accusing eye; he turned the other way, and there was Casey. He curled into a ball, trying to hide his eyes from the ghosts, and cried for his mother. And as he tossed and turned, he found himself spiralling down into a world of ever-deeper despair.

Then, through the darkness, came sounds of anger from up above. His jailers were no longer shouting at him but instead were shouting at each other. And he heard their anger grow until they were smashing things to pieces, and he knew they were fighting viciously amongst themselves.

As he listened, Ruari began to feel stronger. He was no longer the only enemy here. And that, he came to think, might give him a chance. It also gave him new hope. He wrapped his blanket around him more tightly, against the cold and the things that crawled, swallowed back his tears and finally drifted off to sleep.

—∞—

'Glenny!' Harry hailed from a distance as he saw his old army chum trotting along the pathway around the Serpentine in Hyde Park. The telecommunications man returned the wave. He was already blowing hard in the freezing morning air that had left the trees and parkland clad in a seasonal hoar frost. 'Much more than this and you'll be auditioning for Santa Claus,' Harry greeted, noting the straining girth on his friend's tracksuit.

'OK, so I've put on a bit of weight. Occupational hazard,' Crossing muttered, glancing at Harry's flat stomach with more than a little envy. Judging by the gentle glow on the Jones brow he suspected Harry had already done a couple of laps. Typical. He already regretted allowing himself to be talked into an early morning run; there were only so many challenges a man could deal with before breakfast.

'Corporate life getting to you, Glenny?'

'No, not that. It's kids. They eat nothing but crap and chips. I can't keep up. You know what it's like.'

'Domestic bliss.'

'Kids can be seriously damaging to your health.'

'I've heard.'

Twenty years ago the two had been ferocious opponents on the squash court when they had been stationed together in Hereford, their matches always sweaty, aggressive, often epic and usually unpredictable. Neither of them gave quarter, and although Harry hated to admit it, Crossing might even have bested him more often than not. Yet it seemed those days were now a flickering memory for his old friend.

'Come on, gentle lap to warm us up. While you tell me all about it,' Harry suggested.

They set off around the lake, scattering grumbling ducks. 'It's all in the signalling, you see,' Crossing began. 'When a call is made from a mobile, before it's connected, it has to get permission from the system to make sure the user's account is valid for what it wants to do. To make sure the bill gets paid. You can imagine we're pretty hot on that. And all the information's archived, so there're location updates and account credentials and signature streams and—'

'English, please, Glenny.'

'How brief do you want it?'

'How far do you want to run?'

Harry's question was met with a glance that would have sliced the froth off a pint of beer. 'OK, craphead, here's what it comes down to. We got the country, the area, even the mast the signal came through. When you switch on your phone it's continuously looking for the nearest mast. Sometimes it can often see more than one, and then it chooses the hottest signal. And if it's travelling, it will switch masts to maintain the signal.'

'You mean—'

'We can even tell you which direction he was travelling in. Took a little while, mind you, what with all that duff information you fed me.'

'What duff information?'

Crossing waited several breaths before replying, deliberately punishing his friend while trying to pretend he was enjoying the exercise. 'You said the phone call came from Switzerland. It didn't. It was made in Italy.'

They ran on, more painful paces for Crossing while Harry digested what he had been told, grinding out yard after remorseless yard, almost heedless of what was around him, until his friend began to gasp. 'Look, Harry, it's good news. We can trace the next phone call in the same way.'

'Trouble is, they're not communicating by phone.'

'Shit. How?'

'Skype.'

Crossing skidded to a halt on the icy pathway as if he'd thrown an anchor, his eyes no longer glazed but ablaze with agitation. 'Then, my friend,' he panted, 'you are truly fucked.'

Harry stopped and turned to face his friend. Crossing bent over, hands on his knees as he tried to fill his lungs with oxygen, only to discover it came in packets of lung-scraping ice air. A bead of sweat trembled like a dewdrop on the end of his nose. 'Look, Skype uses what's called VoIP. Voice over Internet Protocol. Ugly acronym – you know how we techies love 'em – but it's a system that borders on the beautiful. All the info is routed directly between the two end points and it's encrypted with so much industrial strength cryptography that it's got balls like an elephant. The boys and girls at GCHQ and A Branch hate it. Can't stop it, can't intercept it, not unless you're freakishly lucky, and even if you are it's so heavily encrypted you get jumble, nothing that makes any more sense than the contents of my wife's handbag. It's peer-to-peer stuff. Only works if it's meant for you.'

'You mean the police can't crack it? Trace it?'

'What's to trace? It's got no moving parts, no machinery, it's stunningly simple, fabulously flexible, almost impregnable. You can't bomb it, block it, break it . . .' He was gasping once again, but this time in enthusiasm, on his own turf now. Slowly he straightened up. 'Skype,' he said slowly, the word condensing into a little cloud in front of his face, 'is a kidnapper's wet dream, old chum. Too damned clever for our own good, sometimes we are. You've got your work cut out on this one, Harry.'

—⁂—

Harry didn't wait to change out of his jogging kit, he simply ran on from Hyde Park to Notting Hill. He found a security man blocking his way at the Breslins' front door. The man was typical of his type, an hour every day in the gym and two in the pub, with muscles and stomach to match that stretched the seams of his cheap suit and whose every opinion was fed to him through a pink plastic earpiece.

'Are they expecting you?' the security man asked gruffly, blowing on his fingertips for warmth.

'I very much doubt it,' Harry replied.

The man began to mutter into a microphone at his lapel, and a little while later the front door opened. It was a woman, the housekeeper, Harry guessed, who showed him up the stairs and immediately disappeared. He found Terri kneeling beside the Christmas tree, which was no longer leaning but firmly anchored and upright in its base. She was decorating the tree with tinsel and threading a string of lights through its branches. A pile of wrapped presents waited nearby. She looked up defiantly, but her eyes were raw and her fingers trembling. She seemed older than the woman he had met the night before. Something had happened.

Her fingers led a trail of silvered paper around the tree. 'I'm getting it ready,' she said forlornly, 'for when Ruari comes home. What do you think?'

'He'll love it.'

'Thank you, Harry.' She offered a forced smile, then nodded in the direction of a far door. 'They're in the dining room,' she said, as though they were entirely separate to her, then went back to her task, filling her time, leaving as little space as possible for her fears.

Harry's immediate impression was that the negotiating team had already fallen apart. The men were scattered disjointedly around the room – J.J. sat alone at the table, distractedly drumming his fingers, Archer and Hiley, the risk assessor, had their heads together, muttering, while Sean Breslin sat in the corner in the manner of a chess player, waiting for the next move. At the end of the table was a computer surrounded by trailing wires that fed into other pieces of kit that Harry assumed were for monitoring and recording. The curtains were drawn, covering the windows that overlooked the street, and the atmosphere was thick enough to chew.

'Hope I'm not disturbing you,' Harry began, addressing J.J. 'I know you don't want me here, but I've stumbled across something I think might help.'

From the corner, the older Breslin's eyes burned with mistrust, as if to say that the only way Harry could help was if a hole opened beneath him and he dropped to the Devil, but the son appeared less hostile. 'If you're able to help, then you are welcome,' he sighed. His voice was thick with exhaustion.

'It's the call from Ruari's phone.'

'You know about that?' J.J asked, less kindly.

'I told him,' Terri said. She was behind Harry, standing by the door.

'I'd like to know what else you've heard,' J.J. said, his eyes honed with suspicion, his gaze fixed unblinkingly on his wife.

'The call – it didn't come from Switzerland. It came out of Italy.'

The other men stirred. Patiently, Harry began to repeat what Crossing had explained to him. J.J. listened attentively, Hiley nodded thoughtfully, Archer chewed his cheek, Sean Breslin continued to stare like a hawk. It was left to Terri to show emotion. Harry was explaining about the switching between masts when she moved closer and grabbed his sleeve. 'Where was it, Harry?' she demanded suddenly, urgent. 'Show me, please show me.'

She continued to hold him, as if she was afraid he might

leave without telling everything he knew. It was a gesture too intimate for comfort, and Harry turned back to her husband. 'Would you mind if I used the computer?'

J.J. nodded at the screen, and in a moment Harry was fiddling with the mouse while the rest slowly gathered round, like moths drawn to the flame, even the older Breslin. Harry brought up a satellite image from Google Earth and soon they were staring down upon the Southern Alps from a height that was diminishing all the time. 'Where were the bodies of the girl and the instructor found?' he asked.

Hiley pointed to the screen, locations that were in the vicinity of Zermatt.

'OK, so the call was made from here. Near a place called Ceppo Morelli,' Harry announced. The screen zoomed in until it showed a cluster of rooftops hidden in the foothills.

'But that's barely inside Italy at all,' protested Archer.

'The location updates tell us they were flying east.'

'Yes, but for how long?' Archer muttered, ever the unbeliever and professional pain.

'They were coming out of the Alps. No need to fly in anything other than a pretty direct route. My guess is they continued travelling east.'

'Guesswork's all very good but—' Archer began yet again until Terri cut him off. She was leaning over Harry's shoulder, her eyes fixed to the screen, breathing in his ear, rattling his memories. Her finger began tracing the route from Villars through the places where the bodies had been found and across to Ceppo Morelli, as if she could almost touch her son. 'Thank you, Harry,' she whispered, 'thank you so much.'

'But how do you know all this, Mr Jones?' J.J. said, breaking up the huddle. 'Surely this information is all confidential.'

Harry smiled ruefully. 'I have friends in low places. A bit like a newspaper.'

'Need to check it, of course,' Archer continued doggedly.

'And why the bloody hell didn't we know this already?' J.J. demanded, growing exasperated with Archer's remorseless scepticism. He was Ruari's father, for God's sake, he needed hope as much as he needed to draw breath.

But Archer wasn't to be thrown off course so easily. 'As you say, J.J., the records are confidential, and Mr Jones here has probably broken the law. We have to go through official channels, and in Switzerland that takes time.'

'We don't have time!' J.J. burst out, banging his fist on the table.

'So give them what they want!' It was Terri. She glowered at her husband from the other end of the table; he wasn't the only one who was feeling pain and had a right to express it. An uncomfortable silence spread through the room.

'What *do* they want?'

It was Harry who broke the tension, much to his own surprise. He hadn't meant to interfere, to get himself in the middle of what was clearly a growing battle of wills, but he found himself asking anyway.

J.J. moaned softly, his fists clenched tight with frustration. 'They were in contact again, last night.' He took several deep breaths, trying to summon up reserves of strength. 'It seems this kidnapping isn't about money after all. It's about some diaries. Written by Nelson Mandela.'

CHAPTER ELEVEN

The Mandela diaries. The words rattled through Chombo's mind like a curse, as they did every day. He was sitting on a balcony of his favourite hotel, sipping a cooling beer and gazing out across the swimming pool to the landscaped gardens beyond. The breeze was gentle, the rain gone, yet he could find no peace, and knew he wouldn't, not until Mandela's ghost had finally been buried and his diaries along with it.

The name of the former South African leader was still sacrosanct, the most powerful political force in this part of Africa, and no one dared touch his memory. His official diaries had long since been published but in their wake had come whispers of another, more private and far darker set of scribblings, comments and conclusions written down in his final years that took an uncharacteristically venomous line for a man whose reputation had been built on an infinite smile. But these writings were different, an old man's chance to get even, from beyond the grave. Three months ago word had spread that the diaries were being touted around, that they would not only rewrite history but also screw up a fair bit of the future, too, by humiliating many powerful men. Chombo, so it was said, was one of them.

Like every leader, Chombo was not all that he seemed. He had avoided the retributions and prolific recriminations of the Mugabe years, partly by ensuring that he could never be identified as a threat to the old dog, and in still larger part because of his reputation as one of the original freedom fighters, a man who, even as a boy, had fought for the ZANU guerrillas against the white regime of Ian Smith. He'd run messages, endured many dangers, flitted between bush and barracks to bring instructions to the black troops on whose loyalty the Smith regime depended but on which it could no longer rely. It was even said that when the bush war had spread into the towns, Chombo had helped plant a bomb in Woolworth's in the capital, then named Salisbury, that had killed and injured almost a hundred people. Yet such bravery came at a price. Chombo had been caught and had suffered grievously in the prisons of the white man, and wasn't the scar on his face proof of that, a constant reminder of what he had given to his country? But all this was a lie, a story put around by a few of his friends to kick-start his political career; it had seemed to matter little at first but like so many of these things it had gained a life of its own. He had developed a habit in front of audiences of running the tips of his fingers along the scar, which was deep and slithered down his face from above his eye line to below his lip. The crowd would notice, whisper amongst themselves that it was a symbol of the struggle, of white oppression, and every time he touched it was like the beating of a drum to muster people to the cause. It was an unconscious habit, he said, even to himself; he had never deliberately played up to it, had he?

Chombo's thoughts were interrupted by a servant – no, steward, that was the modern word, and in all things apart from tribal loyalties Chombo was determined to be modern. The man bowed, took a pace closer and refreshed Chombo's beer while a yellow-breasted seedeater hopped along the balcony rail, waiting expectantly for crumbs. Chombo loved this spot. Beneath him a group of school-children was playing in the pool; they were splashing and laughing, like all children should. Theirs was a private school, of course, not one of the gutter schools that had been left in tatters through the Mugabe years, but they were children nonetheless and they deserved their games in the sun. He had to start somewhere, rebuilding his coun-try, and this place was as good a spot as any from which to begin, for this wasn't simply his favourite hotel it was also *his* hotel, at least in part, owned by a white businessman who had felt the need for a friend on the inside of the black establishment and so had sold twenty per cent of the hotel to Chombo. Not that Chombo had paid any money, but the money would come, eventually, from the profits of the hotel, profits that because of Chombo's participation were swelling, which was why he had just that morning agreed to take another twenty per cent stake and . . . And so forth.

This was Chombo's Zimbabwe, modern, clean, thriving, with contented children and respectful staff, and if it didn't represent more than a tiny fraction of the country, then perhaps one day it would, under his leadership. If he survived the election. And the wretched diaries.

Somehow Mandela had discovered the truth, that Chombo's wounds had come not from torture at the hands of white men but as the result of a self-inflicted car crash on the Massachusetts Turnpike while he had been a student in Boston, that he had never played a part in the bush war, that he had never risked his life, except through drunk driving, and that he had never been inside Ian Smith's jails or felt the swipe of his blade. Oh, it wasn't a sin in Mandela's eyes that Chombo had never fought or even that he preferred a master's degree to martyrdom, but what Mandela would never forgive, as a man who had spent twenty-seven years of his life locked away in a prison, was someone like Chombo who claimed the moral authority of African suffering while in fact he'd been screwing his brains out between the legs of white girls on the other side of the world. Chombo was no better than a jackal that had come to steal the carcass after the lions had done all the dirty work. That was Mandela's view, he'd written it down in his diaries, and opening them before the elections would be as good as splitting Chombo's skull with an axe.

He had to stop the diaries, prevent Mandela's ghost rattling its chains. Everything depended on it. That would take sacrifices, of course, but what weighed more heavily on his conscience, one white boy whose name he didn't even know, or children like those who were splashing and squealing in front of him, the future of Zimbabwe? For Chombo, it was no contest. And as he sat there, reflecting on it all, he was delighted to discover that it didn't prick his conscience, not a bit. He was turning over a new page. He smiled in contentment; his file would get thicker after all. He swatted away a fly and called for another drink.

—◊—

'For God's sake, give them the sodding diaries!' Terri demanded, her voice rising.

'You know I can't,' her husband whispered, struggling for control.

'What the bloody hell matters most to you, J.J.? Those diaries – or the life of your son?'

J.J.'s grey, drawn face suddenly flushed with anger. How dare she? 'You know it's not like that.'

'From where I'm standing, it looks very much like that!' Terri broke away. She picked up a photograph of Ruari that stood on the sideboard, one in a funky teenager frame – Harry noticed there seemed to be many more images of the boy about the place since he'd last been here, staring out from every corner. She thrust the portrait defiantly at her husband, her words squeezing through tears. 'He's worth more than any book.'

'I know he is,' J.J. snapped back. 'But how many times

153

do I have to tell you? That's not my decision to make, and getting hysterical isn't going to help him either.'

Her lips moved, but for the moment words seemed to fail her. Instead she cried out in despair. For a moment it seemed as though she might slap his face, she was trembling, tears pouring down her cheeks, but she turned away. 'Harry, help me!' she whispered. Her husband flinched. Then she fled from the room, clutching the photograph to her breast.

'I apologize for that,' J.J. muttered to the others as they listened to her running up the stairs to her bedroom. 'Neither of us had any sleep. It's so very hard . . .' His own eyes were overflowing with exhaustion.

'Which is why, J.J., I think we should call in the authorities. We need all the help we can get,' Archer said.

Breslin turned on him. 'I'll not put my son's life at risk. You know what the kidnappers said!' He was panting in anger, his head lowered like a bull preparing to charge, his lips twisting and ready to abuse the other man for his insensitivity, for taking advantage of the moment, but even as the curses came to his tongue his shoulders sagged in resignation. The man was doing no more than his job.

Hiley joined the game, too. 'It sort of makes sense, Mr Breslin. Our hands are tied without them.'

Breslin turned, feeling outnumbered. 'What about you, Dad?'

'Me?' Breslin senior stirred from his perch in the corner where he'd been sitting quietly. He was a watcher, not a rusher. He scratched his chin. 'Personally, I never was much for running to the police.' As he spoke, his eyes were fixed firmly on Harry. 'And the Swiss police don't seem to be making much progress, two bodies and bugger-all else.'

'Well, they wouldn't, would they, not if Mr Jones is right,' Hiley added.

Stiffly, reluctantly, like the creaking of a rusted drawbridge, J.J. turned to Harry. 'What do you think, Mr Jones?'

'I've got nothing to offer but guesswork,' Harry replied.

'Nevertheless.'

'My guess is that they're in Italy.'

'On the basis of one phone call?' Archer interrupted. 'They could be anywhere – doubled back to Switzerland, or even somewhere in the Balkans.'

'It's possible.'

'But you *guess* otherwise,' J.J. persisted.

'Everything Mr Archer says might be correct,' Harry conceded, feeling awkward and exposed in his sweaty sports kit surrounded by all the suits. 'We can't discount the possibility that the phone call was a deliberate attempt to mislead us.'

Archer nodded.

'But on the other hand, let's assume the helicopter was heading in its intended direction. Look . . .' He led them back to the computer with its maps and began tracing a path across the screen. 'It was coming out of the mountains. There was no need for it to be flying in anything other than a direct line towards its destination. If it were heading south it wouldn't have passed anywhere near Ceppo Morelli.'

'And if it carried on east it could be sitting outside some souk in Turkey by now,' the bloody-minded Archer suggested.

'No, it couldn't even get out of Italy, not without refuelling, which would have left clues. So follow the logic, and the flight path and . . .' Harry's fingers traced a line across the base of the Alps from Ceppo Morelli, across Lake Como, until it hesitated near Verona – 'they'd have landed somewhere short of here.'

'And then?' J.J. pressed quietly.

'Put yourself in their boots. If you were the kidnappers, wouldn't you want to stop somewhere close at hand?'

'So somewhere in Italy.'

'Northern Italy.'

'Even if you're right, it's still a hell of a lot of space in which to hide one boy.' J.J. stood up from the screen and stretched his back wearily. 'So what's your view, Mr Jones? Should we talk to the police?'

'I'll say to you what I said to your wife. It's a decision that only the parents can take.'

'You did? You told her that?' For a second J.J. seemed in pain as he struggled with the idea of Harry talking about such things with his wife. His eyes darted back and forth, searching Harry's face for some clue as to what else they might have discussed, then stood silent, as though coming to a decision. 'May we have a *private* word?'

156

He led Harry back through the sitting room, past the half-decorated Christmas tree, and out onto a small roof terrace directly outside the windows. It stood on top of an extension to the main house that Harry assumed might be a playroom or garden room, the sort of thing that was common as kids came along and families grew. The terrace had been packed up for the winter, its table and chairs piled in a corner, the patio heater covered, the plants in tall stone pots covered in hessian to protect against the frost. Dead twigs lay piled in the corner. Breslin stood at the railings, looking out beneath a dull, lowering sky across the frost-covered gardens, like a ship's captain on his bridge searching the horizon for icebergs. He buttoned his suit against the cold, lit himself a cigarette and sighed, picking a stray flake of tobacco from the tip of his tongue.

'Something just between us?'

Harry nodded.

'I've acquired the rights to the Mandela diaries. They're historic, intriguing, sensational in parts. I'd just done the deal when we last met.'

Harry remembered him bounding up the stairs and the words that had leapt from his lips. *They've signed! We're saved!*

'The diaries are a huge commercial coup. And now we've been told to destroy them, otherwise we'll never see Ruari again. A straight swap. But . . .' He winced, as though he had caught sight of the iceberg, far too close. 'The diaries aren't mine, they belong to the company. They're worth millions. I'm not in a position to do what the kidnappers demand.'

'Your fellow directors wouldn't be sympathetic?'

'We're talking money men – pension funds, venture-capital people, red-neck bankers in Chicago. They own far more of the company than I do. And frankly, the company's in trouble. Without the diaries, the entire newspaper group might go under. So sympathy?' He shook his head. 'Terri doesn't understand, I don't blame her, but there's nothing I can do. I cannot hand over the diaries.'

'Between the rocks and a very hard place.'

'Oh, if only I could lock my wife inside the boardroom with my fellow directors, she'd win them round, either that or pummel them into submission. There's nothing she wouldn't do for that boy.'

'Why are you telling me this?'

'Because . . .' Breslin hesitated. He stood gazing out over the bare winter garden. The tops of the empty trees were bending in a freshening wind, and old leaves were scattering across the grass like rats in search of a new home. 'This is a time of extraordinary pressure on my family, Mr Jones. And while I'm grateful for what you've done, the suggestions you've made, I really don't need you around here making things worse.'

'Look, I've done nothing—'

Breslin tossed away the stub of his cigarette and turned sharply to face Harry. 'I'm making no accusations, but I've seen the two of you together, you and my wife. The chemistry, the tension when you're both in the same room.'

That's only because I'm so pissed off with her, Harry wanted to object. It's only anger you've picked up, nothing else, but Breslin wasn't interested.

'I've no idea what was going through Terri's mind when she involved you, but whatever her motives, they're not shared within the Breslin family.'

'Ah, your father.'

'My father loves Ruari more than any person in this world.' The words carried the unalloyed sincerity of a believer professing his faith in the Resurrection.

'But he doesn't much like me.'

'Neither do I. I don't find it comfortable when my wife's former lover suddenly pops up on the scene. Narrow-minded of me, I know, but that's how I feel.'

Former lover? Terri had said she'd never told him, not outright. Did he really know or was he simply testing the air? No, Harry decided, the man knew. In any case, it didn't seem to make much difference. 'You're being uncomfortably honest.'

'There's little point in being otherwise in my situation. My son's life is at stake. They have already killed two people, I have no doubt they will kill Ruari if it serves their purpose. If we're to save him, it'll take teamwork, not mavericks with their own agendas.'

A winter breeze ruffled through Harry's hair, cut through his tracksuit, it was too cold out here for comfort.

'Beautiful woman, isn't she?' Breslin muttered.

He didn't bother to answer, yet it was true, and more so than Harry dared admit, even to himself. The years had added a fullness that he'd been struggling to ignore.

'Leave her alone.'

'You have to understand, it's never been my intention—'

But Harry's protest was cut short. Breslin had turned his back on Harry once more and was staring out across the leaf-strewn lawn. 'So *petty*, don't you think, these personal issues? When a boy's life is at stake?'

It was Harry's cue to leave. He took it, and didn't look back, so he didn't see Sean Breslin at the window, his hawk-like eyes watching every step, burning into his back until he had disappeared from sight.

CHAPTER TWELVE

Of all the Romanians, Nelu the computer geek was the most important. Like the others he had been conscripted into the Armata Romana, where his military service had consisted of several years being immersed in some of the more sordid techniques of cybercraft. He had been treated like a dog and fed worse than a pig, but it had proved useful experience. In the kaleidoscopic world of international politics the Romanian Army that had once been part of the Warsaw Pact was now a member of NATO, its former sworn enemy, so its conscripts were used to marching to many different tunes. The long-term effect, combined with abject poverty for most ordinary Romanians alongside official corruption on a scale that was almost pornographic, was to give soldiers like Nelu extraordinary flexibility and a burning loyalty to no one but themselves. After his discharge Nelu had kept up his cyber-skills, making a good living racketeering on eBay, selling products he didn't own and making off with the proceeds before anyone could catch him, always staying a cyber-step ahead. Now he had hired out his talents to de Vries. The offer was enticing, a

161

few months messing around with Skype and he'd been promised more money than he could make in two years mugging bewildered punters on the Internet, and the beauty of it all was that for Nelu there was absolutely no risk. Even if they'd kidnapped the Queen of England it was probable that their messaging would have remained secure, yet they'd kidnapped a mere boy, and the authorities didn't know where he was, or even if he was still alive. Yes, Skype was a bloody wonderful weapon, much more fun than getting your balls blown off in the military.

It was moving towards dusk, red ribbons of cloud leaking into the sky in the direction of Venice, when Nelu was driven away from the farmhouse by de Vries and Grobelaar. It was one of the perks of his role, escaping from the claustrophobia of the farmhouse, leaving that to the others. After all, that's what they were being paid for, they were the muscle, while he was the one with the brains. And he used them. It wasn't enough that Skype was such a bomb-proof system, Nelu wanted to go one step further, to add another layer of cover just in case some other nerd in a wrinkled T-shirt had developed software that would change the rules overnight. He sent every message using a different Skype account and from a different location. It was easy, even up on the Carso. Drive around the few small towns on the plateau until they discovered a wi-fi hot spot, usually some public building like a school or hospital whose wi-fi system could be picked up from the road or parking lot outside. Then they would piggyback on it, send their message through someone else's server. So even if a police force or intelligence service somehow managed to track down their location, even to the yard, by the time they arrived they'd discover nothing but an empty stretch of tarmac.

This evening they drove to Opicina, passing the shops and small eating places that were still open, until they found a senior school whose doors had long since closed for the day. Nelu had identified this as a wi-fi hot spot on a previous recce, now they parked as close as possible, away from the bustle of the main road, while Nelu opened up his laptop and set up the call. It took him less than twenty seconds.

It was six days since Ruari had been snatched. The burble of the Skype ring tone carved through the house in Notting Hill like a fire alarm. Hiley answered, rushing from the kitchen where he had been making himself yet another mug of coffee. He was the family's designated negotiator, a role that had been agreed during the last call, when the demand for the Mandela diaries had been put to them. The arrangement suited both sides; negotiation is a skill requiring experience and emotional detachment, qualities that hysterical parents rarely provide. A kidnapping is nothing less than a declaration of war, a vile and degenerate assault upon the innocent, but at the end of the day both family and criminals usually share a common interest – they want an early end to the hostilities. Hiley was a man who could help them achieve that. He scrabbled for the mouse and hit the accept button.

'What have you got for me? What have you decided?' de
Vries asked, speaking into a simple headset. He was sitting
in the car parked within the shadows of the school, yet his
words rang as clear as if he were in the next room.

'Look, can I have a name for you first?' Hiley began.
'Any name. If you don't mind. Jan, Rudi, Willem. I'd find it
easier to call you by a name, whatever one you want.' He
needed to break down the barriers, develop some sort of
personal connection with this man, perhaps even create an
element of trust between them. It might end up making a
crucial difference. Anyway, he hoped to keep this man talking for as long as possible so that he and the sound men
who would analyse the recording could learn from every
minute, every morsel, every castrated South African vowel
and every bit of background noise.

'Call me whatever you like,' de Vries replied testily. 'Just
stop wasting my fucking time.'

'Then . . . Jan. I'll call you Jan. Is that OK?'

'You waste my time, and I get really pissed off. And
when I'm pissed off I take it out on the boy. This morning
instead of giving him breakfast we gave him a bloody good
kicking. You carry on babbling and he'll get the same for
his dinner. Now what about the diaries?'

Hiley sighed. The easy bit was over, now he really had to
earn his money. He had spent most of the morning discussing his plan with J.J. and the others. It had been tossed
back and forth, J.J. had asked many questions, raised many
objections – a stubborn man – but in the end they'd all

accepted Hiley's proposals. Yet it was one thing to persuade them, quite another to throw it at the kidnappers. He
sipped his coffee, winced as his upper lip dipped into the
overheated liquid, then stepped out into the minefield.
'Look, Jan, what you ask, about the diaries. You must know
that's impossible.'

'What's impossible? You have the diaries. Burn the stinking things!'

'Trust me, Mr Breslin wants to be as cooperative as possible, but you have to understand. The diaries aren't his.
They belong to the newspaper.'

'And he owns the stinking newspaper.'

'But he doesn't. He's a shareholder, a significant one, of
course, but nowhere near a majority. And the other share-
holders simply won't agree to destroy a very valuable bit
of property. Would you?'

'Then we'll chop the boy to bits and they can have that
on their conscience.'

'Let's not bother with the conscience bit, shall we? I
don't think it fits either of us particularly well.'

'And the boy's fingers aren't going to fit particularly
well on what's left of his hands if you screw around with
me. So what are you going to give me?'

Hiley's heart leapt. The other man was making threats,
that was entirely predictable, but he was also suggesting he
might be open to some sort of deal, willing to negotiate. A
carrot along with the stick. Hiley sipped again at his coffee,
so focused that he no longer noticed the pain from his lip.

'Mr Breslin is talking to the other directors. Everyone wants to be helpful, Jan. We've been pulling our hair out trying to think of some way we can satisfy you. We're doing our best, truly we are. Look, if we could delete just part of the diaries, or delay their publication for a while. Anything along those lines and there's a chance Mr Breslin will be able to persuade the other directors and we could get this situation sorted.'

'Parts? I'll give you parts. What do you want first, his ears or his prick?' De Vries was shouting now, intent on making his words hit home all the harder when the tape was played back to the family, as he knew it would be. And he could shout as loud as he wanted in this isolated spot; Grobelaar was standing watch on the roadway outside and no one else was going to hear him.

'Come on, Jan, if Mr Breslin could stop publication, he would. But he can't. So we've got to find some other way. Give me a little help here, something I can take back to them.'

'The whole diaries. Or you'll never hear from us or the boy again. You've got five seconds before we start cutting him. Four, three—'

'Jan! Jan! Just think for a moment. Even if the other directors agreed to cover up the diaries, someone would leak them. Nelson Mandela – he's the Black Jesus, his diaries are like the bloody Bible. If we tried to cover them up, you know they'd only end up on the Internet, like everything else in this world. There's no such thing as secrets any more. Look, you're good, I know that, it's obvious you know how this techie stuff works. You know some spotty kid sitting in his bedroom can hack into NASA, or my overdraft, or even the Pope's medical records if he works out what buttons to press. Nothing gets buried forever, and too many people already know about these diaries. But what I've suggested, burying one part instead of trying to bury the whole thing, or at least delaying it until it doesn't matter so much – well, it might just let us keep control. Isn't that what you want?'

Hiley was taking a gamble. He knew there was a possibility the other man would simply end the conversation and they would never hear from him again, and that at some later time, in some distant place, what was left of Ruari would be dug up or dredged from the river mud. Or the silence might mean that the South African was deciding what particularly bloodied part of Ruari's anatomy would be sent to them in order to smash the resilience of the Breslins to pieces. Yet there was also a third possibility, that the silence meant he was thinking, turning over what Hiley had said, wondering if it might work.

After a few seconds, time that seemed to stretch out to eternity, the voice returned.

'I'll get back to you.'

Hiley sank his teeth into his tongue rather than betray the elation he felt. He'd made a significant breakthrough. The first chink of light had appeared through the curtain, but he knew he couldn't leave it there, he had to push further.

'There's one other thing, Jan. It's totally important and if we don't get this there's no point in you calling back. You've got to give us proof of life, show us that Ruari is still alive.'

'He was still alive when I kicked the little shit awake this morning.'

'You have to prove it. Without absolute certainty on that, you'll get nothing.'

It was now Hiley making the demands; the pendulum had swung back, just a fraction. There was another pause before:

'I said, I'll get back to you.' In the car, de Vries pulled his hand across his throat as a signal to Nelu and the connection went dead.

Seven hundred and fifty miles away from where his tormentors were already making their way back along leaf-strewn roads towards their hideout, Hiley was left with a sore lip and sweat trickling down his forehead, mulling over what had happened. The conversation had been long, suggesting the kidnappers were confident they could not be traced, even though the technicians hired by Hiley's firm would be sifting through every byte of the recording in search of clues – Hiley thought at one point he might have heard the muffled sound of a car door being slammed in the background, or was it merely a table being kicked? He didn't know, but the sound boys would work it out.

There were two other matters that were vital to Hiley. The first was that the bastard hadn't rejected his suggestions out of hand. There might be flexibility, and that could go a long way to saving Ruari's life.

The other point was that Jan hadn't responded; even in tone there had been neither anger nor interest, no show of cosmetic outrage, nothing more than a flat 'I'll get back to you', like the dull thud of a package being dropped on a conveyor belt. To Hiley's experienced mind, that meant one thing. Jan wasn't the main guy, he was a messenger, a hired hand who didn't have the authority to think for himself. Someone else sat behind him, giving the instructions, and in a subtle yet significant way, the family had just taken a step in his direction. They were getting closer to the truth.

—⁓—

Two young women picked their way along the pavement in the highest of heels, their tailored coats wrapped tightly around their bodies, suggesting considerably more than they hid. Despite the winter weather, both coats finished high up the thigh.

'Best damned show in town,' Archer declared, loud enough for the two girls to hear. They giggled, leaning on each other's arms for support as they disappeared along the crowded street.

Archer was sitting with Will Hiley and Andy Brozic in Jermyn Street at a pavement table outside Franco's, beneath the protective awning and the red glow of an overhead heater as they watched the world go by. It was a crowded world, filled with Christmas shoppers and those who were still emerging from late lunches. Archer had chosen the location, an old haunt from his police days, a place where confidences could be carried away on the wind rather than shared amongst the nearby tables. Good for business, despite the distractions.

'They're not doing very well, are they, the Breslins?' Archer continued, dragging his attention back to the other men.

'It's never easy in these situations,' Brozic said.

But Archer persisted. 'They've frozen, find it difficult to make decisions. Too busy arguing with each other. You've seen how it is between them.'

'I think even my wife would throw a fit or two in the circumstances, wouldn't yours?'

'My wife?' The question seemed to take Archer by surprise. 'Married thirty-two years. Like an ocean liner, she is, ploughs through it all.' It didn't sound like much of a compliment.

A waiter arrived bearing a bottle and three glasses. Archer tried the wine, a deep, lustrous Sassicia, burying his nose in it a little theatrically before nodding in approval. 'I ordered something red – not a moment for champagne, I thought. Maybe later, when this is all done and dusted, I hope? In the meantime, let's imagine we're in Tuscany, it's July, the women have slipped into their shortest skirts and we're just getting started.'

'Not that we've got much to get started with,' Brozic

ventured as he sipped the wine, discovering it was considerably better than he'd expected. 'The Swiss have given us bugger all, apart from bodies and excuses. Not that they've got a hell of a lot to go on.'

'That's why I think we should pursue the Italian connection,' Hiley said.

Archer was shaking his head. 'Probably a wild-goose chase,' he muttered, 'and even if it's not, you know what happens once you get tied down with the Italian police. End up swimming through cold pasta, we'll lose control of the case completely.'

Control seemed to be important to Archer, Hiley mused, and that was probably the real reason he didn't care for the Italian angle. It wasn't his, he didn't own it, it had come from Harry Jones and Jones was clearly not wanted on this voyage. A pity, Hiley thought. 'So what is it you suggest we do, Brian?'

'I tell you what we do,' Archer said, sniffing into his wine. 'We have a word with my old mates at the Yard.'

'But the Breslins have explicitly told us not to do that. No police.'

'Sometimes, Will, you have to think for your client.'

'Even so . . .'

'A quiet word with my old colleagues in the Kidnap Unit. Meet them for a coffee or a curry, somewhere outside the office. I put to them a situation about a boy in Switzerland who's gone missing – an entirely hypothetical situation, of course. They know how to play this game. Encourage them to put a few ferrets down holes, see if any rabbits pop up. Nothing on the record.' He leaned forward as if he were about to share a confidence. 'Scotland Yard was my baili-wick for over twenty years. I know everyone, how it works, how to get results. I've got good friends there, friends who owe me, you understand? They'll do the rest.'

There was a point to Archer's invitation and this con-versation, but Brozic wasn't yet sure what it was. 'Why are you telling us this, Brian? You know we can't disobey a direct instruction from a client.'

'I'm not asking you to do anything, Andy. I'll do all the work, share any results with you. I want to move things along. This is all about teamwork and I'm really enjoying being alongside you guys, you know. We might do more of it in the future, perhaps.'

'For Mr Breslin, you mean?'

'No, I doubt that. He and the newspaper are going through some choppy water right now, who knows where things will be once this is all over? Anyway, the newspa-per's not the end of my ambition. I reckon there's more to life than prowling around checking up on who stole a box of pencils from the stationery cupboard. I may want to move on after this, spread my wings a bit.'

Ah, so that was the purpose of it all. The invitation. The booze. Archer wanted out, to jump ship, climb on board theirs. Brozic was just about to take up the point when Archer's phone came to life. He'd left it prominently on the table, next to his glass, now it lit up with a text message.

His features creased in concentration. 'You'll have to excuse me, gentlemen,' he declared, 'but duty calls.' And already he was rising from his chair, offering his farewells. 'But please enjoy the rest of the bottle. Be a shame to waste the stuff. In fact, as I'm in a bit of a rush, would you mind taking care of the bill? Bloody cheek, I know, but you'll put it back through to us on expenses, of course, with a suitable mark up. What is it nowadays, fifty per cent?' He laughed, yet the smile quickly faded to an earnest frown. 'Take my advice, though. Get your bills in early. I may be speaking out of turn but . . . amongst friends. The weather forecast's full of clouds for J.J., no matter how this little episode ends. Wouldn't want it to rain on all your good work.' He shook their hands, a little fiercely, and departed. At the corner of St James's Street, he stopped to greet a considerably younger woman. He gave her a lingering kiss on the cheek; a few whispers later and they had disappeared around the corner.

The two security men watched him go. 'So tell me, Will, what do you think of that one?' Brozic asked.

'Our Mr Archer?' Hiley savoured a mouthful of wine, deciding it was more than big enough for him to leave the settlement of the bill to his boss. 'Fifty per cent? The man's hopelessly out of date.' He swirled the remnants around his glass. 'And a touch confused about his loyalties, too, I'd say.'

'Think we can use him on board?'

'Him?' He shook his head. 'I don't think so. I get enough shit from you.'

'Remind me to fire you for insolence some time.'

'Yes, sir.'

They went back to the bottle, and to the passing sights of Jermyn Street.

—⚏—

Early December. Darkness descended by around 4 p.m. that close to Christmas, and although the early night undoubtedly helped the matter, Harry afterwards concluded it wouldn't have made the slightest difference if it had been broad summer. They were going to get him anyway.

He had just walked into his mews on his way home to change into his dinner jacket – he was due at a charity fundraiser. Like many London backstreets his mews had been built for housing stable hands and horses and had a surprising variety of entrances and doorways off it that once led to hovels rather than the up-market urban hideaways that had replaced them, and it was from one of these doorways that three men emerged to block his path. They stood, two on the pavement and the third occupying the gutter, thrown into silhouette by a distant street lamp. The lighting in this area was obscure, practically Victorian, and although it gave a vivid atmosphere, Harry concluded that one day it really would have to be brought up to date. He deserved to see who was about to mug him.

They took a couple of steps towards him. Harry was confident he could take two of them down, and he reckoned he had a good chance even with the third, except these weren't young yobs or addicts looking for a short route to their next fix. As they separated and surrounded him, he realized it wasn't likely to be a fair fight. This was no chance encounter. Two of them were carrying baseball bats.

'Evening, lads,' he began, hoping he might talk them round, before the breath was ripped from his body by a mighty blow to the kidneys. He fell forwards, gasping, into the arms of one of them, before a knee in his groin brought brilliant light to this dark corner of London, but only inside his head. The pain shot like a bolt of lightning from his bollocks through every synapse in his body and tried to push his stomach and all its contents out through his throat. During it all, not a word was said. More blows rained down until Harry was on his back, his head bouncing off a cast-iron basement grille. He knew from their silence and the highly effective manner in which they were beating the shit out of him that these men were professionals. This wasn't a chance encounter.

Harry was no stranger to pain. Many years of practice had enabled him to compartmentalize it, not so that it didn't hurt, you couldn't stop pain hurting, but so that he could still keep thinking even while the rest of him felt as if he were taking a bath in acid. The pain might confuse but it didn't consume. That was the theory, at least. He thought he could see the moon, although it might have been that distant street lamp, and he thought he could hear the cries

175

of disturbed seagulls, but perhaps they were only his own cries. As he struggled with them on the pavement, he found he had a man either side of him, pinning his arms, and they were forcing his right leg to double up so that his knee was near his chin. He wasn't sure what they intended but knew it would be unpleasant, so he tried to twist himself free. They were stronger than he was, but his timing was such that when the baseball bat came down and smashed into his leg, it hit not directly on the knee but a few inches below. It was a blow of immense force, one that for the moment was beyond pain and left him feeling numb. That was when he knew the real point of danger had arrived, because all his experience – of being shot, of being frozen, of being drowned – told him that it was when a man went numb that he died. Better to be screaming in agony; men who were screaming were still drawing breath. But now his body felt as though it no longer belonged to him, he was drifting away, helpless. He was only vaguely aware that his deadened leg was being repositioned – they wanted another go at busting his knee – God, they intended to cripple him. He could see the baseball bat raised high once more, ready to strike the blow, when he thought he heard a scream. Not his own scream but that of a woman, which for an instant seemed to distract his attackers, and he wasn't so far gone that he couldn't twist and wriggle once more, grabbing the basement grille to help him roll on his side, protecting his knee. Another scream rang out, and now it was joined by a man's shout, too; this private quarrel was in danger of rapidly becoming a public spectacle. It wasn't running to plan any more. As Harry curled up, like a foetus in a bloodied womb, he felt a boot smash into the base of his spine, but then they were gone, disappearing like will-o'-the-wisps back into the swamp from which they'd come.

—◊◊◊—

The parameters for success in a kidnap are relatively easy to define. It's one that ends profitably and peacefully. Both conditions are important, because money alone is not enough for a kidnapper. Most kidnaps are carried out by professionals, and those episodes that end in the death of the hostage are by definition failures, because they break the rules and so do damage to the game, making it more difficult to play next time around. And it is a game. Each side has something that the other wants, and if they play the game successfully, both will win.

The problem is that a family that has a loved one snatched away and placed under threat rarely sees it like this. It's not easy to play it as a game when you are terrorized and abused, and your loved ones threatened with death. It places the family under extraordinary pressure, which is the point of the exercise. It gives the kidnappers greater negotiating muscle, helps keep up the price.

That's why the Breslins needed Will Hiley. They needed him to think for them, to talk for them, to untangle the twisted strands, to explain the rules of the game and to lift them above the extraordinary hurt they were drowning in.

The next time de Vries made contact, it was by chance that every member of the negotiating group except for Archer was present, and they huddled in front of the computer. Yet this time there was no anonymous Skype screen; the video link had been activated. Strange shapes began shifting from side to side as the laptop and its webcam were moved, as if it were being held in someone's hands, but then it found its place and the first recognizable features came into view. They were Rauri's. The light was dismal and the quality of the video stream desperately grainy but his face was unmistakable. Even if he hadn't been so filthy and bruised Terri would have screamed, but as she did so his head came up and his despondent features grew suddenly alert, listening, wondering.

'Mummy? Mummy?' he called out, his voice rising, trembling. 'Is that you?'

Even as she tried to hurl questions at him and shout out her love, the screen went blank. Yet the sound continued and in a quality that for their ears was all too graphic. They could hear Ruari crying, as though being beaten into silence, and footsteps climbing a creaking stair, then the banging of a closing door. They had been given what they wanted, the proof of life.

They stood transfixed, staring at the blank screen for several seconds until a voice broke through their trance. It was de Vries. 'OK, six months. You publish nothing for six months.' He sounded almost bored. 'That's as far as we go. Then you get the boy back.'

But if de Vries was expecting gratitude for any concession he was quickly disappointed as Terri began screaming abuse at him. It took many moments before J.J. was able to cajole her into relative silence. She retreated to a corner, sobbing quietly, mouthing the words 'six months' and shaking her head in disbelief. Hiley took up the reins.

'Six months? Jan, you must know that won't work. The diaries will leak, you know they will. We can't keep Ruari's disappearance quiet for that length of time. The Swiss authorities are looking everywhere for him.'

'They think he's dead.'

'You know what they're like. Very neat, the Swiss, don't like having bodies littering the place. And long before your six months are up the snows will have melted and they'll know that he's around somewhere. They're not fools.'

'They can seek, but they won't find.'

'Look, you've got to let us start publishing long before that. Not everything, perhaps, but some parts of the diaries, some chapters. We do it in stages, you tell us what. You've got to give me something here.'

'I'll give you his fucking finger, that's what I'll do. You can publish photographs of that if you want. But you may have to forgive me, I don't have any training in surgery. I'll apologize now for what will undoubtedly be a messy job. Particularly if the little shit struggles.'

In her corner, Terri was writhing.

'You want to keep a kid for six months?' Hiley said in an incredulous tone. 'You must be crazy. The longer you wait, the greater the risk you take. There's got to be a better way than that.'

'A finger and a thumb. You'll get them both unless you tell me it's six months.'

'You know I can't do that, Jan, I'll have to consult the family. But please think about what I've said. I want to get this resolved so that everyone walks away from this, but you know you're in a difficult situation.'

'What do you mean?'

'A South African, hanging out in Italy. You can't do that forever, not in Italy. Someone's bound to notice.'

The silence that fell on them was so profound it seemed as though the connection had been lost. In the Breslin home the air seemed to have been sucked from the room, no one breathed. Then the South African's voice returned. 'Fuck you,' it said in a tone that, whatever it implied, did not any longer seem bored. Then the link was cut.

Hiley gasped in exhaustion and he pushed his chair back from the screen. No one spoke. The negotiator shrugged his shoulders to release the tension, and found his shirt stuck firmly to his back. As he turned he discovered J.J.'s face creased in fury.

'What the hell was the point in that? You went out of your way to provoke him. We don't even know if he's in Italy, for pity's sake!'

'We soon will,' Hiley replied calmly. 'Our guys in the sound lab will analyse it, every breath, every inflection. We'll learn a lot from Jan's reaction.'

'I gave you no permission to—'

'Take them by surprise. Test them. That's how we learn.'

But Breslin would not be assuaged. He stood with his arms stiff and his fists clenched in confrontation. 'It's a bloody huge risk.'

'And one worth taking, in my opinion.'

'It's my opinion I pay you to take.'

'No, sir. You pay me for my judgement. And it's my gut reaction that we just caught him out, that he's in Italy after all. And if we knew that it would be a great help to us.'

'I think he's right, J.J.,' his father joined in. He didn't often do that, join in, so that when he did, they listened.

J.J. responded by marching to a side table and pouring himself a large cognac. The decanter clinked against the glass; his hand was trembling. He stared into the goblet, swirled his thoughts around, sulked, then swallowed. He didn't offer anyone else a drink. His selfishness goaded Terri from her corner.

'For God's sake, do what they say, J.J. Give them what they want!'

'You know I can't.'

'I know nothing of the sort. All I see is you bloody men, all of you, playing your wretched games while the life of my son is at stake!' She couldn't stay silent, but neither

181

could she look them in the eye. She knew she was being unfair. 'I'm sorry,' she blurted. 'It's just . . . I'm so exhausted. Not sleeping.'

'None of us are,' her husband replied, in a manner that implied it was she who was being self-centred.

'I'm keeping you awake.'

'We're keeping each other awake.'

'My fault.'

'It's nobody's fault,' he insisted bleakly.

'Best if you sleep in the spare room for a few nights, per-haps. Let us both get some rest.'

It was a conversation that should have been conducted in private, but they had discovered there was no such thing as a private life when your son had been taken hostage. J.J. hesitated, listening to the crack that was forcing its way between them and growing substantially wider. 'OK,' he said quietly.

CHAPTER THIRTEEN

Harry's leg was agony. His knee was swollen and locked stiff, as was much of the rest of him, and there was a cut and vivid purple bruising on the side of his temple, yet somehow they'd missed any vital part. Nothing had been broken. His attackers had been disturbed, scared off before they could complete their job. Harry stayed hidden at home, licking his wounds.

He had plenty of distraction, there was never any shortage of that in the run-up to Christmas. His parliamentary work had piled up, and with less than a week to go before the recess the system had slipped into its usual pre-holiday panic and produced an even thicker forest of paperwork for him to chop his way through. The previous evening he'd signed more than a thousand Christmas cards with their embossed green House of Commons logo, a huge pile of synthetic goodwill that had been sent over to him by his secretary. Many of the names on the envelopes, too many for comfort, he hadn't even recognized, it was so wretchedly impersonal – Happy Christmas, whoever you are! Remember to vote for me next time! But was there to be a next time? He wasn't even sure of that. Sometimes he just wanted to walk away from it all. Downing Street was still pushing for a decision on the Foreign Secretary's job, but he'd asked them to wait another week. Couldn't make up his mind about anything. He was beginning to sense frustration in Mary's voice, but so what? It was nothing compared to what Ruari and Terri were doing to him. As he sat in his den, with winter rain beating intermittently against the window, he wished he had more cards to sign. Sometimes the wretchedly impersonal was a relief.

On the third day he stretched and was delighted to discover that he could now almost straighten his leg, although every move felt as though it was part of a clumsy student's anatomical experiment. He wriggled his toes, relieved that everything still worked, and decided he'd been sitting by his hearth long enough. He might need a stick to get around but he didn't need to hide away any longer. It was time, he decided, to nail the bastard who'd beaten him up.

Harry limped his way up Dean Street in Soho, his head lowered into a sharp northerly wind that was blowing sheets of abandoned newspaper along the gutters and wrapping them around lampposts. Christmas was celebrated in a different fashion on these streets; a poster in the window of one of the many sex shops instructed him to have a Horny Christmas, while the varied items of underwear on show were covered in suggestive strands of tinsel. A bored woman with too much mascara stared at him from behind the glass-fronted door. He hobbled on.

He was headed for the Toucan, a pub that lay just off Soho Square. It was small, unpretentious, with a black-painted facade and the feel of a comfortable but over-worn jumper found at the back of a closet. On a summer's evening the drinkers from the advertising and media companies that thronged together in this part of London would spill out onto the pavement in their bright shirt sleeves and at times even block the road, but when Harry arrived on a winter's afternoon of frozen ankles and monochrome skies there was as yet almost no one. He clambered down the stairs to the small cellar bar. Everything was cod-Irish, except for the barman, who was from Naples. The bar itself offered two pumps of lager and six of Guinness, which stood like cranes on the dock waiting to unload cargo. A dusty accordion hung overhead alongside an old brass clock that had stopped many years ago. Somehow, down here, time didn't much matter. A couple in over-coats stood at one end of the bar sharing a plate of Rossmore oysters, and in an alcove, his wallet on the table in front of him, an unlit hand-rolled cigarette in his hand, sat Sean Breslin. He looked up as Harry shuffled awk-wardly down the stairs, his gaze running from the cane to the leg and all the way up to the lacerated cheek before he met Harry's eyes.

'Mr Jones, this is a surprise. Had an accident?'

'No accident, Sean.'

Breslin didn't invite him to sit, but Harry did so nonethe-less. He waved at the barman and ordered a pint of the

185

black liquid. Neither of them spoke as they waited for the drink to be poured.

'No, not an accident,' Harry said again, sipping through the head of the beer when at last it arrived and savouring the bite of burnt barley.

'Keeping bad company, then.'

'That's for sure.'

Breslin picked up his own beer, slowly, as if he had all the time in the world. 'Why are you here, Mr Jones?'

'To tell you that if ever you set any of your friends on me again, I'll break every bone in your own legs and enough of those in other parts to ensure you'll never be able to take a crap in comfort again.' There was no animosity evident in Harry's voice, this was professional, like two farmers discussing the weather.

Breslin raised his eyes. 'Ah, been busy jumping to conclusions, have we, Mr Jones?' His accent seemed less polished, more rolling than on their previous encounters, as if this place took him back to earlier days of sea cliffs and mist-filled breezes.

'Take it as a compliment. It seems you're a man of your word, Sean. No sooner have you threatened me than I get chosen for a little Irish punishment. They always liked going for kneecaps in your time, didn't they, the Boys? Not so much with baseball bats but with bullets. Seem to remember they even used the occasional electric drill.'

Breslin drank, wiping the cream from his top lip with the back of his hand. 'This is fine stuff, wouldn't you say, Mr

Jones? Best beer in central London. But I'm surprised to see you drinking it, with your prejudice about all things Irish.'

'Not prejudice.'

'Almighty God, but you go getting yourself beaten up, add two and two together and already you're making it a full Irish dozen.'

'Just three, that's all. You know, we were really close, face to face, the sort of thing that happens when you're having the bejesus beaten out of you. And one of them had been drinking this stuff less than half an hour before. I took it as a small clue.'

'So, it's innocent until proven Irish, still. Not much changes with you people.'

'Let's just put it down to experience, shall we? And I came here to make sure it wouldn't happen again.' He stared at Breslin, who held his gaze, not blinking or faltering. 'We don't need all this, not with a kidnap to deal with.'

'Know a thing or two about kidnap, do you?'

'As, I think, do you.'

'I've heard it happens.'

'Happened a lot back home, didn't it?'

'So it's said.'

'Then let's say we've both got a bit of previous.'

As they stared into each other's eyes, Breslin realized that Harry understood, about him and about his past. Sloppy had filled in some of the detail. Breslin had started out as a bookkeeper in Dundalk, in those days a dump of a town that squatted only minutes away from the hated

187

border with the North. It was a place of squalor; the lane where Breslin was raised had neither running water nor inside toilets. It was also a place of deep-rooted national-ism, where the bars openly displayed their hardline sympathies and where the outhouses and the fields beyond hid a history filled with gruesome secrets. Breslin had started off in the building industry, becoming one of the big players, making his fortune bulldozing the sordid concrete boxes of the slum estates and rebuilding his home town on a tide of European money – a good chunk of which had ended up in the pockets of the IRA. Find a clever book-keeper and every lorryload of bricks or cement or lumber or steel joists would have a percentage added on, insurance companies would be scammed for building-site accidents that never happened, dirty money would be laundered and its grubby roots buried beneath new roads and con-crete foundations. No one had ever been able to nail Breslin for it, but you didn't survive in those days without playing the game, and if you played it well, you prospered. Sean Breslin had not only prospered but branched out, given his son the education that in his day his parents could never afford, then set him up in a local newspaper busi-ness. Two very different generations and, according to Sloppy, the divide was still apparent. The father remained as hard-nosed as he was hard-line, while the son seemed to have put much of his Irish past behind him. Sean didn't care for that, not a bit.

Yet if the father had any reservations about his relationship with his son, they were as nothing compared with what he felt about Harry. If it were a fault to be born British, in Sean's eyes it was a crime to have been in the army in Northern Ireland, and nothing less than damnation to have served in the hated SAS. A record like that could mean only one thing. Harry had blood on his hands. Irish blood. All the way up to his elbows. Even sitting with a man like this was enough to curdle a decent pint. These two men shared a past, and their mutual loathing spilled over in each other's eyes.

'Well, at least we understand each other, Sean.'

'I think we do, Mr Jones.'

'Since neither of us wants to ruin our reputation by being seen with each other,' Harry said, 'I'll be off.' He swallowed the last of his beer and rose stiffly from his seat. 'But one last thing. A bit of advice.'

Breslin sighed. 'Don't let me be delaying you. I swear you've tried to give me more than enough advice for one day.'

'The kidnappers.'

'What about them?'

'All my instincts tell me they're hired hands. Mercenaries. And kidnap isn't their usual style of business. I may be wrong but right from the start they seem to have been in one hell of a hurry, like they have a deadline. Kidnappers often let the family wait for days, weeks, before they get in touch, let them stew, but not this lot. It seemed they couldn't wait to get on with it.'

Breslin stared, didn't respond.

'Don't delay too long, Sean. Time's not on your side in this one.' He leaned on his stick and was limping for the stairs when Breslin spoke.

'In the name of God, sit down and finish yer drink.'

'I already have.'

'Then have another.'

Harry stopped, startled, turned slowly. 'With you?'

The eyes remained as cold as a winter's dawn, but Breslin waved a paw and ordered two fresh pints. He waited until they were making damp rings on the table and the barman had retreated before he spoke. 'I'm beginning to think you sit next to the Devil himself.'

'Because I'm English.'

'Because all too often you turn out to be right.' The admission seemed to leave a bad taste in his mouth, which he attempted to wash away with another swig of beer. 'They're in Italy, just like you said. Their man took a real wobble when Hiley threw the suggestion at him, then those very strange people back in the voice lab say it hit him right where it hurts.'

Harry nodded, but said nothing. Being right about Italy didn't give him bragging rights with a man like Breslin.

'But this stuff about them being in a hurry. Hiley – clever fella, that one – he told them we couldn't be burying the diaries forever, that we needed a time limit. They came back and said six months, but he said that wasn't good enough, that we'd have to start publishing something or the whole feckin' lot would leak. Very persuasive, he was.'

'He's right.'

'Six months. Does that sound like they're in a hurry to you, Mr Jones?'

'Depends what they come back with. There's something in those diaries that simply won't be relevant in six months. And if you were sitting on their pot, you'd give yourself a good margin for safety, wouldn't you?'

'Yeah. That's what I was thinking, too.'

It was the first time they had agreed about anything. They sipped in silence for a moment.

'They've sent proof of life?' Harry asked.

Breslin nodded.

'How is he?'

'Happy as a lamb in April, what do you expect?' Breslin spat sarcastically. He sucked at his unlit cigarette, but seemed to derive no satisfaction from it. His lips grew thin, as though sewn together by someone who'd made a pretty poor job of it.

'Tell me, Sean, how deep were you into things? Back during the Troubles?'

'Let's just be saying that you and I will probably both end up in Hell, but squatting on different sides of the fire.'

'Not on different sides, not on this one.'

Breslin's lips were working now, the first sign of emotion his face had betrayed, and as they parted they poured forth scorn. 'For the love of God, this is not about you and me, nor even you and my daughter-in-law. This is about Ruari.'

'I understand. Your son as good as said you'd crawl across broken glass for him.'

'God help me but I'd even sit down and drink with you.'

'I'm sure you'd prefer the broken glass.'

'Any day.'

'I'd still like to help. If you want it.'

Breslin took a deep swig of his beer, swilling it around to wash a bad taste out of his mouth. He ran a hand through his hair so that it stood up on end as though it had a mind of its own, was cussed, awkward, like the man himself. 'In my country we're forced to hack our living from a hard soil, Mr Jones. We hold on to what we have. We learn to love with a fierce passion, even when we know how often that happiness is sure to be ripped from our hands. I love Rauri, and with every part of my Irish soul. He is the future, my future, even after I'm dead and long gone. So I will accept your offer of help, because you are my enemy's enemy.'

'I understand.'

'And even if fairies build their nests at the bottom of my garden and it turns out that I should live for a thousand years, there's not one of them when I'll be of a mind to trust you.'

CHAPTER FOURTEEN

A bulbous silver moon hung over Harare, swollen with rain. The clouds had cleared, at least for the moment, leaving a sky filled with a million angels' eyes, yet down on the streets the city still sweated. Concrete and Africa made an uncomfortable combination. In Chombo's view it had been a mistake for Africans to mimic the colonial master and adopt his clothing, his language, his way of life. The white man was not suited to this place and neither were his habits, least of all this city, which blotted the landscape like a mausoleum. It had been known as Salisbury but they had wiped that away, given it the Shona name of Harare, yet its puddles were still the same and its stench had grown even worse. In some ways Chombo missed the old days. As he sat on his balcony and listened to the buzz-saw sound of mosquitoes cutting through the rumble of traffic, he reflected on how much simpler many things had been in colonial times. Four words, that was all they had needed in those days. Hate The White Man. A straightforward creed made all the easier by the stupidities of the white-pimp Prime Minister Ian Smith and his absurd henchmen. But old habits die hard, the hate lingered on, except now all too often it was turned on themselves.

During his time in Boston, Chombo had given a lecture to his fellow students about the situation back home in what was then called Rhodesia. He gave many such talks on the campuses that crowded the Charles River basin, evenings of colour and passion, pizza and beer, when he had described the fight for freedom in his home country. Often there was a fee for his labours, and always he found a choice of gullible young women keen to show off their liberal East Coast consciences by inviting him into their beds. One evening in a crowded library he had offered his usual performance, the eyes of his audience filling with indignation as he had denounced the imperialist oppressor, when a young man stood up at the back of the hall to ask a question. He had dark eyes and beard, and was wearing a yarmulke, no surprise there. 'Hey, Chombo, enjoyed the talk, almost as much as I did last year. Long live the revolution,' the young man called out, to the accompaniment of many nodding heads and a scattering of applause. 'You're dedicated, that's for sure, gotta give you that. But if the revolution's over there, man, what the hell you doing here?'

Even then Chombo had known how to play the martyr. 'That is a very good question, my friend. And the answer is this. It is because the revolution cannot succeed without your help, your moral support and your money. And also because,' he proclaimed to the rows of young, eager faces,

194

'Mr Ian Smith's bullets do not recognize the fact that I, Moses Chombo, have a Ph.D.' Well, not quite true, he had a master's and was intending to work towards a doctorate, he'd even got a grant for it, although in the event he would never manage to finish it. That night he had crashed his car, with two drunken teenagers on board, sisters, they'd been badly injured, and his life had taken a different course. Yet in all the years since, and no matter how fast and how far he ran, he could never escape those days and the lie they gave to his legend.

He blew another lungful of smoke into the heavy night air in an attempt to keep the mosquitoes at bay and looked across the rim of his glass at Takere, who was sitting opposite. When first they had formed their alliance he would have invited the security man to share a drink, but not any more, it was enough that he be allowed to sit. There was an order of things, and Takere had to be kept in his place.

'Six months,' Chombo muttered. 'You said they would accept that.' It sounded like an accusation.

'I said they *should* accept that. It is extremely reasonable, in exchange for a child's life.'

The President began to protest, but Takere cut him off before in his narrow-minded mood the man said anything they might both find difficult to forget. 'They are haggling. It is a game. It is to be expected.'

'It is not a problem? I have your word on that?'

'A game. Which we must also play.'

'What is it that you suggest?'

'We must dissuade them from making further demands.'

'How?'

'By reminding them of what will happen if they do not cooperate.'

Takere smiled. Chombo thought it was the cruellest expression he had ever seen. The man actually enjoyed this. And it was as if Takere could read his thoughts because he was nodding. 'To be successful, Mr President, you must learn to be a butcher. It is necessary,' he said softly.

Chombo looked out into the darkness. The clouds were returning, the moon had disappeared and taken with it all the angels.

'Do whatever you have to do. It must remain six months,' he whispered, as the rain began to beat down upon his world.

—ᴡᴡ—

For most of the time Ruari was left in darkness. There were two windows in the cellar, small, less than a foot high and so smeared with dirt they allowed nothing more than a dull light to penetrate for a few hours every day. He had begun to hate the darkness. It left him with nothing but the ghosts, and his thoughts, which grew ever more disturbed. Oh, he hated his captors, of course, but yet somehow in this world of near perpetual darkness he had begun to miss them, welcoming every glimpse, even the abuse they hurled at him. Little Shit was a name he wore with pride.

And even when de Vries and Nelu arrived to record another message, he had learned to squeal quickly, to avoid unnecessary pain, and grew almost sorrowful when they packed up the laptop and left.

The hours dragged so slowly yet surely he had been here for weeks? It was becoming so difficult to tell the passage of time in the half-light – he was fed, he crapped; was beaten, strained to pick up any sign of life from the other side of the door, but it was thick and heavy and he could hear only an occasional muffled noise. So he waited with eagerness for the next time they would disturb him, and didn't care for what reason. Almost anything was better than being left idle and alone.

So when the door to the cellar opened with an unusually purposeful clatter and the light was switched on, Ruari felt a tremor of anticipation. Even though he was temporarily blinded, he knew something exceptional was about to happen. This was more than just another feeding time. He could hear de Vries giving orders, and as his eyes adjusted he saw Grobelaar, and Nelu with his laptop, and Cosmin carrying a bucket. He was fascinated to see that Cosmin's face had recovered from its bruising, and assumed his own must be back to something like normal, although his touch detected a distinct kink in his nose that hadn't been there before. Nelu busied himself with the laptop, setting it on a small rickety table and switching on the camera, adjusting its position until Ruari was full frame. The image was grainy and desperately indistinct, the light bulb gave out only a few meagre watts and wasn't strong enough for anything other than the most primitive of recordings. Ruari felt no sense of alarm.

Eventually Nelu seemed satisfied. He nodded at de Vries, and the men began to draw closer to Ruari, their shuffling feet kicking up dust from the dirt floor. They pulled out masks from their belts and covered their faces from the camera. Strange, it made them look like executioners on the scaffold, Ruari thought. Only then did he begin to feel a sense of menace.

Ruari huddled in the dirt, de Vries towering above him. 'Little Shit, this is a moment you might want to start screaming. Yes, scream your lungs out,' he said.

Then Cosmin dragged his bucket closer and from it pulled a glistening heavy-duty knife.

Fear is a more powerful tool than physical pain. As Terri watched what was happening from her home in Notting Hill, a tremble took possession of her lower lip. She could not tear her eyes from the screen.

They had been alerted to expect a message, so all the members of the family negotiating group had gathered in the dining room, waiting. Now they watched the images that were emerging from the dimly lit cellar. They were blurred and at first difficult to follow, shapes that were little more than shadows, colours that were bleached, but suddenly from the midst of confusion appeared a face. It was Ruari's. He was looking up, wide-eyed, an expression of confusion spreading across his face. Terri gasped, her fingers reached out, as though to touch her son, but froze as the camera picked up the unmistakable outlines of the knife. Anonymous, unrecognizable hands grabbed for the boy. That was when he started screaming.

A child's terror takes hold and grows within a mother, there is no effective defence, and Terri found it ever more difficult to see what was taking place as her knees failed her and her head filled with a silent howl of despair. The shadows closed in around Ruari, there were flashes of the blade, and of his terrified eyes, then more shadows as his face disappeared from view, but if the images were intermittent the sound that came over the link and beat upon Terri's senses was constant. Her son was in torment. For a moment she questioned if it were truly him, his voice sounded deeper, so grown up, a man's screams, not the high-pitched squeals of her baby boy running from a bike crash in the garden, yet no matter how she tried to convince herself otherwise, the eyes that stared at her from the screen, accusing, burning into her, were Ruari's.

Then Ruari's cries grew muffled, smothered behind some restraining sleeve, and the confusion of images began to clear. A hand appeared. In its palm was a small bloodied piece of flesh. A finger.

J.J. threw up. He was ripped through by a moan of despair but he wouldn't leave the room, would not run and turn his back on his son, and in any case he wasn't sure right now his legs would obey him. Then Jan's voice sounded, cold, drained of emotion, its tone emphasizing that this was no rash outburst, no spasm of emotion, but an act that was entirely calculated.

'Next time,' he said, 'we carve off more important chunks. Six months. That's what you give us. Six months. Stop screwing around or we drop the boy down a hole in the ground so deep you'll never see him again.'

The voice faded, the screen went dead. For many seconds, no one uttered a word. J.J. wiped the spittle from his mouth, Terri sat huddled in a corner, sobbing. It was Archer who cut through the atmosphere from his seat by the window. 'Go to the authorities. I don't think we have any other option now.'

J.J. slammed his fist into the table, still trying to fight the idea, but his face was drained of colour, apart from the eyes, which were seared red. Slowly his body seemed to deflate, and with it his resistance. 'How would that work?' he muttered.

'I have a word with the Kidnap Unit at Scotland Yard. They'll go straight into action.'

Hiley shot a sharp look at Archer; J.J. noticed. 'What do you think of the idea, Will?' he asked

The risk assessor paused before saying: 'I think Brian is right.'

'But. There's a "but". I can hear a big bloody "but".'

Hiley had more experience of these matters than anyone here; it didn't make him feel any more comfortable. 'It will take time. Because this is happening abroad it will be handed to a specialist group at the Yard – the Hostage and Crisis Negotiation Unit. They're specialist, elite – which means they're small. Less than ten of them, all told. And because the situation's abroad, it's a consular matter, they'll have to go through the Foreign Office, which will go to their Italian counterparts, who will then brief their own police—'

He broke off as J.J. groaned. 'Sweet Jesus, it sounds about as effective as the United Nations.'

'No, they're already up and running, J.J.,' Archer interrupted, rising onto the balls of his feet. Hiley thought he looked smug. 'I took the liberty of having a word with them a couple of days ago. They're waiting for my call.'

'I thought I told you not to.'

'It was an entirely informal chat, a hypothetical scenario, but they knew what I was about.'

J.J. sighed. 'Dear Lord, what am I supposed to do?'

'Give them the diaries – please,' Terri sobbed, still sitting on the floor in a corner, her arms huddled around her knees. 'Or burn the bloody things!'

'You know that's not possible,' J.J. forced the words out through clenched teeth, shamed by his impotence.

'Then what are you going to do?' his wife fired back.

'I don't know!' They stared angrily at each other, but quickly he lowered his head, not wanting her to see that his anger was a cover for his humiliation. J.J. Breslin had never felt more powerless. His son, his marriage, his newspaper – his world was spiralling out of control and he risked losing everything. He was desperate to fight, but instead was lashing out heedlessly. He couldn't do this on his own, yet even in this crowded room he felt utterly lost. He felt ashamed for his display of weakness, for vomiting, for having no answers, and most of all for not being there when his son had needed him most. He had no idea what to do next, or who he could trust. He rushed from the room before they could see his tears.

—⁓—

Harry sat in the chamber of the House of Commons, tucked away on the green leather benches. It was easy to hide here, no major distractions, except when the party leaders appeared to perform their choreographed stunts. For the last two hours there had been rarely more than twenty Members in the great oak-panelled hall, for a debate on a Care Home and Sheltered Accommodation (Domestic Pets) Bill, and many of those present seemed more concerned with signing piles of constituency correspondence.

What was he doing here? It was the question the Prime Minister was pursuing him to answer. So much of Harry's job as a Member of Parliament seemed menial, sometimes even demeaning, so didn't it make sense to exchange it for the creature comforts of the diplomatic circuit, swap the barrack room for business class? Yet Harry had always felt at home in the barracks, getting muck under his nails, and if he accepted the Prime Minister's offer the only way he'd get his hands dirty was cracking lobster shells. Yet it wasn't as simple as that, he used to love lobster. He'd dived for them off the Massachusetts coast with a thick leather glove to protect him from their claws, but tastes change, lives move on, and leather rots in seawater. That's why he'd decided to hide away in the corner of the chamber, hoping it would help make up his mind about where his life was going, but as another speaker bobbed up and down like a plastic duck in a storm, Harry decided it was pointless. He wasn't going to find the solution to his problems here; he might as well consult a horoscope. He couldn't escape the fact that the answer lay not on any public platform but buried somewhere deep within his private life. What was the point in the public acclaim and having enough letters after his name to fill an entire Scrabble board when at night he went back to an empty house with too many cold corners? The beating from those Irish dog-breaths had brought it home to him. He'd got through it all right, he was Harry Jones, but with someone else hanging around in his life he would have found it so much less painful.

He took himself off from his perch in the chamber and began pacing the corridors of Parliament, but he soon grew bored with offering an invented excuse for the bruising on his face. He found himself out on the Terrace overlooking the Thames, alone except for a curious seagull who hopped along the stone balustrade in the hope of finding something to scavenge. The late-afternoon sun was trying to dry out the puddles, but it wouldn't win before the next bank of cloud arrived from the east. There was a high tide, silt-laden waters slapping the embankment, a bracing wind, a touch of sleet in the air. This was more his environment. Come on, Jones, coal face or diplomatic couch, make up your bloody mind! He was still struggling when his phone rang.

'Ha-rry Jones,' a slow American voice declared.

'Charley! What a pleasant surprise. Tell me all your secrets while you remember this is not a secure phone. I have a seagull listening in.'

'You on some beach as usual, with your hands full of women and wine?' Ebinger asked gently with the studied insolence of an old friend, his deep American tones seeming to warm the air around Harry.

'Sore point right now, Charley. Still, Christmas coming, maybe I can escape somewhere.' Suddenly Harry realized he had no plans for Christmas – something else in his personal life he'd been trying – unsuccessfully – to ignore. 'Are you allowed to tell me where you are?'

'At home,' the presidential adviser said. 'Just packing. Off for a few days spreading American humour and the rules of baseball around Asia and Africa. Putnam was just asking after you. She sends her love.'

In the background Harry could hear Ebinger's wife shouting in greeting.

'We keep picking up rumours we're going to be seeing more of you on this side of the water, Harry. Wanted you to know how thrilled Putnam and I would be about that. And you'd have a very special welcome committee lined up here in Washington, you know that.' The American was extending a welcome, putting on a little gentle pressure, using cryptic language while making sure Harry realized the welcoming committee would include the President.

'Fact is, Charley, I've been meaning to call to ask your advice. But how did you hear about it all? Hell, I haven't even told my hairdresser.'

'You know I'm paid to know everything. I have friends in some very peculiar places, so not much escapes me. If it did, I guess I'd be getting myself fired.'

Harry felt a spot of rain on his forehead, cold, heavy, on the cusp of sleet. It had grown considerably darker in the few minutes he'd been standing here. The seagull, its feathers ruffling in the sharpening wind, flapped and flew away, but as it did so an idea took its place.

'Charley, since you've got friends in such peculiar places, have you heard of the Mandela diaries?'

'Published a while ago, weren't they?'

'No, I mean another set. More private. More pointed. I'm told they're doing the rounds.'

'The diaries that could cause a former vice-president of my country a bout of gut-wrenching embarrassment with his wife and church congregation if the scurrilous allegations contained in them ever saw the light of day?' Ebinger chuckled. The sanctimonious shit in question was from a different administration and a different party; he owed him nothing except perhaps a little retribution.

'In all honesty I'm not sure,' Harry replied. 'Haven't seen them myself. But I'd very much like to. Any chance?'

'How urgent is it?'

'Oh, you know, it's just started raining here. So before it finishes, perhaps?'

'Does it ever stop raining there, Harry?'

Harry could hear Putnam shouting in the background. Her husband's car was waiting.

'Have to go. I'll see what I can do,' Ebinger said. 'And I hope to be seeing you soon, Mr Jones, over here. You can pay me back then.'

—◠◠—

A courier in a dark limousine with diplomatic plates delivered the package. No signature required.

Harry devoured the diaries, cancelling an entire day's meetings to read them in one session. They were an old man's meanderings – no, Harry corrected himself, that wasn't the word, not meandering, there was a point to all these stories. The diaries reflected Mandela's enduring faith in the decency of Man, but showed damnably little trust in the honesty of men, at least amongst many of those he'd been forced to deal with. Mandela's had been an intensely political life – at one point he had been only a step away from the gallows, yet later he walked so historically out of his prison and had wound up not in a crude wooden coffin but in the presidential palace. It was scarcely surprising that his long journey had required many kinds of compromise, deals with men he despised. There had been times in his life when he admitted he was guilty of what many would regard as conspiracy and cover-up, not to protect himself but to defend the cause. It was a case of eggs and omelettes and things that needed to be broken for the wider good. Nothing survives wholly intact, least of all political virtue. Page by page had been written with a sharp nib and a memory etched in the most vivid colours. If Mandela's past crime had been to turn a blind eye, now he sought absolution; and yet, as Harry read and reread the words, his lingering impression was of frustration. Mandela had been so very old when he had written them, and many of those names he mentioned were, like Mandela himself, now dead. Reputations would be tarnished, several wives and widows would be left squirming in embarrassment and outrage at their husband's follies, there would be one Israeli Prime Minister who would never be able to run for election again and even the Pope would have to revise the glowing eulogy he had delivered to the memory of a favourite cardinal, but if there was something in these pages that would justify murder and kidnap, Harry was unable to find it. So he read them again.

And that was when he bumped into what he was looking for. Suggestive coincidence rather than conclusive proof, but many men had been stood against a wall and shot on less evidence than this, so the kidnapping of a child fell easily within its compass. His excitement pushed the last of his aches and bruises from his bones, and he stretched for the phone.

It had been impressed upon the Breslin family by Hiley that they should try to lead a normal life. Not possible, of course, but there was no point in staying at home waiting, worrying, allowing their fears to grind them down. And J.J. in particular had business to attend to. He was passing through his outer office, the area where his secretary held sway, when he heard her fielding a call for him.

'Yes, sir. I'll see if he's available.' She placed her hand over the receiver and raised an eyebrow.

'Who is it?'

'A personal call, he says. A Mr Harry Jones?' Her voice rose in enquiry.

Breslin hesitated for a heartbeat before he took the phone, holding it at arm's length.

Then he dropped it back into its cradle.

—⚏—

She had agreed to meet him in the old red-brick Wren church of St James in Piccadilly, on the wooden pew in the corner where the faithful lit candles and left their messages on the prayer board.

'I'm surprised,' Harry admitted. 'A church.'

'Neutral territory,' Terri said. 'With what my husband thinks about you, I thought we needed somewhere which wouldn't encourage the more lurid edges of his imagination. Perhaps we shouldn't be meeting at all.'

'And yet?'

'For old times' sake, I suppose, Harry.' But her eyes said differently.

He watched as she lit a candle and stood in silent prayer, staring at its flame as the wax began to drip into the tray. 'I love it here,' she whispered. 'My friends and I, we come to restaurants nearby to do lunch – you know, silly, indulgent girls' stuff, big frocks, big wines, ridiculously big bills. Then afterwards I creep in here, all on my own, just to say thank you. I've never taken what I've been given for granted, Harry.'

'I never knew you were religious.'

'Do you have to be, just to be grateful?'

For a moment the candles guttered in a draught. A grizzled man in a tattered raincoat came into the church and stopped as he passed, staring at them in the slow, timeless fashion of the homeless. Then he shuffled off to sit in the warmth of a pew closer to the altar.

'I tried to talk to J.J.,' Harry said. 'I think he put the phone down on me.'

'I'm sure he did. He suspects you and I are having an affair again, or even if we're not that we soon will be. Silly man.'

'I told him that was nonsense.'

'And you expected him to believe you?'

Of course not. And why should he? Harry didn't even believe himself.

'I've been reading the diaries, Terri. It's possible I may have found who's behind all this.' They were sitting at opposite ends of the bench, as though determined to keep a proper distance between themselves, but now she stirred, moved closer.

'It's only speculation,' he continued, 'but six months. That's what the kidnappers are demanding.'

'And sticking to.'

'So what's in those diaries that in six months won't matter?'

'J.J.'s had a team of journalists poring over them. Found nothing.'

'But you have to reckon there's a fair chunk of a safety margin within that – let's say a whole three months. So what's going to happen between now and the end of February that's so damned important it could be changed by the diaries and someone thinks is worth killing for?'

She shook her head, the end of her nose bobbing in anxiety. Just as it had in Paris.

'Try power. And Zimbabwe. There's an election coming up there which Moses Chombo is expected to win. But the diaries might blow a hole in all that, destroy his dreams. He's not the man he claims to be, you see. The idea that he's a hero of the struggle is a total sham.'

Her hand reached towards him, as though trying to haul in the rest of what he knew.

'I think Mandela wrote something like this . . .' Harry frowned as he tried to drag the words from the creases of his memory. '*I offer no profound objection to the fact that Moses Chombo preferred to spend his youth in the company of young white girls rather than with his brothers fighting in the bush. It is a choice that many young men would have made. It is not given to every man to be a hero.'* Harry broke off from his recitation. 'Chombo claims to be a veteran of the bush war, you see, and says he has the scars to prove it.'

Terri had shuffled right across the bench and was now sitting close beside him, not wanting to miss a word. From his pew, the tramp turned to gaze at them in suspicion.

Harry steepled his hands in concentration as he tried to recite more of Mandela's script. *'Yet Chombo chose to watch his brothers die, and at a distance. To return to his homeland and claim their legacy, as he did, is nothing less than to steal their spirit. He has gone down a route that has dishonoured Africa ever since the white man arrived. He is unworthy.'* Harry snorted like a horse after a canter. 'That's the word he used. Unworthy. Can you imagine the damage that verdict would do if it was put about before the election?'

'It's motive, for sure, but scarcely proof.'

'This is a game played in the shadows, Terri. Oh, there are plenty of others who'd happily give their right testicle to stop those diaries being dragged out into the sunshine, but it's the timing, you see. No one has a more pressing motive than Chombo.'

'But we can't prove it,' she insisted once more.

'You don't have to. Perhaps all you need is to whisper what you know, or simply suspect, into the right ear and suddenly you've got a hell of an advantage. Leverage. Negotiating muscle.'

'Whose ear?'

'Chombo's, of course.'

Yet she showed no excitement. Her head fell. 'They cut off his finger, Harry.' She began to sob gently. The exhaustion and anxiety had drained away her spirit, she needed a shoulder to lean on, a hand to grasp, and it was now Harry's she clutched.

His ear began to burn, as though the knife was cutting through it once again. 'I'm sorry. But he'll get over that.'

'I sometimes wonder if any of us will get over this.'

Harry sensed she was talking about much more than just the kidnap.

'They said that if we don't cooperate, do what they insist, they'll carve him up and drop him down a hole in the ground so deep we'll never find him.'

'They said that?'

But for the moment she was unable to say more. She buried her head in his chest, and soon the sounds of sobbing could be heard, echoing back from the marble floor and the high vaulted ceiling.

Slowly, screaming at himself to stop, with his ear burning in warning, Harry put his arm around her. The memories came flooding back. He knew he wasn't over her.

Suddenly Harry found himself staring into the face of the curious tramp. The grizzled old man was smiling mischievously, eyeing the woman in Harry's arms, tapping the end of his nose, joining in the conspiracy. Then he nodded his battered head in approval and was gone.

—⚟—

Once her tears had dried they left the church. It wasn't an appropriate place for some of the thoughts that raced through Harry's mind as Terri nestled in his arms and her perfume set siege to his senses. They walked out into the small courtyard that faced Piccadilly, and there they found a Christmas market in full swing, with ruddy-cheeked stallholders wrapped in gloves and colourful scarves, serving out good humour and mulled wine as they tried to entice the passers-by. The bustle of the crowd was intense, forcing Harry and Terri distractingly close. They stopped beside a stall where a small girl with raised voice and stamping foot was begging her mother for a trinket, a glass globe with a primitive model of the towers of Venice inside. As the girl shook the globe, flakes of imitation snow cascaded over the city.

Venice. They'd been there, as well, not just Paris. He knew from the look in Terri's eyes that she was back there, too, and he wondered what memories she clung to, and whether they were the same as his own.

Venice – that was the direction the helicopter had been heading. But something told Harry the gang wasn't there, couldn't be, not on the water, yet if not Venice . . . ?

He took Terri's arm, swung her round. 'What did they say again – drop him down a hole so deep we'd never be able to find him?'

She nodded: 'Almost exactly that.' And suddenly he had

213

grabbed her hand and was running, forcing their way though the crowd.

A little further along the pavements of Piccadilly stood Hatchards, purveyors of books to many members of the Royal Family and the oldest bookshop in London. When Harry dragged Terri through the doors they found themselves surrounded by a sea of bodies, elbows nudging, tills clattering, telephones ringing. This was its busiest time of year.

'Hello there, Harry. Where have they been hiding you this time?' a voice called out above the throng. A man with short-cropped silver hair and a recent yachting tan waved from behind the cash desk. Roger Katz came close to being as much of an institution as the shop itself, a man who loved books and people to the point that he'd retired several times yet somehow could still be found behind his beloved counter. His enthusiasms bubbled forth, his eyes danced in fascination over Terri and he was about to launch upon a detailed interrogation when Harry raised his hand and brought him to a halt, like a traffic cop.

'Roger – Italy. Geography. Now!'

CHAPTER FIFTEEN

Terri was naked, in her bathroom, bent over and smoothing skin lotion onto her legs when J.J. arrived home. It was late, gone nine, he reeked of tobacco smoke and was exhausted after a day spent fighting with the money men. No women, not this time, not now the Bitch of Blackheath had retired to her lair. As he walked into their bedroom he found the bathroom door open, framing Terri's body like a scene by Degas, misty with steam, her body glistening, one slender leg extended, her breasts falling forward, towels discarded in rumpled piles at her feet.

She looked up. 'Hello, darling.'

The time she had spent in the bathroom had been not just for herself but for J.J., too. Ruari's plight had become their only focus, understandably so, but it had made their lives dangerously unbalanced. Even before their son's disappearance a drift had set in to their relationship that was slowly pulling them apart, but not until she had sat so close to Harry and felt his breath on her cheek once again had she realized how much peril her marriage was in. Her family meant far too much to her to let it slip away without a fight, so she had spent her lonely evening trying to wash any trace of bitterness away, hoping to revive old feelings. He'd been sleeping too long upstairs in the guest room, it was becoming a habit rather than a necessity, it was time to bring his heart and his mind back home. Yet as she greeted him he didn't even bother looking up but slumped wearily on the edge of the bed.

Not the start she'd been hoping for. He was upset with her, that she knew, ludicrously suspicious about Harry, his suspicions far more ludicrous than those she'd been harbouring about him. She wasn't blind. J.J. had been 'distracted' in recent months, and she guessed with another woman. It happened, it hurt, but she could live with it while he got over it, so why was he being so childish about . . . about nothing? Not yet, at least. They had to deal with the Harry thing, better to drag it out into the open where it would shrivel and disappear, wouldn't it? At least, that's what she hoped.

'I've been waiting for you,' she said, trying to sound welcoming as he pulled off his tie and cast it into a corner. 'Harry Jones called, had something to pass on.' She tried to make it impersonal, innocent, as she wrapped a towel around her and came to sit near him on the end of the bed.

J.J. responded by moving away to his wardrobe and rifling through his shirts to select one for the morning. 'He's persistent, I'll give him that,' he grunted.

'He thinks he knows where Ruari might be,' she said, pressing on.

J.J. turned, scowled, said nothing.

216

'The helicopter's flight path was to the north-east of Italy. In fact, if they'd kept going they'd have ended up in Venice, but Harry doesn't think they're there, or anywhere on the coast.'

A petulant pause, but he had to ask. 'Why?'

'Because of what they said. About dropping Ruari down a deep hole. Now, if you're sitting in Venice or anywhere by the sea, they'd be talking about feeding him to the fishes, something like that. They wouldn't suggest dropping him down a hole.'

J.J. didn't respond, still refusing to catch her eye. Terri couldn't tell whether his silence implied scorn or deep concentration. She hurried on. 'They didn't even talk about burying him, digging a hole. They made it sound as if the hole already existed.'

'It was just a phrase.'

'No, it may be more than that. A little beyond Venice there's a huge limestone plateau that stretches all the way to Austria and Slovenia. It's riddled with sinkholes, caves, underground rivers, the lot. J.J., I looked at some travel books this afternoon in Hatchards. That area is like a chunk of honeycomb, it's got holes so big and deep some of them are tourist attractions. You know, after the last war they found that thousands of prisoners had been dumped down there. It fits, don't you think?'

'It might.'

'Yes, it might. And it *might* be worth suggesting that the Italian police take a particularly close look at the area.'

'He conjures all this out of one stray remark from the kidnappers?'

Her exasperation was growing, and beginning to show. 'They've already let slip they're in Italy, they may have let slip a little more. Use it, for pity's sake. It might just give you a little more leverage. What have we got to lose?'

'Have you been seeing him?'

She flustered at the unexpected assault. 'I don't understand, he telephoned, you know that . . .'

'Simple question, I'd have thought. Have you seen him?'

'What do you mean?' But her question trailed off into a fatal hesitation.

'I wondered, you see, how he would know what the kidnappers said. About dropping Ruari down a hole.'

'Just remember, J.J., this is about Ruari, nothing else.'

'I hope so.'

Dammit! She'd been trying so hard, the ridiculous man was being so inflexible, unreasonable. And now she felt vulnerable, and guilty. The Harry thing. So she decided not to mention Chombo. It was a possibility, no more, another of Harry's theories that wasn't going to go down well. Nothing for J.J. to do with it except grow still more suspicious. Yet they needed each other, they'd been married too many years to play childish games. She stood up, moved towards him to give it one last try.

Yet because they'd been married these many years he sensed she was holding something back, so when she stretched up to kiss him, she found only his cheek.

'I'm tired,' he complained. 'Going to bed early, if you don't mind. I'll see you in the morning.' Without another word he took his shirt and began climbing the stairs with a slow, heavy step, dragging his pain behind him.

As she listened to the familiar creak of the treads, she wondered if he would ever sleep in her bed again.

—⁓—

The bare bulb suddenly sprang to life and Cosmin stumbled his way down into the cellar. He was holding a battered tin bowl of bean soup and bread, and as he tried to negotiate the primitive wooden steps his foot slipped, leaving him swaying and struggling for balance. For a moment it seemed as though he would fall, then he recovered and burst into laughter.

'Hey, Little Shit, see that? Not a drop spilled!' He stared in triumph and with glazed eyes at the bowl, then at Ruari, before bending to dump the food beside his prisoner. That's when he almost toppled, spilling a good portion of the soup onto the dirt floor. Up close, Ruari could smell his sour breath. The Romanian had been drinking again, the South Africans must be away.

Cosmin straightened himself, planted his feet firmly for balance, unaware that he was standing in the puddle of soup he had just spilled. 'What, you think I'm drunk, Little Shit? No! Well, maybe a little.' He laughed again.

Ruari groaned, not wanting to meet the Romanian's eye or do anything that might antagonize him. His hand was still a throbbing mass of dried blood and he was terrified Cosmin had come to do him more harm. Yet, as he cowered, expecting more hurt, he began to realize it wasn't as simple as that. Things had changed, and in one respect at least for the better. Like Casey and Mattias he, too, had suffered at the hands of these animals, and that put all three of them back on the same side, didn't it? They were together again. He had lost a finger but through that he had regained his friends and also his self-respect. The ghosts had gone and he was no longer alone. The finger had been worth it.

'We have been celebrating, drinking toasts to you,' Cosmin was declaring, swaying above him.

'To me? Why?' Ruari asked weakly. With his uninjured hand he reached out for the bread on the floor and began eating the thick soup as quickly as possible before Cosmin had the chance to stumble once more and scatter the rest of the meal.

'You are our prince. You make us all rich men. We keep you here six months, maybe more. That costs someone a fuck of a lot of money.' The Romanian sniggered.

Six months? The bread stuck in Ruari's throat and he choked. Yet as he forced his food down, he realized it meant they intended to keep him alive, long enough maybe for the rats to help dig him a way out of this wretched hole. Even now he could see bright red eyes lurking in the shadows, eyeing up the spilt food.

'Any chance I can join the celebration?' Ruari asked.

'You? You want to drink, too?' More rough laughter.

'All I want is a bowl of water so that I can wash.' He held up his hand to Cosmin, covered in black, hardened bandage. His wrists were also raw. The shackles had rubbed through the skin and had formed pus-filled scabs. He had noticed that the scratches on his body and legs were no longer healing so fast, either. 'All I want is to keep clean. Otherwise I'm going to get sick.'

Cosmin stared and scratched himself as he considered the matter.

'At least ask your boss when he gets back, will you?' Ruari said.

'Him?' Suddenly Cosmin's mood had darkened, the high spirits replaced by a sneer. 'Bastard!'

Even locked away down in the cellar Ruari had heard the arguments and raised voices. They were getting more frequent. His jailers sounded like sled dogs snarling over who should get the first bite of the carcass. Ruari might not be the only one to get chunks taken out of him, and that thought gave him heart.

'I wouldn't want to get you into trouble,' Ruari lied.

'What trouble?' Cosmin roared.

'You know, like last time . . .' Ruari stroked his nose, but the Romanian needed no reminding.

'That ugly bastard touch me again and I deal with him, you wait and see, so good he never screw another sheep, not ever! I am boss man here, not him. You hear that, Little Shit?' Cosmin raged, shaking his fist as though he had been accused of weakness. He turned and stomped back up the stairs, slamming the door, but he left the light on.

The rats were enjoying an unexpected feast when the door opened again. Toma brought down a towel soaked in warm water and a supply of fresh bandage. He stood over Ruari while the boy did his best to clean himself up. The Romanian appeared agitated, kept glancing at the open door as though listening for the return of the South Africans, and disappeared back upstairs as quickly as he could, taking the towel with him. Not everyone seemed as confident as Cosmin about who was running the show.

Trieste. A city of aquamarine tints and azure skies that gazes out across the waters of the Adriatic in search of something it appears to have lost. It has a melancholy air, like that of an ageing spinster remembering a long-lost lover and living in the hope that one day he will reappear over the horizon. In the meantime she is not certain what she wants – except that she doesn't want to be Venice, which lies seventy miles along the coast. In the view of Triestines, Venice has thrown away her honour and become a tart. So what if she draws the eye and the crowds? Trieste is highly disapproving, and quietly jealous. And when the blossom is but a faded memory and the leaves have begun to fall, and the grey streaks of winter take hold of the skies, Trieste sits with her back against the Carso, her shoulders hunched and her shawl wrapped tightly around her as she waits for the ferocious Bora wind that charges down off the limestone plateau with such force that it can knock over trams and sweep life off the streets.

Trieste is a complex community. It uses several languages, contains many nationalities, and has been ruled by Austrians, Germans, Yugoslavs, and for a short while was once even nominally an independent city state, and all that crammed into the past hundred years, but now, and for the moment, it is part of Italy. Yet much of it remains illusory. Trieste was the dividing line of the Cold War, the seam of the Iron Curtain so famously described by Churchill with his gravelly voice as stretching from Stettin in the Baltic to Trieste in the Adriatic, the frontier between Europe east and west, always on the fold in the map, where Latin civilization runs out of breath and disappears beneath the Balkans.

It has a main square, the Piazza dell'Unità, a construction of fine Middle European temperament overlooking the sea, where every hour two bronze figures on top of the City Hall are spun into motion to strike the passing of time on a great bell, which can be heard inside the Questura, the police headquarters that sits directly behind the City Hall. It had been dark for several hours when the sounds reached into the office of Inspector Francesco D'Amato of the Squadra Mobile, the Italian equivalent of Britain's CID. He was in his early forties, on the small side of average with colouring that suggested he came from the south, hair that was beginning to lose its black sheen, sloping

223

shoulders and a face that rarely relaxed, as if he were constantly studying a passage from the Bible. He was almost too carefully dressed, in the manner of most urban Italians, yet his office was informal to the point of verging on the unkempt, dominated by a dark wooden desk with two unfashionable armchairs, an old television and a glass-fronted bookcase packed with tired volumes that gave the impression of not having been opened in years. The paintwork was scratched, the walls crowded with police badges, framed certificates, photos and mementos of D'Amato's many trips abroad during his twenty years of service. It was a practical, unpretentious room, but it also contained another accessory of which the inspector was inordinately proud – Simona Popescu, his secretary. The two of them made what he thought was a productive team, since he was conscientious and she was efficient and flexible. There was also the point that working with Simona kept him in the office when otherwise he might have been losing himself in some bar. She was sitting there now, in one of the armchairs, taking notes, her legs crossed, her thigh generously exposed, lips pursed in concentration. And her breasts were rising and falling, like a pump powering up his lust. She wasn't Italian but an immigrant, like so many others in this frontier town, and had worked in the Questura for less than a year, yet she had made her way rapidly from the secretarial pool in the basement all the way up to the second floor. She'd even done shifts for the Chief of Police himself and had developed quite a reputation: reliable, well educated, excellent shorthand and exceptional ankles. In a city where so many young Triestines moved elsewhere in search of more exhilarating challenges, girls like Simona had little trouble finding work and D'Amato was delighted to have her – except, that is, he hadn't had her, not in the way he dreamed of almost every night. And that was becoming a problem. D'Amato, like many other senior police officers in Trieste, was on secondment, transferred from his home in a small southern town for a three- or four-year stretch to combat the endemic corruption that might all too easily take hold when police and criminals are born on the same streets. Good pay, promotion prospects, but challenging in the long watches of the night when home is a long way away and you've left your wife and family behind to avoid uprooting the kids from their schools and friends. A weekend back with them every month, that was all. Mother of God it hurt, in all sorts of ways.

Simona recrossed her legs, her skirt rustling on her thigh. She watched as D'Amato's eyes crawled up her ankles. He uttered something indistinct, she asked him to repeat it, pencil poised, and he came out from behind his desk, that dull institutional slab of furniture with its chrome-framed family photos and piles of too-neatly sorted papers, until he was standing beside her, flicking his finger as he did when he was nervous. There was a bulge beneath his belt, she could see he was stiff, and she struggled to suppress a laugh. He'd propositioned her before, touched her, like many men in the Questura, but that was as far as she'd allowed him to go. Now he sank to his knees beside her with a weird, helpless look on his face, placed his hand inside her blouse and groaned. Simona was twenty-two, was born out of grinding poverty and had always known that her rise from the basement to the second floor wasn't simply because she was good with the paperwork. She also felt sorry for Francesco, lonely sap. So she didn't object as he began loosening her buttons.

'Someone might come in,' she whispered.

'I locked the door.' His lips followed his fingertips, marking a trail towards her nipple.

She'd known what to expect when he'd asked her to stay late, that's why she'd already discarded her under-wear. He gasped when he saw. Now she settled back into the armchair, hooked her legs over its faded arms, and closed her eyes as he started grunting. She'd come a long way since she'd left home. Her father wouldn't approve, of course, but she thought her mother might understand. The womenfolk had learned over many generations that they had to be flexible in order to survive. That's the way it had always been, back home in Romania.

CHAPTER SIXTEEN

Chombo was surprised but naturally delighted by the invitation. It required him to take a flight to Johannesburg in South Africa, but that took less than two hours. Worth it, in the circumstances. Charley Ebinger, the US President's National Security Adviser, was in town and wanted to see him – *him*, Moses Chombo, the soon-to-be strong man of Zimbabwe. It seemed like a rite of passage; instead of Chombo flattening his nose up against the windows of power trying to peer in, one of the most powerful men in the world was opening the door, had issued an urgent invitation, would 'intersect with him' at the airport, to use the hilariously bureaucratic language of the US embassy. Yet however clumsy the wording, it was a request Chombo had no wish to refuse, even though he'd been instructed that the meeting must remain totally confidential and that if any rumours of such a meeting were to leak out the Americans would deny it had ever taken place. The United States had no wish to be accused of interfering with the electoral process in Zimbabwe. But none of that mattered to Chombo. He was on his way.

Chombo's aircraft, commandeered from Air Zimbabwe, drew to a halt in a quiet corner of Tambo International, away from the main terminals. The night air was thinner than in Harare, sweeter, easier to breathe, and the American's black four-wheel-drive limousine was waiting, its tail lights shining brightly in the darkness as Chombo descended the steps. A security man held the door of Ebinger's car for him, and closed it behind him with a muffled thud, like the sealing of a vacuum chamber.

'Mr Chombo, good evening. Glad you could spare the time,' Ebinger said as the African settled into the seat. They were surrounded by thickly padded leather and wood, but behind, beneath and above it, the African knew, lay military-grade armour with windows so thick they could stop a mortar round. They were also darkened, no one would see. It irritated Chombo that Ebinger referred to him by his name rather than by his title. He would have preferred to be addressed as 'Mr President' or even 'Your Excellency', but that would come, and soon, in weeks, after the election. He must try to show a little patience.

Ebinger pushed a button on the console in the arm of the seat and a screen rose to separate them from the driver and guard up front. Chombo's fingers brushed idly across the leather and walnut, he wondered where he was being taken – somewhere to eat, he assumed, at this hour of the evening. Yes, a frank discussion and a fine dinner. He had prepared a list of firm requests – he didn't want to call them demands – to put to the American in exchange for whatever it was he wanted. Mining rights to the copper or platinum, he suspected, and Ebinger would have to do well to match let alone exceed what was on offer from the Chinese, but it was a competitive world and Chombo was willing to be flexible – so flexible that he decided he would add a limousine to his list, one just like this, one that befitted the role of president. He smiled to himself, yet his sense of well-being was not to last.

'I hope you'll understand if we have this little conversation in the car,' Ebinger began. 'It's the curse of the modern world, always trying to crack your nuts for you. You have a drink and the world calls you an alcoholic, you smile at a young woman and they assume you're screwing her. You and me, we have this private conversation and some half-arsed journalist demands a transcript under Freedom of Information. So goddamned distasteful, everyone trying to listen in, don't you think?'

Chombo pulled a suitably disapproving face. He knew this was hokum; the Americans bugged everyone, spent many fortunes on it, and yet with all that listening they still talked shit.

'What I have to say to you, Mr Chombo, is to your considerable advantage, but it's not something I want to read about in tomorrow's newspapers. Nor you, I suspect.'

Chombo stirred. He was sure he'd got it right, it was the mining concessions. Was Ebinger going to offer him a bribe?

'Mr Chombo, I've got some bad news I need to share,'

the American said. 'You're stuck in the middle of your presidential race and your rivals are beginning to play dirt-ball. They're trying to destroy your reputation.'

'Who? Who is it?' Chombo blurted in surprise. 'Tell me who is spreading lies?'

'Can't tell for sure and perhaps it doesn't matter much. What matters is your reputation being on the line.'

The car bounced gently on its heavy suspension as they came off the ramp and onto the freeway.

'It's all about the Mandela diaries,' Ebinger continued. 'You may have heard of them. Seems like one of your opponents is suggesting there are some references to you in them that are – how can I put this? – less than flattering.' He spoke the words slowly, giving them strength. 'You're not alone. There are a couple of former American presidents who'd happily use the diaries for target practice, a Roman Catholic cardinal who'll probably have to spend the rest of his life in confession and a French minister who might even go to jail if they're published, but your problem, Mr Chombo, runs a little deeper than that.'

Deeper than jail? The leather seat seemed to have grown sticky, tugging at his clothes.

'You see, someone has kidnapped the son of the newspaper owner who is planning to publish the diaries. Pretty sick stuff. And they're trying to make out that you're behind it all. The boy was snatched in Switzerland and taken to Italy. They're threatening to kill him unless all the references to you are dropped.'

The African did not stir. Inside the bombproof bubble, the atmosphere seemed stifling.

'What we suspect is this. The kidnap plot is going to be exposed, made very public, in an attempt to implicate you. They might even kill the boy. Even a halfwit couldn't fail to see how catastrophic the impact would be on your election campaign. Let me tell you, Mr Chombo, those guys are first-class bastards. You got yourself some mighty powerful enemies out there. You need to take a good deal of care.'

Chombo's lips moved, but no words emerged. He didn't believe any of this; where was the American going with it all? Suddenly it felt very hot, even with the air conditioning. He was being roasted.

'The United States cannot interfere officially, of course, but will you let me offer you a little advice?'

The African's voice emerged wooden and robotic. 'I am always happy to listen to my American friends.'

'You're a most powerful and influential man in these parts, Mr Chombo. Whatever rogue elements are responsible for this – well, I'm sure you have your ways of finding out who they are and dealing with them. But deal with them *now*. Before this all blows up in our faces. You get that boy released and I'm sure his father will want to show you all kinds of gratitude.'

'How, precisely?'

'By ensuring that the, er ... *unhelpful* bits about you in the diaries get withheld.'

'Withheld? That is a strange term. What does it mean?'

'They get lost somewhere along the trail. Never make it to publication.'

'But how can that be guaranteed? What if those things that are lost become found again?'

'Well, as my daddy used to say to me, you can't walk through the stables without expecting to get a little shit on your shoes. But if you want my entirely private counsel, it's this. Have faith, Mr Chombo. Have faith in the gratitude of a father. Have faith in the fact that the diaries won't appear until well after the election, when you'll have got your feet firmly under that big old desk in the palace, and then – well, who'll give a damn? If any of it comes out later, you'll be able to denounce it as a forgery, lies put around by your opponents who've climbed into bed with the old white colonial press. Hell, handled right, it might even help you.'

'These allegations, they are a preposterous lie.'

'And you would have my help in making that point, Mr Chombo. You have my personal assurance that we would make sure our files on you remain in strict quarantine.'

'Files? On me?'

'Come now, Mr Chombo, you were a political activist during your time in the United States. Sure we have files on you.' Ebinger held his thumb and finger several inches apart to suggest their thickness. 'But no one has any interest in raking over old coals. The young women you injured in the car smash are fully recovered. And the infant son you left behind in Massachusetts is a father himself now.'

Chombo's features creased with astonishment.

'What, you never knew you were a grandfather? Isn't that something? Let me be the first to congratulate you. Your son and granddaughter are American citizens, of course, and to my mind, that just strengthens the bond between our two countries.'

Despite the climate control Chombo was sweating as he was turned slowly on the spit.

'But if we're going to have a gnat's chance of avoiding disaster for you, we have to move quickly. The boy has got to be released immediately and without harm.'

'But . . .'

'Look, three days should do it. If he's set free within three days from now, that's an end to it.'

'But even if I can get him released—'

'I have no doubt that you can. You're a most resourceful man.'

' . . . the father might publish anyway.'

'That's not going to happen.'

Suddenly Ebinger's voice had lost its almost jovial tone and had replaced it with an unmistakable edge of impatience. He was fed up with pretending to this arsehole. The family would cooperate, would hold off publication, he'd had Harry's assurance on that when he'd called on a secure line to the US embassy in Pretoria to thank him for sending over the diaries.

'Glad I could help,' Ebinger had said.

'There's more,' Harry had replied.

233

'More?'

'Something I need from you while you're out there in South Africa. Help me and I'll . . .'

'You'll what, Harry?'

'Do this for me and I won't run off with your wife.'

Ebinger had laughed. Putnam was in her early sixties and a grandmother three times over, not the type of woman Harry usually got involved with, although over the years Harry and his wife had managed to see off a good quantity of his finest bourbon sitting out on the deck of his Silver Springs home. 'Make the same promise for my daughters and I'm your man,' Ebinger had replied.

'Charley, seriously, you might save a young boy's life here. While you're there in South Africa I want you to get to Chombo,' Harry had said, explaining his request.

'But, Harry, you say you can't be sure Chombo's behind it.'

'You'll know within seconds if he isn't. Just don't directly accuse him of anything and if he's got nothing to do with it there's no harm done.'

Yet it had been a pointless precaution. Ebinger could smell the guilt on Chombo, could see it emerging in little tears just below his hairline.

'Three days, Mr Chombo.'

'But the election isn't for another seven weeks,' Chombo persisted.

'Let me explain it to you so you won't misunderstand. The father's not going to publish and take the risk that whoever has kidnapped the boy will try again. He won't want his son staring over his shoulder in fear of retaliation for the rest of his life. There's a deal to be done here, Mr Chombo. Neat. Simple. Three days. Otherwise this is all going to get like a muck yard in a monsoon.'

Chombo's mind was a sheet of newspaper being blown across the gutter in a storm. Files? Grandchildren? He had lost control of this situation, his own life was being held hostage along with the boy. He had no choice.

'You have my word, Mr Ebinger, that I will do everything I can to resolve this most unfortunate situation.'

'And you have my word, too.' The American made his assurance sound very much like a threat.

'I . . . I understand.'

'Then we are one.' Ebinger's tone made it sound as if he'd just been handed an undercooked hamburger. The job was done, time to finish with this skunk. He pressed a button on the console in his armrest and soon the car was drawing to a halt, its door being held open by the Secret Service agent once again. Chombo was startled to discover that they were back at the airport. Ebinger had been driving him around in circles.

No handshakes. And no dinner. In any event, Chombo was no longer in the mood. He had other things to digest. He watched bleakly from the pavement as the tail lights of the limousine disappeared into the African night.

—∞—

It had begun to snow across London, thick flakes of white that muffled the noise of the distant traffic as Harry hurried along one of the many paths crossing Hyde Park. It was already beginning to settle and his shoes left a trail, but one that would soon be covered over and lost. There were no other marks on the path; wiser heads had stayed at home. A night bird called out in distraction but quickly fell quiet. He picked up his pace as he neared the Serpentine, and the lights of a car flashed briefly in recognition before they died as the engine was switched off. Terri emerged through the falling flakes.

'Hello, Harry.'

They stood facing each other, only inches apart. Her head was wrapped in a scarf like a hijab, outlined against a pillow of snow, and she looked beautiful. They didn't touch, didn't embrace, didn't even hold hands as they had done in their charge down Piccadilly towards the book-shop. They both knew their intimacy was dangerous, and were afraid.

They took the path that led around the lake, their passage marked by the rustling of sheltering waterfowl. They walked in silence for a while, listening to the soft tramp of their feet in the thickening snow.

'We haven't heard from the kidnappers for four days now,' she said as they passed a boathouse. 'I'm worried, Harry. They haven't been silent for this long before.'

'Silence is a weapon. Meant to put pressure on you. Make you suffer.'

'Then it's working.'

'But now it's their turn. We've made contact with Chombo. Hit gold, I think. There's no doubt Chombo knew about Ruari.'

She stopped, swivelled towards him, gasped in anticipation, her breath crystallizing in the cold air.

'We've made a little suggestion to him. If Ruari is released, Chombo's problems with the diaries disappear.'

'Released? But when? How soon?'

'We've told him three days.'

She began panting. 'Three days! Can it be? Can it really be?'

'It's possible. Everyone might get what they want out of this.'

A snowflake slid down her nose as she stared at him. 'Except for you, Harry.'

Damn, she could read him so well. She looked up into his eyes, saw pain, understood why. He had always been focused, almost driven, forever pushing on. It was Harry's way. Yet now it was as though his feet were slipping in the snow, and all because of Terri. Her husband had been right, there was something between them still, would always be, but what was he supposed to do about it? Ruari had brought them together once more, but if he was released, this might even be their last time. And there was still unfinished business.

'Why, Terri? Tell me. Why Paris? Did I order the wrong wine or something?'

'It still matters?'

'Of course.' His tone had hardened, like scar tissue.

Her lips trembled in hesitation, trying to find the right words, but they were elusive. She began walking again, head down as her mind cast back all those years, yet now her arm was linked through his, touching once more.

'You were already married, Harry,' she said finally. 'I heard you got back together with Julia. I was happy for you.' A pause. 'I cried for a month when I heard she had died.'

'You didn't know her.'

'I cried for *you*, Harry. I was going to get in touch, but . . .'

'But?'

'I didn't think it would help you.'

They walked on, counting snowflakes, lost in their maybes. It was a while before he spoke again.

'And if I hadn't been married?'

She stopped yet again beneath the leafless branches of a plane tree, where the pale light of a pavement lamp allowed them to see into each other's faces. 'You were married, Harry.'

'But *if* . . .'

She sighed. 'It would still have been the same, Harry.'

'Why?' He couldn't help it, but anger crept into his voice.

'Because . . . !' She almost shouted, protesting at his dumb persistence in making her relive it all, but she pulled herself back. She owed him. 'Because, Harry, I could never have kept up with you. You were a knight in shining armour, always charging off in search of dragons. That's not what I wanted, what I *needed*. Anyway, I always knew that Julia would reclaim you and even if she didn't, you'd be away doing all those things you do.'

'I would have changed.'

'But I didn't want you to change, don't you see that? You're Harry Jones, one of the most special men in all the world. That's why I fell for you.' A sob. 'And why I could never live with you.'

'I could have done anything for you.'

'If you had ever been tempted away from Julia you would have drowned yourself in guilt, and I would never have been able to forgive myself for that.'

'So you went off with J.J.'

'Yes, J.J.' The way she pronounced his name, it seemed to have come as something of a surprise. 'He was never going to be the greatest passion of my life but in his own tightly buttoned way he's solid, he's sincere, kind and dependable – so far as any man can be. And a wonderful father. Don't try to make me regret what I did, Harry.'

'Why? Do you?'

'You bastard!' she sobbed, the snowflakes melting into tears on her face as her fists beat against his chest in protest at being taken to places she didn't want to go.

Then she was in his arms, and their lips met. They were two people wrapped in a cocoon of snow, cut off from their other world, turning back the clock on their lives. Her breath, her skin, the smell of her hair, the sweetness of her tongue, the pressure of her body that he could feel even through the thickness of their clothes. Yet beyond the silence and the snow there was, still, that other world out there, one that was solid and real, filled with obligation, and it wouldn't disappear. Suddenly Harry felt her beginning to shake, and when she opened her eyes once more they were pouring with misery. With a stifled gasp of despair she pushed herself away. Their eyes tangled, but only for a moment, and once again she was running away from him, leaving a trail of footprints behind her, until she was lost in the whiteness and the darkness of the night.

—ᴡ—

Inspector D'Amato stroked the file that was open in front of him, as if hoping that by touch alone he could bring it bursting into life. As it was, the report made pitifully thin gruel, no more than a single page with a photo clipped to its corner. Not much to show for the life of a sixteen-year-old boy and the misery his parents must be going through. He thought about his own son, Vincenzo, who was now eight. He imagined his boy skipping across the cobbles as he emerged from school, with that huge smile of expectation on his face and his satchel covered in football stickers swinging from his shoulder, running innocent and unsuspecting into the arms of a stranger. As a father such thoughts tormented him, yet as a policeman he had to try to take a more detached view.

The Italians knew well about such crimes because not so long ago their country had been the kidnap centre of the world. Even one of their prime ministers, Aldo Moro, had been taken, and countless others were reported to the police – more than a case every week, with many others that never came to official notice. It had been a national disease, until the authorities had got wise to its ways, and the criminals had discovered it was easier to make their millions from drugs and online fraud. A kidnap might drag on for many months and involve considerable personal hardship, while fortunes nowadays could be made with little more than the touch of an Internet button. No contest. So kidnapping had died down, but it hadn't disappeared. And along with the bad memories, it had left men like D'Amato with a wealth of experience. The Italian police had won many more cases than they had lost, but that didn't mean that all the victims survived. Things sometimes went wrong, someone panicked or lost patience, the families played the game badly, or the kidnappers not at all. They had found the body of Prime Minister Moro dumped in the boot of a car, with eleven bullets in his chest. Yes, sometimes these things went terrifyingly wrong. A family might pay out millions and be left with nothing but a lifetime of pain.

His fingers traced across the page once again, like a blind man reading Braille, searching for clues, but he found none. It was typed as thinly as a politician's promise. It was no more than supposition that the boy was even in Italy, mere guesswork that he might be holed up somewhere on the Carso. This wasn't evidence, it was a wish list. As a policeman he found so little promise in it, yet as a father he was determined not to ignore it, just in case. The Carso was desperately difficult territory for his men, its inhabitants mostly Slovenes, insular and suspicious, and the police presence stretched thin on the ground, yet the people of the Carso weren't uncivilized, they wouldn't welcome foreigners arriving to dump trouble on their doorsteps, so it would be worth pushing his men around the place, looking for any fresh trails of dust.

He closed the file and cast it carelessly onto the top of a pile of paperwork that was already threatening to overwhelm a substantial part of his desk, but he had no worries that the file would be lost. Simona would take care of that, just as she took care of everything else around this place. Her talents stretched so much farther than simply getting laid on his desk but it was, he had to admit, in a manner that was more than a little smug, perhaps an added reason for her to keep the desktop from being overwhelmed with paper. The inspector smiled. He was indeed a fortunate man.

—◊—

Three days, less a few hours already. The clock was ticking. Chombo had been taken by surprise and overwhelmed by the assault Ebinger had unleashed on him. He knew he'd been butchered, made to bleed, yet he was an adaptable man. By the time he could see the lights of Harare beneath the undercarriage he'd recovered his wits and almost persuaded himself that he was returning in triumph. After all, he'd got what he wanted, hadn't he?

It was gone midnight when he arrived back at the presidential palace, but he insisted that Takere be summoned to join him, although he knew the security man was almost certainly already in his bed. Even so, when he appeared he was immaculately dressed in uniform; Chombo suddenly realized that he had never seen Takere out of it. He was always on duty, even when he slept, it seemed.

They stepped out into the private garden attached to the residence, behind high walls topped with razor wire, which ensured they were on their own. The night was humid, heavy, filled with the sickly-sweet fragrance of frangipani and ylang-ylang, while the ice in Chombo's bourbon chinked lazily against the glass. It wasn't his first, but he offered Takere neither apology nor drink.

'How is the boy?' Chombo demanded.

'I believe he is well,' Takere replied cautiously.

'You *believe*?'

Takere couldn't mistake the sarcasm in the emphasis and was immediately on his guard. 'I have not spoken to them for a couple of days. If it is important, I will check.'

'Make sure he is well. We are going to release him.'

'But . . .'

'Make the arrangements.'

'I do not understand.'

'It is not important that you understand. What is important is that you do as I instruct.' It was heavy-handed and Chombo knew it, but he had had a difficult day and someone had to suffer. Takere had to learn his place.

'If that is what you want,' the security man said softly.

'I, Chombo, have taken care of matters that you, Takere, said would take months!' He was being boastful, his ill humour swept along on an excess of bourbon. 'You told me there was no other way.'

'Then I congratulate you, Mr President.'

'You will see to it, Takere,' Chombo instructed. He perched his large frame on the surround of an ornamental pond; Takere was not invited to join him, and was forced to stand disconsolately like a whipped schoolboy.

'And you will be sure to reclaim a good proportion of the money we have invested,' Chombo continued.

Takere shifted uneasily, stubbing at the ground with his toe. 'I'm not sure that will be possible.'

'And why not? We paid for an operation you said would last months. It has lasted only days.'

'You will remember that you agreed to their demands for their fee to be paid up front. I do not believe they are the type of people who will dig into their pockets to give us anything back.'

'Then you must persuade them.'

'How?'

'That is your concern, not mine.'

'I can ask. But I cannot promise.'

Chombo swilled the ice around his glass. 'Tell me, Takere, what was your cut from these people?'

'My . . . cut?' The other man struggled to get his tongue around the word.

'Yes, your cut. Your commission, your consultant's fee, however it is described in the small print of the papers which have been signed.'

Takere hesitated only a fraction. 'There were no papers. There is no small print. As you will remember, you never met those people. That is what we agreed. In any event, I am a security man, not a secretary. My only concern is your safety, Mr President.'

'If you dodge bullets as well as you duck my questions, Takere, you will live a long life.'

'It is your life that is my concern, Mr President.'

'I trust you will remember that. So make the arrangements. About the boy.' He finished the last of the bourbon with one final swallow. 'And get me back my money.'

—⁂—

There was never a chance that de Vries would agree to hand back any of the money. He even demanded payment of an additional ten per cent completion fee, but that was never going to happen. Nevertheless, he found the argument for a radically reduced fee intriguing, full of unexplored potential, so much so that he decided to try it out on his own group of Romanians.

'So you get half,' he told them, kicking a log on the fire and raising a storm of sparks. 'Not bad for a couple of weeks' work. Best payday most of you have ever had.'

That was accurate, but not persuasive. 'Is not what we agreed,' Cosmin, the spokesman, said.

'I know, I know. It's tough on us all. I promise, I have done my best, argued our case, but you know what those black bastards are like. They'd screw your mother then demand payment for her pleasure.'

'Is not what we agreed,' Cosmin repeated. There was a dull, dogged tone to his words that began to test de Vries's patience.

'How do you think I feel?' he snapped, poking a finger into his own chest. 'I lose more than anyone.'

It was a lie, and a grotesque one. When he had got them to take their half, he and Grobelaar would pocket the rest. It threatened to be the biggest handout they'd ever enjoyed. But Cosmin, stubborn mule, was still shaking his head. 'No, not what we agreed. We don't accept.'

'Really? You don't accept? A pity,' the South African replied. 'Because you don't have any bloody choice.'

CHAPTER SEVENTEEN

D'Amato often likened his job to his occasional hobby of fishing. A combination of experience and patience, and sometimes grabbing a little luck when it passed by, and good fortune arrived in the form of a burglary, in the hamlet of Rupinpiccolo up on the Carso. Crimes weren't always reported there, the Slovenes did things their own way, had no time for authority, preferred to sort out their own problems without calling in the police. After all, who knew what the hell the wretched carabinieri might uncover once they started poking into barns and kicking over hayricks? But the elderly woman lived on her own, the thieves had taken all her family heirlooms and cash, and what enabled the investigation to float to the top of the slurry pond was the old woman's claim that foreigners were to blame. There wasn't a shred of evidence for this, her views were built on nothing but prejudice and her abject failure to realize what a thieving toe-rag her grand-son had become, but a couple of foreigners had been reported in the neighbourhood and on the Carso such people stood out. She didn't know what type of foreigner, or precisely where they might be found, but that was the job of the police to sort out and not let an old woman suffer.

It was enough for D'Amato to put a couple of his hounds onto the job. He didn't associate the report of the burglary with that of the kidnap of the English boy, not at first, but when the hounds returned with the information that foreigners had bought substantial quantities of supplies at a small local supermarket, not just once but several times in recent weeks, and that they were English or spoke English, at least, and drove a rented car, the questions began to mount in D'Amato's mind. And soon there were enough of them for him to instruct his hounds to return to the Carso and do a little more digging.

— ᴨᴨ —

Ruari's stomach told him something was up. That was how he told time, through his stomach, and he knew they'd missed a meal. It wasn't just late, it had entirely passed by. Not as punishment, he concluded, because then they would have made a point of making him suffer, but for some reason their routine had gone. No one came.

He tried to distract the lingering pain from his finger and his rising sense of unease by turning the dusty cobweb dangling above his head into a street map. His home in Notting Hill was at the centre and his mind followed different strands of the silk, trying to remember where they led. Second right, fourth on the left, and after a while it had to be Earl's Court, or was it Tyburn? Start all over again. It was mindless, but necessary, better than sitting in the semi-darkness hurting and worrying about his stomach, or the men upstairs.

He was wandering down the King's Road towards his favourite pizza restaurant when he heard voices. That was unusual. Occasionally he would hear muffled sounds from upstairs, a scraped chair, a dropped bowl, the slam of a door, but the cellar was deep and the stone floor thick and he had only heard voices once before, at the time of the fight. So he abandoned his walk and concentrated, trying to pick up what was being said. He couldn't make out the words, but there was no mistaking their anger. The voices were rising, growing increasingly strident. What could they be arguing about? It could only be one thing, he decided. Him.

As the aggression mounted, Ruari grew afraid. His finger, or lost finger, the little one on his right hand, had been agony at first, but gradually it had gone numb and did little more than complain, but now it began to throb and burn again, picking up on his anxiety.

He heard a chair topple – no, it was something more than that. It sounded like a chair being smashed to pieces, to matchwood. Then shouts. Noises of fury. More chairs being tipped or smashed. Confusion. A fight. And finally, a terrible cry.

The silence that followed the onslaught screamed inside Ruari's imagination. He had heard no guns, this was no rescue bid, just his captors losing their tempers, and Ruari was in their line of fire. In the quiet of the cellar he listened to his own heartbeat.

The door to the cellar seemed to explode as it was kicked in, with such violence it was left lurching at a sickening angle on a solitary hinge. A curse rang out in Romanian. Then Cosmin was clattering down the unsteady wooden steps. He was sweating, had a wild look in his eye, and a torn lip. And in his hand he carried his knife once again. It was already dripping blood.

—⁓—

The Toucan had made its preparations for Christmas. Two strings of tinsel dangled from the beaten-up brass clock, another was draped across the front of the beer pumps. The cheap plaster bust that sat on a shelf behind the counter between the whiskies had been dressed in a red Santa Claus hat. Harry hadn't noticed the bust before and was taken by surprise as he walked in; it had a prominent nose, sparse hair and appeared to be Prince Philip.

The man in the overcoat who had been eating oysters during Harry's last visit was still there, except this time with a different woman. Their hands and eyes suggested they weren't strangers, and that Christmas was likely to come early for him. Sean was there, too, at the same table. As Harry sat down, the Irishman pushed a fresh pint of Guinness towards him. That was all Harry got as a greeting.

'This is getting to be dangerously like a habit, Sean.'

'You've no need to be worrying yourself on that account, Mr Jones.'

'Not a social invitation, then.'

And already the ingrained animosity was pushing them apart. Breslin was already most of the way through his beer and Harry sensed it wasn't his first.

'We had another message,' Breslin announced. 'Ruari's to be released.'

'Then let's pray they mean it.'

'I'm not much of a one for prayer myself, but I'll not argue with you on that.' He paused, as if he had something difficult to say, and his eyes, always so cautious, settled on Harry. 'I understand you might have had something to do with that, with arranging for his release. I don't know the details, and that pathetic excuse for a policeman Archer is already claiming full credit, but he's just full of gab, the sort that always nibbles at someone else's cheese. That man is about as much feckin' use as a hole in your underwear.'

Harry suspected Sean held a similar opinion about most British policemen.

'Anyhow, I wanted to say thank you,' the Irishman continued. 'On behalf of the family.'

'I appreciate it. I know it's not the easiest thing for you to say.'

'No, it's not, but we Breslins pay our debts.' A final couple of inches of the dark liquor slid down his throat and he nodded to the barman for another, trying to drown his discomfort.

That was when Harry realized. No one else in the family wanted to see him. Not J.J., and after the other night in Hyde Park, not Terri either. Sean had drawn the short straw. 'I think I understand,' Harry muttered.

Sean waited to take the top off his fresh drink before he replied. It was as though he was considering his words, content to keep Harry waiting. 'I'm the head of the family. Ruari's my grandson. My thanks are sincere.'

'And J.J.?'

'He's grateful, too. Would have been here himself, but he sort of has an issue with you and his wife.'

'There is no issue.'

'He seems to think so. And he's a proud man.'

'He's wrong.'

'Now you'll not be asking me to take your word for that, Mr Jones.'

It wasn't a thing Harry much wanted to swear to on a stack of Bibles, either. He'd sweated through an entire set of sheets after his encounter with Terri; she had a rare talent for making a mess of his bed. He decided to change the subject. 'Of course. Jackie Charlton.'

'What are you on about now?'

'It's Jackie Charlton,' Harry repeated, nodding at the plaster bust and at last recognizing the angular features as those of the former Irish national football coach. 'For one lurid moment I thought it was Prince Philip.'

'An English prince? Bury me alive first, but not in here!'

'He's Greek, actually. And the Windsors are German.'

'Then get rid of them, why not? We did.'

The man seemed hard-wired to hate the English, it was as though he couldn't help himself. He'd been suckled on it at his mother's breast, been taught it at school, heard it preached from any number of pulpits, had it sprinkled along with the holy water and sung about in every pub. God and Irish nationalism marched hand in hand, and the English were the Antichrist. That belief was as much part of him as was his name.

'This wasn't your first kidnapping, was it, Sean?' The question sounded entirely rhetorical. 'You were a Provo fundraiser. I seem to remember that kidnapping came in handy for a while when you and your friends were a little short.'

'Somehow I suspect that even you, Major Jones' – he used Harry's old army rank, readily available on Wikipedia – 'weren't entirely an innocent in such matters.'

'We didn't take hostages, we tried to release them.'

'And sure as Christ was crucified you took 'em,' Sean replied, the softness of his voice no disguise for the passion behind his words. 'You just changed the language, didn't call them hostages but political prisoners, imprisoned them without charges and without trial, and even if they did make it to court it was in a secret hearing with a bent British judge.'

'Don't preach to me, Sean. I saw what your friends did.'

253

'By God, you bastards have short memories.'

'What's done is done, Sean.'

'And I'll remember what was done till the day I burn in Hell.'

Sean's face was flushed, the old eyes bright with anger. Then they sank to his drink, which he finished with one throat-stirring draught.

'Tell me, Sean, what got you started?'

His eyes came up again, angry, piercing. 'You really want to know?'

'I do.'

A long hesitation. Then Breslin slowly raised his hand again to summon the barman. 'Two Bushmills, the sixteen-year-old, mind. Make them large. No ice.' Sean gave his instruction without taking his eyes off Harry. 'So, Mr Jones, you're wanting to know what got me started,' he whispered, so softly that Harry was obliged to lean forward to catch the words. 'I'm surprised you of all people should have to ask me that. You see, I was no different from the rest. The winter of '72 it was, and a bloody awful winter, too. I'd spent the afternoon playing football in the park with J.J., he'd have been, what, about five? It was snowing, we ended up building a snowman instead, but the lad never did take much to sport. We got back home, and we turned the radio on, and we heard. Bloody Sunday. Your troops had killed thirteen unarmed civilians in Derry. Half of them teenagers, many of them shot in the back, and the Union Jack a butcher's apron once more. In half an hour your devils turned the clock back three hundred feckin' years.'

Harry was about to challenge him, remind him of Omagh, of Bloody Friday, of Enniskillen on Remembrance Day, of the La Mon fire-bomb massacre and a dozen other examples of the slaughter of innocents that were down to the IRA, but he decided this wasn't the moment. He wanted to listen, not to score points in a game that had no end.

'There were no more bystanders after that.' The tumblers of whiskey arrived; Sean took a sip. 'One of those boys you shot. He was my nephew. Sixteen, that's how old he was, still waiting to pass his exams and lose his cherry. Crawling away on the ground, trying to get to safety. The Paras said he was carrying a weapon; the priest who was beside him all the time and gave him the last rites says that was a lie. All the family got left with was a foggy black-and-white photo of a young kid, bleeding his brains out in a gutter.' Very slowly, he ran his tongue across lips that had dried out with anger. 'You were a paratrooper. Weren't you, Major Jones?'

'You know I was,' Harry responded. Not then, not in Derry, not at that time, but the details didn't matter.

'It was after that I began helping. I was an accountant, a reasonably bright one. Lots of people were at it in those days, raising money for the cause. And very inventive, so we were. Some of the local pubs started running a little lottery, and there were a few insurance claims that needed –

how can I put this to a law-abiding man such as yourself? –
a bit of *massaging*. Then some of the local bookies who were
operating beneath the radar volunteered to pay a little
gentle tax, and if they didn't volunteer they paid it anyway.
Everyone was raising money in their own way – yes, and at
times that might have involved a few unintended holidays
for a banker or a wealthy foreign businessman.'

'Kidnapping's not a sodding vacation, Sean.'

'Everyone had his own means, and it all needed
accounting for. So that's what I did. I was the gatekeeper. I
handled the books.'

'You laundered their dirty money for them.'

'It was better than shooting kids in the back.'

The bar had begun to grow more crowded, but neither of
them noticed. They had gone back to another world,
another time.

'I don't suppose we'll be needing another drink, you
and I,' Sean said, finishing off his whiskey without taking
his eyes from Harry. 'Blood. Family. At the end of the day,
that's what counts, Major Jones, isn't it?'

'I wouldn't know.'

'Then may God forgive me for saying so, but for the first
time in my life, I pity you. Truly I do.'

—⚊—

Sex had its amusing side, Simona decided. She was in the
modest hotel room booked by D'Amato where moments
ago he had finished throwing himself at her, and on her.

He wouldn't use his own apartment, where his wife cast too many shadows, but he had begged Simona to spend the night with him rather than confine themselves to a few trembling moments behind a filing cabinet, so they had decided on the neutral ground of the hotel – an insipid establishment, near the railway station, but it had the benefit of being determinedly anonymous, a place where the inspector was unlikely to run into any of his colleagues. He had no desire to become an object of gossip. He had brought a bottle of Prosecco along with his overnight things, and they'd used tooth mugs, but she'd barely taken a sip before he was on her, in a state of considerable excitement. It wasn't just her naked and youthful body; he'd arrived clicking his fingers, always with the inspector a sign of agitation, and he'd even clicked as he came. Now he lay back on the rumpled duvet, panting, spent, taking sips of Prosecco while his other hand remained clamped to her breast, and sharing the reasons for his turbulent mood.

The case on the Carso. It had come alive, and D'Amato with it. The two Englishmen, or English-speakers, D'Amato explained, had been regularly buying provisions at a local store, but far too much for their own consumption, enough for eight, at least. No one seemed to know why they were on the Carso, or why they had rented the remote farmhouse to which their car had been followed, although it was known that they had paid in advance for three months and in cash. It seemed clear they wanted to

257

stay for some time, yet leave no trace. What was more, D'Amato insisted excitedly as he repeatedly stroked Simona's breast, they had first appeared at the farmhouse less than two weeks before the English boy had disappeared, and there were reports that activity on the road that passed nearest to the farmhouse had been unusually busy on the day of the kidnap itself. 'You see. It all fits!' he exclaimed.

He rolled over to wrap her in his arms. In the light from the bedside lamp she could see the early signs of grey in his hair, and in the mirror the remarkable paleness of his bottom, yet for a man in middle age he seemed to retain plenty of enthusiasm and she could feel that enthusiasm once more brushing against her thigh. This case was clearly getting to him.

'It's not conclusive, I know,' he continued, 'so yesterday I sent one of my undercover officers in an egg-delivery van. Incompetent bastard, he broke most of them. He drove up pretending to be lost, needing directions. He said nothing was right about the place, no work being done, no noise being made, just a guy who answered the door and who made it clear he didn't want a stranger on his doorstep. He wasn't one of the Englishmen, either, some other type of foreigner, broken Italian, a fuck-off scowl on his face. There were other men in the house, the driver was sure of that, but they were keeping their heads down. Then this morning' – so intense was his excitement that he had rolled on top of her once more – 'the two Englishmen with

258

another man in tow drove a few miles down the road and parked outside the research institute in Padriciano. The new man appeared to have a laptop with him, we think he was sending messages from the back seat, piggybacking on the institute's wi-fi service.'

'They can do that?'

'Oh, yes. Oh, yes,' he sighed, as though it hurt.

For a moment she thought he had become distracted because he was inside her once more, shuffling away, and he was gasping, the pitch of his voice rising with every breath, yet his mind was still elsewhere.

'It can be done, my love. Easily. Happens all over the place. Outside schools, libraries, hospitals. Even private homes. All you need is the password and – they're so simple. A five-year-old can guess them. Or you get – software – to do it – for you!'

She stifled a giggle as his forehead creased in concentration.

'The kidnappers. They're using the Internet. To contact the family. You know what I think? I'll bet they're driving round the Carso. Using different wi-fi hot spots. For every message. Makes it almost impossible . . . to – to-to-to – trace!'

He gave a squeak followed by a deep groan, and she could restrain herself no longer, bursting into a fit of laughter that she managed to disguise as a gasp of passion, which happened to coincide precisely with his own climax. Soon he was lying back, the pillows crushed beside his

259

head, staring at the ceiling. He exhaled, long and forlornly, like a deflating air bed.

'Simona, can you imagine what it would be like for my career, me smashing an international kidnapping ring?'

Trieste was, in the eyes of some, a nowhere place where little of significance happened any more. It wasn't an entirely accurate conclusion, for its location on the edge of the Balkans meant that it was used for trafficking of all sorts – drugs, weapons, women – but for the most part such matters passed quickly through and onwards to other jurisdictions. They hadn't had a car stolen in the last month, or a good international bust in years.

'So what are you going to do about it?' Simona whispered.

'Raid the place. Early in the morning. I'm sorry, little one, but I have to leave you in a few hours . . .'

And still the man was insatiable, she had to give him that. It took more Prosecco and yet more sex before his eyes began to flicker and he was teetering on the edge of sleep. She rolled away from him and stole quietly from the bed, picking up her handbag.

'Where are you going?' he asked drowsily, his hand reaching out after her.

'Just to the bathroom. To take care of things.'

He offered up a weak smile, weary yet triumphant, and closed his eyes once again.

Once in the bathroom, Simona reached for her phone, searching for the number of her cousin, Nelu. Simona lodged with his mother, her aunt, and although Nelu had moved to his own place she'd got to know him well, and liked him, despite the fact that he swam in pretty murky waters. Her aunt called the two of them *'Negru si Alb'*, Black and White, as they chatted around her table, and Nelu had chased her around the table, too, when her aunt was away, but she had never let him catch her. And a couple of weeks ago Nelu had gone away, on business so her aunt had declared, with some of those shadowy friends of his, doing whatever they did, but she couldn't say what or where. As D'Amato had talked up the value of coincidence, so Simona had begun to grow concerned, for the dates of the kidnapping seemed to coincide all too neatly with the time Nelu had disappeared. Without wanting to she realized she had become involved, and that meant she had a decision to make, but it wasn't much of one, not for her. *'Familie unita.'* Family sticks together, as they say in Romania.

It wasn't just Nelu at risk. If he was involved with the kidnap and it all went wrong, she was in danger, too, of being thrown out of her job which was her pathway out of poverty, perhaps the only chance she would get. That wasn't going to happen. She began texting.

'Daca cu Englezashu, fugi. Razia politiei dimineata.'

'If you are with missing English boy, get out now. Police raid dawn.'

—∿—

Three days, that was all. But what did that mean? Was it like the three days of Easter, from Friday until Sunday, or did it imply three clear days in between? Harry had been the one to come up with that limit, it was the minimum he thought Chombo needed to tear his plans to pieces so that Ruari could be released and the matter resolved safely – and safely not just for himself but also for the kidnappers. That had to be. There was no chance of them delivering up the boy unless their own safety was guaranteed. Ruari's life depended on that; it wasn't justice, merely survival, but that's what mattered most. The kidnappers had to be allowed to go. So three days it was, give or take a few hours, although no one could say how many, not precisely.

As the hours seeped away, one by one, life in the Breslin household began to alter its pace. Minutes began to matter, change shape, grow longer, become endless as they waited to hear whether their son was alive or was dead. Terri stayed at home, J.J. began to cancel his meetings, they ate through the contents of the freezer and waited up together, surrounded by silence.

That evening, as close to the passing of seventy-two hours as Terri could reckon, she lit one of the Christmas candles she had prepared for Ruari's return and placed it in the window overlooking their street. J.J. watched her, understanding, but saying nothing, suffering in his own way, unable to find words that any longer had meaning. In the darkness that covered the rest of the room, Terri fashioned a nest for herself in an armchair with a duvet and pillow, her legs tucked beneath her and the telephone by her side. She watched the glow of the candle, with every flicker of its flame, and waited for her child to come home.

—∿—

D'Amato knew nothing of three days. He hadn't been told of any deal. A message would reach him eventually, through the labyrinthine processes of international police procedure, but it hadn't yet. Even if it had, he would still have wanted to nail the kidnapping bastards, not turn a blind eye and let them wander free. There was no way he would have deliberately risked Ruari's life but his motives would have been decidedly and perhaps dangerously confused. This was a crime, a sin, a stain upon the honour of Italy and D'Amato's police record, one that required those who were responsible to have their balls burned upon the pyre of justice, otherwise there was neither glory nor advancement for him.

It was four in the morning when he stole from the bed, not yet five when he joined the officers of the Squadra Mobile unit who had gathered on the Carso. It was still as dark as pitch. The surveillance unit that had been keeping watch overnight had spotted a guard, one of the gang who was supposed to be alert, but indolence and complacency had taken a firm grip after two weeks and even the solitary guard had disappeared, presumably to doze by the fire. There was no sign of any other movement. The rest were asleep. Perfect. Take the bastards by surprise.

Only three doors, one front and back, and a side door leading to the outside toilet. On D'Amato's signal, and with all windows covered, the twenty-man assault team would begin by blasting open the doors and hurling thunderflashes in front of them, screaming as they charged up the stairs, fanning quickly into every room, creating maximum commotion, and so quickly that those in bed would be taken by surprise, caught fumbling with their trousers, weapons lost in the dark, overwhelmed before anyone had the chance to react and escape, let alone kill their hostage. All over in seconds.

Yet as the doors to the upstairs rooms were kicked open one after the other, like the rattle of a machine gun, confusion took hold. There were fresh shouts. D'Amato was called. He bounded up the stairs, Beretta in hand, explored every room, opened every cupboard and hatch, kicked over every bed, but it changed nothing.

The farmhouse was empty.

There were many signs of a hasty evacuation. Clothes, books, toiletries, personal effects, were left discarded. Food had been left on a plate, a meal unfinished, with not even enough time for it to congeal.

Only when they got to the cellar at the back did they find their first significant clue. There they discovered not one but two bodies, their faces badly beaten and terrible wounds slashed across their throats.

They were the corpses of de Vries and Grobelaar.

—∽—

His logic, de Vries had thought, was compelling, and with it he could cheat the Romanians on a handsome scale. Cosmin and the others had already been paid fifty per cent of their fee, and while the original agreement with de Vries had been that the other half, less their 'fine' of ten thousand dollars, would be paid on completion, he explained that there was now no chance of extracting any further money from their paymasters. And while de Vries said he was as mortified as any of them by this, he also offered them what he held out as good news. The job was over much sooner than anyone had expected, and they could walk away from it with one pocket full, at least, and without the police forces of several nations breathing down their necks. Home by Christmas. Not bad for a few weeks' work that always held the potential for ending in disaster.

Yet the logic was only compelling if the facts were true, and Cosmin didn't trust de Vries. Why should he accept half his fee, he said, when his nose had been fully broken? So the two of them had squared up to each other, in front of the fire, and had resumed their fight, except this time Cosmin had won. De Vries had been badly beaten, with much smashing of furniture, and after that Grobelaar went down with almost the first punch.

Cosmin had brought his own logic to the affair, which he explained as de Vries and Grobelaar lay bloodied and help- less at his feet. They had the boy and he was still a valuable commodity, worth a mountain of money to them, and far more than de Vries had ever offered. So Chombo could go shag his own grandmother, this kidnap wasn't over, not at all. It had only just begun to get interesting.

And still Cosmin wasn't finished, he pursued his argument like a hound hunts down a fleeing fox. With his boot pressing firmly down upon de Vries's skull, he argued that whatever ransom they might manage to extract from the boy's family, it would go even further if there were two less to share it. The arithmetic was very simple, the logic inexorable, the brutality swift and absolute. De Vries and Grobelaar never had a chance.

CHAPTER EIGHTEEN

It didn't take long for D'Amato to drag himself back from the depths of his disappointment. By the time he had finished his third cigarette he had summoned up two search helicopters, placed the railway station, docks and airport on alert, and ordered roadblocks on all major roads leaving the Carso. However, he wasn't optimistic. It would take more than an hour to drag additional police officers up from Trieste, which stretched the kidnappers' head start. He also had to face another considerable problem. It was all very well blocking the major routes, but there were miles of minor roads and hundreds of tracks that snaked through the Carso like the stretch marks on his wife's belly. For officials such as tax collectors and policemen, it was like stepping into a maze of confusion. He was not optimistic, but he had to go through the motions to cover his official arse, and with that in mind he had already given the surveillance team the most ferocious bollocking of their lives. It was clear they had been incompetent and somehow alerted the gang, and if D'Amato could have his way they'd be dropped down one of the local sinkholes with rocks in their pockets; as it was, they'd be doing night shift stuck on guard outside the police barracks for a month. Somebody had to take the blame, but no matter how much he tried to offload it, he knew that most of it would fall on his shoulders. He'd already talked to the Border Police and would have to do the same with all the neighbouring police authorities and even the Central Operation Service and Central Directorate of Criminal Police in Rome, alert the lot of them, every sniggering bastard amongst them. Admit the failure. *His* failure. The walk from his office to the spot on the carpet in front of the commissioner's desk back in the Questura would seem like a trek to the North Pole.

D'Amato's frustration was extreme. It wasn't just the professional disappointment and the sense of a lost career opportunity, both of which were intense, but also his feelings as a father for the boy they hadn't saved. He wanted to make amends, but knew he was unlikely to get another opportunity. If he were in the gang's shoes he'd have fled well away from the area, probably to the border with Slovenia, only three miles away. They were probably across it already, into the badlands. What they wouldn't do was stay on the Carso, where even now every farmer, bar-owner, cheese-maker, pig-herder, carpenter and quarry man was being turned over by his officers, and in the process almost certainly being turned against them, too. D'Amato knew he and his men had already outstayed their welcome in these parts.

Oh, Mother of God, it would all take a mountain of paperwork to cover over the holes in this operation. That's what police work had become nowadays – the distribution of blame. And paperwork. As he tossed away the stub of yet another cigarette, once again he offered up a prayer of thanks that at least he had Simona to handle all that for him.

—⚬—

Mary Mishcon had been chasing Harry yet again, no longer bothering to hide the frustration that was taking hold inside Downing Street. What's your problem, Harry? For pity's sake, yes or no? As it all ran through his mind he'd spent the night sleepless, thumping pillows. He knew he was ideally suited for the job of Foreign Secretary, thought he might be able to make a real difference in it, and most people would give various valuable parts of their anatomy for the chance. *So what is your problem, Jones?*

There was also a compelling new factor. Getting stuck into a new challenge would give him every excuse he needed not to think about Terri. He was thinking a lot about her once again, but in a different light. All those years ago they had always met on their own, in a closeted world of unreality they had created for themselves during stolen days in Venice, Amsterdam, Edinburgh, even St Ives one blustery, sheet-winding weekend. And, of course, there was Paris. Yet all that was gone. He could no longer even think of her without seeing her with J.J., taking centre stage

269

in a world of entanglements that had nothing to do with him and never would.

With that understanding came acceptance. At last his anger with her began to subside, he started to let go of that stubborn dream, although it left him profoundly depressed. It had been pointless, all those wasted years when he should have moved on, and thought he had moved on, until she turned up in Downing Street. But it wasn't too late.

Yes, the time had come to cut himself off from Terri once and for all. Seeing her again, having her once more in his arms, feeling the storm clouds welling up inside him, had shaken him profoundly, quite apart from his involvement with her son. Typical bloody Terri, she'd always dragged catastrophe into his life. But he'd done as much as he could for her, and for Ruari. It was time to move on.

He'd been hoping for a phone call to tell him that the boy was at last coming back home, but as he waited he wondered who would make that call? A reluctant and remorseful J.J.? Sean, perhaps? Terri? Oh, he hoped not, not her. No, it would probably be that smug bastard Archer, dismissing him like a hotel valet. Harry knew he would be the last to know, bottom of the list.

He stayed longer in the shower than usual, letting the high-pressure stream beat the new day into him. As he towelled himself down he looked at the bedside phone, willing it to ring. *Come on, Jones, time to stop hanging around waiting for others, time to get on with the rest of your life!*

Christ, he needed the distraction. Her Majesty's Secretary of State for Foreign and Commonwealth Affairs. It would take him half the day just to write out his job title. No more room for silly diversions. He made up his mind. He threw the towel into a corner and, sitting naked on his bed, he reached for the phone and dialled Downing Street.

—ɷ—

It was less than a week away from the longest night of the year. Daylight didn't take hold until around eight in the morning, and in Notting Hill it brought with it the reluctant figure of Archer, dragging behind him the news from Trieste. It required careful handling. Bad tidings. He'd been hoping there might be a bonus for him in all this, enough to pay for the flat he wanted to rent for his young Polish mistress, but that prospect had gone out of the window. There might even be worse to come. It had been a mistake to insist to his contacts at the Yard that all communications with the family be directed through him. They're fragile, in no fit state, he'd argued, but in reality it had been so that he could keep hold of the reins, be in control. Yet now the horses were threatening to charge off in entirely the wrong direction.

He found J.J. in the kitchen, washing up his breakfast bowl and mug with meticulous, almost obsessive care. They could perfectly well have gone in the dishwasher, even been left for the housekeeper, but Breslin needed something to pass the time, to disguise the trembling in his

271

hands, so he washed up. He turned sharply when he heard Archer arrive, leaving the tap running.

'They've sent news, J.J.'

'Ruari!' The mug slipped from his hands and cracked against the side of the sink, and suddenly Terri was out of her armchair and close by, gripping the doorframe for support.

Archer knew he was about to step out onto the thin ice of a total screw-up and he wasn't as light-footed as once he had been. Eating at the corporate lunch table could do that to a man. Yet that was where experience came in, and Archer knew the moves, all of them. It was the young guys who rushed ahead and found the ice collapsing beneath them.

'They almost got him this morning,' he said, summoning excitement into his voice. 'In the countryside near Trieste. Missed him by only minutes and now they're searching every farmhouse and outhouse and possible hiding place in the region.'

'They?' J.J. asked, a sudden croak in his voice.

'The Italian police.'

'But . . .' J.J. was shaking his head, trying to get a fix on what he had just heard.

'Road blocks. Spotter planes. Sniffer dogs. The lot.'

'We had a deal, they weren't meant to be there, Brian.' It was Terri, her voice low.

Archer heard the ice beginning to groan beneath his feet. 'Apparently the police stumbled across the hideout.

In the circumstances you can't expect them to turn a blind eye.'

'What I expected was my son,' Terri said.

'Someone messed up.'

'Someone?'

'The police.'

'But they weren't supposed to be involved.' J.J. seemed bewildered, floundering in disbelief.

Archer blanched. The two of them were at it together, which was unusual in this family, joining up to throw rocks at him from both sides and threatening to break through the ice. But what was it his old man had said? Never drown on your own, always do it with company. And right now his father seemed a wise bird.

'You'll remember . . . We decided,' Archer suggested.

'What I remember is that you insisted, Brian,' Terri said. Somehow she seemed stronger than J.J., had a firmer grip on her emotions, had taken charge.

'But we're getting closer. The Trieste police are certain Ruari's alive, the kidnappers are on the run. Who knows, they might even drop him at the side of the road.'

'Or down a hole,' J.J. whispered.

The ice was cracking, giving way. 'That's unfair, J.J.,' Archer replied. 'We all agreed we had no choice. What other option was there?'

'Chombo,' Terri reminded him.

'But we didn't know about him at the time.'

'*You* didn't.'

'The Trieste police didn't, either, that's why they raided the place. They had no choice, it's a major crime, they had to get involved. It's just . . . these things don't always run to plan.'

He was going down. He knew it, could see it in Terri's eyes, flickering with rage, while her husband seemed to have turned to stone, his face a mask, his thoughts in another place, with his son. Terri leaned across him to turn off the tap. When she turned back once more, she looked directly at Archer.

'Brian, I don't think I want you in my house any more.'

It was in the silence that followed that they heard the warble of the Skype connection calling from the dining room.

—∿—

No Hiley this time, they'd sent him to Rome to be ready for Ruari's release, and no Jan, either. The voice at the other end was rougher, the English broken.

'We have your boy. You want him back?'

'But of course!' J.J. shouted.

'How many fingers you want back?'

'Please, no!'

'Five million euro. You get him back for five million.'

'But we had a deal!'

'That deal is dead.'

'Where's Jan? I want to talk to Jan.'

A harsh, callous laugh. 'He dead, too. Very dead. Like the boy will be.'

'We can't possibly—' But Terri had grabbed her husband's arm, squeezed it tight, pleading caution. 'We have to think about this. It will take us time to raise any money.'

'Take all the time you want. Until Christmas. If no five million euro by Christmas Day, the boy end up like Jan.'

'But that's less than two weeks,' Terri cried.

'Get busy, bitch.'

—⁂—

Drinking. On your own again, Jones. He knew he was doing too much of both and neither had brought him happiness. Harry stared into the fire. This was Mayfair, a smokeless zone, so the fire consisted of nothing more than ribbons of designer gas flame, but it was better than staring at a blank wall and an empty glass. Anyway, wasn't he supposed to be celebrating? He'd told Mary he wanted to come to Downing Street to finalize the details on the new job and she'd put some time in the diary for early the following week, so now he sat in his den beneath the stark light of a reading lamp and raised a toast in glorious farewell to his old life as a backbench politician, a life in which he had no real responsibilities apart from his constituents and making an occasional speech that was noticed by almost no one except the record-takers of Hansard. Not much of a life. At least as Foreign Secretary he would be able to pretend.

His melancholy was interrupted by the telephone. It was

Sloppy. 'Evening, you inglorious bastard. Remember you asked me to keep you up to speed on any stories of wickedness and worries around the Breslin camp?'

'Ah, yes,' Harry sighed, trying to summon up enthusiasm from the dregs.

'Well, bingo, old buddy. Word is he's trying to sell. Everything. And in a hurry, poor sod.'

'Sorry, I don't understand . . .'

'Wake up at the back of the class, Jones! The newspaper's up to its rafters in debt and the whisper in the gutter is that the bum-bandits at his bank have recalled the loans, so he's trying to raise new money on everything he's got, including his house. Sounds desperate. Wolves waiting in the wings on this one, old chap.'

'Really?'

'Suggestion is he may even have to bail out of the newspaper. One minute he's telling everyone there's light at the end of the tunnel, next he's desperate to jump ship.'

'Ship in a tunnel, Sloppy?'

'You don't pay me for my command of syntax, old chap. But take it from me, Breslin's for the high jump. There's a smell of death around this one.'

'Thanks, Sloppy. I owe you. But I've got to go. I think someone's trying to kick down my front door . . .'

Sloppy was chuntering on about Harry's taste for desperate women when Harry cut him off. The banging was persistent, along with the ringing of the bell, and as he opened the door he found the last person in the world he wanted to see. Terri. She was standing on the doorstep, her face pale in the lamplight.

'I'd better come in,' she said quietly.

He moved aside to let her in, reluctant, and led her into his den. She shrugged off her coat, allowing it to fall aimlessly on the floor, and when she turned, he was startled how much she had aged. It was more than just the stark, atmospheric lighting; her features were drawn, sallow, the eyes exhausted.

'They still have Ruari,' she said softly.

'Dear God, I'm so sorry,' he said, cautious, defensive, not wanting to get too close to her. 'What happened?'

'A total bloody screw-up. The police, they raided the hideout – near Trieste. Yes, you were right about that, too. It was this morning, before the handover. Found two bodies. They think that one of them was the man we call Jan.'

'What?'

'They're guessing, but the Trieste police believe the kidnap has been taken over by the hired help. Changed the rules of the game. It's all just got worse.'

Harry was shaking his head in bewilderment.

'They want five million euros, Harry. Five million. By Christmas Day. Or they will kill Ruari.'

Harry winced inside. 'Kidnappers have to say those sort of things.'

'I think they mean it. They've already left bodies scattered across Switzerland and now Italy. What's one more? They mean it.'

He couldn't deny her logic. 'You seem . . . remarkably composed, in the circumstances.'

'I don't have a choice. If I wobble, lose control, even for a moment, I'll fall apart. But I'm not going to. Ruari needs help not hysterics.'

'So?'

'J.J.'s running through town trying to find the money. Selling investments. Raising loans.' She was about to say more, but changed her mind. There was no point. With the newspaper already drowning in debt, they'd already discovered that no one wanted to lend them more.

'I heard. Will you be OK with that?'

'It's tough. Sean has said he'll help.'

'It seems he was right. That old bugger never did trust the police.'

She took a step towards him. 'What can we do, Harry?'

'It's not for me to tell you and your husband—'

'No, Harry, *we*! You and me.'

'We?'

'You have to help me!' Her composure was beginning to slip. An urgency had crept into her voice and her body was beginning to shake. 'J.J.'s dying under the pressure, can't think, can barely function any more. The police have no clues, Archer is useless, we sent Hiley to Rome to wait for Ruari's release . . . That only leaves you and me, Harry.'

'Not me, Terri. I have no further part to play in this. Anyway, what can I do?'

'Something, Harry! Do something, for God's sake!'

Do something. The curse of the politician throughout the ages. Harry had never been one to make fatuous promises and he wasn't in the mood for it now, particularly with a woman he desperately wanted out of his life. It wasn't punishment, merely self-protection. Harry shook his head defiantly. 'I can't think of a thing that would make the slightest difference.'

'There must be. You're Harry Jones,' she whispered.

And still he shook his head.

'Even Sean's going to Trieste,' she said, her eyes brimming with accusation.

'What's the point? He's unlikely to stumble over him on a street corner.'

'At least he's trying!'

'He's family.'

She was shaking with emotion, and despite all her defiance suddenly very close to falling apart. She took another step towards him, hesitant, uncertain, within touching distance now. 'Harry, about the other night . . .'

'When you—' Immediately he regretted starting on the thought, couldn't finish it, couldn't be that cruel. But she knew where his mind had lodged.

'When I ran out on you yet again.'

He sipped his whisky rather than respond or look into her eyes, but then quickly cast the glass to one side. Getting drunk wasn't the answer. Her voice was steadier now.

'I ran because I was afraid, Harry. I ran because I care so much about you.'

'Seemed a strange way of showing it.'

'You have no idea what you mean to me, do you?' She was reaching for him, just as she had done in the park.

He took a sharp breath. He had no idea she would stoop this low. 'What I think, Terri, is that you would do anything, say anything, to help Ruari.'

'They're not just words . . .'

'I've done everything I can to help. Now leave me out of this. Please.'

She grabbed his arms. 'You can't be left out!'

'Oh, just watch me.' He tried to turn away, reach once more for his drink, but she held him too tight.

'You can't!' The words came as a wail of anguish, and her hands began flailing at his chest with such wretchedness that Harry was taken aback. Her pain seemed so much more than an act. She was sobbing profoundly, battling to take each breath, her face fallen forward and buried in his chest, the tears real and already soaking through his shirt.

'You can't leave Ruari,' she whimpered.

She raised her eyes to him, the tears flickering in the firelight like a necklace of diamonds.

'Harry, he's your son.'

CHAPTER NINETEEN

Harry had once been close, too close, to a mortar round. It was outside Baghdad, on that mission to snatch an Iraqi general shortly before that first Gulf War. He and his buddy had already been wounded, and then in the dark some outfit of the Republican Guard had started lobbing mortars, pretty lightweight stuff but they'd got lucky and one of the shells had blown Harry and his chum clean off their feet. There were plenty of fragments, too; Harry escaped serious injury but the shrapnel found his partner, and that's what eventually killed him. Harry could never forget the sensation that immediately followed the blast. He had no idea where he was, even who he was, the disorientation was total, his thoughts scrambled, his lungs bursting, until eventually he woke up to find himself crawling through the sand. And that was precisely how he felt now.

'It can't be.'

Harry had to struggle to produce each word, forcing it out, yet even as he tried to deny what Terri had told him he began to doubt himself. Suddenly he realized he had no idea how old Ruari was, early teens to judge by the family photographs, but that's all they were, photographs, already out of date even by the time they were put in their frames.

It had been seventeen years, and then a few months, since Paris. June. The sixth, to be exact. How deeply it had carved its way inside his memory.

She took a step back from him to give him room to breathe, and to think. 'I was already seeing J.J. by then, and I'd decided I couldn't carry on with you, even though I loved you so much, Harry. It's true. I didn't know I was pregnant, and by the time I did, I couldn't even be sure whose child it was.'

Harry's mouth had gone dry, his words seemed to stumble over each other. 'When did you find out?'

'Not until much later. By that time I was married to J.J., and you were back with Julia.'

'And you never let me know.'

'How could I? What would you have done, Harry? Torn all our worlds apart, that's what you would have done. Neither J.J. nor Julia deserved that.'

'How did you find out? About me and Ruari?'

'Oh, Harry, you only have to know you both to see that. He has little features, his ears, his fingers, the shape of his head, that are pure you, but it's inside, in his character, that you find it most. He's wilful. Ridiculously stubborn. Totally determined. Typical Jones.' Somehow she was smiling through her tears.

He turned away, trying to shield himself, only to be forced back. 'And . . . J.J.? Does he know?'

'We've never talked about it. Sometimes I think he's guessed but . . . Harry, he's been a brilliant father to Ruari. He may not be the most gifted athlete, he's rubbish at football and far too serious for his own good, but he loves Ruari and has always done his best.'

'I think he knows.'

'Perhaps,' she said sadly.

'We'll all have a lot of sorting out to do after this.'

'After what?'

'After we've got Ruari back.'

'So you'll help?'

'You do ask the most ridiculous questions.'

And before he could say any more she was in his arms once again, and this time she didn't run away.

—◊—

Barriers had come down, past lies and all the hurts that went with them had been ripped away. From this point their worlds were never going to be the same. The longing was mutual and they said not another word until they had satisfied it. It was madness, it was escape, it was both celebration and selfish distraction, it was love, greed, desperation, lust, all those things. They spoke without words, reliving old times, trying to lose themselves, and when they had finished they lay back amongst the cushions in front of the fire, seeing their bodies as though for

283

the first time, and remembering. It was so much like it had once been – and then it seemed too much so. Their pasts had been irreconcilable, their obligations inescapable, and reliving those long-lost moments served to remind them only that they were buried as deeply and as inextricably as ever within the troubles of the present.

'Have we just made everything worse?' she whispered.

Worse? How much worse could it get? Everything had changed, and not just between the two of them. The nature of the kidnap had changed, too. What had once been political had now turned to money, and a huge amount of it, while the deadline had been cut from months to days. Bodies with their throats ripped out suggested their adversaries lacked any shred of pity, and they no longer had any idea who their adversaries were, or where they and Ruari might be.

'I'm not sure we can handle it any more, Harry,' she said. '*We*', that wonderful, exquisitely tormenting pronoun, so short and yet bursting with significance, for he knew she was back to talking about her and her husband. She sighed, rested her head on Harry's shoulder. 'J.J.'s in another place. I think he's in danger of breaking, Harry. He knows that if he manages to raise the ransom money it will destroy everything he's ever tried to create, but if we don't get Ruari back, that will destroy him even more completely. It's more than one life at stake here. I don't know how much more he can take.' She had just cheated on her husband, but there was no mistaking her care for him. Harry tried to remember whether he had felt like that with Julia.

'Let me help pay the ransom.'

'You?' She ran a finger gently down his cheek until it stopped on his lips. 'No, I can't let you do that. J.J. has enough people trying to crucify him, and you would be the last nail. He doesn't deserve that. He mustn't know about you, Harry, not yet at least.'

'I can't let Ruari suffer simply because J.J. isn't able to raise the money.'

She took his face in her hands, brought it close. 'And I won't let J.J. suffer simply because you can.' This wasn't just about Ruari, it was about them all, and she was taking charge, navigating through the reefs that surrounded them. 'He'll do his bit, whatever it takes. The Breslins are stubborn, too.'

'Ah, I almost forgot. Sean.'

'He's said he'll help, of course. With the money. And he's booked on the morning flight to Trieste. Somewhere to start picking up the threads once more. He says it's better than simply sitting here waiting.'

'He's probably right.' No, certainly right, Harry realized. There was no substitute for having a man on the ground, behind enemy lines. That had often been his job. 'I'll go with him,' he heard himself saying.

'You? And Sean?' She couldn't hide her incredulity.

'Share resources. Experiences.'

'You and Sean?' she repeated.

285

'It's about Ruari, not about him and me. He told me that himself.'

And he reminded Sean of those words when he phoned him a few minutes later, after he'd torn himself away from Terri and thrown on some clothes.

'So you'll be coming with me, will you, Mr Jones?' the Irishman responded. 'Covering all the bases, you say? One man at high table, the other in the gutter. So tell me, which one of us is the better equipped for the gutter?'

'Only one way to find out, Sean.'

'You may be right.'

'I'll see you tomorrow, then.'

Sean was about to put down the phone when he hesitated, another thought in the air. 'Are you with my daughter-in-law by any chance?'

The old bastard knew. No point in dodging the fact. 'I am.'

There was a silence, a short hesitation as Sean digested the news. Harry thought he was working up some form of rebuke, but even as he waited for the outburst of denunciation, the line went dead. He found the silence more damning than words.

They met the following morning at Gatwick Airport. They didn't fly direct to Trieste with Ryanair, the Irish airline, but flew instead to Venice on a rival carrier. When Harry asked why he was told in the curtest terms that Sean had once had a falling out with what he called 'those dozy gombeens at Ryanair' and hadn't flown them since.

It seemed to Harry that the Irish could never let go of a

slight, even with each other. So they had flown into Italy across the dark, silted lagoons of Venice, where they hired a car and took the coastal road to Trieste, which brought them to the centre of the city by nightfall. Throughout the entire journey, although they sat together, Harry and Sean exchanged barely a word.

—∞—

Trieste had once been one of the major ports of Europe, the main outlet to the sea of the Austro-Hungarian Empire, which lavished pomp and riches upon it in a manner they thought befitting their status as the pre-eminent power on the continent. And typical of the Habsburg mind, they ended up with a city that was solid and familiar, logical and spacious, but lacking in any great landmark or signature; it was all trombones and dumplings, with barely a Latin flourish in sight. Whatever eminence the place had came to an abrupt end with two bullets fired at Sarajevo in the summer of 1914 that killed Archduke Franz Ferdinand, the heir to the imperial throne, and his wife, Sophie. Their coffins were brought back in sombre procession through Trieste, and some said the city had been in mourning ever since. A century later it was a small town by the sea, with a population of two hundred thousand souls and declining, its port much redundant, its mercantile princes largely fled, its old quarter that dated back to Roman times half-updated but never finished, a little bit of Austria on the Italian coast where the local *osterias* still served boiled pork

287

in the middle-European way and many of the old barmen in this town of watering holes and coffee shops still greeted their guests with a very Germanic 'Bitte?'. Yet as Harry and Sean made their way towards their hotel on the central piazza, they saw people promenading in the typical North Italian manner, the women walking arm in arm, wrapped in their furs against the winter breeze, the miniature dogs strutting on their short legs and leads, the menfolk following dutifully behind. Some writers complained that Trieste had no clear character, yet it was perhaps nearer the truth to suggest that it had many different characters, and the inhabitants simply hadn't bothered to decide which they preferred. Many newcomers and transients like D'Amato made the glib mistake of identifying character with authority, but when they had passed away or simply passed on, like so many before them, the Bora would still blow, the ferry would still leave for Albania, and Trieste would remain staring out across the Adriatic, as it always had, waiting for whomever or whatever came next.

Yet if Harry was expecting mediocrity, he was pleasantly surprised. Terri, who had made their reservations, sent them to the Grand Hotel Duchi d'Aosta on the central Piazza dell'Unità. The exterior of the building suggested little more than a slice of solid Habsburgian conformity yet inside it was an eye-popper, filled with quirky North Italian delights and period pieces. 'No hardship here, then,' Sean muttered as he gazed around the foyer, 'not that there'll be any time to enjoy it.' They had an appointment the following morning, at ten, with D'Amato.

'Will you be eating in our restaurant tonight, sir?' the concierge enquired. 'We think it is the finest in the city. It's called Harry's Grill.'

'Suddenly lost my appetite,' Sean replied sullenly.

'And I'm going for a walk,' Harry added. 'Get to know this place.'

So they left their suitcases and went their separate ways, Sean heading off into the night while Harry began his walk. He spent no more than two hours, but that was all it needed to familiarize himself with the heart of Trieste – the Piazza dell'Unità dressed in its Christmas fare, the quietly lit seafront, the downcast docks, the Grand Canal which was no longer so grand. Only when he was almost back in the Piazza dell'Unità did he stumble upon the narrow streets of the Old City with its two thousand years of history. They were still adding to it in their own distinctly chaotic fashion; many of the buildings on its largely pedestrianized streets were empty, in the process of refurbishment, their windows barred, their doors blocked, but much of the work had already been abandoned, with weeds encroaching on the fresh render and threatening to swamp the temporary power lines. He walked through a maze of alleys and ate pasta at a restaurant that in the summer would spill out onto one of the paved squares. While he ate he examined his fellow diners, wondering if any of them might have answers to his questions.

Trieste closed remarkably early. As Harry walked back to the hotel, the life of the Old City had already retreated behind curtains and shutters. Even the couple of beggars who tried to waylay him from their perch in a crumbling doorway did so in desultory fashion, as if they knew it was already time to pack up and go home. He stopped under what appeared to be an ancient Roman arch, all crumbling stone and graffiti, listening to the city at night. He heard a cat howling, the distant growl of a scooter, footsteps that faded down a nearby alley, but apart from that there was little distraction. He stood for some while, listening to the city breathing, trying to feel its pulse, and eventually an elderly man wrapped up in muffler and felt hat and bending over his cane came shuffling by. He knew Harry was there but didn't raise his eyes or return Harry's gaze.

Already Harry was beginning to understand Trieste. This was a place of shutters and blind eyes, where people didn't want to know. A wonderful place to hide.

The silence of the city ended abruptly at seven in the morning with the heavy tolling of Catholic and Orthodox consciences. Church bells rang out on all sides summoning penitents to prayer and dragging Harry from his bed. He scarcely needed the encouragement; he hadn't been able to sleep. Every time he closed his eyes Ruari walked into the room, kicking open his door, with his mother not far behind. Harry sat on the edge of his bed, his head in his hands, while the threads of his unravelling life whipped around him. He decided to freshen up with a swim, grabbed a towel and robe and headed down to the hotel's underground pool, an extraordinary construction of mosaics and marble that incorporated authentic Roman footings for what might once have been a pagan temple. He was surprised to find Sean already there, swimming in a practised manner through his lengths, and clearly exceptionally fit for his age and nocturnal habits. Harry wasn't in the mood either to share or to disturb; he turned abruptly and began walking away, but suspected Sean had already seen him.

They didn't join up until shortly before ten to walk to the Questura. A blustery wind scuttled in off the sea, playing tag with the Christmas muzak across the pavement of the Piazza dell'Unità. 'Cliffeckinrichard,' Sean scowled. 'You come all this way, and you get Cliffeckinrichard.'

'It's to scare away the seagulls,' Harry muttered. They marched on in silence.

The Questura was close behind the City Hall, solidly built and unpretentious, the sort of building that wasn't going anywhere in a hurry. As they climbed the steps, Harry realized he hadn't noticed a single police siren in the city, no raging car horns, not even a discarded cigarette packet or sweet wrapper. The streets were unlike any he'd found elsewhere in Italy. A dark-eyed, athletic young woman greeted them in the reception area and took them

291

up to the second floor. No waiting. Nothing but courtesy. They were ushered straight in.

'Ah, welcome – Signor Breslin?' D'Amato extended a hand and raised an eyebrow in Sean's direction to confirm the identification before turning to Harry. 'And you, sir?'

'Jones. A . . . a family friend,' Harry replied, at a loss as to how else he might explain his presence.

'Signor Breslin, if you and your very good friend would take a seat. And coffee, of course. Simona, please bring the gentlemen some coffee.'

'No need,' Sean began, waving a hand.

But the inspector was insistent. 'Trieste is famous for its coffee. You will find at least fifteen different varieties here,' he explained in his excellent but less than colloquial English. 'In the morning it is our custom to take it with a shot of grappa, but this is police headquarters, so you will forgive.' He shrugged and smiled, then his face melted into seriousness. 'I am so sorry that your visit to Trieste should be under such unfortunate circumstances. Please allow me to extend my sympathies to your family, Mr Breslin. Kidnap, it is a crime of beasts, not human beings.' His eyes said he meant it. After a mournful moment he glanced down to the sheets of paper that had been arranged care-fully on his desk, shuffling them around as though to refresh his memory, then looked up once more. 'My officers have searched the farmhouse. There is good news, I think. They have found some ski clothes, a teenager's. They are being tested but I am sure we will find they are your grandson's. It means he is almost certainly alive. We have found nothing that says otherwise.' He decided it wasn't necessary to mention the bloodied bandages they'd also found and were testing in the expectation they would reveal Ruari's blood group.

Simona returned with the coffee. As she bent over to serve it, Harry couldn't help but become aware of the tight body beneath the blouse and demure dress, and the ease with which she filled the space.

'*Multumesc*,' D'Amato muttered at her, accepting his small cup of espresso, his eyes lingering just a fraction too long on her bottom as she left. He swallowed a brief smile of guilt before turning back to his guests. 'You will know, of course, that we found two bodies. South Africans, we believe. We are checking all international databases, but sadly that takes time. Everything takes time.'

'Sometimes too much time,' Sean said.

'I understand your impatience, signor, but until yesterday no one knew for sure that your grandson was being held here. He could have been anywhere in Italy. It was only through excellent police work that we made the breakthrough.'

'But, sadly, your *excellent police work* didn't manage to catch them.' Sean's emphasis stopped only a little short of sarcasm.

'We assume that the gang was in some way alerted. It is possible they saw police cars on the Carso and panicked. In such a place it is so very difficult for the police to – how do you say, keep our heads low? Yet without those cars we could not have found them.' D'Amato spread his arms in frustration, then sprang up to stand beside a large wall map of his fiefdom and began stabbing at it with his finger. 'There is more. We thought the gang had gone to the border with Slovenia.' He traced a prospective path. 'It is only a few minutes away from the farmhouse and it is not guarded even at the main crossing points, not in the new Europe, eh? But we have a report that a boat was taken from the Trieste marina on the same evening.' The finger began stabbing once again. 'At this time of year it could not have been for amusement. So I think it is possible they have taken the boy that way, by sea, down the coast to Slovenia, here, or more likely Croatia. The coastline there is very beautiful, but as you can see, very rugged. They could hide there for months. That is not such good news. I am sorry.'

'What makes you so sure they are not still in Trieste, Inspector?' Harry asked.

D'Amato nodded, acknowledging the merit of the question, and returned to his chair. 'That is possible, of course, but not, I think, likely. We keep looking, you understand, just in case, but I must try to tell you about Trieste, Signor Jones. It is not a big city, very respectable, perhaps a little dull and stubborn. And very law-abiding. The Triestines even hesitate to cross an empty street against a red light. They like their order of things. There is a story, Signor Jones, that when God was making the world, he flew around it with a bag in each hand. One bag contained all the good things in life, the other was filled with disappointment. As he was flying over this beautiful bay the bag with all the good things burst and fell upon the land, and He said, this is unfair, this cannot be the only place on earth with no disappointment. So to make up for all that good fortune, He filled the place with Triestines.' D'Amato smiled, but without humour. 'I can say this, because I am from Campania. So the people here, they are a little suspicious, a little wary. They do not like others bringing their problems and leaving them on their doorsteps. They do not welcome kidnappers. It is easier to do such things in almost any other town in Italy, and the Balkans . . .' His shoulders rose once more, as though shrugging off an unbearable responsibility. 'We shall keep looking. If they are here we will catch them. But I do not think they are. It is a bad place for foreigners to hide.' He pushed his cup of coffee away, he was finished. 'I will let you know the moment I hear any news.' He rose wearily to his feet. 'How long do you intend to stay in Trieste, gentlemen?'

'I'm not sure. We came to see for ourselves,' Sean replied.

'Of course. You must stay as long as you feel it is necessary, and so long as you are here, please feel free to call on me for anything you desire. But I fear there will be nothing more for you in Trieste. If you wish my advice, I suggest you return home, to be with the rest of your family. That is best at a time such as this.' He held out his hand, leading them to the door, but Harry lagged behind, hesitated.

295

'You said foreigners.'

D'Amato turned. 'Did I?'

'You said this was a bad place for foreigners to hide. You think the gang is not Italian?'

'We are examining what was left behind in the farm-house. Much of it could have come from anywhere, but we found a few books, cheap novels. In Romanian. Also a personal music player with some Romanian songs. We think it is possible the gang might be from there.'

'But you have Romanians in Trieste.'

'Signor Jones, we have all sorts of people here. This is a port, an international crossroads. But very few Romanians, perhaps no more than two thousand.'

'Your secretary, the young lady. She is Romanian.'

The inspector's brow creased. 'How do you know?'

'You said thank you. In Romanian. *Multumesc.*'

The inspector's eyes clouded. 'What are you trying to imply, Signor Jones?'

'Nothing. Absolutely nothing. I'm just trying to find out what I can.'

'There is nothing to find out about the young lady, I assure you,' D'Amato replied. An edge had crept into his voice. 'It is not possible that she has any connection with this matter.'

'I wasn't—'

But D'Amato cut through him. 'No connection whatso-ever. I can give you my personal guarantee on that.' Why, she'd been sleeping in his bed when the kidnappers were

296

escaping. He was her alibi, about as good an alibi as you could get, although he had no intention of sharing it with these men. They had suddenly become a bore. 'If you decide to stay in Trieste, please let me know, gentlemen. Otherwise I wish you a safe journey home, and good luck.'

It might have been his imagination, but Harry thought the door was closed behind them on rather stiffer hinges than those on which it had been opened.

—⧸⧹—

They found themselves a table outside the Caffè degli Specchi, across the piazza from their hotel. It was one of the most fashionable spots in town, known as the Café of the Mirrors, where Triestines and visitors had been drinking coffee and wine ever since the days of the emperors, and not a lot had changed since. They sat in the sun, wrapped in their coats against the sea breeze, sipping more coffee as they tried to marshal their thoughts, while the good burghers and ubiquitous bankers, the humble clerks and inquisitive accountants of the city walked past.

'So what do you think?' Harry asked eventually.

'I'm thinking it was James Joyce and Richard Burton themselves who once sat right here, drinking their own coffee on a table at this exact spot.'

'They came here?'

'For sure. Lived here, for a while.'

'What, Richard Burton the film star?'

'For the love of God, not that one. The explorer, the man of many letters. He died here. The man who translated the *Arabian Nights* and who was supposed to have written out a pornographic translation of *The Perfumed Garden*, before his wife burned all his notes.'

'That's probably why I never read it. Never finished *Ulysses*, either.'

'Then, Mr Jones, that's something else we'll not be able to talk about.'

They went back to sipping black mud.

It was several minutes before Sean began again. 'I think that Inspector D'Amato's banging his secretary.'

'What makes you think that?'

'An old man's instinct for such things. When you're a spectator of the game, you see so much more than while you're out there playing on the field.'

His eyes burned into Harry, who grew uncomfortable.

'So let's get this over with, Mr Jones. I'm not sure what's going on between you and Terri, and I'm not a man to moralize. On my old grandmother's grave, if I were D'Amato I'd be banging her myself, but I told you before. Blood. Family. In the end, they're the things that count.'

'I agree.'

''Tis an awful long way to the gates of Heaven, Mr Jones, and I'm not sure I'll ever be making the trip. Too many diversions along the way, things I didn't get right. Just like a politician. A paratrooper, even.'

'Let alone a Provo,' Harry said, finishing off the thought.

'That's right. But you'd better be clear in your mind about one thing. I'm here in this place to protect my family, Mr Jones, not to sit back and watch you pull it apart.'

Harry raised his cup. 'Then, to family.'

'And to Hell with anyone who gets in my way.'

They left it there, for the moment.

The couple next to them vacated their table; a seagull swooped down on the breeze, eyeing the biscotti left on a plate. Harry's ear was burning again. Perhaps it was the effect of the freshening wind, but he had an idea it might be in warning. He pushed aside his cup. 'There's one thing I don't like about this, Sean.'

'Just the one?'

'We know how bloody dangerous the kidnappers are, even when everything was going well for them. Now they've had their plans kicked to pieces. They're on the run, and rushing, too. Why the hell have they brought the deadline forward to Christmas?'

'I wish to God I knew.'

'It's like they're losing control. This isn't a recipe for happiness on anyone's part.'

Sean sucked his cheeks. 'Been thinking along those lines myself. And something else that's been nipping at my mind. In the rush to get out of the farmhouse, to escape, did they let Ruari see their faces? If he has, they're not going to let him get away, not with him being able to identify every single one of the murdering bastards, no matter how much we pay them. You know how the game is played.'

299

'We can't be sure.'

'In their place, would you be willing to take that risk?'

'No, I wouldn't,' Harry replied softly.

The seagull had set down on the nearby table and was scavenging. The waiter advanced, flapping his towel, the bird screeched and took off in fright, knocking the glasses to the pavement where they shattered into a hundred pieces of ice. Muttering to himself, the waiter stalked off in search of a broom. If only their mess could be cleared up so easily, Harry mused.

'So,' the Irishman said, 'what are you thinking the next step should be?'

'You asking me?'

'Looks like it. Just this once.'

Harry didn't answer immediately, staring instead into the dregs of his cup like a fortune-teller in search of an answer. 'D'Amato and the police, you trust them?' he eventually asked.

'Trust?' Sean raised an eyebrow. 'I wouldn't trust them with my shirt on a winter's night.'

Harry's fingers went to his ear. It was still burning, warning him of pain to come. He sighed. 'In which case, if Ruari is to stand any chance, he'll have to be got out, and quickly. Before the Christmas deadline. And we'll have to do it, you and me; we don't have time to wait for the good inspector to find his way out from inside his secretary's knickers.'

'Now there's something amazing. Pretty soon, Mr Jones, you and I will be agreeing.'

'But we haven't any idea where Ruari is. Do you buy D'Amato's idea that he's not in Trieste, that this is the last place they'll hide?'

'The man's about as much use as a chocolate teapot,' Sean spat. 'There must be some reason why they came to Trieste in the first place. They felt safe here, or they know it well, have friends. That's maybe why they got warning of the raid. And wasn't that exactly what we did back during the Troubles when we wanted to confuse the crap out of you lot? Hid right beneath your long British noses, so we did.' Sean threw Harry a defiant rebel look.

'And the speed boat?'

'A feint, a false trail.'

'So you think they're here.'

'Worth a look.'

'May be a complete waste of time.'

'Well, what choice do we have? We've nowhere else to be scratching around, now, have we?'

We. You and me. It wasn't different camps any longer. They had slipped into a different place.

'You know, Sean, you seem to understand the kidnappers' minds pretty well.'

Sean shook his head, knowing where Harry was leading him. 'I was never there myself.' Then his face twisted, almost into a grin, an expression Harry had never seen on him. 'Except for that feckin' horse.'

'What horse?'

'Shergar. Remember that useless lump of horseflesh?'

301

Sean's description was entirely ironic. Like most Irishmen he was a lover of the turf and Shergar had been one of its finest princes, a thoroughbred stallion who had won almost every major race he'd started, often by a record margin, and been worth a king's ransom at stud. Which was why the Provisional IRA had kidnapped him, demanding five million pounds for his return. The horse had never been seen again.

'What happened?' Harry asked, intrigued.

'A total and unmitigated feck-up, from the moment the nag woke up to discover Micky Ahern trying to stick a needle up his arse. Went wild, kicked himself to buggery, and poor Mickey, too. Buried both of them together.'

Sean allowed himself a brief smile, but it faded quickly. It didn't seem a particularly good omen.

'So where do we start, Sean?'

'Only one place we can. The farmhouse. We start there. Go take a look for ourselves.'

—⁓—

Simona was perched on the edge of D'Amato's desk, her skirt riding her thigh. The inspector was smiling, she'd just agreed to spend the coming night with him and was even going to book the hotel for him. She made things so easy. They were sharing a whispered joke when his phone rang. As she leaned across him to answer it, her blouse fell forward, leaving him wondering how he would ever find the willpower to hold out until the evening.

302

She listened for a moment, then held her hand over the receiver. 'It's the English,' she said, in a manner that would have had Sean choking.

He hesitated only for a moment before shaking his head. 'Get rid of them,' he mouthed.

'The inspector is not available,' she said dutifully, then listened a little more before covering the mouthpiece again. 'They want to visit the farmhouse.'

The inspector sighed in frustration, dragging his eyes out of their sockets in order to concentrate. 'Tell them it is a crime scene, not just kidnap but murder, that forensics are still inside, it is not possible.'

Once again she repeated his message, before saying goodbye and placing the receiver back in its cradle. 'They say they are going anyway.'

D'Amato flicked his fingers in agitation. 'What do you think, my little bird? You understand men so well.'

'I think they are going to be trouble,' she whispered.

—⚬⚬⚬—

Sean, who had the keys, decided he would drive. They took the main road up to the Carso, their rented Fiat 1.4 never getting above third as they wound their way up the steep slope, passing the funicular as it hauled itself on a more direct route up to the plateau. Not until they approached the towering obelisk at Opicina were they able to slip into a higher gear. The monument had been erected by some long-dead Austro-Hungarian ruler to mark the spot where

303

the Carso at last gave way to civilization, a milestone of happiness after the long haul across the wilderness of limestone. The views from the edge of the plateau were extraordinary. On their right hand were the snow-topped mountains of the pre-Alps, on their left lay the rugged forests of Slovenia, while in front of them the ground tumbled down towards the streets and the seafront of Trieste more than a thousand feet below, and beyond that still the gentle waiting waters of the bay that stretched out to the horizon where Venice lurked hidden in the mists. In most other countries the spot would be overwhelmed with souvenir stalls and trinket-sellers, but here there was nothing, just the view, understated and undersold like the rest of Trieste. Opicina itself was little more than a village and a stop at the end of the funicular, yet it was the most substantial spot on the Carso. It took them only minutes to pass through and get onto the winding roads that snaked through the scrub woodland and hard-won fields of the plateau with its ancient, crumbing stone walls and old Karsic houses. These houses had a strong, primitive style, and were squat, as though ducking from the wind, heavily shuttered with long balconies covered in vines and good-luck wreaths tied to the gates. At this time of year the wreaths had withered, and were the colour of rust.

They found the farmhouse without difficulty. Where its track turned off the main road a police car was parked. The occupants were sitting, heads tilted back, caps nudged down over their noses, unaware of Sean and Harry's arrival until the Fiat had passed them and was bumping and swaying down the tree-shrouded track. They drove for several minutes before they came across an officer who was altogether more alert. He stepped out into their path, held up his hand, brought them to a halt. Over his shoulder, beyond the trees, they could see the farmhouse, scruffy, anonymous, forlorn, in desperate need of a little pointing and paint.

Neither Harry nor Sean had much Italian, and the officer no English. As they attempted to explain what they wanted, he kept shaking his head and uttering *'Non si puo'* – it can't be done. It seemed like his sermon. Behind him they could see no sign of the forensic teams that the inspector's office had told them were crawling over the place, nothing beyond another solitary officer who was squatting hatless on the step, smoking and gazing languidly in their direction.

'Looks like they're dug in for a long siege,' Breslin muttered.

'Something tells me they knew we were coming,' Harry added.

'D'Amato,' they both concluded as one.

There was no point in further argument. They stood at the side of the track in silence for a few moments. Two days ago Ruari had been here. Yet as Sean and Harry shared a private moment, there was one thought Harry knew the other man couldn't be part of. This might be as close as he ever got to his son.

When they climbed back into the car they had trouble turning, the track was so narrow, hemmed in by tree stumps, and the policeman showed no inclination to help. As at last they set off again, the Fiat clattered into a deep pothole, struggling through it with a jarring clunk of complaint.

'God help me,' Sean muttered, 'but that nice young lady at the car-rental place isn't going to be happy with us for this.'

The car stumbled on. By the time they made it back to the main road, the two dozing officers were awake, waiting for them, watching with suspicion until they disappeared from sight.

'Something tells me we're about as welcome in these parts as a politician with the pox,' Sean observed.

'I'll have to take your word on that,' Harry replied.

It had been a long day since breakfast. They stopped in a nearby village, at a small *osteria* in the lee of an ancient church tower that had been built on the summit of a hill and dominated the surrounding area. As they pushed open the rough-hewn door they were greeted by the aroma of wood smoke and strong cheese; an elderly woman in a red-check apron bustled towards them. This was authentic Carso, Slovene not Italian, the simplest of establishments with green felt hats on the pegs, frills running along the edge of the lace curtains and painted plates hanging on the walls, a little chunk of Austria that had been dropped two hundred years and several hundred miles from its original home. They had no language in common beyond the woman's few words of primitive English, but sign language soon brought forth a spread of prosciutto and neck ham along with farmhouse cheese, spiced sausage and a bowl of freshly grated horseradish. A basket of bread and two tumblers of blood-red Terrano were set down in the middle; the wine was a little rough, thick, and excellent for slicing through the fat of the ham. They ordered a second glass as they picked over the plates. They lost themselves in their thoughts, pondering what lay ahead, and it was some time before either of them spoke.

'Even if they're in Trieste, we've no idea where to look,' Sean eventually muttered disconsolately.

'Then perhaps we're going to have to persuade them to show us.'

'And how in the name of God do you hope to do that?'

'I've got an idea,' Harry ventured. 'You'll probably think it half-arsed.'

'I'll let you into a little secret, Mr Jones. Such an idea from you would come as no great surprise.'

—◊—

Sean remained silent after Harry had finished. He didn't object to what Harry had suggested, but neither did he approve. He simply sat quietly, reflecting, as Harry paid their bill and the woman nodded in gratitude. Sean held his silence, even as they made their way back to the car.

'Something's bugging you, Sean. You don't like the plan?' Harry asked eventually as, still without a word,

Sean started the engine and selected first gear. Sean looked ahead along the steep road that led out of the village.

'No, it's not the plan.'

'Then what?'

'It's you.' The Irishman turned in his seat, his brow creased by doubt. He was staring at Harry curiously, his bright eyes darting, questioning. 'Your plan is certainly half-arsed, but I'll not complain at that since I've nothing better to offer in its place. Yet it requires you to put your neck very firmly on the line, to take a terrible risk. Oh, that's not for the first time, I know, Queen and feckin' country and all that, but I'm sitting here asking myself, why would you be doing that, for my grandson?' The troubled cast in his eye suggested he'd already tried various possibilities and cared for none of them. He left the question hanging in the air as he slipped the handbrake and they set off.

Harry was drawing breath to reply, something vacuous about kids and friends in need, when he realized Sean wasn't paying attention any more. Instead he was staring with concentrated ferocity at the road ahead, and pumping savagely at the brake pedal. Yet the car was still accelerating.

Although the Carso is a plateau, it isn't flat. It has hills for its churches, and inclines, some of which are savage and steep. It was on one of these inclines that the car was now set. The handbrake was useless, but they might have stopped their progress without too much harm by deliberately colliding with the corner of the last house in the village, which they were now rapidly approaching, yet, just as Sean turned the wheel to clip it, a donkey appeared without warning from the alley in front of them, dragging a cart directly into their path. A look of horror from the farmer, a bray of alarm from the beast, and Sean swerved. By then it was too late, they were travelling too quickly.

The first thing Sean struck was a low wall beside a field a little further down the road. Goats scattered in panic. The front bumper dislodged and for a moment became jammed beneath the wheels, slowing them a little, but soon it was flailing like a windmill behind them. Sean clipped the other wing twice taking the next corner, but beyond that was a straight stretch of road that ran between a rock face and a sheer drop on Harry's side. He could see clay-tile rooftops forty feet below; he tightened his seat belt. They were gaining speed and there was never any possibility they would be able to take the next bend, a sharp left-hander, but at least it took them away from the drop. For a few yards the Fiat scraped along a wall of natural rock, leaving bits of bodywork and a shower of sparks in its wake. The window beside Harry's face shattered, tearing at his cheek and showering his lap in fragments of glass. And even as Sean struggled in vain to correct their course, the front wheel hit an outcropping boulder and the suspension struts snapped, hurling the car in the air. When once more it landed on the roadway, with a savage jolt that shattered more glass, the Fiat had only three wheels. They careered on, with no hope of control, metal screaming, like a fairground ride, knowing they would hit whatever lay ahead of them at the next corner. Their eyes met in fear.

'See you in Hell, Mr Jones!' Sean cried as, with a final sickening twist and shriek of tortured metal, the car left the roadway and hurtled towards the waiting rocks.

CHAPTER TWENTY

The car had finished its journey wedged on its side in a deep rocky ditch. The driver's airbag had operated, saving Sean from the worst of the impact, but Harry had been left to the less than tender mercies of his seat belt. When eventually he forced open his eyes, he felt as if he'd spent a week in a cement mixer. He thought he might have been knocked out, but had no idea for how long, or even which way was up or down. The roof was six inches lower than the manufacturer's specification, the windscreen was a crazy pavement of cracks, and there was a nasty smell of burning electricals and petrol. Beside him, Sean was beginning to come round.

'You OK?' Harry asked him.

Sean tested his limbs, then nodded. 'Nothing broken, but I can't move. And if it's all the same with you, instead of hanging around here I'd rather be getting ourselves out before whatever's causing that smell of smoke gets together with the leaking petrol and decides to throw a feckin' party.' He started fumbling with his belt.

Harry struggled with the release on his own seat belt,

groaning as a wave of pain ran up his right side, then leaned across Sean to push at the driver's door, which in their new arrangement was now facing the sky, but it had been jammed by the impact and wouldn't budge. 'You're right, Sean. That girl at the car rental? She's going to be really pissed off with you.'

Sean tried to smile, and winced. 'The brakes went.'

'And there was me thinking you were simply in a hurry.'

'I think it's not just the car-rental lass who doesn't like us.'

'That's good news, Sean.'

'Good news?'

'It means they're still in Trieste.'

Harry was trying to kick out the windscreen and wondering where the blood on his shirt had come from when he heard sounds of a commotion from above their heads. Shouts. Falling stones bouncing off the bent panelling as people scrambled down. Legs. In uniform. Hands, wrenching at the driver's door. A face. The police.

'Praise Mary,' Sean muttered as the officers began to twist him out of his seat and haul him up. More help. And a final pair of hands to drag him over the edge of the rock cleft to safety. He was surprised to see it was D'Amato.

'Inspector, I'm grateful to you,' Sean said as he stumbled into the policeman's arms.

But a frown came over D'Amato's face. He wrinkled his nose. What was that he could smell on the Irishman's breath? 'Signor Breslin, have you been drinking?'

Ah, the Terrano. 'Only a couple of small glasses.'

'Then I regret. You are under arrest.'

—⟋⟍—

They handcuffed Sean, wouldn't listen to his protests, just put him in the back of a police car and drove him away.

'Signor Jones, you will come with me, please,' D'Amato suggested pointedly as they finished dragging Harry to safety. 'I will take you to the hospital. You need attention for the cuts on your face. And a chance to talk, perhaps.'

It was just the two of them in the car as the inspector drove back down. There was already a hint of dusk, a vague redness washing across the sky from the direction of Venice, and it had begun to rain, a fine mist that turned to fog, clinging to the dark trunks of the trees and adding to the sense of isolation, of being cut off.

'There is no way he was over the limit,' Harry said, his tone belligerent.

'We have to be careful in such matters, you understand. It can all be sorted out at headquarters.' He sounded reassuring, trying to take the spark from the air between them.

'The car was sabotaged. When you drag it out, I think you'll find the brake hoses have been cut.'

'Perhaps. We shall look.'

'It's good of you to take such a personal interest, Inspector. Even better if you did something to help.'

313

D'Amato sighed. 'Signor Jones, I regret very much your problems and I will do everything I can to help, on that you have my word. But your presence is not helping here. You will only get in the way of the police investigation.'

'The presence of kidnappers isn't wanted, either, but you've got them.'

'Please, I beg you. Do not cause any further trouble.'

'Someone has just tried to kill us. Add that to a kidnap and two murders. How much more chaos do you want on your quiet streets, Inspector?' Harry snapped.

'I understand your anger and upset. Your experience must have been terrible.' D'Amato was working hard to calm the storm, and already they were pulling up at the hospital on Piazza Osedale. The inspector drew the car to a halt, turned to face Harry, creases of concern playing around the corners of his eyes. 'Please learn the lesson of your terrible accident. For your own safety, I suggest that you make your arrangements to leave.'

'Not without my friend.'

'Signor Jones, if you are right about his drinking, I think you will find he is released, very quickly. In the morning, at the latest. You can both be in your own beds back home by tomorrow evening.'

'And Ruari?'

'At the moment he is in God's hands, not mine.'

'No, Inspector, he is in someone else's hands, murdering shit-heads who are here in this city right under your nose. And if you can't find them, I promise you, I will.'

D'Amato's fingers drummed against the steering wheel. 'Signor Jones, please. Leave.'

Harry was opening the door and climbing out when he paused. 'No, thank you, Inspector. I think I'll hang on in Trieste.'

The drumming stopped. The policeman gripped the wheel, his knuckles showing white. 'You do not understand, Signor Jones. I don't believe I was offering you an option.'

—❦—

The roast-chestnut seller on Via Oriani offered a grin from behind his stall that was broad enough to persuade Harry to stop. The wind had picked up with the sunset and it was close to freezing; he'd already consumed an entire bar of chocolate to keep up his blood sugar but his system was still screaming for more. The chestnut-seller, a dark-skinned man with a colourful woollen hat and a strong look of the North African coast, tested the nuts by squeezing each one to ensure they remained firm and sweet, then threw a couple of extras into the paper cone for good luck. Harry was glad for the chestnuts, and the smile. It hadn't been much of a day.

As so often in his life, it was the ordinary foot soldiers rather than the commanding officers who helped Harry make it through – the Polish chambermaid in his room, for instance, where he had returned to shower and change his clothes, and the junior concierge, Karim. Harry needed to discover the parts of Trieste that were off the beaten path, the sort of detail the guidebooks didn't offer, the immigrant bits, and who better to tell him than immigrants themselves?

There were a couple of thousand Romanians in Trieste, so D'Amato had claimed, but that would be the official figure and thus almost certainly inaccurate. It would make no allowance for the illegals. Yet even if he doubled the number Harry still came up with only four thousand, which suggested a small community, probably tightly knit, and this was a conclusion that both the chambermaid and Karim had confirmed.

But it was the nurse at the Pronto Soccorso or A&E in the chaotic downtown hospital who tended Harry's injuries who had been particularly helpful. The wounds themselves were superficial, blood but no bone, and as she swabbed them down, muttering in admiration as she did so at the work on his ear, he'd noticed the nametag on her chest. Sabic. Another immigrant, and with passable English. She had told him a lot about an area of town called the Little Balkans. It was precisely what Harry needed.

The place she had mentioned was a run-down quarter of rented and largely dilapidated properties off the Piazza Garibaldi, a square presided over by the gilded figure of the Madonna set high on a stone column. From here, along streets on all sides stretched crowded tenements whose bell-pushes told their own stories. There were -bichs and -sics and -vichs, Mohammeds and Radulas and Taroskis, Liu Chens and even a Signor Zhu, often with two or three names scrawled beside a single buzzer. It was the old story – as soon as one of these exotic nametags appeared, the Italians left, if they could. The tide was coming in and the longer they stayed the stickier things would get. Soon it wasn't just one building but the whole street and then the neighbourhood, and now every fourth shop which wasn't an ethnic food store or restaurant seemed to be a recycling centre for second-hand electricals or car parts. The Little Balkans.

It was the bars Harry was most interested in. His lunchtime conversation with Sean in the *osteria* had focused on them, they were the basis for his plan, as much as it was worth, which was less than half an arse now he'd lost Sean, but since when had things ever gone to plan in his life? Now, in the light of the early night as the figure of the gilded Madonna came into view, there was no mistaking the Little Balkans. Crumbling buildings a hundred and fifty years old, five or six storeys high with huge, draught-leaking windows, and bare bulbs shining through. Leaking drainpipes, crudely patched masonry, washing hanging from windows, streets where the supply of paint seemed to have run out years ago, except for the graffiti. The politics of many distant countries were being fought out on the walls with messages that were raw, rough, and often deeply racist. There were even swastikas. As he looked up Harry saw two plastic Santas dangling on ropes from a shutter – trying to get in, or to escape?

In the doorway of a food store that claimed to be a

Chinese pizzeria, its Italian owner was bawling at an Asian employee, who refused to catch his eye, looking away in the downcast habit of an Oriental. Two Muslim women in hijabs scurried by, heads into the wind, and a copy of *Hurriyet* wrapped itself around Harry's ankles. Then he found his first bar. It was typical of this part of town; small, narrow like a railway carriage, with a long bar on one side and little more than a large shelf on the other for drinkers to lean on. Apart from a few bar stools it was standing-room only. A drinking hole. It was still relatively quiet, only the early crowd. Nurse Sabic had told him that these places filled up later at night, and first thing in the morning, before the working hour. The middle-aged barman was testing the flow of lager from one of his new barrels; the tap spat and coughed a couple of times before he was satisfied. Only then did he look up. Behind him Harry could see bottles of cheap whisky along with grappa and vodka, and amongst them several bottles of *tsuica*, the favourite spirit of Romania, distilled from plums. It could kick your head in with a single blow. Harry ordered a beer.

He noticed a copy of *Il Piccolo*, the local newspaper, lying on the bar. It had a blaring headline. *Doppio Omocidio!* 'Double Murder!' Beneath it the story was illustrated with several graphic photographs of the inside of the farm-house. So much for D'Amato and the sanctity of the crime scene. The barman was wiry to the point of looking withered, his narrow face dominated by a huge moustache with nicotine stains beneath his nostrils. His skin was like the bark of an apple tree, and his eyes kept wandering to the side of Harry's face, and the clips Nurse Sabic had applied to keep the wounds on his cheek intact. Harry sipped his beer, didn't want to rush this, waited until he'd gone through more than half the glass before he spoke.

'You speak English?'

The barman shrugged. 'A little.'

'I have lost some property here in Trieste. Some very valuable English property.'

The barman shrugged again, and started polishing a glass.

'I would be grateful if you could help me find it.'

Harry spoke slowly, but the barman appeared not to have heard.

'*Very* grateful,' Harry emphasized.

He reached into his pocket and brought out a new €200 note and placed it beside his glass on the counter, where it lay crisp and flat and clearly visible until Harry covered it with his hand. The barman's eyes began to flicker in uncertainty.

'I want my property back. To buy it back. No questions. And no police. You understand?'

Another shrug, more half-hearted this time.

'I will come back here tomorrow evening. If you can help me, there will be more of these.'

He withdrew his hand, and the barman stared once again at the note with its distinctive sunflower-yellow design.

'What property?'

'A boy. An English boy.'

319

The barman's expression flooded with suspicion. The glass-polishing became more furious.

Harry rose from his seat. 'I will see you again. Tomorrow.'

As Harry turned, the barman placed his own hand over the note and glanced around to see whether any of the other drinkers had noticed. He was relieved to see them all still staring into their beers, oblivious. The barman was nervous, he'd just made almost a week's wages in a couple of minutes for saying nothing, with the promise of more to come. If he made this much for keeping his mouth shut, how much more might there be if he had something to say? He didn't trust the English, he didn't trust drinkers who left their beers unfinished, and he didn't trust this bastard in particular. Fuck him. But he would ask around, anyway, carefully, of course, couldn't do any harm.

Harry got much the same reaction in all the bars he visited, eleven in total, any that had even a hint of a Romanian connection, steering clear of only the Turkish and Vietnamese. When he was finished he hailed a taxi back to his hotel. He was exhausted, a little drunk, and he knew it wasn't wise to walk streets like these when so many knew he had his pockets stuffed with cash. This was already a turbulent part of town, and he'd just given it a bloody good shaking.

—ᴍ—

The men had grumbled about the lateness of the hour and the lack of notice, the theatre tickets that would go unused and the dinner invitations discarded, but they'd all agreed to come. J.J. had insisted. He needed them. They were the three other substantial owners of the newspaper, the men who controlled the voting shares while ordinary share-holders looked on. One of the men, David Carson, was a long-standing partner in the business, a friend of Breslin's from their schooldays who had taken up twenty per cent of the voting shares at the outset and had stuck with them through sunshine and storm, although over the years his business interests had slowly moved elsewhere – into property, a Michelin-starred restaurant that earned better reviews than it had ever done profits, and an expensive third wife. The other two men sitting around the bare boardroom table were more recent arrivals, Laval and Cutter, money men, managers of investment funds who controlled around ten per cent each, speculators who enjoyed prowling through the wood in the hope that the grizzlies would frighten the smaller wildlife into their arms. The atmosphere in the *Newsday* headquarters was out of sorts, artificial, the building unnaturally quiet at this time of night, no bustle, no attentive assistants, no coffee; it had the spartan atmosphere of one of God's waiting rooms in an existential play. Cutter was the last to arrive, and came in glancing purposefully at his watch.

'I'll be brief, to the point,' J.J. said once they had all sat down around the boardroom table. 'I want to sell my stake in the newspaper. Immediately. Tonight, if possible.'

They were men of business, experienced in hiding

emotion and rarely showing surprise, but each one glanced at the others, searching for a sign that he was being played in a game the others were all in on; but they found nothing in each other's faces except bafflement. They turned back to J.J.

'Our Articles of Association say that if any of us want to sell our shares we must offer the others first refusal before putting them on the open market. So that's what I'm doing.'

'But why, J.J.?' Laval said. 'We have a right to know.'

'It's an entirely personal matter – nothing to do with the business, if that's what you mean. This is the last moment I would choose to sell, just when the business is being turned around . . .' He was already starting his sales pitch.

'Convince me,' Cutter said.

J.J. hesitated. 'First I need to swear you to secrecy.' He knew that would be tricky, and perhaps pointless, this was a newspaper they were talking about, but the police in both Britain and Italy had told him in the strongest terms that any publicity would only make matters more difficult, might even panic the kidnappers into doing something rash. The silence had held so far, but for how much longer? J.J. had spent many hours of his sleepless nights wondering if he would have sat on such a good story if it had been someone else's kid. Did he have that much integrity? He hoped so, but didn't know, not for certain. There were so many things in his life he wasn't sure about any more. He placed his hands palm down on the table in front of him and sucked in a deep breath. He had to trust them, he had no choice. 'My son has been kidnapped. I need the money for his ransom.'

They stared speechless at him, their suspicions put to one side, now seeing in his face the signs of extraordinary suffering.

'Jesus H. Christ! I'm gutted for you,' Cutter burst out, his Midwest American tones stretching his words and adding emphasis.

J.J. felt something inside turn to liquid. His stomach had been in turmoil for days, unable to cope with a diet of unrelenting misery, too little sleep, too much caffeine. He couldn't take their sympathy added to the mix. He wanted to scream, to throw things, he didn't want pity, commiserations, empty words, what he wanted was their stinking money! But instead of screaming, he nodded in gratitude at Cutter. 'Look, I know we've been through a difficult patch, but you've all seen the revised business plan. It's strong, robust. This newspaper is headed back where it ought to be. I hope you'll take that into consideration.'

He had rehearsed this, and each time it sounded sicker, more pathetic. The family home, the villa in France, their assets, even Terri's jewellery, they'd had valuers poring over them for the past couple of days; as Terri had told him, those things didn't matter, they could all be replaced. But the newspaper was different. It was the rock on which he had stood all his adult life, the lover he'd spent more time with than anyone else, the creature he'd trained, transformed, held on to through every storm. The newspaper was his life. Now he was liquidating it, ripping off his balls, bleeding to death. And these men knew it.

'Sorry to throw this at you,' he muttered, rolling his tongue around his mouth, wondering what had happened to his saliva.

'Pity's sake, J.J., no apology needed. You poor bastard,' Carson said.

'It has been a pretty terrible few days.'

'I believe I can speak for all of us,' Laval added. 'This is so unjust. Unfair, J.J. You don't deserve this.'

'No one deserves this,' J.J. whispered. He looked around the table. 'So?'

As soon as J.J. reached him, Carson's eyes began to melt with emotion. 'Hell, I'm sorry, J.J. Buy more? God's truth is I was thinking of selling up myself. Will almost certainly have to, in fact. The property business – well, you know how tough that's been.' And there had been whispers of yet another divorce. 'I'm desperately sorry, my friend, but I'm not in a position to help you.'

J.J.'s stomach gave another turn. A good man, Carson. Slowly, stiffly, J.J. turned to Laval. 'And you, Peter?'

'J.J., what price do you want?'

'The best I can get.'

'But you know what the balance sheet looks like. There is so much debt.'

'The business plan, the future . . .'

'The future . . .' Laval said, tossing up the word as though he were juggling a ball. 'The future can only be touched by dreamers. But your needs are today.' He shook his head. 'I'm sorry.'

'Give me a price.'

'Not at any price. Over the last three years this has been the worst-performing investment in my fund – not your fault, I know, but my investors would not understand. I'm sorry.'

He hadn't expected this. J.J. was more aware than any of them of the storms they had ridden, he had been the captain strapped to the helm while they were mere passengers, which was also why he could see more clearly the calmer waters that lay ahead. Or was that merely, as Laval had put it, the dream? Was he too close, too involved, too desperate, to be objective?

He turned to Cutter. 'Ken?'

The American was a small, remarkably bald man, with a scalp that shone, which made his head almost phallic; someone had once described him as possessing a circumcised soul. He had a reputation as being a man who would never knowingly let anyone else get to the fridge first, even his kids. 'I just want to say, J.J., how ripped up I feel about what you're going through. Anything I personally can do to help, you bet I will.'

'Thank you.'

'But if I take another twenty-five per cent of the equity, I take responsibility for the same amount of debt. Look at it. It's huge.' He pronounced it 'ooge', as if he were too tight even to offer up the first consonant.

'We've cut, we've reorganized, we've reshaped and restructured . . .'

'Sure. Things might be much better in six months' time.'

'I don't have six months.'

The American sucked his teeth. 'But right now, you're offering furniture from a fire sale while the cushion's still burning.'

'You buy my share, you'll as good as control the company.'

'I buy your share, I buy your debt.'

'Make me an offer. Or I'll have to put the shares on the open market.'

'OK.' He held up a finger. 'One.'

'One million?' The bastard was trying to screw him. They were worth more than that.

But Cutter was shaking his head. 'One *pound*. That's my offer, with all that debt hanging round its neck. One pound is what the Russian Lebedev paid for the *Standard*, and another pound for the *Independent*. Seems like the going rate for newspapers in trouble.'

'You can't—'

'You know I have to put personal feeling aside on this.'

But the comparison with the *Standard* and the *Indy* is outrageous, you miserable chiselling bastard, my life's work for a pound? J.J. wanted to scream, but didn't. He couldn't afford to show any sign of weakness. He was glad he'd kept on his jacket because he was sweating like a pig beneath it, his shirt drenched. Soon beads of perspiration would burst out beneath his hairline and betray him, reveal his fear. This couldn't go on.

'Very well, I'll put the shares on the open market, see if that gets a better response.'

'But you can't do that for a month,' Cutter replied softly.

Something inside J.J. died. He thought it might be the last flicker of the flame that had kept his hope alive. 'Our Articles of Association require that I give you first refusal, which I've done.'

'They also provide that we have twenty-eight days to think about it.'

'You've thought about it.'

And now the circumcised soul leaked out of Cutter's eyes. 'I want to think about it some more. Maybe in a week or so, I could make you a different offer.'

But nothing like what the shares were worth. The man was feral, couldn't see a wounded animal without attacking, taking advantage. It was his nature. He'd guessed that J.J. was coming to the end of his resources, couldn't beg or borrow much more, so Cutter's reaction had been immediate and instinctive. Leave the sucker twisting on the spit for a week or two, and he'd be even easier to tear apart.

J.J. stood up. He wanted to say something, words that might form a profound rebuke, some epitaph to carve on the stone above the grave they were digging for him. But nothing came. He walked away.

CHAPTER TWENTY-ONE

It was a tradition called *osmizze* that dated back to the emperors, a period of a week or so when officialdom turned a blind eye and allowed the Slovene farmers of the plateau to serve up their own food and wine on their premises without the usual suffocating blanket of permits and price regulation, even without taxation. All that was required was for the farmer to hang a wine flask above the door as a sign he should be left alone. The tradition had been fiercely defended and had survived, flourished even, a mark that even in a world of universal edicts those who lived on the Carso ran their affairs by a different set of rules.

D'Amato and Simona enjoyed the tradition to its full, nestled in a corner of the farmhouse beneath ancient smoke-stained beams, sampling the plates of ham and cheese and sauerkraut soup, followed by marinated pork covered in white flakes of the ubiquitous grated horseradish, and everything washed down with enough Terrano to put them both well over the limit. While he paid the bill in cash she tottered in the direction of his car, and after he had stuck his wallet away he ran after her, anxious not to be apart for even a moment, and marvelling yet again at his good fortune as the seat belt pulled her sweater tight against her body, leaving little to his overheated imagination.

The darkness, as in most places up on the plateau, was profound. They left the hamlet with only the headlights to pick out the crumbling stonework and the twisted shadows of the passing trees. There were no other cars; they were alone. It didn't take long for his eager hand to find her knee. As they began to swing down the narrow, winding road, his hand crept higher, ever more urgent, stroking, searching, until with a gasp of exhilaration from them both it found its place between her thighs. There it stayed as the car rolled gently through every corner, swinging back and forth, one way, then the other. While she moaned, D'Amato screamed inside, he hadn't felt like this for twenty years, perhaps ever. This woman made him feel an entirely changed, more potent creature. Oh, he loved his wife and children but he *lusted* after this girl, which right here and now meant so much more. And she responded, with every slow twist of the wheel along this dark, secretive road that was leading them to a wonderful place. And soon, he knew, it would be his turn.

At last, very gently, she removed his hand, whispering something in gratitude, he didn't hear what, it didn't matter, it wasn't a moment for words. As the road emerged from the woods the view before them opened out and became spectacular – the dancing lights of Trieste, the ribbon of its seafront, and the gracious curve of the gulf marked out by varying degrees of shadow. He pulled over to a spot where they could spend a few moments more, lost in their private world. She lit them both a cigarette; as he took his from her lips, she kissed his fingers.

'Are they still causing you trouble?' she asked after a while.

'Who?'

'The two Englishmen.'

D'Amato, even at a moment like this, didn't require much prompting. Like most policemen his mind kept snagging on his work. 'They still insist the local Romanians are involved.' He took down another lungful of nicotine. 'What do you think, my little bird?'

'My opinion is nothing. But it doesn't make much sense to me. The boy was kidnapped in Switzerland, no? If they were local, why bring all that trouble to their own doorstep?'

'Perhaps.'

'But I'm worried. What will happen to you if the two Englishmen carry on like this?'

'To me?'

'The more noise they make, the more it will . . .' she hesitated, stretching for the appropriate words – 'remind people that you lost the boy. When he was at the farmhouse. It all went wrong. That isn't good for you, is it?'

He raised his cigarette to his lips, could still smell her on his fingers. He gazed out at an anonymous light that was blinking somewhere out to sea. He had to admit she had a point.

'And if they keep making their accusations, it will do nothing but stir up trouble in the community. You know how sensitive we immigrants can be.' She laughed, but he didn't join in. Trieste had a reputation for welcoming immigrants, it was a long-established port, an international highway, had two official languages, Italian and Slovene, and a dozen different religions represented in its churches. It was a melting pot that had been formed slowly and been stirred successfully over many centuries. Yet that reputation was under strain. In recent years, too many immigrants had arrived too quickly, resentment was growing on both sides, the pot was beginning to boil and bubble, and God help whoever was on watch when it overflowed. Not him, not Francesco D'Amato, he wasn't going to allow two bastard Englishmen to start a stampede that would trample across his reputation. If that happened, he would lose everything, including his little bird, and he did not want that, wouldn't allow it. He reached for her hand.

'An English boy, South Africans, strange Romanians – to hell with them all. Nothing to do with you and me, eh?'

She rested her head on his shoulders. 'I would hate anything to come between us, Francesco.'

He kissed her. 'Don't worry, my little bird, it won't.'

No, jumping into that particular cesspit was the last thing on his mind. Even if the Romanian gang was still here, he guessed it wouldn't be hanging around for long, would move on and take its troubles with it. Sometimes, for the greater good, it was better to use a deaf ear.

He started the car once more, driving away with considerably more impatience than they had arrived; it was his turn now, he wanted to get back to the hotel. As the lights of the city flashed past, so much more brilliant than anything she had ever known in her small town in Romania, Simona thanked the gods of good fortune that she had been brought to this place and to this man. They were the answer to her every dream. She had told her cousin, Nelu, that if he wanted any further help then he and the other members of his gang would have to pay for it. She had told him very bluntly; she wanted her cut.

Nelu had begun by expressing gratitude but also marked reluctance, until she had reminded him that without her every member of the gang would have been caught and would be facing a lifetime in some scumbag prison, unless, of course, they'd already been shot. It was, he admitted, a strong point, and what remained of his reluctance vanished when she reminded him of what her cooperation would mean. It was nothing less than a guarantee that they would never be caught, not in Trieste, not on D'Amato's patch. Not while she was at his side.

Nelu was not an unreasonable man. As Simona set out her case, what she suggested began to seem an excellent idea to him. And after a brief but heated discussion it had also come to recommend itself to Cosmin and the others.

333

So now they were six. The gang had just got larger, and far more powerful.

—∽—

J.J. returned to his home in Notting Hill. Unlike previous nights since his son's kidnap, he didn't go straight to the decanter, instead he sought out Terri, who was sitting, gazing listlessly at a book, with one eye fixed on her candle. He stood in the doorway; he didn't need to say anything, she could see it in his tortured face, but he said it anyhow.

'I've failed.' The voice was no more than a whisper, like the rustling of scorched paper. 'I can't raise the money, not that quickly.' On feet of lead he came to sit beside her, the closest they had been in days. She stared at him, knew he was breaking.

'How far short are we?'

'I don't know – around two million.'

'Your father . . .'

He nodded. 'But it's not enough.'

She hesitated, wondering whether the moment had come, whether he was desperate enough for what was coming next. But she had little choice, she had to take the gamble. 'I had a call today. A man named Sopwith-Dane.'

J.J.'s head came up. 'Know the name – something in the City, I think.'

'He said he had a client, a business colleague, who had heard about Ruari.'

'But how? Who?'

'He said his client would be ready to lend us as much as we needed, until we had things sorted.'

'But who the hell—?' Yet already J.J. had answered his own question, and his face twisted. 'It's Jones, I know it is. Your fucking friend.'

'He wouldn't say, J.J.'

But they both knew.

'Does it matter?' she whispered.

'Of course it does!' His face was like a clown's mask, struggling to hide what was inside, but too much pain and fear had been building up over recent days, and now it overflowed. 'There was that film, wasn't there? The one that posed the question, would a man let his wife screw another man for a million? What do you think the going rate is, Terri?'

'Don't, J.J.,' she pleaded, her eyes filling with tears.

'Damn him! Damn him!' her husband sobbed as he buried his head in his hands.

—⁓—

Harry lay alone on the soft, supportive contours of his bed, listening to the sounds of the city at night. He'd barely slept in seventy-two hours and knew he would get precious little sleep tonight while he struggled to calm his fears – not for himself, but for a kid he didn't even know.

Sounds of late-night revelry crept through his open window from a distant corner of the piazza, yet even as the young Triestines stumbled and caroused their way along, Harry reckoned that by most standards the disturbance was modest, subdued, like so much of this city. A poet had once written that when Trieste had lost its pre-eminence as a port its prostitutes had disappeared, and with them they had taken the city's soul, yet the suspicion was growing inside Harry that the Triestines took their professed modesty altogether too seriously; this was still a port, after all, with its swirling mixture of races and humanities, a road to nowhere, perhaps, but also a road to everywhere, and if its solid citizens failed to see any sign of trouble it was only because they preferred to bury their heads in a plateful of cake rather than look out for it as it passed by the shutters.

Harry desperately needed to rest. He had to be sharp and alert in the morning, a danger to others rather than to himself, so he settled back, determined to find sleep, and he thought he was winning the battle until his iPhone came to life yet again. A text message. Even as he opened it, a shard of despair drove itself through the centre of his forehead.

'Where were you? Your appointment with PM at nine this evening?'

From Mary. Oh, sweet Jesus, what day was it? All he could remember was that it was five days to Christmas, five days before the kidnappers' deadline ran out. That's how he measured time now, not in dates and diaries. Too many demands, too much pain, too little time. *Five days.* And still he had nothing more than guesswork and gut instinct to say that Ruari was anywhere near Trieste.

Sleep. *Sleep!* He forced his head back onto the pillows, but he couldn't find it. Wherever he tried to lead his thoughts they ended up in the same place, with Ruari.

As he lay back on the cotton-softest bed in the most indulgent hotel in town, searching desperately for answers, he had no inkling that Ruari and his kidnappers were less than a two-minute walk away.

—◊◊—

Chombo snorted, trying to clear his nostrils and his mind, his barrel chest heaving up and down as he massaged his thoughts. He had come once more to his home in the Eastern Highlands with its well-stocked garden of fuchsias and pine trees and reluctant ceiling fans. There was too much bustle in Harare to get his thoughts into line. His Mercedes SUV stood outside, its sides stained with the red, oily mud of the climbing road that had tossed him about, no matter how carefully the driver had negotiated the broken tarmac. But that would soon change. Everything would change.

Yet still Chombo felt uneasy. Even on the verge of victory, his life was in the hands of others, and in particular the Englishman who controlled the diaries. Would he stick to the deal? He wondered, and he worried. It wasn't his fault that the boy hadn't been released, Chombo had stuck to his side of the bargain, but would others? He hated the uncertainty, and blamed those who had brought it, whom he held responsible. Takere. It was his fault.

Just a few weeks into the New Year, Chombo would no

longer be acting head of state but would be confirmed in his rightful position, and in his mind he was already there, getting on with the glorious task, no longer needing to hesitate or to be patient. He was the President, as good as, and he expected others to respond in the appropriate way, to be respectful, subservient. But Takere wouldn't. The man had been useful, no denying that, but he had one fatal flaw. He had too much power, power that should be the President's. And this flaw showed in the way Takere talked, in the way he held himself while in the Presence, almost as though he thought himself an equal, and there was no equal any longer to Moses Chombo.

As he gazed into the darkness outside his window, Chombo saw everything. Takere was not only disrespectful, he was slow. He would not learn. He had made too many mistakes. He was the one who had brought him the two worthless South African thugs, who had stood in this very room, showing all the arrogance of their kind, and who had stolen from him so much money. They had paid for their failure with their lives, as Chombo had paid for it with his money, and Chombo was sure Takere was sitting on a fat slice of that himself. Yes, this monumental fuck-up was all Takere's fault.

There came a point when a leader had to grow beyond others in order to fulfil his destiny, and that sometimes required things to be done which were unpalatable. Power in Africa was maintained not by reason but by enforcing respect, and nothing squeezes more respect out of a man than fear. You cannot cross the river without getting your feet wet. Yet Takere neither respected nor feared him.

Ah, the river. Chombo's mind went back to the great Limpopo and the fate of the South African journalist. There had been no point in the wretch simply disappearing, leaving no trace and no story behind. It was important that a message be passed on to any who might be tempted to follow, some picture that would discourage them, like a face that could be identified, washed up on the southern bank of the great, grey, winding river while the rest of what remained of him was sufficiently dismembered and unrecognizable to put fear into everyone who saw. The crocodiles that swept along the banks of the Limpopo, as helpful as they so often were, couldn't be trusted to perform such delicate work, and Takere had got his hands particularly dirty that night. He had seemed even to enjoy it. And that was the difference between them; Takere took delight in blood while he, Chombo, shed it only with reluctance. It hurt him, deep inside, truly it did – but what was it that Takere himself had said? To be a successful leader, you must learn to be a butcher.

So there it was. It would be his first New Year's resolution. Chombo would be responsible to Chombo, and to no one else. Takere had to go, his job done, his historic task fulfilled. He would die, as all things must, with his President's gratitude ringing in his ears.

—⋘—

The Old City. A medieval muddle built upon the ruins of a Roman fishing port, a disorderly quarter so different from the rest of Trieste with its well-ordered outpouring of Austrian pride. It was a place of small squares and claustrophobic alleyways, the haunt of troubadours instead of policemen. Some still called it the Ghetto, where the Jews used to live, which they had done for much of their time in harmony with the rest, until Mussolini, yet it stood only a few paces from Piazza dell'Unità with its Habsburg grandeur and Christmas lights. There could be no greater contrast, stiff civic pride versus the ways of the ghetto. On dark evenings when the piazza was windswept and bleak, with respectable citizens scurrying home pursued by their Christmas muzak, inside the Old City the huddled, youthful masses still gathered, eating pizza and getting drunk. The civic authorities had tried hard to reform and rebuild it; fifteen years earlier the place was a rat run, so large amounts of European money had been poured into its concrete and glass frontages, but all those sackfuls of credit still hadn't solved the problem. There was no plan, everything was haphazard, very Italian. The rich wouldn't move in, there weren't enough young people to fill it, so much of it still stood empty, waiting, with faltering plasterwork and boarded windows, hoping for better things tomorrow.

And this was where the Romanians had brought Ruari.

When Nelu had received Simona's message warning that the police were about to raid the farmhouse, for a while he and the other kidnappers panicked. De Vries and

Grobelaar were already dead, their throats slit by Cosmin's knife and their bodies dumped in the cellar, for no better reason than to get them out of the way while the Romanians got drunk. Simona's text had sobered them up remarkably quickly. They had to get out, in a chair-crashing hurry.

That was when the Old City came into its own. The fifth member of the gang, a shy man in his forties with bandy legs and extraordinarily large hands, was named Puiu. Like the others, he had been a conscript but since his discharge he had made his living as an electrician, and until he'd been offered the more lucrative employment of kidnapper he'd been working on the refurbishment of a pair of old town houses at the heart of the Old City, converting them into apartments with the aid of a grant from the city authorities. But the money had run out, the work had come to a halt, the building had been boarded up. So now it stood waiting for Puiu and Cosmin and the others, complete with running water and a temporary electricity supply, and it was even within the footprint of a wi-fi hot spot, as much of the Old City was, which made sending messages so much easier. It also had access to crowded, cosmopolitan streets where their presence would cause no one to lift their heads in curiosity. And Puiu knew how to get access, past the padlocks and flimsy mesh security. Only one drawback, the money tap was about to be turned on once again and the site reopened after Christmas. So they had a new hideout, but they also had a new deadline.

341

Even as D'Amato had been making his way up the winding road to the Carso, the Romanians had thrown a hood over Ruari's head and dragged him up the rickety cellar stairs. He'd been terrified, thinking they were going to cut his throat, too, just as they had done to de Vries and Grobelaar, whose bodies had been staring at him from the corner of the cellar for the best part of a day. It was as close as Ruari had come to breaking; he couldn't stand the thought that his friends the rats might end up doing to him what they had been inflicting these past hours upon the South Africans. So when the gang had thrown him into the boot of a car and he realized they weren't going to kill him straight away, he remained quiet as they sped along back roads then down, always down, until he could hear the sounds of a different world outside the car. Trieste, although he had no way of knowing it. And there was no disguising the anxiety of his captors as they dragged him back out of the boot and into a new hiding place – a building which, judging by the noise, stood in the heart of the city. They dragged him roughly upstairs, his body scraping over every step, raking his back as he tried to curl and protect his mutilated and still inflamed hand. As dawn broke he found himself high up in an attic room, shackled to a floor joist, with the pale light of a new day creeping through a window that looked out over rooftops to the blue-tiled campanile of a distant church. He could hear the city waking, with traffic, bells, even footsteps. And voices.

Yet although he had survived so far, Ruari now knew

these men were going to kill him. He'd seen too much of them, what they were capable of, and seeing it meant he would not be allowed to survive. But here, in the heart of the city, he found reason for hope. There were other people in this new world of his, even if he couldn't see them and could only hear them through a closed window, people who were more than just sullen, murderous beasts. Perhaps some of these people out there were even looking for him. Perhaps, after all, he had a chance.

CHAPTER TWENTY-TWO

In his dreams, Harry was being strafed by machine-gun fire, and Sean was pulling the trigger. He had at last managed to fall off to sleep, weighed down by exhaustion, but it had brought him no peace. His dream was particularly vivid; he was trying to crawl away from the danger, yet he'd got himself tangled on the wire, there was mud in his eyes, his new ear had been torn, and the machine gun was rattling in his ears when it all morphed into a pounding on his door.

'Who is it?' he called out, waking and scrabbling for his wits.

'It's me, Karim,' a voice called out. Harry recognized it as the junior concierge who had been so helpful on the previous day and who had received a generous tip for his pains.

'Come in, damn you.'

A passkey scrabbled at the door and Karim entered. He was a well-presented young man with the dark skin of North Africa and serious eyes that were now downcast. 'Good morning, Mr Jones. A thousand apologies for disturbing you. We have tried to telephone but there was no answer.'

Harry glanced at the bedside phone. Its red message button was glowing. He was alarmed to see it was already ten. He must have died on that bloody wire.

Karim shuffled uneasily as though his highly polished shoes were several sizes too tight. 'I have been instructed, Mr Jones, to ask about your plans. To see if we can help you with any travel arrangements, perhaps.'

Plans? Harry had nothing that would pass muster as a plan, except hanging around waiting. 'Another couple of days, probably,' he muttered, yawning, feeling every limb creaking in complaint. The car crash had roughed him up more badly than he'd realized.

Karim's shoes seemed to have shrunk another size. He was hopping in discomfort. 'I am filled with apology, Mr Jones, but your room is no longer available.'

'Pity. Very nice. But any room will do.'

'I am desolate, Mr Jones,' the young man responded in his quaint and formal English, his head bowing as he tried to remember his lines, 'but the hotel is full. All rooms are already reserved. The management very much regrets . . .'

Harry was just about to make the blindingly obvious point that the piazza was scarcely swamped by crowds, that most people preferred Christmas in the Caribbean, when his mind slipped into gear. This had nothing to do with the management and its imaginary bookings. This was D'Amato putting on a little heat.

'Please,' Karim stuttered, his face a picture of misery.

346

'The management has instructed me to apologize most humbly for any inconvenience.'

'I think I understand, Karim.' Harry collapsed back onto his pillow, trying to clear his thoughts. 'Tell me, if I booked into another hotel, how soon would it be before I found the room no longer available?'

Karim stared, at first uncertain, then succumbed. 'Very quickly, I fear. The reservations are sent every day to the Questura . . .'

'Straight to the police.'

'Yes, sir. I am sorry.'

Harry got out of his bed. He was naked but his years in military service had left him without much modesty. Karim closed his eyes as his guest climbed into his shorts, and when he reopened them he found Harry inspecting the contents of his wallet in a manner that was intended to capture Karim's attention. 'Then tell me, Karim, how much does it cost to rent a car in these parts? A large car, perhaps one that wouldn't be too uncomfortable to sleep in?'

Harry withdrew one of his collection of €200 notes. Karim's face became animated as he watched. 'Around five hundred euro a week. Maybe a little more.'

Harry drew out a second note, and placed the money openly on the bedside table. Then he drew out the same number of notes, after a little thought added another, and began folding them, very tightly.

'I wonder, Karim, whether you would do me a favour?

347

Hire a car later this afternoon, leave it in some very quiet spot, somewhere people will take no notice. Put a couple of sleeping bags in the boot, hide the keys in the exhaust where I can find them. You return it to the rental company at the end of the week. The car won't be driven, there will be no reason for anyone to ask questions.' Harry finished folding the notes and looked up. 'I'd be very grateful.'

As he had watched Harry's performance Karim's eyes had grown larger, like a card player calculating the odds. They seemed very good. 'If – *if* I could help, where would you want it leaving, Mr Jones?'

Harry grabbed his local street map and threw it at Karim. 'Somewhere out of the way. You show me.'

In less than two minutes they were done, a quiet parking area behind San Giusto marked with a red-ink cross.

'Shall I send a porter to collect your bag, Mr Jones?'

'I travel light, I can manage. But thank you all the same,' Harry said, reaching to shake Karim's hand and to pass over his very handsome thousand-euro tip.

—◊—

There was no point in Hiley hanging around any longer in Rome. Ruari's release hadn't happened and he was of more use back home, where the Breslins were delighted to see him; they knew they weren't up to negotiating with the kidnappers themselves. Hiley was soon in action once again.

'Where is my money?' Cosmin demanded.

'First, can I have a name?' Hiley began, as he had done with Jan.

'Santa Claus. My fucking money?'

Hiley sensed there was no point in arguing. Even across the Internet this man managed to give off the aura of serious evil. 'Look, the Breslins are trying to gather it together, trying their hardest, but it's the week before Christmas. You know what that's like. Please, we need a little more time.'

'No.'

'A few more days.'

'What, you want a few more fingers, too? Christmas Day, or Little Shit is dead.'

'But we can't raise five million by Christmas, it's simply not possible. And perhaps not at all. It's an outrageous sum. We could perhaps do a million, we've got almost that together, you could have that now . . .' It was the strategy they had worked out. Try to negotiate, find a chink of light. But the other man was all darkness. Cosmin raised his voice in impatience.

'Stop wasting time! I want five million euros, not a sermon. Or you want I make it pounds?'

'But we must have proof of life. We need to know that Ruari is well, otherwise there is nothing we can do.'

'Little Shit? He is still alive. And kicking. Very much last night. You know our cook, he is – what you call these things? A queer, a goat-fucker. He likes Little Shit *very*

349

much. They had good time last night. Maybe tonight again, too, if you keep wasting my time.'

'Proof of life!' Hiley insisted, growing desperate.

But the connection was cut.

—⚒—

The police were waiting outside the hotel for Harry. Karim nodded in their direction, making sure Harry had seen. There were two of them, lounging on the bonnet of their blue-and-white Fiat parked ostentatiously in the road.

'I think they wish to offer you a lift,' Karim whispered.

'How very kind of the inspector,' Harry replied drily.

Karim began printing out Harry's bill, along with one for Sean. Their two shoulder bags stood to one side in the small, meticulously appointed lobby, which was almost empty, with no sign of the tidal wave of guests that was supposedly about to inundate the hotel. An elegant man in his sixties, immaculately dressed in the North Italian manner, was hovering, waiting, his head bowed and hands clasped as though in mourning. He introduced himself as the manager.

'My profound apologies once again, Mr Jones,' he began, spreading his hands wide. 'This should not have happened.'

'I agree.'

The man's frown deepened as Karim pushed Harry's bill across the counter. Harry was inspecting it when the manager stretched across and slid it away from him. 'I think I see a mistake in your bill, Mr Jones. We do not permit such things at our hotel. If you will allow me?' He folded the bill and pushed it into his pocket. He attempted a smile. 'I hope there may be another time.'

Nodding in gratitude, Harry shouldered both bags.

'A pleasant journey, Mr Jones,' the manager called after him.

'Not without my friend,' Harry replied as he set off.

He walked out onto the piazza, aware that the policemen's eyes hadn't left him for a second, and headed for the Questura, less than five minutes' walk away. It had two entrances, the main one they had used on the previous day, and a less obvious side access. Harry suspected, correctly, that Sean would be relegated to the side door reserved for the local lowlife. Indeed, as he arrived, he found Sean beside the reception desk, looking bedraggled, with sleepless eyes and unkempt hair, shaking hands and saying goodbye to an elderly, stooped stranger. 'My lawyer,' he explained. 'You see, Mr Jones, I've been in Trieste less than two days and already I'm making friends.'

'They throwing you out, are they?'

'I have to admit there are some here who don't seem to have taken to me. That dozy bollox of an inspector, for one,' Sean said, taking his bag. 'The breath test was negative, of course. It just took them a whole feckin' night with me on a concrete bed for them to get the results back and for my lawyer to arrange the paperwork.'

'More friends,' Harry suggested, as they emerged from the Questura to find the policemen with their car parked directly outside. One of them was holding open the back door, indicating they should get in. 'Our taxi. I suspect they want to take us to the airport. Make sure we leave.'

'Not bloody likely!'

But Harry took Sean's arm, whispered in his ear, led him towards the car. 'We are flying from Venice. So take us to the railway station, please,' he instructed the policeman. He got a sullen look in return as the door was banged shut behind them.

No further word was spoken as the policemen drove them north along the seafront, past the old docks to the Stazione Centrale, another sleepy chunk of ancient Austrian architecture that stood behind a small park. After Sean and Harry had climbed out they were followed by the two policemen, who made it very obvious what they were about. Inside the high-ceilinged ticket hall Harry bought two tickets from the machines; they didn't have long to wait, indeed they had to hurry, the train for Venice was due to leave in a few minutes. They joined the gentle throng of other passengers as they waited to board. As Sean stepped onto the train Harry knelt on the platform, pretending to tie his shoelace, and glanced at the barrier where the policemen were waiting, still watching.

By the time he and Sean had squeezed their way through three of the coaches and stepped out onto the platform once more, the policemen had gone.

—∞—

'As sure as Mary's the mother of God, we've got ourselves an informer inside the police,' Sean said, forking his way steadily through a plate of ribbon pasta with clams and tender octopus. It was delicious, and he'd had no breakfast.

'What makes you say that?' Harry asked.

'The raid on the farmhouse – the kidnappers were warned about that, you can bet your army pension on it. And those brake lines didn't get cut by accident. Someone told the bastards that we were around, and where to find us.'

'I agree.'

They were sitting at an outdoor table of a restaurant beside the Grand Canal, a relatively short, straight and narrow waterway that pointed like a finger into the heart of the city. The buildings that ran along the canal were not just warehouses, they were palaces, built by the merchant-magnates of the nineteenth century so that they could count their profits being unloaded from the old wooden sailing ships while enjoying the comfort of their own sitting rooms. Two centuries later, the buildings still stood tall and proud, but plastic debris now lay strewn along the bottom of the waterway and graffiti sprayed on the central bridge entreated passers-by to do unnatural things to themselves. It was a rare expression of crudeness in this part of town. Dominating the canal's far end stood the pillared church of Sant'Antonio Nuovo, and sprawled before it was a Christmas market of stalls overflowing with colourful fruit from southern Italy and craftware from more distant parts; while Triestines browsed up and down, two beggars armed with an accordion and flute preyed upon elderly women, hoping to be bribed with a few coins to go away, but they never retreated more than a few paces before they stopped to dip into the free samples of food on offer on all sides. At the centre of the market was a full-sized Nativity scene, complete with live donkey and goats that were chewing and tugging at the decorated Christmas tree. Music played, the winter sun shone bright, it was a scene of contentment, no one seemed to be in any hurry, but then no one in Trieste ever was – except, of course, for the kidnappers.

It was while Harry was paying the bill for the pasta that he looked towards the seafront, and swore. Sean followed his gaze. The two policemen who had transported them to the station were parking their car on the pavement at the entrance to the canal. They were looking pointedly in their direction.

'You know, Sean,' Harry muttered, casting some spare change on the table as an additional tip, 'I have a feeling that those gentlemen aren't going to leave us alone. They still want us to leave.'

'But wouldn't you be agreeing with me, Mr Jones, that it'd be a terrible pity to leave this place without seeing more of the sights?'

The policemen were now out of their car, shaking their heads in exasperation, reaching for their caps as they prepared to hunt Harry and Sean down. The sun was low, shining into their eyes, and as they approached, one of the officers failed to see the dog crap until it was already underfoot. He stopped suddenly, gave an undignified hop and grabbed his partner's arm for support.

'Stretch our legs, are you thinking?' Sean muttered.

'That is exactly what I am thinking.'

'Then race you to the gates of Hell, Mr Jones.'

They grabbed their bags and ran. With a shout of alarm, the police officers gave chase, but they had lost a few vital yards, and Harry and Sean disappeared into the crowds of the Christmas market. Every few seconds the policemen's heads would pop up, peering above the shoppers as they tried to spot the fugitives, but they had almost lost them in the melee when suddenly Sean cried out. His legs were no longer young, unsuited to running from the police and dodging through crowds, and as he tried to avoid an elderly woman dressed in a huge fur coat tugging a reluctant miniature dog he stumbled and crashed into a stall, breaking the strap on his luggage and spilling it. For a moment he looked at it helplessly. Stopping would lose him any chance of getting away, but the bag had everything in it, including his wallet and passport. He had no time to think, the policemen were gaining. With a curse he abandoned the bag and hobbled after Harry.

They turned one corner, then another, losing themselves again in the crowds. Sean's lungs screamed in protest, his head was pounding, his legs felt like frozen twigs. He couldn't go on much longer, but as he prepared to dash across an empty road hot on Harry's heels he glanced over his shoulder and his heart lifted in relief at what he saw. Which was absolutely nothing. They had lost their pursuers. His senses flooded with relief, and he would have shouted with joy if he'd had the breath, but that was also the moment he realized he had done something very foolish. Drowning his moment of celebration was a roaring sound, a horn blaring in protest. He turned as quickly as he could, to discover a delivery van bearing down on him, almost on top of him. He had been looking the wrong way. And it was too late to save himself, he couldn't move, the van couldn't stop. The last thing he saw was the look of terror twisted across the driver's face.

Sean was hit and hurled to the ground; that in itself came as no surprise. What did surprise him was that he knew anything about it, that he was still alive. He was lying in the gutter, winded, but not badly wounded, with Harry on top of him.

For a moment, in shock, Sean's world stood still. Staring deep into Harry's eyes he saw flickers of concern mixed with grey flecks of relief, then he saw all the way down, to things that lay buried deep inside the other man. Sean couldn't move, every physical reaction was frozen as his thoughts tumbled over a thousand rocks before falling like a waterfall through his mind. His fingers seized hold of Harry as though his life depended on it, as a few seconds earlier it had.

'Luck of the Irish, eh, Sean?' Harry eventually muttered, prising himself off the other man. 'Stupid bugger.'

Harry waved away the offers of help as strangers gathered round. Soon he and Sean were left on their own again, with Sean leaning on Harry's arm, trying to stretch the ache from his limbs. He was still a little unsteady. 'Come on,' he whispered, 'let's go in here for a moment.' He nodded towards the doorway of a nearby church – there seemed to be churches everywhere in Trieste, with their bells and colourful domes and pot pourri of religions. As they entered, he was still leaning on Harry, breathing heavily with shock.

The church was dark, its atmosphere almost conspiratorial, rich with gilt, polished wood and incense. A service was in progress, a bell ringing, a priest's sonorous voice raised in prayer while a scattering of penitents shuffled along behind him. Sean stumbled towards a corner pew and sat slumped, head bowed, automatically making the sign of the cross.

'Thank you for that,' he whispered hoarsely, turning from the altar to Harry.

'I hope you haven't come here to confess,' Harry replied, 'we haven't got that much time.'

'I'm trying to catch me sodding breath,' Sean muttered. 'Anyway, you feckin' heathen, last time I took a look I was a Catholic. I think you'll find this is Orthodox.'

'I take the word of a true believer.'

'Me?' He shook his head wearily. 'I'm not so much of a believer in anything.'

'Except things Irish.'

357

'My country right or wrong?' Sean shook his head. 'Never been that blind. Happy to leave that to the British.' They were sparring again, but there seemed to be no personal malice in it, they had moved beyond that.

'Do you hate everything British, Sean?'

'No, just some of the things they've done in my country.'

'And me.'

'I don't hate you, I—'

'I wasn't at Bloody Sunday, Sean.'

'But you're part of the system that was.'

'I never shot an Irishman in the back.'

'There must have been others.'

'It was a war. People get hurt.' And there had even been one Irishman, an informer, Harry had shot in cold blood – executed, for want of a better word, and Harry had never found one. The man had been on his way to hand over information that would have resulted in the deaths of many others. Rough justice, some would call it. Murder, according to others. 'Looking back, it's easy to think maybe we could have found a better way. But you're part of a system, you don't set the rules, don't get to pick and choose. Perhaps that was one of the reasons I left the army and became a politician. I wanted to set some of the rules, not just follow them blindly.'

Sean was staring at the altar again, his hands still gripped as though in prayer, with a strange light in his eye. Strangely, there were tears gathering, too. The shock, Harry thought, until Sean spoke.

'You know, Mr Jones, the two of us have more in common than perhaps we've a liking for. You get involved, sure you do. You get sucked in, little by little, isn't that the way? Do your bit for a cause you believe in, that seems so right. There are limits, of course, a line you'll never cross, you're not a criminal or one of those crazies, but then . . . Then you wake up one rainy morning and find you've already left that line so far behind you that you can never go back, no matter how hard you run. I'd seen that happen – to others. It was going to be so very different for me. That's why I tried to stick to the money and the scams, claiming for the broken legs rather than breaking them myself, but those hard bastards on the Army Council, men like Adams and McGuinness, they would insist on you taking one more step, doing that little bit more, until it got to a point that you'd lost sight of where you'd come from. All the friends, all the dying. It was too much, we went too far. We ended up killing more of our own than ever you bastards did.' He turned to stare at Harry. 'My mother, God rest her gentle soul, used to say it wasn't important just to see the light, you had to know whether it was a moonbeam or lightning. You had to know the difference, she said. Somewhere along the road we lost all that, lost the moonbeams. Bloody Friday, Bloody Sunday, Bloody Christmas – what was the difference in the end? I wish I believed in God, then maybe he'd sort it out for me. But I don't.' He laughed, drily. 'No, don't you go looking at me like that, Mr Jones. Sure I cross myself, it's what we Irish do, but I was schooled by the Christian Brothers and beaten every day for the terrible sin of wanting to write with my left hand, and beaten all the more when I wouldn't shove that same hand up their stinking cassocks. No, I lost my faith a long time ago, and now I don't believe in anything much, except for my family. That's why I'm here, not for God but for Ruari, and if I'm on my knees praying it's for Ruari, not for myself, just in case there is a God.' He sighed, as though he was worn out by many things, and he looked once more directly into Harry's eyes. 'What's done is done, Mr Jones. Those people who were once terrorists have got themselves some votes and now we call them politicians. I'm a sharp bookkeeper who became a respectable businessman. And you – well, I told you once I'd never trust you. But I don't trust most of the other bastards, either, not even myself at times. And as long as you're here for Ruari, I guess that's good enough for me.'

A confession? A truce? An offering of peace? Harry wasn't sure, but it was good enough for him. They had a job to do.

'Come on, Sean, let's be having you. There's a war to fight out there. Time to give me some of that old rebel shit.'

—⟋⟍—

She found her husband on the patio overlooking the garden. It was a place where, over the years and in the summer, he would sit with his papers while he listened to Ruari playing on the grass below, being there for them if not entirely with them. Now the gardens were empty, frost-bare, and he sat wrapped in a thick overcoat and muffler, his face as grey as the tin sky above.

'I think I've done it,' J.J. said in a strained, reluctant voice, his eyes staring out into the distance, sightless. 'I've got some venture-cap people to give me a loan against the newspaper shares. They buy them if the partners won't, I pay them back if they do.' But the lines carved like mountain fissures across his face said there was not a word of good news in the whole affair. 'Either way we lose the newspaper for a fraction of its worth. And everything else, too.'

Terri stood near to him. It was Christmas cold but she couldn't feel it, could feel nothing except his pain.

'Five million. He's worth it, isn't he?' he asked.

'Of course he is.'

'But what if . . . what if we don't get him back, Terri?'

The thought had never left her.

'And what about us?' he added.

It was a moment they both knew had to come. Total, brutal honesty. It was what kidnap forced upon families. There could be no hiding place from the truth. This wasn't just about Ruari, it was about them all. Was it right to destroy everything they had, just for one? It was the question they could no longer avoid, along with many others. His eyes were on her now, fearful of many things.

'Are you in love with Harry Jones?'

'You know a part of me has always been in love with

361

him, J.J., for old times' sake. But that has never, ever got in the way of my love for you.'

'And now?'

Even at moments of total honesty it wasn't always possible to answer. She simply didn't know, wasn't sure.

'Are you still sleeping with that woman from the bank?'

He flinched. How did she know? How long had she known? His mind raced, it had never been more than a little game, of no great consequence, it wasn't the same as Harry Jones. But the more he protested to himself, the more confused he grew. He shook his head. 'No, I'm not,' he told her. Then he added: 'I'm sorry.'

'Me, too, J.J.,' she whispered. Her hand brushed gently on his sleeve as she left.

—⚶—

Harry and Sean were single-minded men in pursuit of mayhem, and they had preparations to make. They checked out the car where Karim said it would be – a Renault estate with the keys smuggled up its exhaust and two new sleeping bags on the back seat. Sean had nothing but the clothes he stood in, so there were purchases to make, a couple of fresh shirts, a waterproof, underwear, toiletries. Some bottled water and chocolate. And cash for Sean in case of emergencies. 'Never thought I'd be selling out to the Brits,' he muttered, stuffing notes into his pocket. But first, and most important, was a new mobile phone for him, an iPhone to match Harry's. If their mayhem was to have any chance of success, they needed to remain in touch.

By the time they had finished, dusk was beginning to fall. 21st December, the longest night of the year, and the lights of the city began to ignite and multiply along the streets. A change had come over the two men since their conversation in the church; Sean had grown quiet once again, withdrawn, as if he had already said too much. Harry took the lead in making all their arrangements while Sean hung alongside, like a fish swimming into a current, marking time with a languid flick of its tail, refusing to rise to any bait or distraction. He kept looking at Harry, reassessing, both curious and cautious about what he saw.

They rested in the Renault for an hour until darkness had taken full hold. 'I think it's time,' Harry said as the bells on the city clocks began tolling seven. 'You ready?'

Sean didn't reply, merely climbed awkwardly out of the car. He was stiff, aching from Harry's body tackle and his encounter with the pavement. Harry would have preferred to walk, it wasn't more than fifteen minutes at a stroll, a chance to clear his mind, but watching Sean hobble took the point out of it, so they hailed a taxi and directed it to the Little Balkans. There they began their bar crawl, retracing Harry's footsteps of the night before.

They had decided that Sean would go into the bar first, order a beer, find a corner into which he could fade. Some minutes later Harry would appear, order his own drink, making sure the barman saw the crisp €200 note in his wallet – only one, he didn't want there to be so much on show it would encourage a mass mugging – and when the time was right he would quietly press for news. So they began. At the first bar they got nothing but a scowl of suspicion from the bartender, which grew even deeper when Harry promised to return the following evening. It was much the same story at the second, and barely different at the third, where the bartender tried to spin a story that he reckoned was worth the money but was nothing more than froth on the bar-room floor. The patter was established; Harry would leave, followed a little later by Sean, and they would head on a short walk through the crumpled streets of the Little Balkans to their next encounter.

They stopped for a slice of pizza after the fifth, at an Anatolian takeaway that stank of old fat, but the Little Balkans wasn't a place to be fussy. Harry wasn't sure he'd seen a true Italian during the past hour; many of the faces were considerably darker, some distinctly Asian or African, their expressions strained, their skin sallow, telling unfinished tales of hardship.

It happened in the sixth. Sean had tucked himself into the corner of a bar barely wider than a railway carriage, hiding beside a cooler cabinet with a cracked door that had been clumsily repaired with gaffer tape. The place wasn't busy but was filling as the evening drew on, its three tables occupied, while the other drinkers stood and leaned, and already some were leaning farther than others. The barman had a distinctive mouth beneath his moustache, with a chipped front tooth and a gold molar, and neither his clothes nor his hair had received much attention for a couple of days. When Harry walked in he went directly to the same spot he'd occupied on his previous visit and ordered a beer; the barman poured it carefully, wiping the spillage from the bottom of the glass with a towel, his eyes alert as he pushed it across the bar. Harry paid, once again taking care to display the note in his wallet.

'Is good,' the barman muttered. 'You wait.'

Harry took the top off his beer then left the rest untouched. A puddle of dampness from his glass began to spread across the varnished wood in front of him, while in the reflection of the smudgy mirror he examined the other punters. He learned nothing except that a good number of them were excessive and even desperate drinkers, if their dull eyes and unsteady hands were to be believed, but did desperation make them more or less likely candidates as kidnappers? He couldn't tell. And perhaps the barman wasn't to be trusted, anyway. After a while Harry arched his eyebrows in impatience. 'Is good,' the reply came back once more.

Then two men who were sitting at the back of the bar got up to leave, emptying their glasses and pulling on their jackets, but as they passed behind Harry they stopped, and stood either side of him at the bar. The barman exposed his chipped tooth. 'My money,' he demanded. Harry knew it could be a set-up, a mugging in the making, the easiest way in the world to deprive him of his money, but he had no choice. He opened his wallet, so wide that they could all see he had only a single large note in it, and slid it across the bar. The barman grabbed it in the same moment that one of the men touched Harry's sleeve and turned towards the door.

The newcomers were younger than Harry, dark, very Latin, as Harry knew most Romanians were, unkempt, and seemingly fit. His excitement mounted, along with his caution. He would have to be careful with these two, no matter what they intended. One led him to the door while the other followed close behind. Parked directly outside was an old white Transit van with battered bodywork, and faded lettering on its side suggesting it had once been used by a food-delivery company in Germany. The engine was already running, pouring out a stream of oily smoke as the two men opened the rear door and pushed Harry inside. They followed him, closed the door, and said not a word as they were driven off into the night.

It was only after they had turned the first corner that one of the men drew a gun on him.

CHAPTER TWENTY-THREE

Sean hobbled out into the street as the Transit van drove off leaving an acrid cloud of badly burned diesel. The street lighting in these parts was poor, and his eyesight old, and he couldn't get the registration details, but that wasn't so important. He fished out his new phone and switched to the tracking app that Harry had installed that afternoon, the software that linked his phone with Harry's and recorded each other's location by using updates from GPS and WiFi access points. A street map of Trieste flashed up on the screen; Sean was relieved to see a small avatar moving away from the point at which he was standing. It was heading south, towards the seafront. He studied it carefully as the avatar moved slowly through the grid of streets. There was no rush. If Harry's plan worked, his phone would lead Sean straight to him.

—◊◊◊—

They searched Harry thoroughly, took away all the contents of his pockets, including his phone and wallet, then threw a blanket over him so that he could see nothing, but they didn't harm or threaten him, apart from waving a gun in his face. And although he was travelling blind, the sounds he could hear told their own story. The traffic remained heavy, slow-moving, suggesting they were still in the city centre, and he could hear voices aplenty from the pavement. The van creaked and complained at every opportunity, its best years far behind it, and as they drove on Harry grew relieved, for clearly this was no simple mugging, they could have done that inside the van then dumped him on any backstreet. It seemed these men were interested in more than a few hundred euros. Harry estimated they hadn't been driving more than ten minutes when the van began to slow, whining down through the gears, pulling off the main road and onto streets where the traffic was lighter. Then they were reversing along what was a narrow alleyway, judging from the sound. They stopped, someone was banging on the door, Harry was dragged out, not violently but still swathed in his blanket, across a small rubble-strewn yard then through a creaking door before being hustled up two flights of stairs. He knew from the hollow echo that the property they were in was empty, and from the glimpses of builders' rubbish at his feet that it was under reconstruction. He wasn't surprised to discover, when at last the blanket was pulled from his head, that he was in a room of raw plaster walls and naked pipework, strewn with builders' gear and with nothing but a single bare bulb for light. In addition to the two who had brought him here there were two others; they were all armed, and all those arms were pointing directly at him.

They searched him once again, this time more thoroughly, took his belt and his footwear. They bound his hands in front of him with his belt, not tightly but sufficient to ensure he could pull no surprises, and the inspection was intimate enough to leave his trousers flopping around his ankles.

'What did the bastard have on him?' Cosmin demanded.

'Only these,' Sandu replied, holding out a wallet, pen, loose change, wristwatch and phone.

They spoke in rich Latin tones that Harry found easy on the ear, even if he understood no more than a few words of the language. Good morning, good evening, good night, please, thank you, more wine, cheers – a menu of words he'd picked up on a night out with a hard-drinking Romanian delegation during a visit to NATO headquarters in Brussels. He couldn't follow any of this conversation but he knew what Cosmin was about. The Romanian inspected his shoes carefully before tossing them to one side, took the pen apart and threw its pieces after the shoes, grabbed the wallet, emptied out the small amount of beer money it still contained, ripped open the lining to see if anything else was hidden inside. He did the same with Harry's coat. Then he picked up the phone. Cosmin looked at it suspiciously, turning it over in his hands; he'd had enough trouble with phones. He didn't want to mess around with it in case it sent some sort of signal, but he knew that many phones could be tracked even when they were supposedly switched off.

'What do you think, Nelu?' he demanded.

'Get rid of it,' Nelu replied.

Harry watched as they talked. He could tell that these were serious men, tough, not fools, and not amateurs. He sat propped against the wall, his hands tied, struggling to drag his trousers up his legs, surrounded by armed men, knowing they would be happy to kill him, and knowing in his own turn that he would have to kill every one of them.

Cosmin and Nelu finished their discussion about the phone. It had not been switched on. Cosmin placed it on a workbench and began walking around it, staring. Then he took a heavy hammer, raised it high above his head and beat the phone to fragments.

That was when Sean's tracking signal went blank.

—ᴍ—

'What the fuck you want?' Cosmin demanded roughly, at last turning his attention to Harry.

'The boy.'

'Talk.'

'Can I get out of this?' Harry asked, holding up his bound wrists.

'Fuck you.'

'OK, I'm a friend of the boy's family. They asked me to come here to do two things. To make sure the boy is still alive. And to make sure he is released safely when the ransom is paid.'

'How you do that?'

'The ransom will not be paid until I talk to them over your Skype link. I will make sure the money is paid in the way you want, and also that the boy is released at the same time. Everyone goes home happy.'

Cosmin started nodding thoughtfully. The mention of Skype was some sort of proof that this man had a connection with the family, which meant he might be useful. It also meant he could be seriously dangerous. He wandered across to inspect Harry more carefully, bent over him, examined the wound on his face. Harry's nose filled with garlic and stale sweat.

Cosmin appeared satisfied. He straightened up. 'What is your name?'

'My name is Harry Jones.'

Harry didn't even have time to scream as Cosmin's boot hit him flush on the chin. His senses were swirling, tumbling over and over in a remorseless current, then they began closing down, drowning. Just before he passed out he realized that these people knew who he was. Then he gave up the struggle to stay afloat and his world went black.

—⁓—

Sean had decided that the tracker solution Harry had insisted on had severe limitations. The first problem was that, for some reason he didn't understand, it had given up the ghost. The second was that although he had followed the marker until the moment it disappeared from the screen, its accuracy in the dense inner city left a lot to be desired. In fact, many of the smaller streets and alleyways weren't even marked, and for a moment Sean panicked. He was no longer a young man, even at the best of times he had little faith in his abilities with things technical. Every muscle and joint in his body was screaming at him and he was entirely alone, without even a dog to lick his boots.

Yet the signal had given out somewhere in the Old City, that unmistakable maze of twists and turns, alleyways and side streets that was to be found only in this quarter, so it was here that Sean came. His hobbling was getting worse; his knee had taken a sharp knock when Harry had thrown him out of the path of the delivery van and it was making its misery felt. It was swelling, stiffening, so much so that he was forced to purchase a walking stick, a twisted hardwood cane with a gnarled, heavy head like a shillelagh. It made him more mobile but did nothing to lessen the pain, and he found the pavements of the Old City a challenge. This part of town was built against a hill, on top of which stood an ancient fort and the somewhat less ancient cathedral of San Giusto, and down from which tumbled a chaos of medieval passageways. Hard walking for any elderly man, let alone one with a dodgy knee. Every street tested his strength. He passed up and down, searching for what he wasn't quite sure, hoping to discover a battered white van tucked away behind every corner even though many of the alleys and passageways were absurdly narrow, barely wide enough for two donkeys to pass, and some even smaller than that. But he could find no sign of Harry.

The restaurants and bars began to close; the craft shops were already dark, most of the other buildings hiding behind their shutters. The Old City was closing its eyes, falling asleep. Sean found himself walking through the central Via del Teatro for the third time when he stumbled on a paving stone and almost tripped. His knee erupted in protest, leaving him bent over his stick, sobbing in pain. He was exhausted, cold, he knew he had to rest. There was nothing more he could do tonight. With an awkward and tender step, he shuffled his way back to his refuge in the car.

—∿—

'I have booked your ticket home,' Simona said as he came into the bedroom. She used her office voice, tinged with sadness, as though this was business. She pushed the covers distractedly away, exposing her naked body.

As he saw her stretched out on the bed D'Amato's cheeks flushed with anticipation even as some other part of him filled with guilt. 'You know I must go home for Christmas. But I'll be back soon.'

'When?' she asked, trying to pretend it was a matter totally without significance. He knew she was playing, teasing; it was her way.

'As soon as I can.' He began ripping off his clothes. They had agreed to go out to dinner, but he was late, again, and if he had to starve for this woman he knew every stab of hunger would be worth it.

'You're always in such a rush, Francesco.'

'I am sorry, my little bird.'

She stared in accusation. 'And you haven't even had time to get presents for your children.'

'I know.'

'So I have bought you some. The things they want.' She waved in the direction of a small pile of packages wrapped in colourful paper that sat on a side table.

His eyes grew wider still. 'You are truly amazing,' he gasped in admiration. Did this woman not have everything a man wanted in a lover? 'But . . . how do you do all this? How do you know what they want?'

'Simple. Your e-mail. You should never have told me your password.' And now she laughed.

'You can run my entire life!' he exclaimed, dropping his shorts.

'But, Francesco, I do. Except you must buy your own presents for your wife. I think we must draw a line somewhere, no?'

'Christmas! Four days. So close. I lose track of it all, there is so little time,' he complained, throwing himself onto the bed beside her.

'Which is why I have also bought your present for me.'

As she laughed, he kissed her and he began to stroke her

body, watching in timeless awe as he saw it coming to life.

'So what do you want for Christmas from me, Francesco?' She was breathing on his body, ruffling the hairs on his chest.

'You know what I want,' he gasped, losing all trace of judgement as her lips began to nibble their way slowly down his body.

—⁂—

Terri was staring into the flame of her candle at the window when J.J. arrived home. He threw his jacket onto the back of a chair; it slipped, fell to the floor, he didn't bother picking it up. That was out of character, he was usually so particular about his clothes.

'I've done it, got everything in place,' he said, yet it sounded like an expression of defeat. He collapsed into a chair opposite her.

Without being asked she got up and poured him a drink.

'Thank you,' he whispered, surprised, as he took the glass, grateful. It was the first thing either of them had done for the other in days. He sipped, feeling the whiskey cut through his exhaustion. 'I had to take the last quarter-million from Sopwith-Dane. Thought you should know. A loan. I told him I could offer no security, he said his instructions were that it didn't matter.' He paused while the thought hovered between them. 'It's time to decide, Terri. Do we pay the ransom?'

'How can we say no?'

'It will cost us everything we have.'

'And if we don't, it will cost us even more.'

He stared deep into his glass. She thought she could see a tear fall, splashing into the whiskey. 'I agree.' The voice seemed to come from far away.

'Can't we rebuild it all, J.J.?'

It seemed to take all of his remaining strength to drag his eyes up from his drink and look at her, his wife of seventeen years. 'I'm not sure,' he said, 'I think it may be too late for that.'

—⚒—

When Harry regained consciousness it was still dark. He had been brought to a different room, dragged there judging by the grazing he felt on his back, a room that was higher up the building, with a mansard ceiling – the attic, he assumed. He could see very little, tasted blood in his mouth from a split lip. He tried to stretch but found himself shackled by his wrists to a steel joist. His thoughts were scrambled, like a scattered herd, and it took him some time to round them up.

They knew who he was. One mention of his name and it had all fallen apart, and there was only one person he could blame for that, from whom the information could have leaked and put these thugs on their guard. Inspector D'Amato.

Harry felt his first nibble of despair. There was no one to help him, no one even looking out for him, apart from an old Irishman with a dodgy leg who couldn't even cross the bloody road without almost killing himself – which meant Harry was on his own, except, as the first blush of a grey dawn began to squeeze through the windows at either end of the room, he discovered he wasn't entirely alone. As his eyes and senses adjusted, he saw on the other side of the room the outline of another figure, shackled like him, stretched out on the floor and asleep. He stared into the half-light, and made out the pale but distinctive features of a young man.

It was his first sight of Ruari. His son.

—ᴡ—

Harry must have fallen asleep, for he woke some time later to find someone hissing at him. It was Ruari, from across the room.

'Hey! Hey!' he was calling softly. 'My name's Ruari Breslin.'

'I know.'

It was still early, not yet full daylight. Harry struggled to see his son, even from a distance of no more than ten feet, but that might have had something to do with the maelstrom that was gathering in his eyes. The boy was older than his photographs, of course, with a bandaged hand, a bent nose, a grime-smeared face and almost a month's worth of youthful hair on his cheeks. Harry's chin, too, the same stubborn set of the jaw. And his mother's eyes.

'Who are you?' Ruari whispered.

Who was he? What sort of damned-fool question was that? I'm your father, you little idiot! Your bloody father! But there was no way Ruari could know, or should discover that, not right now, not here. It would be something for later.

'Did my dad send you?' Ruari asked, eagerly, and Harry twisted inside. How many battles was it possible to fight all at once?

'I'm a friend of your family. I've come to get you out of here.'

'Great start.'

'I've found you, haven't I?' Harry replied, feeling pained by the teenage sarcasm, but hurt far more by knowing it was entirely justified. 'Thanks, Dad,' would have been so much better. But at least the boy's reaction showed that he wasn't cowed, that even after everything he'd gone through he still had a sharp edge.

Any further discussion was cut short as a figure loomed in the doorway and switched on the light. It was Sandu, his hand resting on the pistol at his hip. 'Hey, *bastarzi*! Shut up,' he snarled, 'or you get nothing to eat but piss and wind for breakfast.' He glared at them, checking their bonds, then cast them into semi-darkness once more before disappearing back into the adjoining room.

Harry nodded in the guard's direction. 'How many?' he mouthed at Ruari.

Ruari held up five fingers.

Not bad odds, as these things went. Pity he was so

tightly shackled, and the armed guard just feet away. Harry had been in worse spots, of course. Problem was, just at the moment, he couldn't remember when.

—∿—

Sean woke with the dawn, and groaned. He'd fallen into a deep sleep, in need of every minute of it, but during the night his immobile knee had swollen all the more and was now so stiff it would not bend. At this rate he'd have trouble simply falling out of the car, let alone chasing kidnappers. He tried swinging his leg round and cried out in pain. He sat still for a moment, panting, focusing, cursing, feeling every one of his near-seventy years and a dozen more besides, knowing he had to try again. By the time he'd succeeded in twisting and levering his body out of the car, his cheeks were moist with shame for his uselessness. He placed his injured leg on the ground, put a little weight on it, gasped in agony, even though he had his stick. Jesus, Mary and Joseph, it felt like he'd been feckin' knee-capped. Knee-capped, him! Suddenly he had an image in his mind of Harry, and the bastard was laughing at him.

He straightened himself up to his full height of five foot ten – or was it less than that now, at his age? It had been so long since it mattered, so long since anything much mattered, except this. 'To hell with you, Mr Harry Bloody Jones,' he muttered, and with clenched teeth began to hobble down the uneven paving into the Old City.

379

—ᴍ—

It was to be a day of reckoning, a day that must inevitably result in someone's death, yet for Sean it got off to an inauspicious start as he tapped his uncertain way through the streets of the Old City, hoping to see by daylight something he had missed the previous night, and gratified that as he moved his knee seemed to ease a little. But still he found no clue. They were here, somewhere, buried inside this maze, but he had no idea where.

It was the troubadour in the Via San Sebastiano who gave him his first gleam of inspiration. The man was dressed in a simple dark suit of many stains and had bells on his hat, drumsticks strapped to his feet, cymbals on his elbows, a horn at his lips and a stringed instrument in his hands. The level of noise he made was extraordinary as every sound bounced off the nearby walls before running off into the surrounding streets. Sean sipped coffee as he watched the man's pointed beard twitching and marking time to every beat. After he had finished his repertoire he moved on to a different pitch, and soon Sean could hear the clash of the cymbals and beat of the drum once more snaking through the town.

When he was young Sean had possessed an exceptionally fine voice. Even while the Christian Brothers had been beating him for using his left hand, and four-fold when they found him using it beneath the covers, they'd allowed him to sing solos in the school chapel. 'And you just

380

remember, while you're being at it, lad, that Jesus sits at God's right hand, not his left,' Father Benedict had told him as he had whipped him yet again. Sean's voice had been a beautiful, soaring treble that deepened to a bar-filling tenor with age. Now, as the coffee warmed his throat, he was well aware that he hadn't used it for a while, like so much else, he reflected ruefully, but it was never too late. 'Time to dust it down and give it a bit of an airing, Sean, me boy,' he muttered to himself. So he took up the pitch in the doorway of the abandoned building, recently vacated by the troubadour, and began. He looked every bit the street singer. His trousers had been through several adventures, his shoes had lost their shine, the eyes were raw, he had two days of grey stubble on his chin and he was leaning on his stick. But when he dropped his jacket to the pavement in front of him and started to sing, his voice reached into every corner of this narrow square. He began with 'Danny Boy', following it with 'The Wearing o' the Green', a rebel ballad, with its searing expressions of hatred for the English, and soon he was back home, many years younger, and far away from this strange and dangerous place.

By the time he finished he had collected several euro coins. He sang another song, then moved his pitch, and did the same several times over in the ensuing hours. He couldn't linger in any one place, didn't have time, not if he were to have any chance of covering the troubled streets in this part of town. No one had time, not today.

—ʍ—

Harry still clung to a distant hope that he might be able to bluff his way out. When Cosmin appeared, rubbing his finger around his gums and sipping from a mug of coffee, Harry confronted him. 'What the hell is this?' he demanded, waving his manacled wrists. 'You don't understand.'

He got nothing in reply but the toe of Cosmin's boot aimed expertly between his ribs.

'I came here to help you,' Harry gasped, doubling up with pain as the other man passed nonchalantly by.

Cosmin continued picking his teeth until suddenly he seemed to have found something that surprised him. He stopped, stared suspiciously at his finger, then turned. 'You want to help? OK, you help. Nelu!' he cried, summoning the computer operator, who came tumbling out from the next room. 'We talk. With Little Shit's mummy and daddy.'

In Notting Hill, Hiley had moved into a spare room of the Breslin home. With the deadline approaching and the money at last in place, they would need his expertise to nail down the final details, and it was he who answered the summons of Skype. J.J. and Terri hovered close at hand. They were surprised to see that the kidnappers had activated the video link, and their surprise turned to alarm when they saw Harry's bruised face, with his mouth gagged, emerging from the screen. The picture was very tight, offering no background except a meaningless wall.

'Have you got my fucking money?' Cosmin began. No preamble. Just aggression.

'We must have proof of life, that was the deal,' Hiley replied, struggling as he watched Harry, knowing what he saw implied disaster.

'Proof of life? I give you proof of life,' Cosmin snarled.

They could not see, could only hear, a boot being buried in Harry's ribs. His face contorted in agony.

'See! Alive,' Cosmin mocked.

'The boy. What about the boy?'

'He's here,' Cosmin replied. 'Isn't he?' He jerked up Harry's head by the hair until he was staring directly into the camera.

Harry, with his mouth bound, could do no more than wince and nod.

'We still need to see him,' Hiley insisted.

'When I see my money.'

Hiley turned to J.J. and Terri. Whatever hope there had been of Harry releasing Ruari was now gone. They had no option. Slowly J.J. nodded.

'We have your money. Five million euros,' Hiley said.

'Good. But that five million is for the boy. We now have your friend, too. Another million. The price is now six million.' And he laughed. Sure, this Harry Jones could help all right, by getting them more money. Now they had Simona on board they had to find an extra share, and six million split so neatly between them all.

'The deal was five million!' Hiley protested.

'Now it is six.'

'We can't! We simply cannot. It's not possible,' J.J. gasped from the background.

'That's what you said before, about five.'

'But . . .'

'I give you time. Until this evening. You have many friends. Call them.'

'Listen. We cannot do this.' Hiley's voice was adamant and slow, hitting every syllable, hoping it might get the message across.

'This evening. Tonight,' Cosmin repeated. 'If you don't . . .'

Suddenly Harry's head had been jerked up again, exposing his neck, and a large blade was being drawn slowly across his throat.

'Mr Jones will show you tonight what happens to the boy on Christmas Day. Unless you pay. You understand?'

'I understand you very well,' Hiley said grimly.

The connection went dead.

CHAPTER TWENTY-FOUR

As the hours passed, the guards relaxed, sent out for pizzas – another benefit of being in the inner city, they no longer had to put up with the malevolent muck Sandu passed off as cooking. Even the prisoners got a slice. And when the pizza was finished and the cartons thrown into a corner, Cosmin led the other Romanians off for a game of cards, leaving just one, Puiu, the electrician, on guard. Harry spent the time inspecting his manacles, but they were secure and firmly locked. No way out. As the hours drew on towards evening, he sat propped against the wall, looking across at his unknowing son, feeling the bite of fear.

When Puiu began to look bored Harry tried to talk with Ruari, but all he got for his efforts was a Romanian curse and another kicking. So they sat in silence. The two windows at either end of the room remained closed, the sounds of the city muffled, but they could hear the bells, the buzz of noisy scooters, and occasionally even make out shouts from the streets below, yet up here in the attic it was a one-way process; Harry could have screamed his head off and it would have been heard by no one but pigeons and seagulls.

Then Harry heard the strains of the song.

'Oh, Danny Boy, the pipes, the pipes are calling, From glen to glen, and down the mountain side . . .'

He stiffened. He'd never heard Sean sing, but how many other daft bastard Irishmen were out there on these streets?

'But come ye back, when summer's in the meadow . . .' The words bounced off the walls of the Old City ghetto, echoed upwards and crept into the room.

Sean had chosen his moment well, Puiu was taking a leak. Harry searched around desperately; he had to find some way of letting Sean know where they were, some means of making a racket, but there was nothing within reach, even of his feet, except for a couple of discarded takeaway boxes and a broom. On the workbench there was any number of useful items, a hammer, a bucket – God, he could have marched to war behind their noise – but they were hopelessly out of reach. The nearest tool was a scaffolding clamp, lying discarded on the floor and well beyond his grasp, the sort of thing he would gladly have used to beat out Cosmin's brains, if only he could stretch that far.

'And I am dead, as dead I well may be, You'll come and find the place where I am lying, And kneel and say an "Ave" there for me . . .'

He could hear Puiu pissing in the bowl; Harry doubted the man would stop to wash his hands. He was running out of time.

He was a good two feet short of the clamp, but by stretching himself full length on the floor he was able to hook his foot around the broom, which came tumbling towards him, and by grasping the handle between his knees and feet he was able to reach behind the clamp and sweep it towards him. But the bloody thing was heavy, obstinate, the broom kept brushing over it, and Harry could hear Puiu finishing in the bathroom. Yet with every awkward jerk of the broom head, the clamp scraped and inched its way across the bare floor, until at last, stretching to his limit, he hooked his toe inside it. Even as the figure of Puiu appeared in the doorway, Harry swung his leg and hurled the clamp across the room. It smashed through the window, accompanied by an explosion of glass that went clattering down into the street below, followed by a waterfall of splinters that sang out like wind chimes in a gale.

Harry knew he was taking a terrible risk with the retribution Puiu would inevitably wreak upon him, but what had he got to lose? Cosmin was planning to slit his throat in a few hours' time, and the man was a psychopath who took pleasure in keeping to his word. In any event, Puiu's wrath was tempered by concern; this screw-up had happened on his watch, while he wasn't watching, and he was all too aware that Cosmin's temper was best avoided. So Puiu decided he would play the whole thing down, explain it away as an accident, a stumble over all the crap that others left lying around the floor. After all, what did it matter, it wasn't as if anyone was storming up the stairs.

For the moment, he decided, it would be enough to remind this English prick of the pain that came with screwing around with a man like him. He started swinging his boot.

Harry had taken beatings all the way around the world, from West Africa to Afghanistan, some on home turf and even from Irishmen outside his own home in Mayfair, but never had he taken a bloody good kicking with such a sense of satisfaction.

—⁓—

It was a broken window, no cause for alarm, just one of many minor distractions in the Old City that disappeared as quickly as they came. But Sean heard it, the clatter of falling iron and the singing of tell-tale glass shards. Only trouble was, he couldn't find them. The maze of passageways was too confusing, filled with derelict homes and reconstruction sites where broken glass lay scattered on all sides, and where some of the alleys were so narrow it was impossible to see up to the windows on high. He knew that the sound could have come from only a handful of nearby streets, but although he hobbled back and forth and through them all, he couldn't be sure. So when he had exhausted himself foraging for signs that would not be found, he sat himself down in a derelict doorway at the heart of these cramped streets and alleys, rolled himself a cigarette, and waited. An old woman in threadbare woollen tights passed by and tried to sell him some mistletoe, but otherwise no one disturbed him.

But what did a kidnapper look like? Sean had seen two of them in the bar when they picked up Harry. Young, dishevelled, like a million others, and all male, he guessed. So he sat patiently, trying to translate the meanings of the graffiti on the walls, studying the little spirals of rubbish picked up by the wind, and casting a builder's eye over the half-finished streets around him.

It was Sandu he saw, one of the men from the bar, who had suddenly appeared through a fug of tobacco smoke and was walking down the street towards him. For a moment Sean was anxious – would Sandu recognize him, too? But Sandu was young, with all the arrogance of his few years, and to him Sean was nothing more than an old man on a doorstep, someone of no consequence. He strode past.

Sean didn't go after him. He didn't want to leave these streets, where Ruari was hidden, and anyway he couldn't have kept up, his leg was once again unbending iron. But within a few minutes Sandu had reappeared carrying a plastic bag of supplies, and this time Sean followed, hoisting himself up on his stick, trying to ignore his screaming knee. The Romanian didn't even bother looking behind him as he led Sean all the way to the safe house.

—✺—

With every hour and with increasing desperation, J.J. had been trying to make contact with Jimmy Sopwith-Dane, but the man was nowhere to be found. He tried the two

389

numbers for his office, and even his home phone, although it was an unlisted number and supposedly unobtainable, but such things had never worried the news desk of a newspaper. He left messages everywhere, yet there was no reply. The news desk even sent a messenger to the City but found his office closed. It was as if Sloppy himself had disappeared along with everyone else.

It was well into the short December afternoon before any of his frantic messages were returned. Sloppy's secretary called. She apologized for not doing so earlier, but she and the rest of the skeleton staff had all been out to lunch, which judging by her speech had been an indulgent one. Of course, Christmas. And that's why J.J. couldn't talk to Sloppy, because he was off trekking through some sticky Asian jungle and completely, utterly, hopelessly out of touch.

'But you don't understand,' J.J. pleaded, 'I must get in contact with him right now.'

'I'm so sorry, sir, but you don't understand. You can't.'

Sloppy was the one chance they had of being able to raise the money which might save Harry's life, and that chance was being paddled up some impossibly muddy river in Borneo.

—⁓—

Sandu looked carefully to either side before he entered the building, but peered straight through the bent man leaning on his stick a little way down the alley. Sean smiled grimly; maybe at last he'd found one advantage in getting old. The building into which Sandu had disappeared was a run-down town house of crumbling stucco that had once been gentrified, but had since gone through many periods of decline and neglect. The site was fenced off from the alley with mesh barriers, but carelessly, they didn't meet in the middle. Immediately behind them was a tall Venetian door of old oak that had once been painted green and whose missing glass panels had been replaced by stray off-cuts of chipboard. The door was secured by a formidable padlock, but the hasp to which it was attached had been unscrewed. To those who knew, it was open house.

The building was five storeys, including the converted attic, but the windows on the top floor couldn't be seen from the alleyway below, no matter how far Sean crooked his neck. Yet on the rubble at his feet was broken window glass. He knew this was the right place.

He'd found it. But what was he to do? In usual circumstances a call to the police would have settled everything, but the old Irishman in Sean trusted policemen very little and Inspector D'Amato not at all. He remembered the last time D'Amato was supposed to have resolved the situation, at the farmhouse, and in particular he remembered the corpses that had been left behind. No, this was family, and family troubles where Sean came from were sorted without running to others for help. That had been the rule for hundreds of years, it's what had kept Ireland together, just as it had equally successfully kept Ireland apart. The Irish way. Sean would have to do the job himself.

Yet how, what was he to do? He had only one good leg, no weapon, and no idea what lay waiting for him inside. He knew there would be only one way to find out, and he'd only get the one chance. It had to be tonight. Before he ran out of strength, or courage, or found himself picked up by the police.

It was already growing dark, the alleyway was poorly lit by a single distant lamp, but as he craned his neck he could see a glow of light from the top floor. He was up there, Ruari. Sean knew the boy would die unless he got him out, might even die in the attempt, but better a half chance than none at all. He had to try. 'Jesus, Mary and Joseph, give me strength,' he found himself muttering. Old Irish habits die hard. And old Irish men die hard, too, he told himself. Anyway, what did an old man have to lose?

In the rapidly fading light, he studied the building one more time, analysing its construction, imagining what it might be like inside, working out what he was going to do – going to *try* to do. He'd done it once before, for one of his insurance scams. Which meant he knew just how great was the risk he was about to take. With one last crick of the neck upwards, he shuffled on.

He found what he was looking for three streets away, on a small parking lot at the back of the Grand Hotel Duchi d'Aosta. A group of youths were gathered around their scooters, exchanging cigarettes, working out how they might spend their evening.

'Anyone speak Irish?' Sean asked, interrupting their chatter.

At first he was met with suspicion but then one of them replied, 'English. A little.'

'Then I suppose that'll have to do,' he sighed. He produced a €50 note from his pocket. 'I've run out of petrol,' he said, 'and as you can see I'm not much of one for the walking. I wonder, if I gave you this, could you bring me back one of those plastic cans of fuel? And keep the change?'

The youth began to nod and smile. There would be plenty of change from that.

'And if I gave you another note when you got back, could you be bringing me two?'

They were all nodding now, their English and their evening greatly improved. Sean handed over the first note. 'Five minutes,' the youth said, grinning as he started up his scooter.

—ɯ—

The computer screen sprang into life once more. Cosmin appeared wearing a mask.

'You got the money?'

'You must give us time,' Hiley replied, already pleading.

'I give you time. Now time is up. I don't think you bastards take me seriously.'

'We do! Of course, we do. It's just—'

But Cosmin wasn't listening. 'Screw you! I give you warning. Now I show you what happens when you not listen.'

Harry knew the time had come. They were going to kill him. Yet the moment of greatest danger was also one of opportunity, when they would release him from his tether to the steel joist. His hands would still be bound, but it would give him a chance, so he hoped. But they knew what was in his mind. They had their guns and boots ready, and the broomstick, and after they had kicked the wind out of him they threaded it behind his back and through the crook of his elbows so that he was completely powerless, couldn't even curl up to protect himself. He was kneeling, defenceless, when another boot came flying in, straight into his groin, and he fell to the floor retching in pain. Tears began flooding from his eyes and nose, he looked up to see the masked figure of Cosmin towering over him.

'You'll be the first one I kill,' Harry cursed, but he was choking and the threat disappeared in an eruption of phlegm. Cosmin laughed, mocking, then he dragged Harry by the broomstick towards the webcam that Nelu was placing in position. They knelt him down in front of it, he didn't resist, he couldn't. He was going to die trussed like a chicken.

'You want blindfold?' Cosmin asked.

Harry shook his head.

'Good. So you watch yourself die.'

CHAPTER TWENTY-FIVE

Sean let himself into the house with great care. It wasn't easy, walking with a stick while carrying two cans of petrol. He had to put them down in order to open the old door, inch by inch, groan and creak, expecting that any moment its groaning and creaking would bring some scurrying guard, because he was sure there had to be a guard. Open the door, just a foot or so, creep inside with the first can of fuel, go back outside, fetch the second can, return, close the door, breathe again. It seemed to take forever yet he'd got almost nowhere.

It took even longer to adjust his old eyes to what he found within the house, for there was very little ambient light. He was in a hallway so filled with builder's clutter that it threatened to trip him at every step, and there was a staircase hugging the wall as it wound its way upwards. Sean was relieved to see it had a banister rail and was constructed of stone, no ancient creaking wood to betray him. And he didn't mind the clutter, either, with its off-cuts of wood, old pots of paint, plastic sheeting and even a gas cylinder, all excellent combustible material. He poured the contents of one of the cans over the lot until petrol was slopping at his feet. Then, leaning on the banister, he began climbing, dragging his bad leg behind him.

There was a guard, as he suspected. Toma was sitting on the first-floor landing, his automatic pistol beside him, yet his attention was not on the staircase but upwards. Sean saw him clearly from the turn in the stair, the guard's face bathed in the light from above as he tried to make sense of the noises and snatches of conversation drifting down, wondering if they had done it yet. Because Toma knew that Harry was going to die. Cosmin enjoyed killing, would even give up his share of a million extra euros for it, the bastard. He was unbalanced, clinically insane, Toma thought. He was glad to be getting out of this mess in a day or two.

Toma was wrapped up in his thoughts. He never heard the gentle kiss of soles on stone as Sean crept up behind him, or the rustle of a sleeve as the shillelagh was raised high, or the swish of parting air as it came down with such force on the side of his skull that it killed him without a cry.

—m—

'We have to talk about this, we want to help you,' Hiley was saying, pleading, really, but his voice carried no confidence. His eyes were fixed on the screen that was bursting to its edges with the image of Harry, and Cosmin standing beside him. Harry appeared dejected, resigned, his shoulders slumped forward in defeat, but his eyes were fixed on

Ruari, who sat directly opposite him against the other wall, his face fixed in horror. Harry tried to reassure him with all sorts of messages that he wrapped up in his stare, but which he knew Ruari had no hope of understanding. Yet if he were to die, Harry thought, he could do it in worse ways than staring into the boy's eyes. Not that he planned to die, he still intended somehow to spring from their clutches and overpower them all, even though he was bound and they were armed, his legs were numb from the kneeling, and he'd been in this business long enough to know that sometimes plans just don't work. So, for the moment, he kept staring at his son.

'Now, you tell me one more time,' Cosmin was growling, 'you got five million, yes?'

'Yes.'

'But you not got six million.'

'No.'

'So now I show you I am serious businessman and this is serious business. You mess with me, so this one will die. And if I not get my five million by tomorrow, the kid die, too.'

'But you said Christmas Day. Tomorrow's the twenty-third,' Hiley protested. It was a pathetic objection, he knew, but he was desperate to keep the other man talking. 'Just give us a little more time!'

'You got five million, so you give it to me now. I send instructions. Anyway, Christmas Day fucking banks are all closed, no?'

He began laughing, hideously and almost uncontrollably. Hiley squirmed and tried to find something else to say, yet suddenly his thoughts dried to dust as a blade appeared in Cosmin's hand, catching the light as it twisted. From behind Hiley's shoulder, Terri let forth a cry of dread. Harry's hair had been grabbed, his head wrenched upwards, his throat exposed, the blade pressing hard against it.

J.J. buried his head in his hands, Terri ran from the room, Hiley was still pleading that they could sort things out when Cosmin at last stopped his insane laughter.

'Now you shut the fuck up. And you watch your friend die.'

———

Sean was exhausted by the time he made it to the top of the staircase. There was a moment when he thought he'd never make it, dragging his leg, and the petrol can, along with Toma's automatic pistol. By the last step he was perspiring profusely, the sweat running into his eyes, so at first he couldn't make out what he saw through the doorway that as yet had no door. He saw Harry, on his knees. Ruari, too! And something unspeakable was about to happen. He could try to use the pistol but he wasn't sure how, he hadn't had a chance to inspect it in the darkness of the stairwell, and even if he took out one or two of them it wouldn't be enough. Anyway, he was a bookkeeper, not a gunman; he knew his limits. Instead, he unscrewed the cap of the remaining can and tipped it gently onto its side until he saw a steady trickle of petrol. Then he stepped into the room. At first no one saw him. All eyes were on Harry.

'Well, bless me, I'm glad to have found you all, every man-jack of you,' he announced with a theatrical flourish, holding his head at an awkward angle to one side like a fool. 'I'm guessing this belongs to you.' He held out the pistol innocently by its barrel.

Everyone in the room turned towards him. 'Who the hell are you?' Cosmin growled.

'Me? The name's Sean Breslin,' he replied guilelessly. 'I'm the boy's grandfather, so I am. And I found this thing downstairs, thought I'd be returning it to you.' He tottered on his cane and placed the pistol on a nearby chair before straightening himself in a way that suggested every muscle in his body was screaming in objection. 'But don't let me disturb you,' he said, nodding towards Harry. 'Go ahead. Feckin' Englishman. I'd give you a hand myself if only I could stand up straight.'

They watched this innocent, doddering old man, spell-bound.

'But there's just one thing,' Sean began again, patting his pockets in search of something. 'When a man's about to die, he deserves a final smoke, doesn't he? That's the rules.'

They were still watching transfixed as he produced a cigarette and a book of matches, lit the cigarette and sucked in a first lungful of nicotine with an expression of content-ment that suggested it solved all the problems of the world. He took another, shorter drag, then inspected the burning tip, blowing on it before he tossed it over his shoulder onto the landing.

—⚬—

Sean had no clear plan. He knew he wouldn't be able to rescue Ruari on his own. He needed some outrageous stroke of luck, a quixotic roll of the celestial dice if he were to have any chance. But while he had no clear plan, he knew the kidnappers had a plan, one that was detailed and fixed, and because of that it was vulnerable, and he could throw it into chaos. So that is what he did.

By the time he threw the cigarette onto the landing, enough fuel had spilled, slurped and dripped its way down the stairwell to create instant chaos. Much of the petrol in the lower hallway had already evaporated, leaving the stairwell filled with highly inflammable fumes, and now a river of flame was running down to meet it. It all exploded in a most satisfactory fireball – just as it had when he'd torched a debt-ridden development back in Dundalk to claim the insurance.

In expectation of this eruption of anarchy, Sean had already taken a step to one side, so that he was out of the direct path of the fire as it roared up the stairs and burst through the attic doorway. It was Cosmin who took the worst of the blast, knocked off his feet while it passed almost harmlessly above Harry's head.

The chaos grew. Sean picked up the pistol and tried to fire it. Nothing happened, the safety was on, but now he was standing in the light he was quickly able to locate it and began firing, wildly and like the total amateur he was, and a fraction of a second before Sandu recovered his wits and began firing his gun, too. Sandu was still firing when one of Sean's bullets hit him in the heart and threw him to the ground.

It was Harry who had reacted to the fireball first. Even as lurid flames were swirling above his head he threw himself sideways to the floor, knocking the broom handle through the crook of his elbows and giving him back some mobility, although his legs were dead from all the kneeling. Cosmin lay stunned beside him on the floor; Harry grabbed the pistol at his belt and began firing. Soon bullets were flying on all sides.

No one was ever entirely sure whose gun shot Puiu and Nelu. Sean was still firing but so was Sandu, wildly, blindly, even as he lay dying, his finger frozen on the trigger. It might have been him who shot his friends; Harry finished him off with the last round in the magazine.

There was no time for relief. Fire was already coursing through the building, taking hold, the stairwell was filled with tall flames and greedy, choking smoke. There would be no way out down there.

'Did you think this one through, Sean?' Harry demanded, trying to manoeuvre himself onto his reluctant knees.

'The roof. There'll be some sort of access,' Sean replied as a gas canister exploded down below, thrusting a fresh blast of flame and acrid smoke into the room.

But there was a cry of alarm. It was Ruari. As Harry turned he found Cosmin lunging towards him, his face twisted in torment, a cry on his lips and his knife in his hand. Harry still had his hands bound and could barely move, while Cosmin had weight, speed and a weapon. As fights went, this was unlikely to be an even one.

Yet as Cosmin charged, Ruari threw himself forward, feet first, tangling with Cosmin's ankles in a way that would have earned him a dismissal from any soccer pitch. The Romanian toppled like a huge oak, his full weight crashing directly on top of Harry.

For what seemed like an endless while, neither of them moved. Then Harry grunted, heaved the Romanian off him. Cosmin rolled over. His knife had buried itself deep between his ribs. He was still alive, his eyes flickering wildly, the breath rasping, but he could barely move, his entire body numbed by shock.

'I was never going to kill you, Mr Jones,' he blurted as Harry bent over him. 'All for show. You know the game.'

'Sure.'

'Please, help me. Don't let me die like this.' His eyes stuttered down to his wound, which was already beginning to seep alarming amounts of blood.

'Don't worry,' Harry reassured him, 'I guarantee the fire will kill you before you bleed to death.'

Cosmin began whimpering as Harry reached into his pocket to relieve him of the keys to Ruari's manacles. He moved across to the boy, released him, touched him, that first time. 'You saved my life, Ruari. Thank you.'

'You're welcome, Mr Jones,' he replied, innocently. 'But Granddad saved us both, didn't he?'

'Yes, but unless we get out of here in about thirty seconds, there won't have been much bloody point.'

Smoke was rising through the gaps in the floorboards, it was getting very difficult to breathe.

'What do you reckon, Sean?' Harry shouted across the room as he helped Ruari to his feet; the boy's muscles were weak, refusing to coordinate, and he almost fell again before Harry grabbed him.

'Try the next room. There has to be a roof access or skylight or something.' Sean waved them on. Strangely, he was sitting down, slumped against the wall. 'My feckin' knee,' he explained. 'It's killing me.'

'I'll be back for you, Sean,' Harry cried, hauling Ruari through to the next room where the guards had slept. There was a knife in there, which with the boy's help he used to free his wrists. And as Sean had promised, there was a trapdoor, in the middle of the ceiling. The cold fresh air hit Harry in the face as he forced it open, but already the smoke was chasing close behind, the fire seeking out this fresh source of oxygen. Out in the night air he could hear the sound of sirens, emergency vehicles, summoned to the blaze, and they came with great speed to a cramped, congested quarter like the Old City. But they wouldn't be there in time.

It was a struggle to get Ruari through the trapdoor. He

didn't have the strength to haul himself up, and Harry had barely enough to lift him, yet in the end it was done.

'Try to get onto the roof of the next building,' Harry instructed as Ruari stared down from above.

'Where's Granddad?'

'Right behind us.'

'But I don't see him.'

'You must get away from the fire.'

'No way. I'm not going anywhere without Granddad,' Ruari answered in a manner that said there was no point in Harry arguing the matter. 'And you promised to go back for him.'

Harry stared in admiration at his son. 'Then I suppose I'd better fetch him.'

Back in the room the smoke was much thicker, the floor-boards at the end already in flames. Sean was still sitting against the wall. Harry crawled to his side. 'Come on, you old Irish arsonist,' he muttered, grabbing him beneath the shoulders, but as soon as he tried to lift him he realized something was desperately wrong, and it had nothing to do with his knee. Sean was a dead weight, his eyes glazing, his skin sallow, and beneath his jacket Harry found a hideously neat and desperately serious bullet hole that was already making one hell of a mess of Sean's shirt. Their eyes met. There was nothing to be said. Neither of them was going to lie. Yet Sean saw the pain that had fallen upon Harry.

'What's the matter with you, Mr Jones, never seen an Irishman die before?'

Harry had no words. He'd been around death many times, but found nothing to say.

Then Ruari's voice came through the fire, calling for his granddad. It revived the old man. He grabbed Harry's sleeve, dragged him close, coughing, the words rattling in his throat, and not just from the smoke. 'You take care of that boy for me, you hear?'

There was something in his eye that Harry didn't understand. 'What do you mean?'

Sean held on to Harry all the tighter, pulled him closer still. 'I know he's your son.'

'But . . . how? Who told you?'

'You did. When you knocked me out of the way of that van and fell on top of me. First time I ever looked at you – you, as a man, as a member of the human race and not just as a feckin' Brit.' His breathing had grown desperately laboured, his chest pumping but taking in so little air. 'I looked into your eyes and I saw Ruari. That's when I knew.'

'And yet you still . . .'

'I've loved that lad all his life. No reason to stop because of you.' There was pride in his expression. Then he lost focus as pain from somewhere deep inside took hold and twisted his face.

'In another life, Sean, you and me, it would have been different.'

But already the pain had passed, and they both knew it would never return. A wry smile crept across the

Irishman's lips. 'I'll be keeping that place warm for you. See you in Hell, Mr Jones.' And he was gone.

—〜〜—

The fire was taking a firmer hold, the smoke blinding Harry. A floor joist gave way at the far end of the room with a roar of warning. Harry had to go, and he couldn't take Sean's body with him. He left it, crawled away, but when he looked back for the last time it seemed to him that the old man was still smiling.

He found Ruari peering down anxiously through the trapdoor. 'Granddad. Where's Granddad?'

'I'm sorry, Ruari. He didn't make it,' Harry said as he hauled himself up onto the roof.

Ruari was about to protest when there came a terrible groan from the dying building and a fountain of sparks burst through the open hatch. There could be no going back. Ruari was struggling, trying to peer down into the blaze, willing his grandfather to emerge, but Harry held him. 'He'd been shot, Ruari. He died in my arms, not in the fire,' Harry said as the boy sobbed in fury at the flames. 'Almost the last thing he said was that he loved you.'

'I know that,' the boy whispered.

'And right now, I think he'd want you to get off this roof.'

Lights from emergency vehicles were flashing from sur-rounding streets, more sirens were approaching, at last help was near at hand. 'Too bloody late as usual,' Harry

406

said. He and Ruari were clambering to safety on the neighbouring roof when a small access hatch opened at its far end and a figure climbed out. It was D'Amato.

'Mr Jones!' he called as he approached, advancing with care along the narrow gutter barely two shoes in width that stood between the sloping roof and the low parapet. 'And is this the boy? It's a miracle!'

'An Irish miracle,' Harry muttered, unimpressed by the policeman's new-found enthusiasm.

The Italian took Ruari's hand and shook it with considerable force. 'I am Inspector D'Amato and I am very pleased to see you!'

'Thank you, Inspector.'

'Forgive me for asking but did anyone . . . in there . . . ?' He was having trouble framing his question. 'Is there anyone else left?'

Harry shook his head. 'Not a soul, Inspector.'

Glints of strange excitement seemed to be dancing in the policeman's eye; Harry put it down to the reflection of the flames, and more than a passing dose of guilt.

'We must get you to safety,' D'Amato declared. 'You first, young man, I think.' He took Ruari's outstretched arm and led him with care along the narrow guttering until they had reached the access hatch. 'There is a ladder down from here,' he announced. 'It's old, not very safe. One at a time. When you get to the bottom you go straight down the staircase. Quickly, please, it is already a little too warm up here,' he instructed.

'But you and Mr Jones—'

'We will follow.'

Flames were eating through the other roof and Ruari needed no further encouragement. With D'Amato's help he located the ladder and in seconds had disappeared.

When D'Amato turned back from the access hatch and stood up, Harry was astonished to discover he was holding his gun. 'Your turn now, I think, Mr Jones.'

'What the—'

'I am sorry, but I cannot allow you to tell your story. You understand that, don't you?' He was standing in the cramped guttering, a little unsteadily, unseen from the streets below, vanishing and reappearing as he was caught in the flickering emergency lights, yet all the while the gun remained steady in his hand and fixed on Harry, who backed off a couple of steps. D'Amato edged after him.

'I intended none of this, Mr Jones, I beg you to believe me, but I have been very stupid. A woman. Yes, a Romanian woman, my secretary. You can imagine the details, and how impossible it will be for me if they come out, as they will if you ever tell your story. I will lose everything I have, my career, my family, all that I have ever lived for. You see, I have no choice. It is you or it is me.' Self-pity was beginning to flood into his voice.

'How the hell do you expect to get away with it?' Harry demanded, forced to shout above the growing roar of the fire. 'The boy has seen me, he knows I'm alive.'

'Ah, but it is very dangerous up here on this rooftop, anything might happen. And I have spent a lifetime listening to some very imaginative alibis; I think there will be little difficulty in inventing one that is suitable.'

'In cold blood? Your family must be very proud of you.'

'It is for my family that I am doing this! Please believe me, if there were any other way . . .' The self-pity had risen, he was all but sobbing in misery. 'Forgive me. But I must kill you.'

'Then you'll have to kill us both,' a voice came from behind him. D'Amato turned, awkwardly in the narrow gutter, and peered over his shoulder. It was Ruari.

'Please, no, not you,' D'Amato protested.

Harry edged a little closer, D'Amato twisted round yet again, unbalanced, in danger of toppling. He steadied himself, but with difficulty as he kept turning to face one, then the other.

'You may get one of us, you're unlikely to get us both,' Harry said, shuffling closer still.

D'Amato twisted back and forth frantically, thrusting with his gun, struggling to keep his footing as he tried to get them to back off. Suddenly he froze, staring at Ruari. Dear God, he was a family man, with his own son, little Vincenzo, waiting for him at home – a boy he hoped one day would grow to have the stature and courage of this young man. He couldn't kill him; it would be like killing his own.

D'Amato wasn't a man of profound character. He wanted to shoot himself but he couldn't do that, either. Instead his knees buckled and he collapsed onto the roof, where he lay letting forth a pitiful wail of despair.

CHAPTER TWENTY-SIX

Harry was desperate to be alone with Ruari, to have the opportunity to talk with him, but as soon as they emerged from the burning building they found themselves in the hands of the Italian police and medical support services. There wasn't a moment of peace to be found. In any event, what was Harry to say? The things he had on his mind weren't his decision alone. Better to wait until they were home.

The Italian authorities still had many more questions to ask, more gaps in the troubled story to fill, but none of it was going to happen over Christmas, so it was late the following afternoon when Harry and Ruari took their seats on the Cessna Citation executive jet that J.J. had chartered to bring them back home. Even then they weren't alone; a nurse and one of D'Amato's colleagues sat alongside, just in case. In case of what, Harry wasn't entirely certain. Ruari, with all the impossible energy of youth, was already showing a remarkable physical recovery kick-started by a couple of decent meals and a bucketful of ice cream. But there would be other wounds that would take longer to heal. He was slumbering now, as they climbed above the Alps and left the city lights of Trieste far behind.

Harry was less fortunate. As the adrenalin drained away, the effects of the repeated kickings and brutality made themselves felt, leaving him in considerable pain. He'd also picked up some first-degree burns to his back and shoulder. The doctor who had treated him had kept exclaiming in surprise as he discovered the patchwork of old injuries that covered so much of Harry's body. 'It seems you have a remarkable capacity for recovery,' the doctor had encouraged, running his fingers over old scars. But the truth was that Harry didn't recover as quickly as he once had. His body was talking to him, telling him it was time to change, to move on to different things. With Terri, perhaps? As he looked below and saw the peaks of the snow-smothered mountains bathed in brilliant moonlight, Harry realized how much was waiting for him at the end of this journey.

Ruari sat on the other side of the narrow cabin. He still called him Mr Jones. Harry had been going to object, suggest he call him Harry, but somehow that didn't seem right, either. Yes, so much sorting out to do. Harry sat back in the soft executive leather, closed his eyes, couldn't sleep. The strains of 'Danny Boy' kept slipping through his mind.

As soon as they landed at Biggin Hill airport, Harry discovered why the Italian police officer had accompanied them. They taxied to a halt in front of the squat terminal tower; usually it was an orderly and unpretentious area, but now it was lit by television lights and filled with a jostling crowd of newsmen. The Squadra Mobile were already playing the press and had proclaimed a glorious victory. A kidnapped boy delivered from the grasp of his tormentors, success snatched from the jaws of evil – it was a powerful story and the Italian was here to make sure it stayed that way.

And standing out in front of the posse of media men, waiting on the floodlit apron, were J.J. and Terri.

Ruari saw them, could barely hold his excitement, stomped his feet as the cabin door opened and the steps were lowered. Harry watched as he cried with anticipation. 'Dad! Mummy!' He seemed to fly down the steps and into their arms.

Harry hesitated, hung back. His presence wouldn't help the fragile sanity of the media, would raise too many questions that, right at this moment, he didn't want to answer, and indeed couldn't answer. He was the last off the plane, and from the bottom of the steps he watched J.J. and Ruari, bound together, hugging each other with a joy that bordered on desperation as they moved to talk to the journalists. J.J. was, after all, a newspaperman as well as a father.

Harry stood in the shadows of the plane, watching from a distance.

'How do I thank you, Harry?' a voice whispered at his shoulder. It was Terri.

Thank him? He could think of a million ways. 'He's one remarkable kid.'

'Of course he is. He's ours.' Her eyes were filled with pride, and gratitude, and a million other things that were all getting twisted together.

'What happens next, Terri?'

She didn't answer at first. Tears began to trickle down her face. Then she whispered, 'I love you, Harry.'

And Harry knew. Whatever happened, however this finished, was going to cause exquisite and enduring pain. He turned back to where J.J. and Ruari, still arm in arm, stood in a puddle of television lights, telling their story. 'He thinks J.J.'s the finest father in the world.'

'He is.'

'And as a husband?'

She shook her head slowly in bewilderment. 'What can I say? You know what I feel about you. You've got to decide for us, Harry, I can't do it any longer.'

He took her in his arms, held her tightly, tenderly, stared into her eyes. 'You'll sort it out.'

Her lip trembled; she didn't understand what he was saying.

'I love you, Terri. Ruari, too. Extraordinary, isn't it, this father thing? I'm not so very good at it, I guess, it's all so new, but somehow it's come to mean everything to me.'

'You'll be brilliant at it, Harry.'

'What? Start being Ruari's father by destroying his world? If I split up his family he'd never forgive me. And I could never forgive myself.'

'But you . . .'

'It's not about me, is it? It's him. And he's a very special young man. He saved my life, you know, I couldn't be more proud to call him my son, but what he's become has nothing to do with me. That's down to you. And J.J. You've done an extraordinary job, both of you, created something, *someone*, who is quite exceptional. I have no right to break that. I owe it to Ruari.'

'But you and me, Harry . . .'

'Oh, there may come a time when you can tell Ruari, when we can both tell him, perhaps, but that's not now and it may never be. You and me, we're not really what matters in this. It's Ruari, our son. And whatever happens, we'll always have him.'

'And so much more.'

The tears were showing no hesitation any longer, tumbling down her cheeks. He wanted to brush them away, with his fingertips, with his lips, but he daren't. Yet she wouldn't let him go.

'The other night, Harry . . .'

'Yes.'

'I'll never regret it.'

'We'll always have that,' he whispered, struggling to smile. 'And to hell with Paris.'

She stretched up to kiss him, on the lips, sweetly, without a hint of shame, as only lovers can do. Then she walked away one last time to stand by her husband and son.

The media, like a shoal of fish, turned their attention to her, the tearful and overjoyed mother. As the cameras flashed and she tried to field their frantic questions with nothing but a smile, J.J. looked over his shoulder, still refusing to let go of the boy. He saw Harry, held his eye, as he mouthed two words that were as sincere as anything he had ever said in his life. 'Thank you.' Then he turned back, and with his wife and son, walked off into the night.

—✺—

The media scrum broke up. A young woman detached herself from the rest of the press pack and walked over towards Harry. 'Mr Jones, isn't it? Bit of a surprise to see you here.'

'Just a family friend,' Harry muttered dully.

'What happened to your face?'

'Fell off my bike.' He tried to walk on, but the reporter pursued him.

'So what do you think about the other news?'

'What other news?'

'The appointment this morning of Anne Trowbridge as Foreign Secretary. There'd been rumours you might be offered the job.'

'I think it's excellent news all round,' he responded drily, hoping he had smothered his surprise. 'I may even be forced to celebrate.'

'How?'

He sighed. 'Start with a pint of Guinness, I think. There may be several more to follow.'

—✺—

They buried Sean in the cemetery of the church in Dundalk where he was christened. It was a few days after Christmas. A small ceremony, a family affair, very private. J.J. had written Harry a long and deeply personal letter in his own hand, spelling out his gratitude and inviting him to the funeral. In similar vein, Harry replied, talking in detail of all the things Sean had done in Trieste, of the admiration he would always hold for him, but in the circumstances declining to attend. He didn't need to spell out what those circumstances were.

He travelled on his own to Dundalk a couple of days later. It was the same day that the news came through from Zimbabwe. There had been a coup on Christmas Day; the interim President, Moses Chombo, had been ousted and had not been seen since. The new government was headed by a security official of whom the media knew almost nothing. His name was Takere.

It was snowing when Harry reached the graveyard, much like Sean had told him it had been on that Bloody Sunday, when his world had changed. He found the grave without difficulty with its freshly turned soil and flowers. He knelt beside it, ignoring the dampness creeping around his knees, and remained like that for some time. Then, slowly, carefully, he dug a hole in the soft earth with his fingers directly above the point where he thought Sean's heart would be. From his pocket he pulled his General Service Medal with its purple and green ribbon, his name etched on the rim and with its clasp that

417

marked his military service in the British army in Northern Ireland. 'Time to bury many things, old friend,' he whispered as he placed it in the hole and smoothed the earth over.

—⟪⟫—

Newsday began publishing extracts from the Mandela diaries early in the New Year. They were an instant sensation, not just in Britain but also around the world. Too many famous names were implicated for the diaries to be ignored. The serialization rights earned several fortunes. The newspaper survived. And so did the marriage.

Acknowledgements

Trieste. Why did I choose it? Perhaps because I knew so little about the place. Hadn't Winston Churchill once mentioned it as marking one end of the Iron Curtain? Perhaps it was that alone, and the fact that I was all too aware of my ignorance, that nudged me into making a few enquiries. Rather like Harry, I had no idea what I was stumbling into.

What a city! Trieste is filled with intrigue, romance, an extraordinary history and many wonderful people. One of the pleasures I've encountered in writing *Old Enemies* is the opportunity it has given me to get to know the city and those who live there, and I can only hope the many new friends I made will be content with my inevitably partial and incomplete description of its many attractions. An old and very cosmopolitan friend, Alexandros Kedros, started the process in his typically expansive style, supported by his lovely niece, Olympia Pappas, and her mother, Isarina. Their stories inspired me as much as their own friends and family who live in Trieste were later able to educate and entertain me – and in formidable style. They introduced me to Giulio Campos, who passed on much of his love of his home city, and in particular they introduced me to the former British consul in the city, John Dodds, who not only has been tireless in answering my questions but made my visit such fun, even when the rain threatened to sweep us off the Carso. John himself introduced me to others, and perhaps the most helpful and inspiring of these was Inspector Manuela de Giorgi, who is currently head of the Border Police Office. I owe her and her colleagues in the Trieste police a huge vote of thanks. Their assistance was as genuine as my entirely fictional character of Inspector D'Amato is flawed.

Before I leave Trieste I must recommend the finest book about the city, written by Jan Morris, which is entitled *Trieste and the Meaning of Nowhere*. Her beautiful and mesmerizing descriptions capture the elusive, sleepy character of the place better than any other, and anyone thinking of visiting the city should devour her book. It's not necessary to agree with all her conclusions in order to relish an exceptional piece of writing.

Old Enemies has required me to delve into the murky and unpalatable world of kidnapping, and I have many people to thank for explaining so much of what takes place. Dr David Claridge of Janusian Security Risk Management was extremely helpful, and my distant cousin, Peter Dobbs, also had a hand in getting me underway. My old friend from Downing Street days, Barry Strevens, has also been kind and introduced me to Phil Atkinson of the Serious Organized Crime Agency. Both of them provided time and invaluable advice, while Tessara Coutts gave me all the inspiration I needed to set a scene in a hairdresser's. She cuts my hair and tells me about cats, and does both wonderfully.

The expertise with helicopters of John Edward Taylor and Jamie Murray freed my imagination to fly through the Alps; the hospitality of Kevin Hughes helped me construct the scene based upon Brokers wine bar in the most relaxing of circumstances, and James Body, my neighbour from the other side of the hill in Wiltshire, taught me more about modern communications than I ever knew. I also hope my friend Cosmin Baduleteanu will forgive me for turning him into a ruthless criminal, while another friend, Will Hiley, celebrated his fiftieth birthday during the time this book was being written. I have marked an extraordinary evening of birthday celebrations by appropriating his name for one of the characters.

Three old friends deserve special mention. I can't remember how many times I've thanked Andrei Vandoros in my books, and *Old Enemies* turns out to be no exception. His limitless knowledge and generosity never cease to lighten the sometimes heavy burden of writing, while between them, Ian Patterson and David Foster continue to provide the inspiration and very special advice that allow Harry to grow larger with every adventure.

Rachel and the boys have, as always, been there to massage my weary shoulders and turn furrows into laughter lines through the long months of writing. James and Liz

Barnes, to whom this book is dedicated, are two of the finest friends I have ever had. I thank them from the bottom of my heart for all they have done, and for all they mean to the Dobbs family.

Michael Dobbs.
Wylye, September 2010.